A DEATH MOST QUIET

J. HAHN

J. Hahn

Printed in the United States of America
First Printing 2021
First Edition 2021

ISBN: 978-0-578-92718-3

10 9 8 7 6 5 4 3 2 1

Cover Design by J. Hahn.

A DEATH MOST QUIET

Special thanks to the Yale University Art Gallery.
Cover art image:
Dead Bird - John La Farge, American,
1835–1910, M.A. (HON.) 1896.

Special thanks to:
Michele Morin
Will Hahn
Juliet McVicker
Lila Webb

This book is dedicated to my mother, who taught me that life is precious.

PART I

MADAME X

I

WHERE THE SUN IS SILENT

It took me three years working as a crime reporter for the *Times* before I learned who he was. And once I knew his name, there was no letting go. Being on the outside, I only saw glimpses of the whole, otherwise obscure vignettes, seen alongside anecdotes, told to me by those who knew him. They were like old photographs seen through a stereoscope. Maybe that's an unfair reference for a modern world. Then again, perhaps that's the best way to explain it.

Knowing what I know now, I can't say that my search was abundantly fruitful. I don't know that anyone will ever understand him, but I've tried. And in trying, I've found myself to have more in common with him than I'm comfortable with. Any judgments about the person, or what he's done; I leave it to you, to make up your mind. In general, I'd say that at our worst we're all capable of terrible and ugly things. At times when I'm most hopeful, I think we all deserve another day, and maybe even one more after that.

It's a cynical view of the world, but it's not unfounded. Naturally, I didn't start out this way, but I can't remember a time when it wasn't there. Being a witness to the crimes and violence, night after night, can turn a man toward pessimism, but the bureaucracy of the job made it even worse. As journalists, we were fighting for scraps; looking for anything that wasn't fed to us by the

NYPD. There was rarely anything to be had. The days of print news were all but over. It had been dying for decades, though no one wanted to admit it. Paper is for the purists, and in case you haven't heard, there aren't too many of those around anymore. Once the NYPD started using Twitter, it was all over. Social media and self-published press releases allowed the department to control the narrative, avoid hard questions, and inform the public faster than we ever could. I did my best to portray the truth as I saw it, but we were all pulling water from the same well. We were all telling the same story, in the same language. After three years of self-imposed insomnia, my life seemed to mimic the nocturnal habits of a fruit bat. Only after this realization did I resign myself to re-wording press releases, like everyone else. I can say that I was one of a few who still went out to crime scenes; the last of the 3 A.M. radio-vampires. I'd like to say I did it out of professional pride, but it was equally a matter of personal curiosity.

Until that point, the great love of my life had been literature. From Faulkner to Plath's *Bell Jar*, and the great Truman Capote, I had long been enamored by diction and the confines of the page. But now that was changing. It was as if those hours spent in the company of such writers had been a preamble. They'd been pointing me toward it all along. Yes, the crimes were often hideous and unsightly, but they were more than that. It was human nature in its truest and most unabridged form, and it was there for anyone to see, if they cared to look for it.

It was around that time that the lines between work and my personal life became blurred. Not long after they were indiscernible. I found myself more interested in the anthropology of it all, and I focused more on causality rather than brevity and word count. The facts relative to crime reporting seemed to matter less than the crimes themselves. I wanted to know the dark mechanics of it, its movements and subtle gestures. Were some people just bad; irredeemably predestined? Or was it something that we all had a share in, a common strand of corruptibility that made otherwise good people do devious things? Was it a sudden drop, like a cut elevator cable, or was it a slow, tectonic slide, akin to the earth moving under our feet? Capote warned about giving your heart to a such a wild thing.

Because of these questions, I became a student again, and although I wasn't far from Cooper Square, this wasn't NYU. How does one learn about such intricacies from a distance; from outside the crime scene tape? Sure, I could acquire the distilled, underlying facts, but the emotional substance and physical palpability of murder and madness were always just out of reach. I wasn't getting the answers I was looking for, so I went to find my own subject. I had learned all that I could from books. There was only one option left. I began responding to suicides.

Every correspondent in the city would turn up for the homicides, but no one cared about the suicides; in Hollywood maybe, but rarely in New York. No one wanted to hear about the lonely death of an otherwise forgettable person; certainly not in the open folds over Sunday breakfast. But for me, these deaths held all the forensic elements of a murder, because the inarguable fact remained that someone was killed by a person. They held the tragic evidence of motive, and mental illness, loneliness and death; often paired with the violence of a murder. These secret characteristics, still reverently held, were less guarded than those of a criminal nature. Police procedure was far less stringent, because a suicide would never go to trial. There was no crime, no suspect, no victim; at least not as far as the State was concerned.

After months of quiet attendance, and much to my surprise, police investigators began allowing me unprecedented access to these scenes. I was let in with the strict understanding that I wouldn't report the details of the suicides, or disclose the names of the deceased. They recognized in me a shared interest, and in return I kept my promise. I became an ally, and eventually a friend to many of the patrolmen and investigators of the NYPD who served as my guides, like Virgil, through those deep places where the sun is silent. My education had begun, and it was through these unnamed tragedies that I came to know the stench of decomposition, the shot patterns of a twelve-gauge shotgun, and the life cycle of blow flies.

Prior to that, I was sure that things happened for a reason and that we lived in a world that was relatively safe and peaceful; a believable fiction with all the relevance of a destination wedding. I untied my blindfold and turned my back on the mirage. Some people have their fitness clubs and Caribbean vacations. I had Friday night photo-sharing with the interns at the Medical Examiner's Office, and 'off-the-record' choir practice with officers from the 13th Precinct.

In those early years, what proved to be most significant was the fragile trust of an NYPD detective, Edward McCuen. He would become the Captain of the NYPD's Crime Scene Unit, responsible for the forensic investigation of every major homicide in the five boroughs. For years, I preserved his trust and enjoyed his friendship, while I pursued a carefully guarded secret —his secret: a man named Anselm Winterbottom.

I first saw Winterbottom in January 2010, at the scene of what would later become known as "The Flatbush Killings". I knew most of the detectives in all the major crime units, if not by name, then by face. But he was a stranger. In his late forties, he had dark brown hair and sheltered an average build beneath a drab, canvas field jacket; the kind often worn by bird-hunters. You could imagine my surprise when I watched this stranger get escorted beneath the tape, to meet directly with Captain McCuen. I began seeing him at every major crime scene, but he was never so openly on display. It made me wonder how long he'd gone unnoticed, giving rise to the possibility that I'd been seeing him for years without realizing it. After months of contemplation, I felt compelled to ask McCuen about him. When I did, my friend of many years paused for a moment, sipped his coffee and said, "I don't know who you're talking about—and you can't ever ask me about him again." As his friend, I took comfort in the fact that he didn't lie to me outright, but I felt slighted by his abrupt refusal to say any more. From that moment on, I couldn't let it go. I needed to know who he was, and the more time that passed without answers, the more determined I became. I knew even early on that I'd have to betray my friend to learn his secret.

In writing this, I'll tell you what I know; less from my recollections, and more from those of my reticent friend, Captain Edward McCuen. It wasn't until after his retirement from the NYPD, that he spoke more candidly about his enigmatic friend, Anselm Winterbottom. I learned a great deal, and yet some things he kept hidden from me, even in the days before he died. I felt like he was protecting someone, or maybe he was just keeping an old promise—secrets told to the wind will surely be revealed to the trees. Even now, I'm haunted by a few unanswered questions. The worst part is, I don't know if they even matter. I suppose that's the difference between curiosity and obsession. There's always one more unanswered question.

The events of most interest began in late September when the nights fall heaviest in lower Manhattan. The hours just after midnight had passed into relative obscurity, except for a murder-suicide on Monroe Street. I heard the call come over the police frequency and those of us on scene had already put most of the pieces together. It was an old familiar swan song. Wife cheats on husband; husband kills wife, then turns the gun on himself. I wasn't at all surprised to see McCuen standing in the doorway. It was in moments like these that I admired him most. His dedication was eternal. I had met his wife, Catherine, and she was remarkable, but I found it difficult to believe that she could be so understanding of his absence, so regularly. I'm sure that it took its toll. Yet, there he was, like Wellington at Waterloo, right in the thick of it.

As personnel from the Medical Examiner's office carried two amorphous body bags from the entryway, McCuen's cell phone rang. I watched as he bowed his head in quiet disappointment, signaling that the night was still young. He had hours to go before he'd sleep. Given the distance between us, I couldn't make out what he was saying, but I could tell it was bad news. When he hung up the phone he quickly dialed an uncatalogued, but well-memorized phone number. I moved closer and strained to hear.

"I have something for you," said McCuen. "The Bethesda Fountain—when can you be there?"

Just then a transmission crackled over the radio of a nearby patrolman. A body had been found in Central Park.

II

THE BETHESDA FOUNTAIN

McCuen arrived at the Bethesda Terrace just before 2:00 am. and was greeted by the lead investigator of his team, Lt. Thomas Whelan. Whelan was the youngest member of the Crime Scene Unit, but he was far from inexperienced. He had been personally selected by McCuen. It was never spoken of, but everyone knew that he was McCuen's heir apparent. Every police detective has an expiration, and McCuen had outlasted most of his peers. As for Whelan, he had yet to reach his prime, and still had much to learn. The difference in their ages was magnified by a youthful arrogance, and a less noticeable fear of failure, induced by the fact that his father was a Deputy Inspector. His shortcomings aside, Whelan was a notch above the rest, and completely devoted to his work, and his tutor.

Upon seeing the unmarked cruiser enter the park, Whelan rushed to meet McCuen on the stairs that cascaded through the Terrace. The tempered veteran, and a youthful mind, converged among the echoes of their footsteps, bouncing off the encaustic tiles that lined the terrace.

"Another Victorian dress?" asked McCuen, anxiously.

"Yes, sir."

"Well, we've got ourselves a serial."

The two men continued on toward the open air of the courtyard. It'd been nearly a decade since McCuen had seen the bronze angel that stood atop the Bethesda Fountain. He used to take his daughter to the park when she was young, but he never paid much attention to it. But this night was different. He was drawn into the angel's downward gaze and followed the folds of her robes, which clung to her legs in contrapposto; seemingly drenched in the waters, she presided over. With wings outstretched, she held a lily in her left hand, blessing the waters beneath her. He was seldom reminded of such old-world beauty; it seemed so foreign in the city he had come to know. In the daytime he may have felt differently, but in that moment the angel felt more like some dark spirit; a harbinger of a sinister benediction. In the outer circumference of the fountain, he could see the night's dreadful work. There, lying on the bricks of the terrace, was a pale, corpse eerily adorned by a black Victorian dress.

"We haven't identified the body," said Whelan. "She's a Caucasian female, brunette, approximately thirty-five years old, about 5'8", 130 pounds. A patrolman from the Park Precinct found her. Also—the killer placed a white rose in her left hand."

"A romantic," scoffed McCuen, looking up at the bronze angel. "How refreshing." Continuing to survey his surroundings, he called out to the investigator who was hovering over the woman's lifeless body. "Adams, anything on cause of death?"

"Manual strangulation, for starters," she replied. "The bruising's pretty faint, but it's there. It's also possible he used a chemical agent, maybe chloroform, or halothane. Toxicology will have to confirm."

Maya Adams was a forensic pathologist, and a crime scene analyst who had worked closely with McCuen for six years. A graduate of Boston University's Criminal Forensic Science program, and with a degree in Psychology from

Stanford, she was an invaluable resource. "I'll know more once we move the body, but until then—that's all you get." She held back a smile, knowing full well what McCuen's answer would be, and how Whelan would react.

"Do what you can without moving the body," replied McCuen. He had just tipped his hand.

"Yes, sir," said Adams, looking back at Whelan, smiling. Whelan tried to hide his disappointment, and before he could speak, McCuen jumped in.

"Yes, Tom," said McCuen. "He's coming—he'll be here in twenty minutes."

"Sir, with all due respect—"

"In the meantime," interrupted McCuen. "Let's do what we can before he gets here, and maybe he won't be able to tell us anything we don't already know."

"Yes, sir."

"Tom, one more thing," continued McCuen. "Let's move the outer perimeter back another hundred feet, I don't want anyone getting pictures of the crime scene, or the dress. By order of the commissioner, there is to be no mention of the Victorian dresses to the media, at least not yet."

"I'll get right on it."

Whelan and Adams returned to their work while McCuen made his way back to the Terrace to await an unlikely ally. He spent the next twenty minutes pacing the bricks along the edge of Terrace Drive until a taxicab grabbed his attention. A lone figure exited and was escorted by a patrolman to where McCuen was standing. Every time they met, McCuen questioned whether he should have called him. This time was no different.

"Anselm," said McCuen, handing him a cup of coffee. "Thanks for coming."

"Late nights, and dead bodies," replied Winterbottom. "—how did it come to this?" Without another word, the two men began their descent toward the fountain. Once inside the privacy of the terrace walls, McCuen spoke.

"I was hoping you could go easy on him this time."

"Ed—"

"He's quite capable if you just give him a chance—"

"Look—he's a grown man, for Christ's sake," replied Winterbottom.

"Anselm, please—"

"I'm surprised you would say anything—he's actually the only reason I keep coming out to these things," continued Winterbottom sarcastically. "Why sleep when you can hang out with Tom and look at dead bodies all night?"

"Are you finished?"

"No, I'm serious—dead people really bring out his personality."

"Ok—are we done?" said McCuen. "If you won't do it for his sake—do it for mine." Winterbottom stopped dead in his tracks, forcing McCuen to pause.

"I don't owe you any favors," said Winterbottom, sternly. "And we both know why I'm here."

"Have it your way," replied McCuen, as he continued down the steps, leaving Winterbottom to sit with his objection.

After a brief and uncomfortable silence, Winterbottom followed him.

"Look, you called me here—so here I am. I didn't come here to make friends, and you know I'm no good with people."

"I've noticed," smirked McCuen. "Just do what you can—and try to go easy."

As they emerged from the terrace, Winterbottom turned toward the fountain and the bronze angel in the distance. His interest was piqued as he slowly rotated the styrofoam coffee cup in his hand. His appreciation for the scene was immediately felt; a bronze statue and a centuries-old fountain made for a far more interesting setting than the back alleys and putrefied shipping containers that had awaited him in the past.

"Good morning, Anselm." said Whelan briskly as he approached. Winterbottom glanced over at McCuen, as if to ask for permission to respond. The look wasn't at all out of place in that way, because McCuen often felt like his keeper; a father to an idiosyncratic man-child.

"Hello, Tom," replied Winterbottom awkwardly.

After a brief and equally uncomfortable stalemate, they followed McCuen to the fountain. Winterbottom's attention was immediately drawn toward the lifeless figure beneath it. Without a word, McCuen exchanged a small flashlight for Winterbottom's coffee cup, and he watched as Winterbottom was pulled in. The darkness was parted periodically, by the sudden burst of the flashlight, pointedly fixed on some harrowing aspect. Winterbottom was analyzing everything around him; his head carefully pivoting from one object to the next, without giving the appearance of any singular focus. To an outsider, he would have appeared lost; confused, like a blind man amidst the murmurations of a flock of birds. Standing over the body, he craned his neck slightly to one side, then the other. McCuen likened such movements to watching a young boy staring into a pool of water, attempting to reason with his own reflection. There was a purity to it all, and a fascination that was palpable, but they all knew better than to call it innocence. It was a vigorous exercise, and the workings of an intricate cognition that could never be fully understood, or interpreted.

Then suddenly, Winterbottom backed away and stood quietly on the bricks as his lungs exchanged the crisp, pre-dawn air. With his hand cupping the right side of his face, and his left arm tucked across his chest, he undulated his fingers, like a mechanical adding machine, tapping away like the keystrokes of a typewriter. McCuen had come to anticipate such ritual gestures, as they were clearly linked to the process of deduction. Whelan likened it to some unearthly trance, but it was far from paralytic. It was quite the opposite. There was something beneath it all, moving him, like some great engine.

Winterbottom studied the delicate folds of the black dress, from its bustle, to the ornate stitching on the sleeves and collar, down to the three large bows on its front. He looked at the body, the exposed lower arms and hands, and her frozen stare; a light extinguished. He captured the faint impressions of the killer's ghostly hands; the bruising that wrapped around her neck on either side. Unlike for most people, her eyes and vacant expression held no more value to him than any other inanimate object. The eyes are the windows, but only for the living. His assessment was as devoid of emotion as it was efficient. It was impervious to distraction. A moment after, and without warning, he turned to McCuen and the others.

"Thank you for not moving the body. It makes things much easier."

"Adams, can you give him a rundown of what you've got so far—"

"That won't be necessary," said Winterbottom, calmly. "I'm sure it's all in order. Thirty-year-old female found murdered in Central Park, wearing a Victorian-style dress. The most probable cause of death being whatever happened to her neck, and something for toxicology to sort out."

He had summarized it well, but something was missing.

"And?" replied McCuen.

"And, that's it," he replied.

Even Whelan could see that he was holding back. McCuen exhaled in disappointment and nodded to Whelan and Adams, signaling that he needed to speak to Winterbottom, alone. Careful not to draw unwanted attention, McCuen approached him and leaned in close.

"I didn't call you here because I missed your shining personality. And just because I asked you to treat Tom like a human being, that doesn't mean I want you to agree with everything he says."

"Ed, what do you want from me—I'm tired."

"This woman's been murdered, and I need your help. We've done all that we can do, and we've done it well. Now I need you to do—what you do."

"Maybe there's nothing left for me to tell you," said Winterbottom in defiance. "You've got a team of experts—I see the same things you see. I'm not a fucking magician—although, if you'd like, I could let my eyes roll back in my head—and maybe quote some Rasputin, we could see if that works for everyone?"

"Actually, that's a pretty god-damn accurate account of what just happened!" barked McCuen.

"I shouldn't have come."

"You didn't have to."

"You know that I do," snapped Winterbottom, sharply. Then he turned away and looked down at the ground. "I'm running out of time, Ed. If I do this for you—this is the end of it. I need everything."

"I already gave you everything," replied McCuen. "We've been over this a hundred times."

"You gave me nothing—at least nothing I didn't already know."

"That's all there is!"

"No—" replied Winterbottom. "I want to be free of this whole thing—once and for all."

"Has it ever occurred to you that I might be trying to help you?" said McCuen. "You've got to let it go."

"You know I can't! That's why you keep calling me."

Realizing that their voices were raised, the two men walked further away.

"Do this for me—just one last time," pleaded McCuen. "And when it's finished, I'll give you everything. You have my word."

"The entire case file?"

"Yes, fine—I'll give you the entire case file," agreed McCuen.

"Okay."

McCuen knew the agreement could have profound repercussions, but that was a line he had crossed years ago. With nothing lost between them, they walked back toward the fountain to discuss the killing with the others, who were anxiously awaiting Winterbottom's full-throated assessment.

"If I had to guess, the killer administered a dose of chloroform to her nose and mouth, and he's most likely right-handed—judging from the directional smearing of the victim's lipstick. He's also got relatively large hands as seen from the subtle bruising on her neck. Adams, what do you call that one again?"

"Manual strangulation," she replied.

"Thank you."

Winterbottom often asked her questions that he already knew the answers to. When they first met, she thought it was his way of being kind, but she soon realized that he was just doing it to make Whelan feel irrelevant.

"As for the dress—yes, it's in a Victorian style, but it's not Victorian—the stitching is modern, and so is the weave of the warp yarn."

"What the hell is a warp yarn?" interrupted Whelan.

"Tom, let's not pretend that you don't have a dress just like this one. Anyway, it's not important—just know that the dress was made recently."

"Either way," replied Whelan. "I'm sure we can all agree that she didn't wear a Victorian dress to Central Park. The killer must have—"

"Actually, Tom—that's precisely what she did."

Whelan stopped and shifted his stance in obvious disagreement with the idea.

"People don't go walking around Central Park in Victorian dresses." Whelan continued in disbelief. "She must have been abducted—probably at random—"

"She wasn't abducted," snapped Winterbottom, cutting him off. "And this wasn't random. I know it seems unlikely—but she wore the dress to the Park. I'm sure of it. In fact, she's been wearing the dress for most of the night."

Whelan shook his head in disbelief, scoffing at the idea. McCuen and Adams had their doubts as well. Smiling, Whelan continued.

"When was the last time you saw someone wearing a Victorian dress in New York City?"

"David Bowie—in 1983, but that's beside the point."

"I'm not buying it," snapped Whelan. "The dress was put on post-mortem, or he killed her in it somewhere else, and dumped her here. There's just no way she wears a dress like that to Central Park. Adams, you've gotta back me up on this—"

"He makes a good point, Anselm."

"Ok, let's slow it down a bit," said McCuen. "Let's assume our killer abducts her, then dresses her up, like some sick doll collector—"

"Instead, let's not waste any more fucking time," said Winterbottom, coldly. "She wore the dress here—and she was killed, right here, wearing it—not before."

"Okay," replied McCuen, doubtfully. "Show us."

Winterbottom walked over to the corpse and pointed to the dead woman's neck. "There are traces of liquid on the veiled portion of the dress."

"Yes—okay?" replied McCuen.

"Remember that guy, last year, on Cobble Hill—the anesthesiologist who tried to euthanize his cat using chloroform?"

"Yeah, I remember him," replied Adams. "He killed his elderly parents with a meat clever —but he used chloroform on the cat."

"Right," said Winterbottom. "That night, you told me that chloroform dries more slowly than water."

"Yes, it does."

"Okay—it was raining until about ten o'clock tonight. The ground is dry, but there are liquid smears on the dress, just below her neck. It's not rain—I think it's chloroform, and if you get close enough, you can smell that sweet chemical smell."

"Presumably, chloroform," corrected Whelan, still not convinced about the dress.

"Yes, Whelan, for Christ's sake—*presumably* chloroform."

"Come on, Anselm—," interrupted McCuen. "Whelan—you too. There's a dead woman at your feet. Let's focus on that."

"As I was saying," continued Winterbottom. "Presuming it's chloroform on her dress— which it is, that would mean that she was wearing the dress when the chloroform was administered. Not to mention that if the body was carried here, the heel straps on her shoes wouldn't have left such deep trace lines on her feet. She walked here wearing those shoes and the dress—and she was murdered right here in this spot. If the killer didn't come here with her, he at least knew she'd be here."

"Okay, I'm convinced," said McCuen. "Anything else?"

"Yes—and it's bad news for you. She's wealthy—and more likely than not—so is her killer."

"What makes you say that?"

"Her hands," replied Winterbottom. "She's never worked a day in her life. Not to mention the fact that if the light catches it just right, there's a thin, diamond band in her hair, just behind her head. If it's real—it's worth over $10,000 dollars. The killer didn't steal it, which tells me he didn't need to, or else he's completely psychotic."

"I don't think we can rule out the killer being psychotic," said Adams. "She's been strangled at the foot of a bronze statue depicting a Greek goddess."

"True—he could be psychotic," conceded Winterbottom. "But if he is—he's not very good at it."

"Are we really having this conversation?" added Whelan.

"The angel's holding a lily in her left hand—not a rose." Winterbottom continued. "A psychotic killer transfixed on a ritual killing wouldn't mess up such a detail."

"Maybe he was just interested in the act itself?" said McCuen. "You know—the thrill of it all?"

"Maybe, but something's not right."

"To be clear—there's a lot that's not right about this, Anselm," said Adams.

"He's psychotic," repeated Whelan. "Sometimes it's just that simple."

"I wouldn't rule it out, but it's a bloodless killing," continued Winterbottom. "He literally put her to sleep before gently strangling her to death. Where's the violence? She's lying at the foot of a sacrificial altar, and he decides not to shed a single drop of blood? That doesn't seem psychotic to me. It doesn't even look like he tried to have sex with her. Doesn't that seem strange to anyone?"

"Yes," replied Adams. "It's uncommon, but what difference does it make—crazy people do crazy things."

"Killers kill people for a reason," replied Winterbottom. "The crazy ones kill for crazy reasons, but they still have reasons. There's no sign of severe trauma—so he didn't do it out of anger. Sure, you could make an argument that he was seeking power and control, but if that was the case, you'd expect him to exert that power and control—he would have tried to have sex with her. He killed her for a different reason."

"Yes—," said Whelan. "Because he's psychotic."

"Maybe—but that's not a reason."

"Thank you."

"It's more concerning than that," added Winterbottom. "People follow predictable patterns. They all have their quirks—like the guy from Cobble Hill, or that guy in Fort Greene, who did all those terrible things with fluorescent light bulbs?"

"Norman Tate," replied McCuen in remembrance.

"Yes, Norman Tate," echoed Winterbottom. "Pathologically, Tate and the guy from Cobble Hill were different in superficial ways, but they both followed the same measurable decline, or deviation. They all moved through similar incremental, deviant acts, driven by a need for satisfaction. If you look at people closely enough, everyone follows a general pattern of behavior. Inside that general pattern, there are subtle nuances that make each one unique." Then he turned to McCuen before proceeding. "Ed—you've seen it more than any of us. Haven't you felt that criminals, specifically murderers, are all playing from the same sheet of music?"

"Yes, for the most part."

"Adams, you know the profiles better than anyone. What would you say is the consequential difference between male and female serial killers?"

"Well, male serial killers hunt their victims, who are typically total strangers. Female serial killers tend to lure their victims from among people they already know."

"Brilliant," replied Winterbottom.

He was flattering her again, and twisting the knife into Whelan, all at the same time. "The general pattern is that they all kill people," Winterbottom continued, "—but inside that behavioral pattern they vary slightly, in their approaches and appetites. The more those appetites are gratified, the less satisfaction they feel, and they move deeper and deeper into deviance."

"And this one's different?" asked McCuen. Winterbottom rarely showed any sign of emotion, aside from contempt, but McCuen could see that he was genuinely disturbed by what he was seeing.

"Yes—this one's different," he replied, solemnly. "Some of what he's done gives me the impression that he's a novice—like the chloroform, and the gentle strangulation. It's as if he's unsure, or even lacking the urge to kill at all. But, in contrast—he goes to great lengths to set up a ritual murder, adorned with a Victorian dress, which shows a more refined pathology. Not to mention his proficiency. He's killed her in the middle of Central Park—and he did so without leaving a single bruise on her forearms. He applied precisely enough force to subdue her swiftly, without undue injury. This murder's too pristine to be his first—he's more experienced than he's letting on. Calling him psychotic is an oversimplification—he's intentional and well-practiced. What disturbs me most is that he's shown incredible restraint."

"Is that such a bad thing?" said Whelan.

"For our purposes, yes—that's a very bad thing," replied McCuen. "Serial killers get caught because of their lack of restraint. Most often—they become more and more violent, and less and less focused on getting caught."

"And if what we've seen tonight is restraint—what happens when our killer loses control?" added Winterbottom. "We could be dealing with a killer of the worst kind."

Winterbottom paused, and McCuen returned to something that had been bothering him from the beginning.

"So why would he put a white rose in her hand, and not a lily—like the statue?" asked McCuen. "And what would he gain from playing the novice?"

"I'm not sure," answered Winterbottom. "—but something's missing. Maybe we're focusing on the wrong thing."

He paused briefly before speaking again.

"Maybe the fountain, and the angel don't matter to him at all," he said, burying his hands deep in his jacket pockets. "Maybe this wasn't meant to be a sacrificial killing. Maybe it's just a public place—maybe he's just trying to get our attention."

Winterbottom looked at the corpse again.

"Yes, I think that's it," he said. "—he's trying to get our attention—which means he didn't get it before."

Winterbottom looked at McCuen inquisitively.

"When was the first body found?"

McCuen paused and nodded in concession, while Adams and Whelan shook their heads in astonishment.

"There's no fucking way," smiled Whelan, looking at McCuen. "You told him—you had to have told him."

McCuen shook his head in denial.

"No, I didn't tell him," replied McCuen, as he faced Winterbottom. "The first victim was found three days ago, in a rooftop apartment in Midtown. She was strangled to death, wearing a Victorian dress. Her name was Emma Strauss—the heiress to one of New York's wealthiest banking families."

III

THE OBSESSION

That night, while McCuen was leaving Central Park, I was across town at *The Times*, quietly awaiting the piercing tones and eerie, green glow of the fax machine. As much as I tried to manufacture some kind of justification, deep down I knew that I'd already betrayed him. It wasn't a clear betrayal, not by any means, but I knew it was wrong, and it left me feeling like Cassius. What made it worse was the fact that McCuen had no way of knowing what I'd done.

Earlier, on Monroe Street, when McCuen dialed that number on his cell phone, I began plotting. I noted the time that he made the call and having divined that he was speaking to his nameless associate; the rest was easy. As his friend, I knew his cell phone number, so I simply contacted an acquaintance of mine. I'll call him "Bob" for the sake of anonymity. Bob worked for McCuen's cell phone carrier, and I asked him for any information associated with the phone number that McCuen had dialed that night. Of course, initially he refused on the grounds that it was entirely illegal, but then I reminded him about an unpublicized story from six months ago, relating to a prostitution sting on Canal Street. After that, Bob was quite eager to help me get the information I needed. He said that he'd fax it over within the hour; three had gone by and still there was nothing. I began to think it was a bad idea to put so much faith in a married man who spends his Tuesday afternoons trolling for hand jobs in Chinatown.

As I considered the ramifications of what I had done, the fax machine came to life and delivered a single page of information. It was hardly the windfall I was hoping for. The phone number was linked to a landline assigned to *"Edmund & Gray Importers"* with a listed address on Lexington Avenue on the Upper East Side. An internet search for the business yielded almost nothing. From what I could tell, Edmund & Gray Importers was a brokerage firm for rare antiquities, but little more than that was advertised. It had to be the right phone number; Bob may have been a lot of things, but he didn't strike me as being incompetent. I had to assume I was on the right track. But doing so, I was faced with something worthy of speculation.

Why was the Captain of the NYPD's Crime Scene Unit calling the phone number of an antiquities dealer at 2 A.M.? I could really only be sure of two things: he wasn't buying Ming vases for Catherine, not on a police salary, and he wasn't on the take. Anything else was a possibility. Others might not be so quick to dismiss corruption on his part, but I knew him better than that; he just wasn't capable of it. Any detractors would only have to set foot in his house to see that he had no interest in luxury or antiquities. It was sparse and clean, like how I imagined his childhood home was growing up. It reminded me of the houses staged at nuclear testing sites; quaint, and well cared for, but mostly uninhabited. All that aside, the man himself was the best proof; his personal integrity was beyond question, beyond reproach.

Later that morning, I began calling antiquities dealers throughout the city. No one seemed to know anything about Edmund & Gray Importers. In the process, I was subjected to the most eccentric arm-twisting I've ever experienced. At one point, a purveyor from the East Village, side-stepped my initial questioning and before I knew it, I was seriously considering the necessity of a pair of hand-carved, wooden medical mannequins from the turn of the century. Fortunately, I was shaken from my stupor by the unmistakable sound of a squawking Macaw coming from the other end of the line. It ended any chance of its owner completing the sale. It did nothing to answer my inquiry, but it cemented my suspicion that despite the appearance of worldliness, antiquarian dealers have an intrinsic patrimony to carnival folk and Barbary pirates. Frustrated by my lack of progress, I decided to call Edmund & Gray, directly.

"Edmund & Gray Importers, how may I help you?"

The voice on the phone spoke with the syntax of a bygone era. I felt like I was speaking to Eleanor Roosevelt.

"Yes, hello," I said, half surprised that anyone answered. "I'd like to schedule a viewing of your inventory."

"I'm sorry, sir, you must speak up."

"I'd like to schedule a viewing of your collection," I repeated more loudly. "Would your broker be available today, or tomorrow?"

"I'm afraid he's no longer taking appointments. Have a nice day."

Then she abruptly hung up the phone. It seemed like Edmund & Gray Importers had little to do with antiques at all. That afternoon, I got stuck. The traffic in Midtown was a mess, and it took me thirty minutes to get to Lexington Avenue. I overshot my destination on account of it being one of six adjoining row houses. I parked just south of it and moved up the sidewalk to where a small plaque was affixed to the fifth house in the row. It read: Edmund & Gray Importers. There was nothing about the building that suggested it was engaged in any kind of business at all, and its tall, narrow facade was composed of three obvious levels, faced with brownstone bricks. It was more a residence than a business, boxed in by other houses. As I coaxed to life the last of a pack of Dunhill's, I wondered if it was occupied at all. After pacing the block a few times, I discarded my cigarette and approached the main door. I knew that the woman who hung up the phone could more easily close the door, or just not answer it at all. Having already tested the doorknob with a gently half-turn, I opted to walk right in.

Once inside the entryway, I climbed a short staircase into an open foyer and found myself faced with a secretary-style desk, resting vacantly beneath an unlit desk lamp. The room itself was lined from floor to ceiling with bookshelves, holding a sizable collection of antiquarian books, including topics from art history, philosophy, physics and quantum mathematics. Aside from the scholarly texts, the room's decor was spartan, and showed a predilection for the European style. Even in the room's low light I had the sense that the tables, chairs and other furnishings had traveled far. It was as if I had stepped back in time, and around the world, all at once.

Behind the desk was a wide staircase which led to the upper levels of the house, and to the right was a single closed door, under which a sliver of muted sunlight could be seen. Hoping to find the room empty, I pushed open the door. Finding it unoccupied, I began surveying the room. It was a large narrow space, almost entirely empty except for a high-backed leather chair, a desk, and a mattress that lay disheveled on the floor, amongst a scattering of discarded papers. It was as if I had entered a third-world, presidential palace, in the aftermath of a revolution. It seemed looted; stripped of all luxury and convenience, yet its high ceiling and ornamental trimmings, preserved a sense of omnipotence.

The large window to my right, which looked out across Lexington Avenue, was veiled by a linen curtain. Most out of place were the four computer servers that occupied the far corner of the room. Near to them, on the opposing wall, was an enormous chalkboard. I could see that it had been well used, with the dust from its previous contents vigorously pushed across its surface; its secrets well kept. The numerical formulas that were visible and clearly marked were every bit as elusive as its former mysteries. The chalkboard was crowded with symbols, the likes of which I'd never seen in Calculus. This was far more advanced. As I turned to look around the room a second time, I realized that I had overlooked its most peculiar characteristic. The entire wall facing the door was shrouded by an enormous curtain. It was massive, at least twenty feet long; more than enough to draw envy from Baum's great Wizard. It had the visual weight of a Renaissance tapestry, and in how it fell there was little doubt that it concealed something profound. I approached it with the intent to push it aside when I was ambushed by a familiar voice.

"May I help you, sir?" said a woman from behind me.

I turned and found myself facing a petite woman in her seventies, no doubt the very same woman I had spoken to on the phone. She had silvery hair which had been formally subdued behind her head, and her face seemed to balance a sense of gentle kindness with quiet ferocity. My presence had clearly awakened the latter.

"I'm sorry, ma'am. There was no answer at the door."

I felt tension in my chest and cringed on the inside, betting on her appreciation for decorum and social etiquette. Before she responded, she exhaled and smiled. I was in the clear.

"That's the trouble with doorbells," she replied graciously. "You have to push them, in order for them to work properly."

A stern look spanned across her face, as she let her words sink in, like teeth.

“Now, if you don’t mind?” she said, signaling a necessary return to the adjoining room.

Back in the library, she sat down at the desk and motioned for me to approach.

“Now, how may I help you?”

“Yes, I’m looking for a matching pair of wooden medical mannequins from the turn of the century—”

“As you can see, our inventory is quite limited at the moment,” she said, standing again.

“I was hoping to schedule an appointment with your broker?”

“Our broker is out of the country, at the moment.”

“When do you expect him to return?”

“I wouldn’t know, he’s quite unpredictable—and arrogant—a miserable person, really.”

“I’d really like to speak to him directly, could you tell me his name—”

“Pardon me?” she said, straining to hear what I was asking.

“His name? Could I have his name?”

“There’s no need to whisper, young man!” she said in frustration.

“What’s his name—what’s your broker’s name?” I was nearly shouting.

“I’m afraid that would be most inappropriate, and there’s no need for shouting!” Only then did I realize that during the exchange, I had been softly escorted to the front door.

“I really just need his name—and maybe a way to contact him? Or, maybe I could come back later?”

"I'm afraid not," she replied. "But you may have my name—Mrs. Agnes Bruce," she smiled gently. "And there will be no need to call on him a third time!"

Then she slammed the door in my face.

* * *

That same morning, Winterbottom had accompanied McCuen to the Odessa, in the East Village, for breakfast. They often met there for early morning meals to discuss those things that eluded them. When they arrived, they sat at a familiar booth by the window. After placing their order, McCuen presented Winterbottom with the reports and photographs from the scene of the first murder, the killing of Emma Strauss.

"She was found by her housemaid, three days ago, but she was murdered sometime the night before. As you'll see in the photographs, she was wearing a white and gray Victorian day-dress, a neck bow and a black blazer."

Winterbottom turned the photographs horizontally, and back again, as he shuffled through the folder. Coming to the photographs of the corpse, he saw the dress that McCuen had described. Strauss was lying on her back, pale with rigor mortis, like a life-sized porcelain doll. On the floor beside her turned-away face was a white Victorian boater hat.

"It's not exactly a seductive looking dress is it?" said Winterbottom. "What about her apartment?"

"There were no signs of forced entry, and no indications of a struggle. Toxicology confirmed that chloroform was used before the killer strangled her to death."

"Were there any marks on her neck?" asked Winterbottom.

"No, not externally, but at autopsy they found bruising of the trachea, and on the inside of her gums. We think the bruising on the gums was from him administering the chloroform, and the bruising on her trachea came later when he strangled her."

"And we're certain she was strangled?" asked Winterbottom. "The chloroform could have killed her if it was administered in a high enough dose."

McCuen took a sip of his coffee before answering.

"The Medical Examiner found petechiae on the inside of her eyelids."
"What's that?" asked Winterbottom.

"When someone is strangled, the capillaries in the eyes rupture. It's called petechiae. It only happens when the air supply is cut off."

Unfazed by the subject, Winterbottom cut into his Eggs Benedict, skewering a section of yoke before continuing to sort through the crime scene photos.

"I'm not seeing it," said Winterbottom. "Did he leave a white rose?"

"No," replied McCuen. "The Victorian dresses are indisputably linked, but why he left the second victim with a white rose is beyond me."

Winterbottom's expression became fixed and his tone flattened.

"Why didn't you call me when it happened?"

"I did," replied McCuen, recognizing Winterbottom's contentious-ness. "I called you three times, to be exact—I even drove to the house, but you weren't there."

McCuen watched him as he sat back and sipped his coffee, eventually settling into a more leveled posture.

"I was actually concerned about you," McCuen smiled. "You know—like maybe you had gone out to dinner with friends, or something dreadful like that."

"Hilarious," said Winterbottom dryly, turning his attention back to the crime scene photographs. "What's this?"

"We found some of Strauss' clothing in the master bathroom. It seems as if she'd changed into the dress just before she was murdered."

"She was waiting for him?"

"It looks that way," said McCuen.

"Was she assaulted—sexually, I mean?" asked Winterbottom, still scanning the folder for the Medical Examiner's report.

"The Medical Examiner doesn't think so."

"They don't think so? That's helpful," snapped Winterbottom.

"It's more complicated than you think," he replied. "They can say, with relative certainty, that she wasn't assaulted when she was conscious. However, she may have had consensual sex before she was killed. Oh, and there is the potential that she may have been assaulted after she was unconscious—just to be clear."

"Holy shit, that's definitive," replied Winterbottom, shaking his head. "Fucking doctors."

"I know, they're paid a lot of money for not having any answers," joked McCuen. "All that aside, the fact that she put on the dress suggests that our killer's an acquaintance—perhaps even a lover."

"Putting on a dress is one thing. Putting on a Victorian dress is another," said Winterbottom, staring into his coffee cup.

His eyes were fixed on it, but he wasn't chasing the origins of its flavor. His mind was searching, adrift in what was yet to be realized.

"What else do we know about her?" he asked.

"She's the daughter of a wealthy Austrian banker," replied McCuen. "She also worked as a model by day and played the extravagant socialite at night. In recent years she focused on philanthropy, spending most of her time and money supporting the arts, as well as sustainability projects in Africa."

"What about her husband?" asked Winterbottom noticing her diamond ring in the post-mortem photographs.

"William Stanhope," answered McCuen. "He's a millionaire investment banker—they were engaged to be married. We've confirmed with his secretary that he was attending a gala at the Los Angeles Museum of Art at the time of the murder. Interestingly—some of her friends said that Strauss has been somewhat estranged from Stanhope, as of late. I've instructed Whelan and Adams to keep digging. If he didn't kill her—maybe her reputation did."

"How so?"

"Strauss has a well-publicized history of promiscuity," replied McCuen.

"Promiscuity—isn't it appalling when women start acting like men," said Winterbottom, sarcastically. "I'm sure her fiancé's a real catch."

McCuen's cell phone rang just as the server began pouring two fresh cups of coffee. By the time she had turned away, McCuen had hung up his phone.

"They identified the woman from the park—Olivia Alford. She's the wife of Walter Alford, the founder of Tripoli Financial."

McCuen sat back against the red, padded booth. Given the news, it did little to comfort him.

"How long do we have before the assholes down at Police Plaza start looking over your shoulder?"

"I'm surprised we've made it this far," replied McCuen. "I'll try to hold them off a little longer, but if they assign someone from headquarters—I can't have you around."

"And what about our arrangement?" asked Winterbottom.

"We made an agreement," said McCuen. "I'll get you the file—regardless of what happens."

"Thank you, Ed," replied Winterbottom, sincerely. "In the meantime, I'll do my best to help, but we're running out of time, and I'm not referring to the police commissioner. The second murder occurred within three days of the first. Our killer won't give us that much time again."

"You think he'll progress?" asked McCuen.

"For as strange as this one is—if he's human, he won't have a choice. The murder of Olivia Alford was only slightly more violent than the first, but it was far more theatrical. The same thing that made him kill in the first place will make him more insatiable and violent. By now he's already planned the next murder, and it'll be harder and harder for him to resist the urge to kill again. But, like I said before—this one's different, at least in appearance. Only time will tell." Then Winterbottom stopped abruptly. "But you know that better than I do."

McCuen sipped his coffee and nodded in acknowledgement.

"Eighteen years is a long time," continued Winterbottom. "It's one thing to hear about this stuff on the news—or to read about it in books. It's a different thing entirely to breathe it in."

"A few more years, and I'm done," replied McCuen. "And retirement, that'll be worth it." Winterbottom caught him looking all around the diner, through the windows, and out onto the street.

"You won't ever be like them, Ed," said Winterbottom. "I've been trying to be like them my entire life. It may be for different reasons—but you and I can never be like that."

"Well, in a few years—I'm sure as hell going to try."

"Even if you retire, it won't change anything. You've seen too much. You can't suddenly turn a blind eye to it." Winterbottom smiled. "Saying it—doesn't make it so. The mirage fades as soon as you've got a mouthful of sand."

"Maybe, but they're not all that innocent, and they seem to be doing just fine," said McCuen, looking at the people sitting in the restaurant.

"They're like children, Ed," continued Winterbottom. "They want to believe that the world is a safe place, and that monsters don't exist—but you and I know that's not true, so we can never be like them."

Beyond the conversations of the other diners, McCuen's gaze became fixed on the front window and the people passing by.

"Do they ever think about it?" he asked. "Do they ever realize that they're—"

"—At the mercy of the stranger standing next to them?" said Winterbottom.

"Yeah," replied McCuen, surprised that Winterbottom could so easily summarize his thoughts.

"Most never do—not in any meaningful way. They all think they're special. Deep down, they know there's awful stuff out there, but they call it something else, or try to push it out of view. Mostly, they just don't think it'll happen to them. Call it ignorance, or indifference, but really it's selfishness; in that way—they're like sheep."

"Sheep?" asked McCuen, feeling like he had missed a part of their conversation. "Why do you say that?"

"W.D. Hamilton—" replied Winterbottom, suddenly realizing that he had gone too far, too fast. "Never mind—it doesn't matter."

"Tell me—why are they like sheep?" asked McCuen. "I'm curious—and who the hell is W.D. Hamilton."

"It's called *Selfish-Herd Theory*, and moving just beneath its surface in all its grand majesty is mathematics. Geometry to be more precise. I know that sounds strange, but that's what it is—instinct and predictable geometric patterns."

Winterbottom watched as McCuen drank the last of his coffee. Then he proceeded to explain.

"In 1971, Hamilton, a British evolutionary biologist, theorized that herd animals, specifically sheep, were not in fact a tight-knit group that stayed together for protection, but instead stayed together in order to increase their individual odds of survival. Essentially—each sheep is trying to avoid being eaten, at the expense of those around them."

"Safety in numbers," said McCuen.

"Yes, but that's an incredibly honorable way of putting it," said Winterbottom. "The saying implies that the group of individuals will all be safe if they stay together, but that's not the case. Being in a herd only increases an individual's chances of survival. Furthermore, the safety of any individual in the group is obtained at the expense of the other members of the herd. The welfare of the group as a whole isn't even a consideration. More recently, the theory was tested and they found that when a flock of sheep is threatened by a predator, the sheep all attempt to get to the center of the flock where it's safest. They all move in recognizable, geometric patterns in an attempt to predict where the center of the flock will be when the predator strikes. And so in that way, as humans—we're predictably selfish, like sheep. We move through our days in well-established patterns—avoiding any threat to the status quo, and when something bad happens, nobody really cares unless it happens to them."

"I have more faith in people than that."

"Maybe you shouldn't."

"Maybe," conceded McCuen. "Either way, our wolf isn't hunting because he's hungry." They continued in silence, watching the people moving by, until long after the waitress had cleared away their plates and empty cups.

"I need to ask you for another favor," sighed McCuen, reluctantly. "We're heading to Long Island tonight to meet with Walter Alford. Can you come?"

"Ed, that's a long drive—"

"I know, and it probably won't be worth it—I just thought—"

"You know what—why not?" replied Winterbottom. "That way I'm guaranteed not to make any new friends."

Then Winterbottom stood up and placed some money on the table.

"You're leaving?" asked McCuen.

"If I'm going with you tonight, I need to get some sleep," replied Winterbottom. "What time can you pick me up?"

"I'll be there at five—Alford's flying in from Scotland this afternoon," replied McCuen. "Based on my conversation with his assistant, this will probably be our only chance for an interview. He's a busy man."

"A busy man, whose wife was just murdered," said Winterbottom. "At least I'll be able to get a few hours of sleep."

"You do that," said McCuen, smiling. "Don't let a little thing like a serial killer get under your skin." Winterbottom pulled on his jacket and smiled.

"He's going to kill someone—whether I get to sleep, or not," replied Winterbottom coldly. "And don't confuse my interest with empathy, Ed. Even though I've agreed to go with you tonight, the fact remains that if it weren't for our little arrangement—I would've left you in the park."

IV

THE TALL GRASSES OF BROOKLYN

After my eviction from Edmund & Gray Importers, I finished the rest of the day at the office. On my way home, I found myself dwelling on the fact that Lexington Avenue wasn't much of a detour. I paid dearly for my curiosity and quickly found myself mired in bumper-to-bumper traffic. I arrived just before five o'clock and watched people and cars coming and going until I could move closer to the house. I eventually maneuvered into a parking space within view of the front door. From the darkened interior of my car, I patiently waited. If I was lucky, maybe I'd get a better look at him. The house was quiet and dark, in stark contrast from the other row houses whose windows were illuminated. They were like the chambered frames of a silent movie. In one, I could see a man talking on his cell phone, uncomfortably seated at a mahogany desk, while in the adjacent room, under lamplight, a brown-haired woman sat alone, nervously twirling her hair. In the next house over, a younger couple of obvious means was working in the kitchen, preparing for company. Despite their best efforts, they seemed detached, each secretly hoping their guests would arrive early, and rescue them from the awkward closeness. At the far end of the row, there was an older woman preparing for a more formal outing, perhaps the opening performance of *Madame Butterfly* at the Met. I watched her shuffling from room to room, carefully applying her makeup, and checking her work in the various mirrors of the house; one in every room. Even a distant onlooker like myself could see it. She was consumed by it, paying acute attention to those undeserved alterations of time. She would continue applying concealer until her taxicab arrived. Yes, I'm convinced she'd brave the poisonous forests of the Amazon to find that ancient fountain, like Ponce De Leon, or Orellana. These windows were occupied, but they were no less lonely than the darkened window that was my focus. They reminded me of the paintings of Edward Hopper; inhabited, but not wholly alive. And the people inside them appeared more like automatons, reminiscent of the Karakuri puppets of ancient Japan.

It wasn't long before my attention returned to the fifth row house from the left, still dormant and dark. It looked as if there was a gap in the buildings, a house forgotten. The only sign of life was a subtle blue glow that failed to fully penetrate the curtained window. Having been inside the house, I knew that the light was coming from the large computer monitor. He was inside, working in the darkness.

Suddenly, a set of headlights approached, and an unmarked police cruiser pulled up in front of me. I watched as McCuen hurried across the street, stopping briefly at the front door. Immediately, the light in the window went out. The door to the row house opened and the two men hurried to the car. Something was unraveling, but I had to let them go, or risk being seen.

* * *

From the house, McCuen and Winterbottom made the long drive south to Brooklyn, to an abandoned lot on Franklin Avenue. As I would later learn from McCuen, Winterbottom refused to meet publicly with him and his team, a circumstance that McCuen attributed to his eccentricity. As for McCuen, bringing Winterbottom anywhere affiliated with the NYPD was out of the question. His team had accepted the premise that Winterbottom was an investigatory consultant, a title that McCuen had hastily invented, but he knew that their allegiance to the idea was fragile at best. To be safe, McCuen had kept Winterbottom's full name from them, and it was only after several cases that he provided them with his first name. Both men had their secrets and relied on the other to keep them. Winterbottom also refused to allow anyone other than McCuen to access his sanctuary on Lexington Avenue, making places like the Franklin Avenue lot a necessity.

Winterbottom claimed ownership of the lot, and the chain-link fences and locked gate offered McCuen's team adequate privacy amongst the knee high grass that had taken back what once was theirs. For this night's purpose the empty lot was especially convenient because it was on the way to their ultimate destination. McCuen and Winterbottom had arrived early and opened the gate in preparation for the others.

Without a word, Winterbottom began an inexplicable ritual that McCuen had grown accustomed to. Winterbottom began walking along the perimeter of the lot where the grasses were highest. He walked slowly and with a careful cadence, as if wading waist deep in water. He moved through the darkness, allowing his hands to brush against the tall stalks and seed heads. It had taken McCuen a year to recognize that Winterbottom always walked in a counterclockwise direction. He didn't know why, or what purpose it all served. All he knew was that Winterbottom was complicated. Perhaps, in his mind, he was opening a door, turning a key, or maybe he was winding a clock, taking back the hours from the day. After all, this was just one of the many aberrations that McCuen had come to know. Maybe it was as simple as the feel of the lush green grass, or the sound of it brushing against him, a welcome change from the steel and concrete of the city.

McCuen found himself, once again, questioning his own judgement, and wondering how he could trust such an unpredictable person. A man who didn't own a cell phone, who refused to drive a car, and in fact, only recently resigned himself to riding in them. A man so coarse and oppositional, that he had no friends to speak of, and at times showed significant signs of Asperger's syndrome. He was irritable, unsympathetic, and self-centered. In essence, he contradicted much of who McCuen was, and acted in opposition to all that he believed in. So why was he there? Because McCuen needed him. In conjunction with all of Winterbottom's shortcomings was the mechanized efficiency of unparalleled genius. It was his lack of empathy and the absence of human emotion that allowed him to see a clear path to the facts and circumstances.

For Winterbottom, what mattered most was raw information; all that was tangible, and all that was probable; nothing else. He could comprehend aspects of human behavior in a way that only an outsider could, seeing it through a microscope and binoculars all at the same time. As a child who found social interactions challenging, Winterbottom grew up studying human behavior as a means of survival. All he ever wanted to do was blend in, and so he watched, and imitated those around him, so he could vanish; disappear in plain sight. Although he never acquired these natural inclinations for himself, he learned to understand them in a way that others took for granted. It was the reason McCuen excused his callous nature, and on that night, it was the reason why he was standing alone in the dark, with the man who walked the tall grasses of Brooklyn.

It wasn't long before a car lumbered over the patch of loose gravel at the entrance to the lot. Whelan and Adams emerged and quietly joined McCuen in the stark glow of the headlights.

“Has he wandered off again?” smiled Whelan.

“He won’t be long,” replied McCuen.

They stood in the quiet air for nearly five minutes before Winterbottom returned. “You both look like hell,” said Winterbottom, coming out of the darkness.

“Thanks, Anselm,” replied Adams. “You’re not looking so good yourself.”

“Chasing the dead will do that to you,” he replied smiling, though she could tell that his mind was elsewhere. “What did you find?”

“The only common thread between our victims are their husbands,” said Whelan, as he handed McCuen a dossier. “According to several sources, Alford and Stanhope have been harsh business competitors for the past few years.”

“But they’re not the only ones,” interrupted Adams. “Apparently, John Fields, a billionaire investment banker, is also a part of the fray. Some of the more dramatic people we spoke to said that the dealings between the ‘Three Kings of Wall Street’ are more akin to war than business.”

“Recently, Alford had to surrender most of his real estate holdings,” said Whelan. “We’ve compiled as much information as we could on both Olivia and Walter Alford, including brief biographies, financial investments, and a summary of their philanthropic work.”

Adams pulled the file from her satchel and handed it to Winterbottom.

“I figured you’d enjoy some light reading for the car ride.”

She knew that for Winterbottom the drive would be the equivalent of crossing the Atlantic Ocean in a barrel.

“Thank you, Maya,” said Winterbottom, sincerely. “This will help.”

* * *

If wealth and power could be represented in blood and bone, Walter Alford would be its absolute configuration. The only living heir to a fortune as old as the country itself, Alford commanded admiration, if for no other reason than for his tenacity. Born just after the end of World War II, he witnessed the boom of the postwar economy, and developed an appetite for success. Much like his father, he adopted a business strategy similar to the military tactics used during the war. In his prime, he'd accept nothing but total surrender, and more often than not, he would get it. In the course of his lifetime, he built a tremendous empire and left many of his rivals financially broken. Despite his brutal successes and corporate conquests, Alford adhered to a rigid form of decorum which had long since been abandoned by his younger competitors. He would crush you financially, and tear at your pecuniary corpse like a crow, but in victory he would offer some form of consolation, most often in a subsidiary company worth a fraction of what he had taken from you. In other words, he was brutal, but not barbaric, which made him far more gracious than some. Millennials are the real cannibals of Wall Street. In the post-crash world we live in, the stock market will never yield another Warren Buffett, but it's a feeding ground for schools of hungry piranhas. One of them could never take down a bull on its own, but en masse, they could strip it to the bone. In recent months, and in keeping with the allegory, Alford had been wounded, and the piranhas were circling. The old king was in decline. Many believed that he had failed to accept that the corporate world was changing, and at seventy-four years old, adaptation was too difficult.

The perception of his personal life was as expected, having married Olivia, a woman less than half his age. Some felt their relationship boiled down to her need for money, and his desire for a trophy. Others said that the merciless financier was genuinely in love with her. As Winterbottom poured over the financial reports and magazine articles, his mind began swimming through the possibilities. Possession and power, love and money, these were all reasons enough on their own. Men had killed for much less.

After a long drive, and upon arriving at the gatehouse, Winterbottom detached himself from his reading. As Alford's mansion came into view, they were all struck by the breadth of his estate, Whelan and Adams shifting in their seats to take it all in. It was a towering building with a large mansard roof, supported by broad stone walls. Built in the Beaux-Arts style of architecture, it was a monument to the wealth and prosperity of the previous century. As they moved down the driveway, Winterbottom's attention lingered on the dormant gardens and the short-limbed trees of the estate. When they arrived, he exited the car quietly and followed the others to the front entrance where they were greeted by Alford's personal secretary.

"Good evening, Captain McCuen," said the man waiting for them at the front door. "My name is Averill Becker, Mr. Alford's personal assistant—we spoke on the phone."

"Yes, thank you," replied McCuen. "I'm grateful to you and Mr. Alford for meeting with us on such short notice."

"He's glad to be of help, but I'm afraid he's quite distraught, as you can imagine," continued Becker. "Please try to keep things as brief as possible. He wouldn't want me telling you this—but frankly, he's not entirely well, and I worry that at his age—"

"I understand, Mr. Becker," said McCuen. "We'll be brief."

"Thank you, Captain."

As they walked through the entryway of the house, Winterbottom stayed in the back of the group, following Whelan and Adams. As they moved through the atrium, McCuen looked over his shoulder, catching a glimpse of Winterbottom in the rear of the pack. Not much further on, he again looked over his shoulder, watching as Winterbottom moved along the corridor behind him. He seemed distracted; more so than usual. Winterbottom's eyes were darting around from the ceiling to the floor, as if tracking a lumbering housefly nearing the end of its life. McCuen quickly introduced Becker to Whelan, so that he could drop back and talk with Winterbottom.

"What is it?" said McCuen under his breath.

"This was a mistake," replied Winterbottom, nervously. "I shouldn't be here. You know I'm no good with people."

"It's going to be fine," said McCuen. "Was it the car ride?

"No."

"There's no need to be nervous. I'll do all the talking. I just need you to take in as much as you can. You don't have to say anything—in fact, I'd prefer that you didn't."

"It's not that," said Winterbottom, cautiously.

"Then what is it?"

"Well, there's a very real chance that he'll recognize me." McCuen froze in mid-step.

"You know him?" whispered McCuen, angrily. "Yes," replied Winterbottom. "I mean, technically."

"Please tell me you're talking about his secretary?"

"No—I'm talking about Walter Alford."

"And you're just telling me this now?" McCuen snapped rhetorically.

"Look, I'm sorry, Ed. We met a few times in passing—but it was years ago."

"We were in the car for nearly two hours, and it never crossed your mind?"

"It didn't occur to me until I was inside the house."

"Jesus Christ, Anselm—you've been here before?"

"It was a long time ago!" scoffed Winterbottom, nervously chewing his lip. "What do you want me to do?"

McCuen began shaking his head as they continued to walk down the hallway. His mind began racing as he came face to face with what might happen. He looked behind him, but the front door was nowhere in sight. They were stuck. He had no choice; they had to continue on, and hope that Alford didn't recognize Winterbottom. If he did, McCuen wouldn't be able to offer any reasonable explanation, and that could mean the end of McCuen's career.

"Just stay back with Adams," said McCuen, sternly. "And watch for anything that seems out of place. If we're lucky, he'll be too upset about his wife to recognize you. Whatever you do —don't say a word."

"Okay."

Collecting himself, McCuen cut past Whelan and Adams and rejoined Becker at the head of the line.

They continued into a room framed by marble floors and dark mahogany, as Becker's pace slowed. At the center of the room was an enormous white marble fireplace, adorned with Grecian figures, carved in high relief, a tribute to wealth and decadence. Standing beside it, staring into the open fire, was Walter Alford.

Even as an older man, Alford's athletic frame echoed his early days as a member of the Yale crew team, but the appearance of youthful strength was quickly betrayed by the hard-drawn lines of his face. He wore dark, Merino wool pants and a shirt that was undone at the collar. No amount of luxury or fine clothing could disguise the fact that he appeared utterly defeated. After being introduced, McCuen skillfully introduced his colleagues, avoiding the need to recite names and ranks. As McCuen had hoped, Alford only cast a momentary glance in their direction.

"I'm willing to help in any way that I can, Captain," replied Alford, grimly. "I imagine that in these cases, hard questions must be asked. In order to spare us both undue delay and frustration, I encourage you to be blunt, and direct. I assure you I'll do the same."

Alford then looked back into the fire, resting his forearm against the mantel.

"To start—let me say that I didn't kill Olivia."

"I appreciate your candor," said McCuen. "Perhaps you could tell us more about your relationship with Olivia, and the time leading up to her death." Alford turned and slowly lowered himself into a tall leather chair beside the fire.

"Olivia and I met seven years ago, at a gala for the Metropolitan Museum of Art. She had recently been appointed to the Board of Directors for the museum, and having been introduced, I was happy to play the role of the unwitting, billionaire with an affinity for the Arts. She was radiant. Two years later, we were married."

"And more recently?" asked McCuen.

Alford became rigid, instantly feeling the discomfort of McCuen's inquiry.

"Things have been strained between us," replied Alford, despairingly. "There's no fool like an old fool who thinks he can hold the attention of a woman half his age. I can't say that she was ever unfaithful, but over the past year I've grown suspicious of the possibility." Alford again shifted toward the fire.

"If she had been unfaithful—any idea who it might be?" asked Adams.

"No."

"Is there anyone who would've wanted to harm her?" asked Whelan.

"Not that I can think of," replied Alford. "I've made plenty of enemies, but I can't think of anyone who would take it this far. Not even those goddamned redistributionists. For years I've been receiving threatening letters from environmentalists and animal rights activists, but they've never threatened Olivia. More recently, it's been those socialist brats, but I doubt they had anything to do with this."

"All the same, I'd like to get copies of any recent threatening letters, or communications, if you have them," said McCuen.

"Yes, Captain, I'll have them sent over first thing tomorrow." Alford looked to his secretary, Mr. Becker, and received a nod of confirmation.

"If I may, Mr. Alford," asked Adams. "Can you tell us where you were at the time of your wife's death?"

"That's easy enough," he replied. "I was in Scotland—in the Outer Hebrides—when I was notified that her body had been found."

"Would she have had any reason to be in Central Park that night?" asked McCuen.

"She had no interest in the park."

"Did she have a driver that night?"

"No, I don't think so. We have an apartment on the Upper East Side. She usually stays there when I'm away. As I understand—it's already been searched."

"Yes, that's correct," replied McCuen. "And we'll be returning her belongings to you as soon as we can." Alford sunk lower into his chair.

"Have any of her friends reached out to you?" asked McCuen.

"I'm afraid they haven't—but that's not surprising. Olivia had many friends, but we lived very separate lives. I never cared for her friends, and I'm sure they feel the same way about me. You'd have better luck checking her cell phone."

"Unfortunately, we haven't recovered her phone," replied Whelan. "But we should have the records within a few hours."

"If I had been here—maybe things would be different."

He nodded to Becker, who promptly poured him a glass of scotch. Hearing the fatigue in his voice, and sensing that their time was short, McCuen attempted to steer the conversation in a new direction.

"Who are the business rivals that you mentioned earlier?" asked McCuen.

"In the corporate arena everyone's a rival," replied Alford, taking a generous swallow. "We're all fighting for the same thing, but a few of us have risen above the rest."

"The Three Kings of Wall Street," said McCuen, smiling.

"So, you've heard," said Alford, bolstered by McCuen's comment. "I don't know when it all began, but I've tried to distance myself from it."

"They say that you're the wealthiest of them all," said Whelan, adding buoyancy to the balloon.

"Well, I've lasted the longest," replied Alford.

"Is it true that you, Fields, and Stanhope have something against one another," continued Whelan.

"Men want what they can't have—that's always been true," replied Alford. "But men want what other men have—even more. They would say that I'm ruthless, but I've always respected my adversaries. This younger generation—is abhorrent. They've had everything handed to them, and their sense of entitlement is astounding. Fields and Stanhope may not be as young, or contemptuous as some of the others, but they're no different. It used to be about building something great, but now it's all about the show. Fast cars and beautiful women— trinkets and idols."

He took a last sip.

"The worst part is that before they're done, they'll inherit far more than their own family fortunes. They'll have mine, too. I have no children, and when I'm gone, they'll lay siege to what I've built."

By this time, Winterbottom's interest in the marble fireplace had drawn him closer, and he began admiring its ornate carvings, which seemed to dance in the fire's light. McCuen watched, helpless to stop him. It took less than a few seconds before he drew Alford's attention.

"Do you recognize it?" asked Alford, pointing to the mantel.

Winterbottom seemed surprised to be spoken to.

"I'm afraid not," said Winterbottom nervously looking back at McCuen. "Is it Roman?"

"Greek—from the fourth century," said Alford, clearly disappointed in Winterbottom's assessment.

Then Alford set down his glass and turned his attention back to the mantelpiece.

"*We men are wretched things*," he whispered just loud enough for his guests to hear. The fatigue in his voice signaled that their time was running out.

"Is there anything else, Captain?"

"That's all for now—thank you, Mr. Alford. We'll do our best not to trouble you any further."

With that Mr. Becker escorted them back to the front entrance and asked McCuen to contact him directly if he needed any further assistance.

For the first ten minutes of the car ride, no one said a word. They all felt as though they had wasted precious time. It was procedurally necessary to meet with Alford in person, but very little had been gained. Whelan was the first to break the silence.

"His alibi's solid enough."

"And incredibly convenient," replied Adams. "That makes two wealthy men who were hundreds of miles away when their spouses were murdered. And for what it's worth—she was cheating on him."

"Maybe," said McCuen. "But I don't think he cared enough to kill her for it."

"It's more than enough for some people," she replied.

"If he was worried about her having an affair, he wouldn't be paying for an apartment in Midtown, and taking off to Scotland for weeks at a time." McCuen paused before lobbing another possible motive. "If he killed her, it was because she was going to take his money."

"Another good reason," said Whelan.

Pausing, Whelan smiled slightly, and looked at Winterbottom who was staring out the car window.

"That Roman fireplace was something else, huh?"

Adams held back a smile while they waited for Winterbottom's response. Even Whelan felt disappointed when it never came. Winterbottom's mind was turning again.

"We men are wretched things," said Winterbottom, repeating Alford's words. "That marble mantelpiece depicted the Trojan War. He was quoting the Iliad."

"How does that help us," asked Adams.

"It doesn't," he replied, returning to the window. "In fact, it may be entirely irrelevant."

"Help us out here, Anselm?" said Whelan.

"Kings, gods, and men—all at war with each other," replied Winterbottom. "The Iliad— the Trojan War—it was fought over a woman."

V

THE GAME

The morning came quickly, and found Winterbottom rushing out the front door, just as McCuen pulled up. On the way back from Long Island, McCuen had arranged an interview with Thomas Fields for that morning, but they were running late.

"I should've warned you," said Winterbottom. "Everything east of Lexington is closed off. Just stay on it until Seventy-First Street." Looking back at the house, McCuen saw Mrs. Bruce closing the front door.

"How's Agnes doing these days?"

"Oh, god!" replied Winterbottom. "She's driving me crazy, Ed. She's all up in arms because a man came by the house yesterday asking for me."

"Who was it?"

"I don't know," replied Winterbottom.

McCuen smiled, remembering his first meeting with Mrs. Bruce, the woman he once described as a hurricane dressed like a schoolteacher.

"Did she pretend to be deaf again?"

"She does it every time," said Winterbottom. "The poor bastard didn't stand a chance."

Eager to learn what had happened overnight, Winterbottom shifted the conversation. "You didn't find any more dead women in old dresses did you?"

"Nothing came in last night."

The inevitability of the next murder sank deeper into McCuen's stomach.

"You just reminded me—before we get there, is there anything I need to know? Did you and Fields have dinner last week, or perhaps you were the best man at his wedding—anything like that?"

"No—I've never met Thomas Fields."

"Are you sure?"

"Yes, I'm sure," replied Winterbottom. "And I'm sorry for last night—it was careless of me. I've had a lot on my mind lately."

"It all worked out," said McCuen. "But you do realize what it would mean for me if anyone found out about you."

"I know, Ed," replied Winterbottom. "It's not like I want that kind of attention either."

"Good," said McCuen.

A ten-minute drive turned into a thirty-minute crawl, and by the time they turned onto Park Avenue, they were late for their meeting with Fields. When they arrived, McCuen parked on the street and they hurried up to Field's rooftop apartment. At the front door they were greeted by a stern Frenchman whose demeanor varied little from the mahogany door he had opened for them. He was tall and thin, with a disposition hinting toward a singular dedication to his work.

"This way, please."

The man escorted them into a room that was expansive and modern; a fitting antithesis to Alford's old-world mansion. The room's minimalist decor initially masked the fact that it was in a state of renovation. Paint colors had been swept across the walls in swatches, and rolls of fabric were spread across the floor. More bolts of fabric were stacked in the corner, near a selection of marble tiles, all up for consideration. At the far end of the unfinished room stood Mrs. Esmé Fields, the wife of Thomas Fields. She was busily directing a team of personal assistants, when the Frenchman caught her attention.

"How do you do, gentlemen," she said kindly. "Captain McCuen, I presume."

"Yes, Mrs. Fields," replied McCuen. "I'm sorry to interrupt like this, but we were hoping to meet with your husband. Is he available?"

She looked to their escort for the answer.

"Is he still here, Lucien?"

"No, I'm afraid he had an appointment on Wall Street that was most pressing."

"Thank you, I'll see to these gentlemen."

She was holding a binder of various fabric swatches, as she spoke to her secretary. "Let's get a sample of the Egyptian Ivory for the East wall and order the Makrana tile for the floor."

Her secretary nodded and hurried away into the next room.

"I apologize for the mess," she continued. "They say that change is good, but who knew that a master bedroom renovation would eventually take over the rest of the house?"

She was beautiful, and yet Winterbottom sensed that she was burdened by something. He stopped well short of having pity on her, but he could see that she was withdrawn, as if passing through life more like an observer than an active participant. It was a sadness much deeper than a contemporary seclusion.

As the daughter of a French Diplomat, Esmé spent much of her childhood cloistered behind embassy walls and in private schools. Her world existed between 7th Arrondissement and Park Avenue. It would be wrong for anyone to fault her for it; you can't know what you haven't seen. In that way, she would never know the simple pleasures of life, as much as most would never recognize the sweeping veins of Makrana tile. For her, the world was always screened; seen from fifty stories up, through tinted windows, chauffeured car doors, and idle dinner party conversations. It lent to her a naïve urbanity which implored forgiveness for any pretentiousness that was felt. As Winterbottom watched her, he was reminded of the iridescent plumage of the *Paradisaea Apoda*, and its remote inaccessibility. Yes, she was beautiful, like the bird; there was no denying it. But a bird in a gilded cage is a caged-bird, nonetheless.

"Thank you for your willingness to help, Mrs. Fields," said McCuen, politely. "But I'm afraid we need to speak with your husband directly."

"I understand, Captain," she replied. "Thomas said it had something to do with the murder of Olivia Alford."

"Yes, I'm afraid so," said McCuen.

"What a dreadful thing," she replied. "I wasn't that close with her, given our husbands' business, but she was always kind to me."

McCuen then saw an opportunity he couldn't ignore.

"What exactly is the nature of your husband's business with Mr. Alford?"

"Well, Captain, I can't say that it has much to do with business at all. They hate each other. They always have."

"May I ask why?"

"I'm not sure," she replied cautiously.

"You're not sure of why they hate each other—or you're not sure if it's okay for me to ask?"

She was nervous, and her voice quivered with trepidation, but the comment made her smile.

"Captain, I want to help you, but what does it matter if Thomas hates Alford or not?" As she spoke, she continued to work and they followed her into the adjoining master bedroom. The entire room had been stripped clean from floor to ceiling, and the walls were being primed a solid white. Even the mattress cover had been removed from the bed, exposing its swollen foam.

"I'm just trying to understand it all," continued McCuen.

"I can't see what any of this has to do with Thomas?"

"We're looking for anything that might help, Mrs. Fields. It's really a matter of ruling out motives more than anything else," said McCuen. "Did he know Olivia well?"

"Of course," she replied. "They served together on the Board of Directors for the Metropolitan Museum of Art. Thomas is one of their principal donors and often worked with Olivia on fundraising efforts."

As they spoke, she ran her hands across a sheet of Belgian linen.

"Captain, you can't possibly think he had anything to do with Olivia's murder? He could never do such a thing."

"No, Mrs. Fields," replied McCuen, trying to reassure her. "We're not suggesting anything like that— we just need to understand the nature of his connection to Olivia and Walter Alford."

She shifted her posture and crossed her arms.

"Perhaps, it would be best if you spoke with Thomas directly."

"I intend to," said McCuen. "But two women have been murdered—and there will be a third unless I can stop it."

She began pacing and let out a heavy sigh.

"Alright—but you must be discreet," she insisted. "I don't want to say anything that would upset Thomas—he's a very private person."

"Of course, Mrs. Fields."

She returned to the main living area and signaled for Lucien and the remaining assistants to clear out of the room. When they had all left, she continued.

"Thomas's father, George Fields, was once a good friend of Walter Alford, but even as friends—they were terribly competitive. Whether it was business, the stock market, or sports, they were always trying to outdo each other, or at least that's how it was told to me."

"I take it they had a falling out?" asked McCuen

"Yes—to put it lightly," she replied.

Then she stopped suddenly.

"The Seneca Club," she said remembering its name. "That's where it all began."

"Where what began?" asked Winterbottom.

"They started playing this game, at the club. I've only heard Thomas speak of it on one occasion. It was all very secretive—boys being boys, and all that sort of thing. It was because of that game that old George and Walter Alford grew to hate each other. In a matter of months George had squandered nearly a hundred million dollars, and his mental health began to deteriorate, rapidly. Eventually, Alford won the game and George committed suicide."

"What was this game they were playing?" asked McCuen, curiously. "I really don't know the specifics, but Thomas could tell you."

"Were they betting on something?"

"No," she answered, confidently.

Winterbottom could see that she was holding back and jumped in.

"You said that George Fields squandered a hundred million dollars—on what?" Her posture stiffened and she exhaled nervously.

"Paintings," she replied. "They were all buying these paintings—but I don't really know much about it."

McCuen could hear the regret in her voice for having said as much as she did. Worried, she continued.

"Thomas was a young man when his father died. Rightly, or wrongly—he's always blamed Alford for what happened to his father."

McCuen could see from her trembling hands that he had pushed her far enough. "Thank you, Mrs. Fields," said McCuen. "And I'm sorry if I've upset you."

"It's alright, Captain," she replied. "I apologize for my hesitation—it's just that I've never dealt with anything like this before. I'll have Thomas contact you as soon as he returns. I'm sure he can be more help to you than I've been."

"I look forward to speaking with him," said McCuen. "And in the meantime, please take every precaution."

"Thank you for your concern," she replied. Then she pushed a call button on the nearby light switch, signaling for the porter.

McCuen thanked her again, and soon noticed that Winterbottom wasn't with him. Walking down the hallway, he found him in the foyer, speaking quietly with the Argentinian maid. As he approached, he could hear only the last few words the woman said.

"Las paredes oyen."

As the car doors closed, McCuen unleashed his newfound enthusiasm.

"I'll get Adams and Whelan working on the Seneca Club, and I'll try to meet with Fields, this afternoon if I can—"

"Would you mind dropping me at Madison and East Eighty-First Street?" interrupted Winterbottom, unsympathetically.

It was as if he hadn't heard McCuen at all.

"Why—where are you going?"

"I'll let you know if it pans out," replied Winterbottom. "But, I'd also like to modify our arrangement. I'd like the case file, tonight."

"Anselm, I said I would give it to you—"

"I missed something that I shouldn't have—but if I'm right, I'll have fulfilled my obligation to you. Just be sure to bring the entire case file with you tonight. I'll call you as soon as I have something."

VI

THE SINGER SARGENT PORTRAITS

Within the hour, Winterbottom had left a message for McCuen to meet him at the Metropolitan Museum of Art, in the wing dedicated to American Art. The museum would close in a few hours, so McCuen, Whelan, and Adams rushed through the galleries housing artifacts from China and Japan before entering the American wing. They proceeded to the second floor, where they found Winterbottom waiting for them. He led them through several adjacent galleries to Gallery 771, where they were confronted with five life-sized portraits housed in ornate gold-leaf frames. Each depicted a woman wearing a Victorian dress.

"These are what our killer is after," said Winterbottom. McCuen and his team were speechless, slowly turning in circles as their eyes moved from one painting to another.

The portraits were by the famous American artist John Singer Sargent and dated back to the late 19th-century. The first was a dual portrait depicting a husband and wife. In it the woman was wearing a plain dress, in white and gray, beneath an informal walking coat. She was holding a straw boater hat in her right hand. Her dress and hat clearly matched those worn by Emma Strauss on the night of her murder.

The portrait of Mr. and Mrs. Stokes, as it was titled, was every bit a study in grey and black; perhaps even more so than Whistler's famous portrait. Middle neutrals and stark blacks dominated the composition, and combined with Sargent's liberal use of turpentine, they make the painting come alive, despite the stern postures of its subjects. Mrs. Stokes' fair skin took shape in the delicate smearing of *blanc d'argent* and an almost undetectable hint of *cadmium yellow light*, highlighted by subtle touches of *Chinese vermillion*. The woman smiled, reservedly, as the shadowy face of her husband could be seen lurking behind her. I would later learn that Art historians have noted that Mrs. Stokes and her husband were just recently married when the portrait was painted. Although newly married, any viewer could see the strain between them. It's as if Sargent had used despondency as a medium, rolling it in with the linseed oil. To enrich the painting's complexity, Sargent wanted to paint Mrs. Stokes standing beside a Great Dane, in homage to a Van Dyck portrait from the 1600s. However, Sargent couldn't find a suitable dog, so he asked Mr. Stokes to stand in its place. It was an interesting parallel to what was known about Emma Strauss and her estranged and brooding fiancé, William Stanhope.

The second portrait in the gallery was that of Charlotte Louise Burckhardt, known to the art world as *The Lady with the Rose*. It featured a stunning young woman wearing a black dress, carefully balancing a white rose between her left thumb and forefinger. The dress was familiar to them, and the white rose had an unmistakable presence in the murder of Olivia Alford.

As they all remained quiet, Whelan and Adams took particular notice of the slight band of diamonds painted into the woman's hair.

These masterful portraits held untold subtleties far beyond their subject's physical qualities. Rendered form, composition, and pigments; traces of *raw umber, ivory black,* and *alizarin crimson*; every bit as detailed as those of the forensic nature found at each crime scene. Oil and pigment, chloroform and death. The thoughtful brushstrokes on canvas, and the purple contusions on the neck; an object brought to life, and a life expelled from its form. They had become portraits of murder. Before much attention could be paid to the remaining paintings, Winterbottom spoke.

"These two portraits leave little doubt about their connection to the murders, but what is of paramount concern are the remaining portraits in the gallery. Any one of these portraits could be our killer's next work."

"How many portraits are there?", asked Adams.

"Dozens of paintings are on display," replied Winterbottom. "But the museum has eighty of Sargent's portraits in its overall collection."

"That gives our killer a lot to work with," said Whelan. "But—even if these portraits could point us toward his next victim, how will we know which one will be next?"

"We won't," replied Winterbottom, despairingly. "But it's not as bleak as you think."

"Thanks to good old-fashioned, Victorian-era male chauvinism—and because men are generally arrogant, self-involved assholes—less than half of the portraits here are of women. That gives us much better odds. More importantly, these paintings prove how intentional our killer is. The white rose from the park was placed in Olivia Alford's left hand, exactly matching the Sargent portrait of Louise Burckhardt. These details, and the dresses themselves, suggest a level of obsession that goes far deeper than murder itself. The killer has been in this very gallery, we can be sure of that. He's stood where we are standing now. He's studied these paintings, intimately. These paintings—and this museum, is our connection to the killer. This is where we start."

Winterbottom paused and walked to the adjacent wall of the gallery. "Regardless of what comes next, I can assuredly say that our killer is working up to his greatest masterpiece."

Winterbottom turned to the last portrait in the line. It was one of the most famous portraits of all time, Sargent's finest work, the portrait of Virginie Amélie Avegno Gautreau, more commonly known as *Madame X.* The portrait depicted the slight and delicate frame of Gautreau; her powdered white skin in stark contrast with a pitch-black satin dress. Her pose was purely feminine, and provocative, even for modern appetites. The painting was lavish and stirred seduction against a background of deep yellow ochre and burnt sienna. Many know the painting, but few are aware of its history.

Madame X was Sargent's most prolific work, but at its introduction at the Salon in Paris in 1884, it stirred rumors of the artist's obsession with his subject. Its seductive nature was so apparent that its title was chosen in order to provide anonymity for Gautreau, who was hoping to avoid a public scandal. Not to mention that after its shocking reception, Sargent repainted the shoulder strap of Gautreau's dress to make it appear more securely fastened, hoping to dampen its original, carnal rendition. A testament to his own affections for Gautreau, and the painting itself, was the fact that Sargent kept the painting all for himself for over thirty years.

"This portrait will be his grand finale," said Winterbottom. "The culmination of his devious work."

"We've been given an opportunity in these paintings," said Whelan. "But like you said before—they don't tell us anything about who the next victim will be."

"You're right—we have a lot of work to do," replied McCuen. "However, given the information regarding the Seneca Club, and the fact that Olivia

Alford served on the Board of Directors for this very museum, our killer is likely connected to both. We have to find out how."

"But he could be anybody," said Adams. "A museum donor, a disgruntled security guard, or just a day member coming to look at the paintings."

"Security guards and day-visitors, aren't members of the Seneca Club," said Whelan. The connection between the murders and the club is too strong to be a coincidence. We need to get the membership list, and cross-check it with anything we can find out from the museum."

"That might be a challenge," replied Adams, doubtfully. "The club's entire premise is based on the secrecy of its membership."

"I'll handle the Seneca Club," said McCuen. "You and Whelan see what you can learn from the museum—I want everything from gallery surveillance, lists of employees, acquisition files, and auction records. We need to know exactly how involved Emma Strauss and Olivia Alford were with these paintings." As Adams and Whelan left the gallery, McCuen carefully eyed his surroundings to ensure that he and Winterbottom were alone.

"A deal's a deal," said McCuen. Then, without another word, he opened his coat and handed Winterbottom a small, unmarked thumb-drive. "Just as you requested—the complete case file." Winterbottom reached out to accept it, just as McCuen pulled back slightly. "I don't suppose I could talk you out of this."

"No," replied Winterbottom, solemnly. "You can't." McCuen placed it in his hand.

"I hope you find what you're looking for," he said.

Winterbottom paused and looked at the thumb-drive in his hand.

"You've risked quite a lot for me," he said. "Thank you, Ed."

"Well, you have what you've been looking for—every last piece. I don't suppose you want to come with me to the Seneca Club?"

"It's on my way home—why not," replied Winterbottom. "Besides, I think I'd like to see this one through to the end."

VII

THE SENECA CLUB

The Seneca Club was more than just a men's social club for New York's wealthiest citizens. It was far more exclusive than that. Its members included three former U.S. Presidents, foreign diplomats, politicians, professional athletes, and business executives from around the world. But what set it apart from any other social club was that it required each member to maintain financial assets upwards of twenty-million dollars, or else be expelled from the organization. With a moral foundation that equated wealth with self-worth, one can understand why a group of rich, white men might not see the offense in naming their social club after a tribe of native Iroquois. Or perhaps they were aware of the indignity, and just didn't care. How many terrible things have been excused by the words "to the victor go the spoils" and "boys will be boys?" In actuality, the club was far worse than it appeared. Inside, its members had the privacy and protection to be themselves, to say what they felt, and to act as they pleased. As McCuen and Winterbottom pulled up to the front entrance, all of Winterbottom's worst assumptions were realized.

"Ed, there's a fucking statue of an Indian at the front entrance!"

McCuen ducked his head to see out through the passenger side window.

"Well, look at that—there it is," said McCuen in disgust.

"I hate this place already."

"Come on, maybe it's a symbol of the great respect they have for Native American culture." As they walked up the steps to the front entrance, they passed by the life-sized statue of the great Seneca warrior, Chief Red Jacket, who had fought alongside the Americans in the War of 1812. "You have to admit, it's an impressive statue."

"Yes, it is," said Winterbottom. "Any thoughts on why it's standing outside the club?" His point was well taken. "I'll bet you a hundred dollars they don't have a single, respectful example of native culture inside. If you still have faith in humanity—here's your chance to prove it."

"That's a steep price—but I'll take that bet," replied McCuen. "And, if you're right—I'll let you burn down the building." Of course, McCuen was being facetious, but knowing Winterbottom's tendency for literal interpretation, it made him feel a little uneasy. Inside the club, they proceeded to the main desk where they were greeted by a squirrel-like man, wearing tortoise-shell eyeglasses, a tailored gray suit, and an obnoxious chartreuse bowtie.

"Welcome, gentlemen," he said. "How may I help you?"

"We'd like to inquire about membership to the club," said McCuen. "We'd also like to get a list of your current members."

"Well, sir, this is a private men's club," replied the man at the desk. "I'm afraid the names of our members are strictly confidential. Only active members are allowed access to the membership list."

It was as McCuen feared, and he wasn't willing to push the issue and risk tipping off the investigation. "Thank you for your time."

McCuen nodded to Winterbottom and turned toward the door. "We're going to have to find another way."

“There’s no time for that,” whispered Winterbottom. He turned back to the man at the desk, carefully hiding his disgust for the man’s bowtie. “If I became a member of the club, how long would it take to get access to the membership list?” asked Winterbottom. The man at the desk looked annoyed by the question.

“I’m afraid we have very particular requirements for membership. Our bylaws state that you must—”

“I know what the bylaws say—I’d like to become a member,” snapped Winterbottom, trampling over the man’s response. A look of surprise and disdain flashed across the man’s face as he quietly assessed Winterbottom’s field jacket and worn Australian trail boots.

“Our annual membership is $120,000.00, but the club’s bylaws dictate that a minimum of twenty-million dollars must be maintained at all times, in order to be granted full membership —”

“Yes, I’m aware—”

“Thank you for your understanding—”

“I’m Anselm Winterbottom.” The man froze at the mention of the name. His reaction was precisely why McCuen never disclosed Winterbottom’s true identity to anyone, not even Whelan and Adams. It wasn’t a name that was commonly recognizable, but for anyone acquainted with the *Forbes* list, it was the equivalent of being a Saudi prince. Without prompting, Winterbottom produced his passport, bank account information, and birth certificate, that as eccentricity would have it, he carried with him as a matter of principle at all times. The clerk carried the documents, along with an astounded expression, into the adjoining room for verification. Within minutes he re-emerged.

“Mr. Winterbottom, please excuse this most inadequate introduction to our club."

"That's quite alright," replied Winterbottom, impersonating someone with social grace. "Circumstances being what they are, I can understand your unpreparedness. People seem to think I've disappeared. Just last week someone told me they thought I was dead. Can you imagine? It would've been more thoughtful of me to call ahead."

"Thank you for your understanding. I'll have your membership approved by the end of the day—"

"That's fine," said Winterbottom. "But I would like the membership list now, as a courtesy—I'm sure you understand." The man paused at the unorthodox request, unsure of what to do.

"Well—why not?" he said nervously. "You certainly meet the requirements. I'll have it for you within the hour."

"Thank you," said Winterbottom. "Oh—and we'd also like a tour of the club, while we're here." His request had nothing to do with the investigation and everything to do with his bet with McCuen.

"Yes, of course—follow me," he replied. The man led them up a nearby staircase to the upper chambers of the club. Along the way he spouted off the historical significance of the building and its furnishings, not once mentioning Chief Red Jacket. Every wall of the club was covered with paintings from the early Colonial period, but as they neared the end of the tour, they had yet to see a sign of anything indigenous.

"The least they could do is put a god-damned tomahawk on the wall," whispered Winterbottom, as they proceeded down the upstairs corridor. Finally, they came to the end of a long hallway where the man led them into a large gaming room. It was set up like the grand ballrooms of the 19th-century with tables and chairs neatly arranged around a long central bar that stretched the length of the room. The room itself seemed large enough to host a polo match, quite oversized for the handful of gentlemen huddled in the far corner of the room. On the table was a menagerie of empty glasses, and the billowing plumes of cigar smoke suggested they were nearing the end of a long game of Shanghai.

"Look," whispered McCuen, pointing to a series of Native American portraits on the far wall. "See—a respectful homage to native culture."

"They don't count," said Winterbottom, dismissively.

"Like hell, they don't," said McCuen. "What could be more respectful than classical portraits?"

"Ed—they're hanging above the bar."

"Assholes!" muttered McCuen, recognizing the discriminatory stereotype. He had clearly lost the bet. As the squirrel-man continued to spout off about the club's prestigious clientele, they saw a man break away from the card game in the corner and walk to the bar. It was William Stanhope, the fiancé of Emma Strauss.

"Would you permit us to sample the scotch selection in private?" said Winterbottom.

"Of course, Mr. Winterbottom—and the servers will be happy to answer any questions you might have." The man signaled his approval to the head bartender. "I'll be at the main desk if you should require any further assistance." With that, Winterbottom and McCuen walked to the bar and stood next to Stanhope.

"Mr. Stanhope," said McCuen. "I'm Captain McCuen, with the NYPD—we spoke on the phone the night Emma was killed." Stanhope leaned on the bar and drew back slightly, waiting for his vision to adjust. Given McCuen's presence in the club, Stanhope's confusion was understandable, but he was also quite drunk, and his pending order for another drink made it clear that he intended to remain so for the immediate future.

"I'm surprised to see you here, Captain," remarked Stanhope. "The police business is more lucrative than I thought."

"We didn't expect to find you here, either," replied McCuen. "With that said, you may be able to help us with something."

"I'd be happy to," replied Stanhope. Taking his refilled glass, he walked with them to an empty booth in the corner.

"How can I help?" he muttered as he sank into his seat.

"You were in Los Angeles on the night Emma was found?"

"Yes, and I told the other detectives as much when we last spoke." His recollection indicated a small but welcomed shred of sobriety.

"We'd like to know why you were at that gala in Los Angeles?" said McCuen. "And before you answer—you should know that we often ask people questions that we already know the answers to." McCuen's voice had suddenly shifted to an unforgiving tone. It was a technique he had mastered over the years. Its effectiveness relied on his amicable and even presence, but when it shifted, even slightly, people felt as if the floor was giving out from under them. Stanhope was sitting down, but he felt it just the same. Clearing his throat, he replied.

"Then you must know about the paintings," he said, as he sat up straighter. Then he smiled clumsily and finished his glass of gin and vermouth in one hearty gulp. After a heavy sigh, he continued.

"I went there to meet with a private collector. I was trying to acquire the Sargent portrait of Mrs. Frank Millet."

"Thank you for being honest with us," said McCuen, as he pressed forward. "Who else is playing this game?" Stanhope realized that he had been cornered.

"It started with myself and a few other members of the club."

"This is a murder investigation—we'll need names," insisted McCuen. Stanhope reluctantly continued.

"Walter Alford, Scott McClarendon, Stephen Bennett, and Thomas Fields—but, I doubt they'll admit it. We took an oath of secrecy, on our honor—for whatever that's worth. The whole thing started right here in this room, actually. I may even have been drinking at the time, if you can imagine." He sank further down into his seat and undid the top two buttons of his dress shirt.

"Fields had heard about the game from his father, it was originally a thing between old George and Walter Alford. After George Fields died, Alford was quite happy with the prospect of a new generation of players. He set out the terms, and we all placed the names of well-known artists into a hat. We drew the name of John Singer Sargent, and just like that his portraits became our pursuit. Every year, the player with the fewest Sargent portraits in his possession is eliminated from the game, and expelled from the Seneca Club for life. McClarendon and Bennett already hated each other and the thought of the other being expelled from the club was too much to pass up. I was the club's newest member at the time, so I took it as my opportunity to gain the respect of the old guard—men like Alford."

"And what about Fields?" asked Winterbottom.

"Thomas and I were good friends back then, we did everything together, but mostly, he resented Alford for what happened to his father. He was playing to get even."

"We were told that his father committed suicide."

"He did," replied Stanhope. "Did Thomas tell you—or was it Esmé? It was probably Esmé, I don't think she even knows the whole story. It's a carefully guarded family secret."

"I'm intrigued," said McCuen. It was all Stanhope needed to continue.

"George Fields was a raving lunatic. I don't just mean he was a little off—I mean he was a full-blown psychopath. When he was sixteen, he raped and murdered a fourteen-year-old girl in Vienna, but his family's influence kept it out of the papers and spared him from going to prison. Instead, he spent the next eight years hospitalized at the Creedmoor Asylum in Queens. He was diagnosed with schizophrenia, and anti-social personality disorder. He was released from the hospital early, and being the only heir when his father died, George became one of the richest men in the world. The newspapers, most of which he owned, portrayed him as a titan of industry, but in reality he was deeply disturbed." Stanhope reached for his empty glass again, and signaled to the bartender for another. "After Thomas was born, George's behavior became increasingly unpredictable. The game with Alford had become an obsession, and he spent millions on Neo-Classical paintings. They were after the paintings of Ingres, back then. Rumor has it that he offered two hundred million for the *Grand Odalisque*, but the Louvre wouldn't let it go. Eventually, he was declared mentally unfit, and lost financial control. In the months before his suicide, he was seen stumbling around the grounds of his estate—talking to the trees. On the morning that he died, he told Thomas that he was late for tea with Joan of Arc. Shortly after, he blew his brains out with a pair of dueling pistols."

"Did Alford know about his hospitalization and the murder in Vienna?"

"Probably not, but he knew that old George wasn't all there—he just didn't care. He's a ruthless son of a bitch."

"And how does Thomas play into all this?"

"Hardly at all," replied Stanhope. "Sure—he was drawn into playing the game by Alford, but Thomas is nothing like his father. He inherited his empire, and he hired the most brilliant financial minds he could find to bring it back from the dead. He's more interested in living the life of a billionaire, than working like one."

"How so?"

"The man is decadent—or at least he used to be," replied Stanhope. "It's hard to imagine, but not so long ago he was a living Bacchus—before Esmé came along. Then just like that, he shut it all down. No more parties, no more women, no more drinking, and no more games. She probably saved his life, but she ruined a great deal of fun for the rest of us." Stanhope stretched his arms out along the upper cushion of the booth. "I shouldn't have been surprised when he dropped out of the game."

"He's not playing?"

"Not anymore," said Stanhope catching his breath. "He resigned just after McClarendon and Bennett were eliminated. He hasn't graced these hallowed halls since, leaving just me and Walter Alford to fight over the portraits."

"And where are McClarendon and Bennett now?"

"I have no idea," replied Stanhope. "I haven't seen them since they were expelled from the club, last year. They tied for last place—how fitting. Bennett quietly walked away, but McClarendon made quite an exit. He toppled over tables and threw a chair out of one of the windows. He was always a classy motherfucker."

"Would any of them have reason to kill Emma?"

"No," replied Stanhope, sharply. "No one would—except for me." He said the words so casually that McCuen and Winterbottom questioned what they had heard. "Relax guys!", smiled Stanhope. "I didn't kill Emma, but there's a very good reason why we never got married. You might as well hear it from me, first. Emma was having an affair."

"Who was she seeing?" asked McCuen.

"I wish I knew," he replied. "It could have been anyone."

"Then how can you be so sure she was having an affair?"

"I would catch her lying about where she'd been, or where she was going."

"Did you ever ask her directly?"

"No," replied Stanhope.

"Why not?" asked McCuen. "You don't strike me as someone who beats around the bush."

"I didn't ask her because if I had—then she would have asked me the same question." Just then the bartender delivered his drink. He quickly took another swig.

"And who were you seeing? Olivia Alford?"

"No—absolutely not."

"Then who?"

"Anyone I was seeing—had no idea about Emma."

"How can you be so sure?"

"Because—hypothetically, of course—the women I see, I only see once, and they're paid well for their discretion." Stanhope emptied his glass.

"Fair enough," said McCuen.

"Anything else?" asked Stanhope impatiently.

"Yes," said McCuen. "Who else knows about the game and the Sargent paintings?"

"Only the players were supposed to know about it—but here you are, so someone's been awfully chatty." Winterbottom shifted in his seat.

"There's one thing I'm curious about," said Winterbottom. "How do you know who's winning?"

"That's the beauty of it," replied Stanhope. "We don't. Sure, you can check auction records and public sales—but you can never really know for sure. We'll find out in three days." Just then the bartender delivered Stanhope a fresh glass of gin. "Now, if you'll excuse me, gentlemen, I'm quite thirsty and I have more money to lose." He stood up and rejoined the Shanghai table just as they were getting ready to deal in another hand.

* * *

As they were leaving the Seneca Club, McCuen received a phone call from Thomas Fields, indicating that he would be available for the remainder of the afternoon. Under the spell of intrigue, McCuen and Winterbottom proceeded directly to Park Avenue. When they arrived at Fields' rooftop apartment, they were escorted directly to his study. Fields was sitting at his desk when they arrived and he rose immediately to greet them.

"Captain McCuen, I'm sorry about this morning," said Fields. "I hope that Esmé was of some help to you."

"She was very gracious," said McCuen. "And thank you for seeing us—I'll try not to take up too much of your time.

"Can I get you something to drink?" asked Fields. McCuen diligently refused, and Winterbottom opted to follow McCuen's lead. After pouring a glass for himself, Fields turned to them and continued. "Well, how can I help? Olivia was a good friend—it's terrible what happened to her."

"Mrs. Alford is of course a matter of interest," replied McCuen. "But, I was hoping we could speak to you about the Sargent portraits."

"I don't understand."

"The arrangement—with your friends at the Seneca Club?" said McCuen. It was clear that Fields was uncomfortable talking about it so openly.

"Yes, of course," he replied hesitantly. "It's been a while since I—" Then he stopped abruptly. "What does that have to do with Olivia's murder?"

"We believe that Mrs. Alford's murder is connected to the Sargent paintings." Fields began shaking his head in confusion before turning to the window.

"I was a member of the Seneca Club, and I played Alford's game. I assume you already know the details—"

"Are you still playing?"

"Certainly not," he replied, raising his brow. "I finished with that over a year ago. Those paintings caused me nothing but trouble."

"I can understand wanting to move on," said McCuen. "But letting go of what Alford did to your father—that can't be so easy?"

"No, you're right, Captain," said Fields. "It's not. I'd never deny hating him, and I wouldn't pass up an opportunity to ruin him, if given the chance. When I started playing the game, that was my intention, but men like Alford feed off other people's misery. I watched it happen to my father, and instead of following in his footsteps, I decided to take a different approach. By resigning from the game—I was starving the ravenous, old dog."

"And what about Stanhope? What's he playing for?"

"You've been busy, Captain," replied Fields, impressed at how much they had learned. "I really couldn't say why, or if, Stanhope's still playing—I haven't spoken to him since I left the club. Initially, I thought he did it to impress the other members. If he's still playing, I assume his motivations haven't changed." Then he smiled. "He was the one who told Esmé about the game in the first place—the man drinks too much." Fields then took a drink from his own glass. "It seems like you've been well informed, but in case you haven't already heard, McClarendon and Bennett were playing too. McClarendon retreated to Stockholm after the market crashed. He's been successful overseas, but he'll never regain what he lost. As for Bennett, he's dropped off entirely, but I can assure you that neither had anything to do with Olivia's death."

"Why do you say that?" asked Winterbottom.

"I've done business with both of them. They just don't have it in them."

"And what about Alford and Stanhope, do they have it in them?" Fields' jaw tightened at the question and he paused briefly before answering.

"Alford's more ruthless than he pretends to be and there have been rumors that he harmed Olivia in the past. As for Stanhope—I can't believe that he would kill anyone, but I suppose you just never know. If nothing else—he's unpredictable."

"Was Olivia having an affair?" asked McCuen.

"It's possible," he replied. "But if she was—I'd be the last person she'd tell. We were colleagues, but hardly confidantes." Just then Mrs. Fields entered the room, surprised to find that her husband had visitors.

"I'm sorry to interrupt, darling—I didn't know you had guests," she said. "It's nice to see you again, Captain." She smiled and nodded politely. "I just needed the sketches from Axis Mundi."

"They're on the desk in the living room," said Fields, placing his drink down on a nearby table. Mrs. Fields nodded and quietly left the room, leaving McCuen to continue his questioning.

"What happened to the Sargent paintings you acquired?"

"I sold most of the paintings at auction. There are only so many Sargent paintings, so as you can imagine, Alford's little game has created quite a rise in price over the years. Actually, I was able to turn a decent profit. It's to the point where even Sargent's watercolor sketches are fetching nearly a million apiece."

"Weren't you worried they might go to Alford and Stanhope?" asked Winterbottom. "At that point—I couldn't have cared less." Winterbottom savored the response, while McCuen forged ahead.

"I'd like to go back to the night of Olivia's murder," said McCuen. "When was the last time you saw her?"

"We spoke the night she was killed—at the museum. There was a fundraising event that night to celebrate the acquisition of another Sargent portrait—*The Wyndham Sisters*. Board members all dressed up like the subjects of Sargent's portraits. Olivia was dressed as *The Lady with the Rose*, and I was dressed as the portrait of *Dr. Samuel Jean de Pozzi*."

"Would Emma Strauss have been invited to this event?" asked Winterbottom. "I'm sure she was," said Fields. "But I don't remember seeing her that night. The museum should be able to tell you if she attended."

"Thank you, Mr. Fields," said McCuen. "I appreciate you taking the time to meet with us. We don't quite understand the motive behind these murders yet—and I'd like you and your wife to take all necessary safety precautions."

"Thank you, Captain," replied Fields. "My security advisor, Lucien, and his team have been briefed, and I can assure you that we're in excellent hands."

"Good," replied McCuen. "I'll be in touch if we have any further questions."

When they returned to the car, Winterbottom was noticeably silent. A darkened mood had stayed with him ever since leaving the club. McCuen was trying to weave together all the strands of information that they had been given, and he assumed that Winterbottom was doing the same. They both felt as if the fatal hour was quickly approaching.

"The museum gala explains why Olivia Alford was wearing a Victorian dress in Central Park," said McCuen.

"Yes—and it explains why Strauss willingly put on the dress for the killer," replied Winterbottom.

"I'll have Whelan get a guest list for the museum gala. If our two victims are on it, maybe our killer is too."

"What about the dresses?" asked Winterbottom. "Did you get the DNA analysis from the lab?"

"It came in this morning," replied McCuen. "The dresses from both murders contained traces of DNA belonging to a Caucasian male, but only one of the samples had enough genetic material for a full profile comparison. They're running it through the database now."

"And our *Kings of Wall Street*—is their DNA in the database?"

"No," replied McCuen.

"I didn't think so," said Winterbottom. "Can you get a search warrant for their DNA?"

"We're miles away from probable cause, Anselm. No judge in the five Burroughs would allow a warrant for DNA—not without more evidence. Not to mention the fact that the District Attorney probably plays tennis with half of our suspect pool. I don't like it any more than you do, but that's going to make things much more complicated." As the daylight shifted, the streetlights and traffic signals of Midtown came alive. After a brief silence, Winterbottom spoke.

"I'm sorry, Ed," he said regretfully.

"It's not your fault—we'll figure out another way."

"It's not that," said Winterbottom, cautiously. McCuen looked over at Winterbottom, he was holding up an empty scotch glass.

"Anselm—"

"Before you get upset—yes, I took Fields' scotch glass." Then he reached back behind the seat and pulled a satchel onto his lap. "I also took one from the Seneca Club from our delightful friend, William Stanhope."

"Anselm, you can't just take things without—"

"No, Ed," said Winterbottom, sharply. "You can't take things without consent—because you're a Captain with the NYPD. I can—because, as we both know, I am most definitely not. Now—since you're already angry, you should know that I took Alford's scotch glass, too. We've all got problems—apparently I can't stop stealing glasses, and rich men drink too much—I can't decide which is worse."

"There are rules, Anselm!" barked McCuen. "This is how killers get away with murder."

"This killer's already gotten away with two murders," replied Winterbottom. "And there will be others, unless we find him. These are exigent circumstances—and if the law doesn't make exceptions for that—then it should be broken!"

McCuen offered no response, and shook his head in frustration.

"Tonight's the night," said Winterbottom. "He's going to kill another one, and another after that—"

"I know," replied McCuen, more frustrated than angry.

"We're out of time," said Winterbottom. "Swab the glasses and compare the profiles with the DNA from the dresses. It's our only chance. If the DNA matches—then we can stop him—if it doesn't, then we're no worse off than we are now."

"Even if I did that—it would take days for a DNA comparison."

"I know," replied Winterbottom disappointedly. McCuen nodded in agreement, and in doing so they both reconciled themselves to a haunting realization. A woman would be murdered that night and they were helpless to stop it. As they drove, they watched the sun moving closer to the horizon. It was dark and vibrant, the color of a blood orange. Passing over the Williamsburg Bridge, above the opaque waters of the East River, Winterbottom felt compelled to say aloud what they were both thinking.

"It's a strange feeling—isn't it, knowing that someone will be murdered tonight? I mean —it happens every day, but to know it with such certainty—"

"Yes, it's a strange feeling," replied McCuen.

"Do you ever get used to it?"

"No," replied McCuen. "—not really." After a long pause, he looked over to Winterbottom. "Maybe a walk through the tall grass would do you some good."

"I think it would."

When they arrived at the Franklin Avenue lot, Winterbottom disappeared into the darkness, while McCuen sat alone on the hood, radio in hand, waiting for what the night might bring. His mind was turning. It eventually found its way back to the first time he met Winterbottom, and the circumstances surrounding the Safra Bank Heist.

VIII

THE SAFRA BANK HEIST

As a crime reporter, I had covered the Safra Bank Robbery, but I didn't learn of Winterbottom's involvement until several years after McCuen had retired from the NYPD. McCuen had been in charge of the Crime Scene Unit for four years when it happened. Despite the robbers getting away, it was far from well-orchestrated. The consensus was that the suspects were not 'professional' bank robbers, although McCuen hated to use that term. Regardless, the perpetrators made off with nearly $90,000 in cash. McCuen's unit had obtained a fair amount of forensic evidence, but nothing panned out. Within a few weeks he and his team had exhausted all leads, and the case went stale. If compared with the other cases he had worked, there was nothing special about it, other than how elusive it was. Even the best investigators, if they're being honest, will tell you of at least one case that haunts them; a case that they just couldn't close out.

For McCuen, this was it; a case that by all accounts should have been straightforward, but for whatever reason—be it fate, or just plain old bad luck—he couldn't break it open. And so, it hung like an albatross around his neck, and he carried the metaphorical carcass with him for another four months.

Then one morning, a man named Paul Brunelle walked into the 19th Precinct, asking to speak with McCuen. The man was in his mid-thirties and had a lengthy criminal record. Before McCuen could say a word, the man handed him a letter that read as follows:

This man was one of three, who robbed the Safra National Bank. He is represented by legal counsel and hereby invokes his Miranda rights. However, he is willing to cooperate with the investigation and assist with the apprehension of the remaining suspects.

- A.W.

At the time, the initials meant nothing to him, and as for the letter and the robbery suspect, McCuen thought the whole thing was a setup, some kind of prank. He knew the guys in the drug unit weren't beneath paying an informant to mess with him, but the man appeared genuinely anxious. Risking years of ridicule at the hands of his colleagues, and knowing that a third party can't invoke Miranda rights, McCuen invited Brunelle into an interview room and poured him a glass of water.

"Look, I appreciate you coming in, and you're free to go—anytime," said McCuen. "But I'd like to ask you a few questions—"

"He said that you'd try to ask me questions," interrupted Brunelle, nervously. "I'm invoking my right to remain silent and to not answer any questions at this time."

"Did he tell you to say that too?" asked McCuen. The man didn't respond, but his body language was affirmation enough. Then the man's eyebrows jumped in remembrance.

"Oh—he told me to give you this," said Brunelle, handing McCuen his red backpack. "He said that you should be the one to open it." McCuen cautiously opened the backpack and found that it contained $30,000 in cash, evidently the man's cut from the robbery. The situation had just outgrown anything the guys in the drug unit could cook up.

Within three weeks, the remaining two suspects were arrested and later convicted for their involvement in the bank robbery. Brunelle was given a reduced sentence for his cooperation, and his legal representation had been fully funded by an unnamed third party. When the trial was over, and once he was out of earshot of the District Attorney, McCuen asked him why he had turned himself in. Brunelle said that he had been approached by a man who offered to pay him $50,000 to turn himself in.

"I needed the money," Brunelle said. "My cut from the bank job was only $30,000—and he even offered to pay for my attorney."

"How did he find you?"

"I have no fucking idea," he replied. "I was holed up in my apartment—and then out of nowhere this guy calls me on my cell phone. He tells me he knows that I robbed the bank and that if I turned myself in—and roll on the others, he'd give me $50,000. If I didn't—he was going to call the police, anyway. What choice did I have?"

"Come, on," replied McCuen in disbelief. "You expect me to believe that?"

"You can believe whatever you want. That's how it happened."

"Ok, but who does that?"

"Hell if I know," said Brunelle. "But he sure got your attention."

In the weeks that followed, McCuen continued to receive communications from Winterbottom through couriers. Using the information he gathered from the *Times*, NYPD press releases, and whatever other methods he had at his disposal, Winterbottom was able to make subtle, but accurate predictions relating to a number of McCuen's cases. These predictions never resulted in such a watershed moment as the Safra National Bank Heist, but his efforts were of undeniable value. Sometimes it would be as simple as indicating the most likely place that a suspect would ditch a gun, or where he might live; things like that. Other times it was more complex, like predicting the make and model of a suspect's vehicle based on the age, race and gender of the suspect. At times it made McCuen cringe, but it wasn't profiling; it was predictive. It was all based on recorded data, statistical analysis, and human behavioral science.

The simple truth is that there are formulas and algorithms that can be applied to everything, and the numerical results are in themselves very telling, if you know how to apply them. The numbers don't lie. Of course, the results were never enough to convict anyone all on their own, but, more often than not, he was correct. Winterbottom's suggestions often led to crucial evidence, but it was rarely ever admissible in court. Winterbottom wasn't an investigator, or even a specialist, at least not in a way that the courts would recognize. He wasn't even authorized by the NYPD to be working on investigations. But the advantage to McCuen was never about evidence. Winterbottom's calculations gave him the advantage of time, and when there were lives at stake, nothing was more important than that.

When they first met in person, McCuen avoided any questioning as to why Winterbottom had gotten involved in the Safra Bank investigation. The same was true for their second meeting, and the next after that. By the time he learned who Winterbottom really was, his interest in the heist seemed to matter less and less. Maybe McCuen had convinced himself that Winterbottom was just a wealthy benefactor interested in doing the right thing.

As McCuen stood in the Franklin Avenue lot, he was visited by an unsettling thought. He found himself wondering how Winterbottom was even able to find Brunelle. How could he accomplish such a feat, and with such ease?

In that moment, McCuen remembered the thumb-drive and his thoughts swerved toward suspicion. Had baleful seeds been sown from the beginning? Having given the thumb-drive to Winterbottom, the feeling was inescapable and more firmly felt than ever before. Had it all been about getting the case file from the beginning? The information itself was harmless, but how would it be used? Whatever Winterbottom was planning, McCuen was a part of it now. These thoughts stirred in him, while he waited, and they lingered even as Winterbottom leaned against the car next to him.

"Any divine revelations?" asked McCuen, quickly hiding his concerns. "Maybe you could drum up a miracle for us."

"There are no such things—you Irish-Catholics are just superstitious."

"You're the one walking in circles," smiled McCuen. "Besides, we need all the help we can get."

"Well, I'll keep walking in circles, and you keep praying the rosary—we'll see who gets an answer first."

"Do you mean to tell me that billionaire mathematicians don't believe in miracles?"

"No, not generally," replied Winterbottom.

"But some do?"

"Yes."

"So, you're saying I picked the wrong goddamned mathematician?"

"Yes—most definitely," replied Winterbottom. McCuen smiled and looked out over the grassy lot.

"Now, since we have some time—let me ask you something." From his tone, Winterbottom could see it coming. "Do you not believe in God on philosophical grounds, or is that a mathematical truth?" As much as he admired Winterbottom's gifts, one of McCuen's favorite exercises was to point out the limits of them. Because he couldn't engage Winterbottom on complex theoretical terms, McCuen relied on circular reasoning and oversimplification. It was amateurish and juvenile, but he enjoyed it all the same.

"Are we really doing this, now?" said Winterbottom.

"Why not, if you can disprove the existence of God—that might clear up a lot of things for me."

"I can't disprove the existence of God—but I can't prove it either," replied Winterbottom, growing tired of McCuen's taunting. "I also can't disprove—in mathematical terms—the occurrence of miracles, mermaids, or unicorns."

"So, basically, what you're saying is—miracles can happen," said McCuen, smiling.

"Would that make you feel better?" replied Winterbottom.

"Yes, it would."

"Ok—miracles can happen—just not in Crown Heights."

McCuen laughed to himself, and they both sat quietly listening to the distant sounds of the city. It wasn't long before the silence became too unsettling.

"I have to say—this one's got me worried," said McCuen. "Any one of them could be our killer. It's hard to tell the wolves from the dogs."

"—and the sheep are in the meadow," replied Winterbottom. "There's nothing we can do but wait." As he spoke, a pair of headlights cut through the vacant lot and pulled through the open gate. Whelan and Adams exited the car at a hurried pace, signaling that their search had been fruitful.

"Give me good news," said McCuen turning toward Adams.

"The museum confirmed that Emma Strauss was on the guest list for the masquerade ball, however, on account of being dead—she didn't attend. We also checked in at all the major auction houses in the city and pulled records for the last two years. We found hundreds of bids and purchases made by our "Three Kings." Fields' bidding history stops abruptly—right around the same time that Bennett and McClarendon lost their stake in the game."

"Which backs up what he told us," replied McCuen.

"The records also show a flurry of purchases by Alford and Stanhope," said Whelan. "The curator at the museum confirmed that our buyers have also made several purchases from private collections."

"This is where it gets interesting," said Adams. "Three months ago, the Board of Directors at the museum proposed a vote for the deaccession, or removal, of *Madame X* from its permanent collection—which would have made it eligible for sale, or exchange."

"That would make it the ultimate prize for anyone playing the game," said Whelan. "It was only being considered because the museum had received an offer for the exchange of a significant collection of famous American paintings. The deal was proposed by an obscure collector named Willard Somerset. Ultimately, the Board of Directors voted against the deal. Olivia Alford cast the deciding vote."

"You've got my attention," said Winterbottom.

"In the past year, Somerset's bidding history has equaled Stanhope's and Alford's, beginning right around the time that Fields withdrew from the game."

"They found another player," said Winterbottom.

"Good work," said McCuen. "Now, who the hell is Willard Somerset?"

"We don't know," said Whelan. "There's no record of him in our system."

"That's pretty unusual," said McCuen in disbelief.

"There's not even a parking ticket," replied Adams.

"What about the auction houses and the museum?"

"We tried," replied Whelan. "All they had was an out-of-service phone number."

"Well, it's the goddamn modern age," said McCuen. "There's gotta be something on him. Keep looking—we need picture of this guy, and preferably an address. Subpoena his bank records if you have too. I'll meet you back at headquarters in an hour, no one goes home until we find Willard Somerset."

McCuen felt bolstered, but he was hesitant to call it progress. For all they knew, Somerset could be an innocent third party, just another player in the game, or an unaffiliated admirer of John Singer Sargent. They would have to find Somerset to know for sure. In the meantime, McCuen's attention returned to a more visceral concern. Driving through Midtown, McCuen had become increasingly uncomfortable.

"What is it, Ed?" asked Winterbottom, cutting through the discomfort. "You're distracted —and not in the *'I'm chasing a serial killer' kind of way."*

"Why did you want the file?" said McCuen, nearly cutting him off.

"You know why."

"Anselm, there's nothing in it that can help you. I've been over it myself—hell, I've been over it with you more than a dozen times. So why ask me for it now?

"I just want to go over it again."

"It's an NYPD investigation—" said McCuen.

"But it's hardly an active one, Ed. It's been five years."

"Then why now?"

"I need answers, Ed," pleaded Winterbottom. "You should understand that more than anybody." Winterbottom shifted in his seat and anxiously readjusted his posture before continuing. "It doesn't stop for me, Ed—it never stops." After a few moments, he closed his eyes and surrendered a deep breath, beginning to settle down. "I just need to make sure I haven't missed anything."

"But what good is it—,"

"What have I got to lose, Ed?" His voice sounded desperate. "Tell me—what have I got to lose?" To that question, McCuen could offer no rebuttal, and maybe it was just that simple. Maybe he just couldn't understand it. Maybe nobody could unless it had happened to them. Whether Winterbottom was being honest about the case file or not, McCuen had no choice but to keep driving. His mind was hardly reassured, but he knew that he would need Winterbottom in the coming hours. Instead of pushing the issue, the two men headed to the Odessa. There they sat quietly in a corner booth and drank coffee, until McCuen's cell phone reverberated across the stainless steel tabletop. It was the call they had been waiting for and hoped would never come. Another woman had been murdered; her body had been left on the sidewalk at the intersection of Wall Street and Broad Street, under the Corinthian columns of the New York Stock Exchange.

They arrived at the scene just after nine o'clock, and Whelan and Adams had already begun their work, hovering over the stiff and contorted body of a woman lying on the sidewalk. She was wearing a gold satin dress, adorned with pearls and silk embroidery. The woman's neck appeared to be broken, and she had been stabbed three times; a level of violence not seen in the other two murders. Closer inspection revealed even greater brutality; the woman's Achilles tendons had been severed. The killer had acquired a taste for blood.

"Well—that's different," said McCuen, looking down at the woman's feet.

"Yes, it is," said Winterbottom. "I thought the killer would choose the *Hammersley portrait* for his next victim—you know—the one with the red velvet dress."

"I was talking about her severed tendons," clarified McCuen.

"Yes, of course," said Winterbottom, still examining the dress. "—that too."

"A group of late-night brokers found her on their way back to the office," said Adams. "We think she's Greta Mallory—a well-known dancer with the Metropolitan Ballet." The fact that the woman was a ballerina made her severed tendons the cruel equivalent of pulling the wings off a butterfly.

"*La Carmencita*," said Winterbottom, reciting the title of one of Sargent's most prized portraits. The dress worn by the woman was an unmistakable homage to the painting, and the killer had even adorned the dead woman's face with thick, white makeup. It was an added detail from the portrait itself.

The painting was being housed at the Met, temporarily on loan from the Musée d'Orsay, in Paris. The subject was Carmen Dauset Moreno, a Spanish-gypsy dancer who had attained noteworthy success throughout Europe and the United States.

"It's believed that Sargent first met Moreno in 1889," said Winterbottom, "— at the Exposition Universelle in Paris. Historians say he quickly became infatuated with her, calling her a 'bewildering creature.' If the rumors were true, she was Sargent's lover for a time. In the months after they first met, he painted several portraits of her, including *La Carmencita*—a painting that received a resentful reception by patrons and critics. Any exception taken was certainly not on artistic grounds. The painting was masterful—the problem was with the subject. By that time, Sargent had painted some of the wealthiest people in the world: Robert Louis Stevenson, Isabella Steward Gardner, Theodore Roosevelt, and several members of the House of Lords. Many took offense that a gypsy dancer was held in such high esteem—painted as their equal."

Looking up from his cell phone, Whelan interrupted.

"Fingerprint comparisons came back—she's Greta Mallory," said Whelan.

"Does she have any connection to the other victims?" asked McCuen.

"She went to the Museum gala the same night Olivia Alford was killed," replied Adams.

Winterbottom canted his head to look more squarely at the dead woman's face.

"Ed—"

"I see it," said McCuen. He slowly stretched a pair of nitrile gloves over his hands and let out a heavy sigh. Reaching into the woman's partially closed mouth, McCuen pulled out a small scroll of paper. He carefully unrolled it, as Adams shined a flashlight over his shoulder. The note read: *"Every time I paint a portrait, I lose a friend."* It was a quote from John Singer Sargent, himself.

"There's more," said Winterbottom, pointing to the woman's left hand. McCuen turned and plucked a small envelope from between the corpse's fingers. He carefully held it up to Adams' flashlight, noting the shape of its contents. Without a word, Whelan handed him the tactical knife that he carried on his belt.

"Thanks, Tom." McCuen carefully ran the blade of the knife across the bottom edge of the envelope, careful not to disturb any DNA that might be preserved in the envelope's adhesive seal. Inside, there were two tickets to the Metropolitan Opera for the upcoming performance of *Madame Butterfly*. "It seems we've been invited to the Opera."

Adams approached with an evidence bag and McCuen carefully placed the tickets into the bag to be processed for fingerprints. As McCuen peeled off his gloves, Whelan hung up his cell phone and rushed toward them.

"Digital forensics pulled the GPS data for Emma Strauss' and Olivia Alford's cell phones. Both of their phones located to the same apartment building in Bushwick, the night before they were killed. They also had contact with an unregistered cell phone number. I cross-checked the auction records and found that the same phone number was used to bid on a Sargent portrait, last July. That bid was placed by Willard Somerset."

"Where's the apartment building?" asked McCuen.

"Marcus Garvey Boulevard, but it's a four-story building—there's got to be fifty apartments inside."

"And there's no way to know which apartment is his," said Adams.

"You and Whelan finish up here—don't rush it," said McCuen. "Anselm and I will head to that address—meet us there as soon as you're done."

McCuen and Winterbottom ran to the car and sped towards Bushwick with the blue lights strobing against the street signs and passing cars. Winterbottom wondered if McCuen had considered the odds they were up against, but he hesitated to say anything.

"I should've asked if you wanted to come," said McCuen.

"I would have told you, if it was a problem," replied Winterbottom. "I do have somewhere to be later—but it can wait."

"I'll do my best to get you back home before midnight."

"Thanks," said Winterbottom. "Do you really think we'll be done by midnight? It's not going to be easy narrowing down which apartment it is."

"It might be easier than you think," replied McCuen. "How well do you know Bed-Stuy?"

"I try to avoid it if I can," said Winterbottom.

"I worked Bed-Stuy for five years—I think you're going to like it," replied McCuen, smiling.

Given what was at stake, it would've been foolish to think that McCuen was being dismissive. Instead, Winterbottom got the sense that he was preparing to take whatever action was necessary; the killer had to be stopped. It was both refreshing and troubling all at the same time; the ardent rule-follower had taken a step closer to the edge of the precipice. Regardless of inner determination and will, the fact remained that they were trying to locate a single apartment among fifty.

As they pulled onto Marcus Garvey Boulevard, and turned off the headlights, they stared across the street at their objective. It was a rectangular labyrinth of apartments, shielded by a worn brick facade and traversing fire escapes. It wasn't the kind of place that would attract wealthy socialite women, but it certainly wasn't the worst place to live in Bed-Stuy. Other than a small group of men lingering in front of the main entrance, it seemed as if the entire neighborhood had gone to sleep for the night.

"So now what?" asked Winterbottom.

"We wait," replied McCuen. "If we go to management—the tenants will get tipped off. Landlords hate getting their doors kicked in by the police."

"So that's it?"

"Yes—we wait," repeated McCuen.

"What exactly are we waiting for?" asked Winterbottom.

"Sometimes, you just have to wait," replied McCuen.

They sat there for an hour, as the cold night air slowly infiltrated the unmarked police cruiser. Winterbottom sank deeper into his jacket, watching as a pedestrian passed by on the sidewalk. Then, without warning, McCuen pushed open his door. "Here we go." Winterbottom looked at the building, trying to see what he had missed.

"What are we doing?" he asked in surprise. McCuen didn't answer him and just quietly walked across the street at a hurried pace. Winterbottom instinctively followed, wondering why McCuen was walking right up to the apartment building. The group of men in front of the building had moved to the corner, lingering just outside the reach of the nearby streetlights. McCuen walked straight toward them. Within a few yards of the group, McCuen called out to them, but Winterbottom couldn't make out what was said. One of the men who was wearing a hooded sweatshirt turned as McCuen grabbed him by the shirt and punched him in the face, knocking him to the ground. A second man closed in and was met with a subsequent haymaker from McCuen. It all happened in an instant, and for Winterbottom, it was jarring to see a man so uniquely tempered and reserved, carrying out such exacting violence. As fast as the man with the black shirt had fallen, he was up again, and running away with the others. The man on the ground was cupping his bleeding nose, while McCuen stood over him. Winterbottom arrived just in time to see McCuen ripping three bundles of heroin, from the man's sweatshirt pocket. McCuen unsympathetically rolled him over and pulled a knife out from the man's waistline.

"What's this for?" asked McCuen, waving the knife at the man before throwing it in a nearby trash can. "Listen to me carefully," he said, sharply. "—because in case you haven't figured it out, I'm in no mood for fucking around! You get one chance to go home tonight—do you understand me?"

"Yeah," mumbled the man, still holding his nose.

"I don't think you do!" said McCuen.

"I hear you! I hear you!" said the man, adamantly.

McCuen helped the man up and leaned him against the front wall of the apartment building. Winterbottom watched as McCuen pulled two photographs from his pockct. "What's your namc?"

"Suggs," replied the man.

"Suggs—I'm feeling better about you already," said McCuen. "Now, I'm going to show pictures of two women, okay. I don't want any bullshit about how you don't know them— alright?" Suggs nodded that he understood. McCuen showed him photographs of Olivia Alford and Emma Strauss. The man looked at the photographs carefully and slowly nodded his head.

"Yeah, I've seen them here—coming and going."

"Which apartment did they go to?"

"Oh, come on, man—" sighed Suggs. "Don't do this to me—not right here."

"Suggs," said McCuen. "It is what it is."

"Okay, wait, wait—It was apartment #348—#348."

"Are you sure? Or, are you just guessing?"

"I'm sure—but I don't know whose apartment it is. The manager says he's some Wall Street somebody—but I never saw him. Those women you're looking for—they definitely come and go."

"Together?" asked McCuen.

"Hell, no," said Suggs. "At different times—they're not as special as they think."

"Okay, Suggs." Then McCuen kicked the bundles of heroin into a nearby puddle on the sidewalk.

"Ah, come on, man!" yelled Suggs as McCuen stepped on the drugs, grinding them into a slurry. They all watched it dissolve into a murky pool.

"You can go home now, Suggs."

"But all that product—I'm fucked!" McCuen reached out and gave him a fifty-dollar bill, knowing that he was just a runner. If he returned to his boss with no money and no drugs, he'd be in for far worse than a beating. Suggs accepted the offer and disappeared into the night.

"Somebody call the fucking United Nations," said Winterbottom, still reeling from what he had just witnessed. "Diplomacy really suits you, Ed. What language was that again?"

"I can take a lot of things, Anselm—but a lesson in manners from you—is more than I can handle right now."

"It just doesn't look good—a white cop beating up a black man like that."

"I don't give a shit what it looks like!" barked McCuen.

"This is why people hate cops," said Winterbottom, fuming. McCuen walked up to him and pointed to the heroin that was dissolving in the murky puddle beside them.

"Who do you think he's selling that shit to—in this neighborhood? Rich white people? No—he's selling it to poor minorities. I know who he works for, Anselm—and his boss laces his heroin with an ungodly amount of fentanyl. We've investigated hundreds of fatal overdoses in just the past two weeks. They've all been linked to his heroin. So, in case you care to look beyond what your eyes can see—that over there—was enough fentanyl to kill ten people." Winterbottom was silent as he pondered what McCuen had told him. "If he had been white—I would have hit him just as hard." Before Winterbottom could speak, McCuen continued. "You're in it—right now, Anselm. This is the real world. There's no Monday morning quarterbacking from the safety of your goddamn living room. Out here, you die if you get it wrong—remember that."

Without another word, they hurried to the nearby apartment building and climbed the stairwell to the third floor. As they moved along the hallway, they took careful account of each apartment number they passed. With their intended destination still several doors away, McCuen signaled for absolute silence. At the apartment door, McCuen listened for any sign that the apartment might be occupied. He expertly slowed his breathing, and listened again. Still, there was nothing, no shuffling of feet, no moaning of the floorboards.

"Okay—let's get back to the car," whispered McCuen. "Whelan and Adams will be here soon—we'll need to get a search warrant."

"How long will that take?", asked Winterbottom.

"A few hours," said McCuen.

"Are you serious?" whispered Winterbottom. "You beat the shit out of that guy just so we could wait for a search warrant?"

"Anselm—we can't cover all the exits—"

Before McCuen could finish, Winterbottom turned the doorknob and rushed inside. The uncontrollable impulse to enter the apartment immediately faded, and Winterbottom paused just inside the unlit entryway. McCuen calmly stepped through the door behind him, having drawn his Glock the second the door began to hinge. The only light was coming from the open door, and it was hardly enough to pierce into the depths of the apartment. McCuen moved in front of Winterbottom, who had pressed his body flat up against the wall, realizing that he had just willingly entered the den of a presumed serial killer.

It was then that they heard a shuffling sound coming from the far end of the apartment. Someone was inside.

"That wasn't very smart—now was it," whispered McCuen sternly, as he walked passed Winterbottom. His eyes were fixed on the dark void at the end of the corridor. "It's going to get a lot darker in here. Stay close, but make sure you stay behind me." With that, McCuen closed the door behind them. Winterbottom watched in horror as the last slivers of light were shut out by the closing door. Instinctively, he turned toward it, as if the last few breaths of oxygen were escaping from the room. It was pitch black now, and he could hardly see his own hands in front of his face. It was precisely why McCuen had closed the door. With it opened they would've been backlit. They would've been easy targets, like silhouettes, or fish in a barrel. Slowly their eyes began to adjust to the darkness, and they were able to make out vague shadows and shapes in front of them. Winterbottom could feel his heart pounding, and he began nervously clenching his fists.

McCuen drew a small flashlight from his pocket, but he didn't turn it on. He just continued to move forward, down the short hallway, toward the heart of the apartment. It was cloaked in darkness, but they could see most of the living room. It was empty, except for a chair and a small couch. Moving more quickly, McCuen turned a blind corner and was able to see into a very small bathroom to the left. He ducked in and pushed back the shower curtain, finding it empty. As McCuen exited the bathroom, he could see Winterbottom waiting for him. Focusing on the danger that awaited them, McCuen turned toward the next room, and the narrow doorway that opened up into the kitchen. As Winterbottom followed him, his hands brushed up against the couch and neighboring chair. He suddenly drew back, repulsed by what he had felt. They were covered by thick, plastic drop cloths, bringing to mind a grisly purpose. He rushed to catch up with McCuen, who had yet to enter the kitchen. As McCuen was about to move forward, something shifted further on in the darkness. McCuen waited for nearly two minutes before stepping forward. Without warning, he sent a quick burst from his flashlight into the kitchen, but from where they stood, neither man could see clearly inside. As McCuen turned, he ignited his flashlight again, flooding the kitchen with light, before quickly returning to the darkness. In the light, Winterbottom had seen the small table, the refrigerator, and the kitchen countertop, before it all went black again.

McCuen was waging a physiological war with his flashlight. By using it sparingly, he was preserving his own night vision without making themselves a target. The shorter the burst of light, the less time it would take for their eyes to adjust to the darkness. If the killer was inside the apartment, his eyes would also have to adjust. They would need every advantage they could get. McCuen increased their odds by keeping his right eye closed whenever he turned on the flashlight. It was a trick he used often when he was serving overseas, and throughout his law enforcement career. If needed, he could shoot in the darkness without his dominant eye having to adjust. It was a matter of split seconds, but it could be the difference between life and death. At the moment, however, it was only a slight advantage. They were unwelcome visitors in an unfamiliar place; reaction was all they would have, which put them in serious jeopardy. Kneeling low in the kitchen, Winterbottom looked across the countertop, and felt a sudden pull in his stomach. It was a sickening feeling.

"Ed—," he whispered. "There's a missing—,"

"I saw it," whispered McCuen, calmly, never taking his eyes off the doorway ahead of him. Winterbottom continued to stare uneasily at the countertop. On it was a wooden knife block; one of the knives was missing. Just six feet away, was the last room in the apartment: the bedroom. Even in the darkness, McCuen could tell that the room opened up to the left. It was a blind corner. Without wavering, he slowly approached the doorway as Winterbottom reluctantly followed. McCuen motioned toward the light switch on the wall just inside the room. Winterbottom slowly extended his arm past the threshold and with unsteady hands he flicked the light switch on, but nothing happened. The pounding in his chest was now gripping his throat, echoing into his neck. It flooded his carotid; his pulse was deafening.

Knowing what danger awaited him McCuen rushed inside. With his flashlight illuminated, he could see that the furnishings were covered in thick plastic drop cloths and sheets, just like the living room had been. He drew the narrow cone of light back and forth throughout the room, focusing on the corners, while Winterbottom carefully stepped behind him. The bedroom was larger than either of them would have guessed, and they carefully made their way closer to the bed. Then the light of the flashlight caught the edge of something moving. Suddenly, a black cat leapt onto the bed, and meowed at both of them, disturbed by the bright light. McCuen slowly relaxed, but guardedly continued to the other side of the bed.

Winterbottom sighed and pulling the heavy sheet off the mattress; no cat should have to sleep on plastic. The crinkling of the plastic seemed clamorous in the empty room. As their breathing settled, McCuen turned again to the cat sitting on the bed. Winterbottom smiled.

"Of course, it had to be a black cat", said Winterbottom.

Suddenly, a figure burst out from under a nearby sheet, and pummeled McCuen who was half-facing the other way. Before Winterbottom could react, the man had laid his shoulder into his abdomen, knocking him to the floor. By the time Winterbottom had opened his eyes, all he could hear were the footsteps of their assailant running down the hallway and out the front door.

Winterbottom sat up slowly as McCuen pulled himself off the floor, holding his jaw. He rushed through the apartment, but stopped as he reached the front door. McCuen knew it was futile. The killer was gone.

"God damn it!" said McCuen, in frustration, still sore from being hit. Winterbottom joined him in the half light of the open doorway.

"It wasn't a total loss," he said, holding up the collar from the black cat. It had the owner's name inscribed on it: *Willard Somerset*. Winterbottom tossed it to McCuen. "Who knew that black cats could be so lucky," said Winterbottom, smiling.

"This hardly solves the case," replied McCuen, holding up the cat's collar.

"I was actually talking about your jacket," said Winterbottom, pointing at McCuen's right side. Looking down, McCuen could see that the right side of his jacket had been slashed open by the killer, a narrow miss. It was no doubt the work of the missing eight-inch kitchen knife.

* * *

I was parked on East 89th Street, watching the house, when McCuen dropped him off that night. Winterbottom entered the house, and I was about to pull away when I saw him re-emerge. He walked down to the corner where a taxi was waiting for him. I followed him along FDR Drive to Pell Street, in Chinatown where he quickly disappeared into the night. I had no choice but to head for home.

What I didn't know then, was that Winterbottom had walked north to Bayard Street to a small noodle shop with no sign. The entrance was off to the side of a larger, more popular Chinese restaurant; you'd hardly know it was there. The restaurant consisted of two small tables and a rear kitchen. Under the greenish glow of the fluorescent lights, the space seemed unwelcoming, adorned by an empty aquarium, and a single Chinese calendar on the wall. Winterbottom approached the counter and looked over at an older man who was seated in the corner of the restaurant. He turned back to the counter and rang the bell for service. After a few moments of silence, he rang the bell again. Out of the backroom, adjacent to the kitchen, came a twelve-year-old Chinese boy.

"Stop ringing the goddamn bell—you stupid motherfucker!" shouted the boy. "Every time, stupid, fat, white man ring bell, too much!" Winterbottom's eyes widened. He was shocked and looked back to the older man seated in the corner. The man raised his eyebrows and looked the other way, not wanting to draw the ire of the boy at the counter. "I heard you the first time, dip-shit!" scoffed the boy as he stared angrily at Winterbottom. "What you want?" Winterbottom was quiet for a moment as he collected himself.

"I'd like some egg rolls—you rice eating little bitch!" The young boy's mouth dropped open slightly, and his brow became tense.

"Fuck you, bitch!" yelled the boy. "I'll slap your asshole!" Winterbottom tried to keep a straight face, but he couldn't help it. He burst into laughter and leaned over onto the countertop, shaking his head. The boy's face began to soften, and he started to smile.

"What I say?" said the boy. "Mr. Anselm—did I say it wrong?"

"You're doing much better, Jian—you almost had it," laughed Winterbottom.

"Ah, man—what'd I say?"

"It's alright, Jian," replied Winterbottom. "It's—*I'll slap YOU, asshole'*—

not *'I'll slap YOUR asshole.'* In general, you never want to slap someone's asshole."

"But I got you good with the rest—fat, stupid white man!"

"Yes—you did," smiled Winterbottom.

"Come on," said the boy. "I'll take you to him." Winterbottom followed Jian through the kitchen and down into the basement of the restaurant. They passed through several rooms filled with older Chinese men, all playing Pai Gow. Not a single person diverted his attention to Winterbottom. It was as if he were invisible; they preferred it that way. Finally, Jian knocked on a door at the end of the corridor, and they were greeted by a middle-aged Chinese man.

"Anselm—" said the man, warmly. "How are you?"

"I'm well, Chen. Thank you."

Knowing that the two men had important business to discuss, Jian returned to the kitchen. "Did you get it?" asked Chen, as he walked Winterbottom through what appeared to be a vault door. Inside the room, there were three Jugene supercomputers.

"Yes, I got it," said Winterbottom, holding up the thumb drive that McCuen had given him. "But you have to be careful with this one, Chen. I don't want this coming back to either of us."

"Not to worry," said Chen. "The hardest part's already been done. The system's been storing data for the last six months, and now that we have the drive, I can have the download to you in less than an hour." Winterbottom handed him the thumb drive.

"Will they know there's been a breach?"

"Maybe—if they look hard enough," replied Chen. "But they won't know who did it, or why."

"I expected more from you, Chen," said Winterbottom. "Maybe I should've gone to the Russians?"

"Don't be an asshole," said Chen, laughing. "If you want someone poisoned, you go to the Russians, but for cyber-attacks—we're the only real choice."

"What about the Iranians?" replied Winterbottom. "Or the North Koreans?"

"Now you just sound stupid," snapped Chen, as he began tending to a nearby computer server. After a moment, his smile faded, and he took on a more somber tone. "Anselm, we've known each other for a long time, and I know the rules—no questions—but are you sure you want to do this? I can't figure out why the hell you would want to get—"

"It won't make sense to you, Chen," said Winterbottom, cutting him off.

"Look, I don't need to know—I don't want to know, but if you're having doubts—"

"No," replied Winterbottom, sternly. "Finish the download—I'll handle everything from there."

"And then what?" asked Chen, sensing Winterbottom's fatigue.

"Then—I'll leave, and you won't ever see me again."

Chen had expected as much, and tested the weight of the thumb drive in his hand.

"It'll be done within the hour," he said, reverently. Winterbottom handed him a thick, tightly sealed manilla envelope. The two men shook hands, bowed to one another, and parted ways.

IX

ANSELM WINTERBOTTOM

That night, I couldn't sleep. By 3 AM, I had given up on trying and dragged myself into the office. It was Saturday, and one of the first signs that my interest in McCuen's mysterious friend was becoming a problem. The city database showed that Edmund & Gray Importers was owned by Agnes and Margaret Bruce. I had searched for both names in the newspaper database, but there were no results. Having met Agnes, and knowing that my search only covered the last three years, I had to submit a special request to the Archives Division for all articles relating to Margaret Bruce. There was a decent chance of her name coming up, but I didn't expect such a timely response from the trolls in the basement. They were miserable, which in part I understood. With the changes the internet had imposed on print publications, half of them were laid off, and the rest were forced underground, into the lowest level of the building. That was where my empathy for them stopped. Lack of sunlight and boredom weren't valid excuses for the contempt that they were peddling. It had become a common occurrence for archive responses to come back accompanied by alpha numeric pictograms of a middle finger, or when they were feeling less creative, they'd just write: "Fuck off" in the subject line. With that said, the pictograms were a vast improvement over the previous pictures they used to tag onto internal emails. It was clear that they had too much time on their hands, and not enough of a paycheck to worry about losing it. They had Human Resources whistling in the dark.

Much to my surprise, the email response I received that morning didn't have a hint of sarcasm or angst. There wasn't even any name calling. I had learned to expect it from them, and in its absence, I was a little disappointed. Anything was better than a mundane email. I hadn't complained to Human Resources, but someone did. It appeared that the resulting sensitivity training was paying off. As I downloaded the email attachment, I noticed that the body of the email contained a small arrow pointing down to the corner of my computer monitor. I tried to scroll down, but I couldn't. What was it pointing to? It wasn't until I sat back in my chair that I noticed a sticky note affixed to the lower corner of my computer monitor, just beneath the arrow. The note featured a rudimentary drawing of a penis which made me smile. The Archive trolls had gone low-tech; under the radar. Welcome back, you miserable sons of bitches.

When I clicked on the attached file, it opened to a front-page article from December 21, 2012. The door had been kicked wide open. The headline read: *"Billionaire's Wife and Daughter Victims of Fatal Hit and Run."* Margaret Bruce was the wife of the billionaire mathematician, Anselm Winterbottom. She was killed, just a few blocks from their home on Lexington Avenue, while walking their five-year-old daughter to school. They were run down by an unidentified black Mercedes. The driver was never identified by police.

The name Anselm Winterbottom meant nothing to me, at first. It wasn't until I began looking deeper that I could understand the full weight of his influence. There was really no other way of saying it; he was one of the greatest minds of the century, although most people would never know his name. He was a pioneer in quantum physics, and his work in integrative technologies, and integer factorization had influenced everything from cell phone technology to

GPS satellite technology and artificial intelligence. For those more versed in the field, he was like Godel, or perhaps Turing, only more diverse. Put most simply, he was a modern-day Albert Einstein, only the application of his work was more widespread.

His work with predictive algorithms and behavioral analytics made his mark on the world and influenced nearly every aspect of modern life. It allowed companies to predict what people wanted before they knew that they wanted it. Driven by a complex system of data-farming from internet searches and social media platforms, he could predict consumer behavior. His work streamlined inventory operations, sales, deliveries, and most importantly, it managed risk. These algorithms fueled healthcare innovations and established the foundation for the medical diagnosis of illness by artificial intelligence. When applied to the environment, his efforts bolstered agricultural industries, and sustainability efforts, by analyzing local weather trends, thus maximizing fruit and crop yields. In less than a decade, his influence had spread to nearly every sector of our society, from air traffic control and military technology, to more commonly-used systems like wastewater management and automated traffic lights. He had a hand in every laptop computer and cellphone, facilitating the efficiency and ease that we now take for granted.

For baseball fans, Winterbottom's work could be best described as the sabremetrics of human behavior. In fact, baseball was one of the few industries not influenced by his work. That was all Bill James. (McCuen later told me that Winterbottom ironically felt that analytics was blasphemous when applied to such a sacred game; a sentiment that he didn't feel applied to our society as a whole.)

Anselm Winterbottom. No one had heard a word from him in nearly five years. In the wake of the tragedy, his laboratories and advanced technological initiatives were suddenly shutdown and dissolved. Without a digital trace, he disappeared. I hardly had time to revel in the discovery of his name before I was overtaken by an even greater question. Where had he been for the last five years? And what was his connection to McCuen? It wasn't entirely clear, but the accident surely had something to do with it.

It happened on December 21, 2012, at eight o'clock in the morning. Winterbottom had returned home the night before from a technological summit in Reykjavik and had slept in. He had promised their daughter, Grace, that he would take her to school that morning, but his wife, Margaret, had dutifully taken his place. Grace had her mother's disposition, and much to the relief of her father, she showed no signs of the cognitive irregularities that plagued him as a child. She was attending the Dalton Institute, just a few blocks away from their home on Lexington Avenue. At the intersection of Lexington and East 89th Street, Margaret took Grace by the hand as they waited patiently for the pedestrian signal. In an especially cruel twist, Grace had forgotten her lunch on the kitchen table, and Winterbottom, still half asleep, hurried to catch them before the 89th Street crossing. They were halfway across the street when he called out to them. Margaret looked back just as a black Mercedes Benz ran through the red light and slammed into them. He watched helplessly as his wife and daughter were thrown into the air. He watched them as they fell; their bodies lying broken on the street. The driver emerged from his car in a panic, before seeing Winterbottom rushing toward him. The man jumped back in his car and sped away.

In the hours that followed, police interviewed a few witnesses, but no one was able to give a more detailed description of the vehicle. Winterbottom had seen the man's face, but the resulting report boiled it down to a white male in his mid-thirties, wearing a suit and tie. The only other evidence, which was provided by a nearby witness, was that the car had a New York registration plate.

And that was it.

Before Margaret, Winterbottom only had numbers. As a child he secretly studied numerical patterns in everyday things, like clock faces, and rotary telephone dials. He counted the offshoots of tree branches, observed the flight patterns of birds, and in the solitude of his room, he studied the moves of Kasparov. When he was given a more formal introduction to mathematical formulas his world became an ocean unto itself. It was as if he had been spoken to in his native language for the first time. What followed was like a deluge. After graduating from MIT, he was given a fellowship at Oxford. Within two years, he had authored a number of proofs, upending decades of established quantum mathematical theory. In addition, he had presented a number of new theories in his preferred field of behavioral science, and analytics. For ten years, he rarely slept more than four hours a night and he seldom spoke to anyone. He had become fascinated by the order of things and the simple predictability of numbers, but he was never at peace. Even at the height of his success, he became increasingly aware that his mind had limits.

Looking to the history of mathematics and those prodigious men and women who made their mark in the field, it was easy to recognize that brilliance was often accompanied by tragedy and madness. Kurt Godel was the first that came to my mind.

Godel was an Austrian-American mathematician, one of the greatest minds of the twentieth century. He was a pioneer and a prodigy, but he was haunted by his own thoughts. He developed a fear that people were trying to poison him, and he would only eat food cooked by his wife, Adele. In 1977, Adele was suddenly hospitalized for six months. During that time, Godel refused to eat and died of starvation.

Alan Turing was a famous British mathematician who committed suicide in 1954 by eating a cyanide-laced apple. Then of course, there was Ludwig Boltzmann, who was known for his work in statistical mechanics. He hung himself while on vacation with his family.

Winterbottom had surpassed many of his predecessors, and although he showed no signs of serious mental instability, he was always on guard against it. As he continued to push the boundaries of existing mathematical theory, he became increasingly reclusive. It was at this time that he met Margaret.

She was working at Stanford as a Professor of Humanities, when he was visiting the University as a guest lecturer; one of only three lectures he gave that year. It was anything other than love at first sight. They had a deep respect for each other's intellect, but neither had the time, nor the interest. It would take four years for their friendship and mutual respect to grow into something more. Even as friends, she knew that a mind so beautifully complex was equally troubled. Just as he feared being lost to its revolutions, she was afraid of becoming the linchpin holding him in place. Eventually, their combined fears weren't enough to stop the inevitable. Not long after they were married, Margaret shifted away from academics. With her mother, Agnes, she founded Edmund & Gray Importers, a charitable foundation, focused on acquiring rare antiquities, with the sole purpose of returning artifacts to their native countries.

During that time Winterbottom continued his work, but he did so at a more even pace. When Grace was born, he withdrew from his work almost entirely. Numbers seemed to matter less to him. I imagine that those years were the most peaceful years of his life. And then, in an instant, out on Lexington Avenue, it all came to an end.

I suppose only those who have experienced such a tragedy could fathom the depths of his despair, though I'm sure McCuen genuinely tried. For Winterbottom, I'm tempted to say he died that day, but from what I've learned about him over the years, I think he would disagree. He would say that he wished he had. He was alone again, and the anchor that had kept his mind tethered for so long was gone. It wasn't long after that he found himself haunted by numbers of a different nature.

X
THE OPERA

After the incident at Somerset's apartment, and his trip to Chinatown, Winterbottom exiled himself to his work. At four o'clock, McCuen called to remind him that they would be attending the Opera that evening, and to be ready by six. When he arrived, Winterbottom still wasn't ready.

"I told you to be ready by six."

"I'm sorry, I lost track of time," said Winterbottom. "And let's not get too excited about an invitation from a serial killer."

"Said the man who broke into his house last night," replied McCuen. "We just can't be late."

"—Or he might kill somebody?"

"I'm the one who has to explain it to the Commissioner if we're late," said McCuen, begrudgingly.

"I'm almost ready."

"Where's Mrs. Bruce?" asked McCuen.

"She's out for the night—fight club," replied Winterbottom, dismissively. What he called fight club was actually a weekly Cribbage game at the Fifth

Avenue Presbyterian Church. Her presence was sorely missed, as McCuen watched Winterbottom fail his third attempt at a Double-Windsor. Although, time didn't matter as much as McCuen was letting on. Unbeknownst to Winterbottom, they were actually an hour early. Leaving Winterbottom to struggle with his tie a little longer, McCuen turned his attention to the rest of the room. Looking down at his feet, he followed a cluster of ethernet cables and wires that snaked across the parquet floor. They all converged on a row of eight towering computer servers standing against the wall. In mass, they presented an eerie contrast against the lathe and plaster walls. They hadn't been there a week ago. McCuen looked to the adjacent wall of the room and the great curtain that was covering it.

"You've been busy," he said as he approached the center of the curtain. Looking up from his tie, Winterbottom suddenly noticed that McCuen had grown curious.

"Yes—I started working again."

"On what?"

"Numbers," said Winterbottom, vaguely. "I can show you later—when we have more time. Ready to go?"

"I won't argue with that," replied McCuen.

Once they were in the car, McCuen's mind became set on the task ahead of him. There was no way to prepare for what the night might bring. The killer had proven himself to be unorthodox, and with his grim invitation to the Opera, it seemed like he was toying with them. Up until the most recent murder, the public had been kept in the dark. It was a decision made at the highest levels of the department and the Mayor's office. However, his latest killing, on the steps of the New York Stock Exchange, had forced things out into the open. A murder at the Metropolitan Opera would send panic throughout the city.

As they continued down Lexington Avenue, Winterbottom looked at his wristwatch, noting the time to himself.

"Take East 83rd Street," he said. "It'll be quicker."

"It's much shorter to go—"

"Trust me—it'll be quicker," said Winterbottom, cutting him off.

Before McCuen could continue the argument, his phone rang. Winterbottom couldn't hear what was said, but McCuen's reaction was more telling than words. McCuen activated the car's lights and sirens and pulled hard against the steering wheel. They were turning around.

"There's been a murder at the Seneca Club," he said.

"And what about the opera?" asked Winterbottom.

"I've got under-covers and a tactical unit at the Opera House, they can manage until we get there."

Before long they were standing on the steps of the Seneca Club, beneath the shadow of Chief Red Jacket. A woman's corpse had been dumped on the steps, dressed in white. Her face had been badly beaten, and her neck had been violently twisted. Most noticeably, she had been stabbed multiple times. The white satin dress, that billowed at the shoulders, was identical to the one worn in Sargent's portrait of Ada Rehan. From the position of the body and the presence of lividity, it seemed likely that the woman had been killed earlier in the night and then placed on the steps of the Seneca Club.

"Whelan's going to have a field day with this one," remarked Winterbottom. McCuen didn't respond. While Winterbottom struggled to discern certain aspects of the killing, McCuen focused on matters of a more pertinent nature, such as why the killer bothered to invite them to the opera, if he knew they'd be diverted to the Seneca Club. Was it all a part of the game he was playing, or was it that the killer had no plan at all? Was he a man of devious intellect, or a wild beast, serving more animalistic urges. As the two men pondered the corpse's disposition, patrol officers conducted a canvas search of the surrounding area, looking for witnesses.

Compared with the other paintings in Sargent's catalogue, the portrait of Ada Rehan was just another portrait. It was well executed, but hardly remarkable. As an Irish-American actress, Rehan found fame in her performances of Shakespearian comedies, garnering the respect and admiration of George Bernard Shaw, Mark Twain and Oscar Wilde. When Sargent painted her portrait, she had already retired from the stage, and was nearly forty years old. Rendered against a Baroque tapestry, Sargent painted a formidable figure, beautiful and vivid. The painter had captured a form of beauty not often appreciated, a spirit of elegance that surpassed youthful exuberance. It was the ability to see his subjects so intently that made Sargent's portraits so celebrated; his vision and artistic skill transcended a mere physical likeness. He captured their essence.

What Sargent achieved artistically, the killer equaled in depravity. The dead woman closely resembled the subject's age and general appearance, but her face had been severely beaten. It was the result of unbridled rage.

"Why the white satin dress?" asked Winterbottom, still hung up on the red velvet dress from the *Hammersley portrait*.

"Anselm, the woman's been stabbed and beaten beyond recognition," replied McCuen. "I really don't care what color the dress is."

"It just seems odd to me—"

"I think you're missing the bigger picture," said McCuen sharply, attempting to focus on the matter at hand. Adams arrived shortly after and began examining the body, while Whelan tried to get a list of members who were in the club that night. McCuen anxiously waited for them to finish their work, acutely aware that the opera was about to begin.

"There's a lot of them," said Adams. "—but the stab wounds are mostly superficial. They missed all the major organs and arteries. I don't think any of them would have killed her."

"So it's strangulation, again," said Winterbottom.

"It looks that way, and blunt force trauma to the head." Then Winterbottom looked curiously at the white satin dress again.

"Why is there so little blood on the dress?" he asked. "She was clearly wearing it when she was stabbed. I'd expect more bleeding—even if the wounds were superficial."

"That's because she was stabbed after she was already dead," replied Adams. "If the heart isn't pumping—the blood isn't in any rush to go anywhere,"

"Is that normal for serial killers?" asked Winterbottom. "—to stab people after they're already dead?"

"It's common enough that they have a name for it," replied Adams. "It's called picquering. Some killers develop an arousal response from piercing skin with sharp objects. It's one of the many creepy things that serial killers do."

"Fair enough," replied Winterbottom. "But why would the killer progress from non-sexualized behavior to deviant sexual behavior?"

"I don't know," said Adams.

"You make a good point, Anselm," replied McCuen. "But you said it yourself—this one's different."

Just then Whelan emerged from the Seneca Club and shuffled down the front steps, followed by a man in his mid-twenties who was visibly shaken by the events of the evening. McCuen ducked beneath the crime scene tape and met Whelan as he approached. Looking over Whelan's left shoulder and seeing the man hurrying toward them, McCuen spoke.

"Were you able to get any names?"

"No," said Whelan under his breath. "And this poor bastard's a nervous wreck."

"How hard should we push him?" asked McCuen.

"Go easy—he might pass out." As the man approached, Whelan spoke out loud. "Captain —this is the night porter for the Seneca Club, and unfortunately he says he can't help us—"

"Captain, I'm sorry—" said the porter. His voice was wobbling. "Even if I were allowed to give out the names of our members, I don't have access to the attendance list. Only the Club Manager can do that—"

"We're trying to catch a murderer, and we need those names," continued McCuen. "You don't want another person to die, do you?"

"Oh, god," said the man squeamishly, as he looked over at the woman's lifeless body. He covered his mouth and quickly turned away.

"When do you expect the Club Manager to arrive?" asked Whelan.

"I have no idea—" said the porter. "He didn't tell me he was leaving—I just came down from the barroom and he was gone." As the porter spoke he looked over McCuen's shoulder and he saw a familiar figure walking toward them from up the street. "Wait, there he is." They all turned to see a man walking toward them in the distance. Even from fifty yards away, McCuen could see that it was the squirrel-man with the tortoise-shell glasses and the chartreuse bow tie. The porter began waving his hand in the air. "Over here, Mr. Somerset—over here." McCuen turned sharply to the porter.

"Willard Somerset?"

"Yes," replied to the porter in confusion. "Do you know him?"

Before McCuen could turn around, Somerset began running in the opposite direction. McCuen and Whelan rushed after him on foot, while Adams pushed Winterbottom into a nearby police cruiser. McCuen could never have guessed that Somerset would be so athletic, but he was very quickly breaking away from them. He ran down the remainder of 60th Street, before dashing around the corner. As they approached the intersection, they saw him sprinting across 5th Avenue, recklessly dodging the oncoming traffic.

Charging ahead, McCuen and Whelan bolted past a discord of screeching brakes and car horns, as the oncoming cars broke into abrupt halts and subtle swerves. Whelan jumped to avoid being hit and slid hard against the sidewalk. McCuen saw him fall, but continued on without stopping. Against the clusters of lights and sounds, it was hard to make out if he were chasing a man, or an apparition. He ran harder as he watched Somerset turn into the Southern entrance to Central Park. By then, Whelan was back on his feet and hurried to catch up. Aware of what was ahead of him, he found comfort in finding his Glock still firmly planted in his holster. It was chambered and ready to deliver a swift end if needed.

As they raced through the park, McCuen's lungs began to heave, and he could feel his legs beginning to tire. As Whelan caught up, they could see Somerset cutting through the darkness, his pace was unimpeded. Following him deeper into the park, the lights and sounds of the city were muted by the oaks and elms, and an eerie silence came over them. Knowing that Adams was looking for direction, McCuen keyed his radio.

"He's heading north on Park Road—toward the Central Park Zoo."

As they closed in on Somerset, his movements became increasingly frantic. He reeled around to see his pursuers as he moved with sharp, but nimble steps.

Then suddenly, he leapt over the short wrought-iron fence bordering the zoo and darted between the brick pillars of a nearby pergola. He had vanished. Whelan stopped and listened for the shuffling of Somerset's footsteps. There was nothing. Whelan drew his gun and slowly peered around the pillars, scanning the darkness for any shifting movements. Breathing heavily, McCuen joined him, huddling behind a nearby pillar. Knowing that he was close, they moved cautiously, aware that danger awaited around every corner. Together they moved slowly to the wall of a nearby building. As they approached the end of the brick wall, they heard the rustling of the bushes and the fast tapping of footsteps on the bricks. He was running again. Both men burst into a sprint, following Somerset onto Park Road, before scurrying back across the traffic lanes on 5th Avenue. He was nearly struck by a van and a cascade of approaching cars. Whelan and McCuen continued after him, squeezing between car bumpers as they traversed the street. He was running in circles.

Turning the corner, McCuen's feet slid out from under him, slamming his shoulder and ribs against the sidewalk. Despite the rain dampened sidewalk, Whelan had retained his footing and was gaining on Somerset. Then, much to his surprise, Somerset ducked under the awning of a 5th Avenue apartment building. Whelan charged ahead, as Somerset fumbled with a key to the front door. As Whelan neared the entrance, an unmarked police cruiser jumped the curb in front of the building. Before the cruiser had stopped, Whelan threw himself at Somerset, knocking him into the foyer. Somerset's wiry frame collapsed onto the marble floor and slid hard against the opposing wall. The chase was over, and the battered Willard Somerset offered no resistance.

Adams, Winterbottom, and McCuen pushed through the doorway just as Whelan was placing Somerset in handcuffs. Adams helped him to his feet and leaned him against the wall, patting him down for any weapons. Exhausted from the chase, Whelan loosened his tie and sat down in the corridor to catch his breath.

"Nice job, Tom," said McCuen, placing a hand on his shoulder. Whelan just nodded, in response. Before approaching Somerset, McCuen leaned closer to Winterbottom.

"It always surprises me," he whispered. "They never look like depraved killers, do they?"

"No—they don't," replied Winterbottom. "It's what enables them to get so close to their victims—the ones that can't be charming, or handsome, pretend to be harmless." Then he paused and looked at Somerset, who was curled up against the wall, sobbing. "Although, I'm still not sure about Mr. Somerset."

"I'm going to need more than that," said McCuen. In that moment, Somerset became aware of his situation and buried his face in his hands. Undeterred, McCuen continued. "Mr. Somerset, we haven't been formally introduced—but we met at the club the other day. I'm Captain McCuen—I'm with the NYPD, and I'd very much like to speak to you."

"I didn't kill that woman," cried Somerset.

"That's fine—but just so you know, you don't have to answer any questions—"

"I didn't kill her!" he shouted, turning against the wall. His face turned red as the veins in his neck and forehead surged beneath his skin.

"Ed, hold on," interrupted Winterbottom, pulling at his arm. "Look at his hands."

Much like his figure, Somerset's hands were small and slender. They couldn't have made the wide-reaching bruises that were found on Olivia Alford's neck. The fact couldn't be ignored. Fueled by necessity, McCuen rolled Somerset against the wall, unlocking his handcuffs. He let out a heavy sigh of relief, before turning to face McCuen again. He was met with a hardened expression. His nerves let loose again, and he began to shake, recognizing that he was far from being exonerated.

"Captain—I didn't kill that woman!"

"Then why don't we start with why you were running from the police?" asked Whelan, moving in closer to Somerset.

"The dress—" screeched Somerset. "I saw the dress she was wearing! I brought it to her —but I didn't kill her, I swear!" He began shaking and crying uncontrollably. "Please, you have to believe me!"

"Give us a reason to," replied McCuen.

"Please—I can't."

McCuen slammed his open hand against the wall, inches away from Somerset's head.

"Okay—I'll show you," cried Somerset.

"Show us what?"

"The apartment—upstairs."

Cautiously, they followed Somerset to a fifth-floor apartment, where he unlocked the door and invited them in. Walking into the living room, they saw it was richly furnished, but most noticeably, it housed a vast collection of early American paintings. The canvases crowded the walls of the apartment and spilled over onto the floor, leaning in rows around the perimeter of the room. The majority of them were the works of John Singer Sargent. Looking past the paintings, they all came to a dark revelation. Standing in front of the windows, overlooking the city, were four bare dressmaker forms. Through the cracked lenses of his tortoise shell glasses, Somerset could see that they were all taken in by them.

"I brought her the dress yesterday—just as he asked."

"Who asked you to bring her the dress?" snapped Whelan.

"Mr. Fields," replied Somerset. "This is his apartment." McCuen turned to Adams, he didn't need to say a word. She walked away from Somerset to make a phone call.

"Why would Fields want you to deliver a dress to that woman?" asked McCuen.

"He said it was all a part of the game," said Somerset, as he motioned to the paintings in the room. Nervously, Somerset continued. "A few members of the club have a gentleman's agreement, and whoever gets the most John Singer Sargent paintings—"

"Yes, we know," said McCuen. "But we were told that Fields stopped playing the game."

"He did," replied Somerset. "But he hasn't stopped collecting portraits." The revelation reeked of obsession and brought to mind a menacing suspicion. Had the maniacal twists of the father been carried on by the son? As they awaited Adams' return, Somerset continued. "He has me do the bidding for him—under my name. He gives me the money and tells me which paintings to buy. Never any landscapes, or watercolors from Sargent's time abroad. No—he's quite infatuated with the portraits."

"So why doesn't he buy them himself?"

"Mrs. Fields," replied Somerset, adjusting his glasses. "He doesn't want her to know about them. He doesn't want anyone to know about them. That's why he keeps this apartment."

"So what do the dresses have to do with it?" asked McCuen.

"I don't know, exactly," replied Somerset, uneasily. "He never said. When they arrived here at the apartment, I recognized them, of course—but I never knew what they were for. He left precise instructions on when and where I was to deliver them." Having mentioned the dresses, Somerset was revisited by a sick feeling in his stomach. He could see the dead woman's body in his mind, and it rested on his chest like a millstone. He trembled again as he thought of his role in all of it.

"And what do you get out of it?"

"Pardon me?" said Somerset, distracted by his thoughts.

"What do you get for helping Fields?" repeated Whelan. "Oh, yes—Hans Hofmann," replied Somerset, grimly.

"Who?"

"Hans Hofmann—the Abstract Expressionist," he replied. "For every five Sargent paintings I purchase for Mr. Fields, he buys me a Hofmann. I was hoping for Song of the Nightingale, but I'm afraid after all this—it may not happen."

While the others were speaking with Somerset, Winterbottom quietly broke away and began searching the apartment. He walked along the narrow hallway and could see a room at the far end. The apartment was dimly lit and the room at the end of the hall was no exception. Oddly, the door was closed, and as if gifted with magnetic properties, the brass doorknob pulled him closer. Standing in front of the door, he stopped. He twisted the knob and slowly pushed the door inward. The weight of it creaked against its tired hinges. Cautiously, he stepped into the room to find a dresser, and a mattress, stripped of its bed linens. Like the apartment in Bed-Stuy, the furnishings were covered in plastic drop clothes. Standing starkly beside the bed was an empty dressmaker's form. Winterbottom called out to McCuen, who rushed to the bedroom. Somerset and Whelan followed closely behind.

"There's another dress," said Winterbottom.

"What did you do with this one?" asked McCuen, sharply.

"I took it to Mrs. Fields, this afternoon," cried Somerset. "It was the *Madame X* gown. He said it was for their anniversary—and that she'd be wearing it to the opera this evening." At his words they all rushed to the door where they found Adams waiting for them.

"I just spoke to the lab. The fabric samples from the victim's dresses contained male DNA. It matches the profile from the scotch glass that Anselm took from Thomas Fields. It's him. He's the killer."

"You two—get to the opera," said McCuen, sharply. "Anselm—you're with me, we'll head for their apartment. We need to find Mrs. Fields, immediately. Let all units know to take Mr. Fields into custody and approach with extreme caution."

McCuen and Winterbottom sped to the Fields' apartment, hoping that Whelan and Adams would find Mr. and Mrs. Fields still at the opera. As the car tires skidded onto Park Avenue, the police radio reported that Mr. and Mrs. Fields had left the opera early. McCuen and Winterbottom were close, and he called for every available patrol unit to converge on the Midtown apartment.

"You can't come with me this time," said McCuen, as he parked his cruiser. "Not until we have him."

"Okay," replied Winterbottom.

"Just wait in the car."

As he approached, McCuen was met by two patrol officers who had just seen Field's car entering the underground parking garage. McCuen and the patrol officers rushed to the rooftop apartment, knowing that they were running out of time. At the door, they were greeted by Field's head of security, Lucien.

"I'm sorry, sir—Mr. and Mrs. Fields have retired for the evening."

"This is a police emergency—we're coming in."

"I will need to see official paperwork, sir—"

"We're going in," barked McCuen. "I can walk past you—or over you. It's your choice." The man quickly moved aside and accompanied them into the foyer. Suddenly, they heard Mrs. Fields screaming from inside the apartment. McCuen ran through the living room and into the master bedroom where he found her in a desperate struggle with her husband. Fields was towering over her, crushing her forearms in his grip. Suddenly, there was a silvery flash in the darkness, and a knife could be seen on the floor at their feet. McCuen aimed his gun at Fields and yelled for him to stop. Fields turned to see Captain McCuen, and the patrolmen; their guns were pointing at his upper torso. His eyes had a wild appearance to them, maniacal and darting. Surprised by McCuen's presence and his current predicament, he let go of her wrists and cautiously raised his hands.

"Captain!" he shouted, breathlessly. "Thank God you're here! She—she attacked me!" Before he could take another step, the officers grabbed his arms and placed him in handcuffs.

"Wait—what are you doing!" yelled Fields, as they pushed him out of the room. "It's not what it looks like—I can explain!" By the time they had escorted him out of the room, Mrs. Fields had sunken to the floor, sobbing against the bed. McCuen did his best to console her and patiently waited for her to catch her breath. She kept shaking her head in disbelief, clutching her arms close to her body.

"I don't understand," she cried softly. "He tried to kill me."

As the apartment filled with NYPD personnel, McCuen wrapped Mrs.

Fields in a blanket and walked her to the adjacent room while officers conducted a search of the crime scene. Out of view from Mrs. Fields, Whelan and Adams discovered a small vial of chloroform in Mr. Fields' closet, and in his suit coat pocket they found a white handkerchief, still dampened with chloroform.

Over the next hour, McCuen kept her company while they finished their search. Despite all of her asking, he couldn't formulate an adequate explanation as to why her husband had tried to kill her. How does one explain such a thing? As police personnel began leaving the apartment, Winterbottom quietly entered the room. McCuen had forgotten about him and hurried over to send him away. Mrs. Fields noticed him entering the room and instinctively wiped the tears from her eyes.

"Anselm, you can't be here," said McCuen, sharply.

It was as if McCuen wasn't even there. Winterbottom just continued to stare at Mrs. Fields. There was contempt in his eyes.

"You were asking why your husband tried to kill you," said Winterbottom to Mrs. Fields.

"Anselm—what are you doing?" interrupted McCuen, grabbing him by the arm.

Winterbottom forcefully pulled away from him.

"But I know that he didn't." Winterbottom's assertion took McCuen by surprise. Seeing Winterbottom's unbroken gaze, McCuen turned with the futile hope that she hadn't heard what was said. The noticeable change in her demeanor told him that she had.

"That's enough!" barked McCuen, desperately trying to gain control.

"He didn't try to kill you," continued Winterbottom. "In fact—I suspect he hasn't laid a hand on you, in quite some time."

"How dare you!" she shouted angrily.

"Anselm!" snapped McCuen in disgust. "You're leaving, now!"

"The dresses were clever," said Winterbottom, calmly. "You planned it perfectly."

"Captain, who is this man?" she demanded. There was an edge to her voice.

"Your husband didn't kill those women," said Winterbottom. "You did."

"How dare you!" she shouted. "Captain, do something—get him out of here!"

As angry as he was at Winterbottom, McCuen could see that something had shifted; he saw something in her that he hadn't noticed before. She was no longer the fragile victim, a tender lamb. Instead, she was sharp and fierce. He turned slowly toward her, looking for vindication. Having lost her sway over McCuen, her eyes nervously darted back and forth between the two men, and she sneered before letting out a howling scream. "Lucien!"

In an instant, the Frenchman burst into the room and aimed his gun on McCuen. Seeing Lucien, Winterbottom instinctively swatted a ceramic vase from the nearby desk, hurling it into the air. The vase tumbled between the two men, well in front of the Frenchman, but it gave McCuen time to react and draw his Glock. Lucien's first two shots strayed off to the right of McCuen and pushed through the paneled linen on the far side of the room. Then a volley of bullets followed, rattling against the opposing wall. By the time the vase had fractured against the tiled floor, the Frenchman was writhing on the ground, with three holes in his belly. His gun was lying beside him on the floor. Unshaken, McCuen kept his gun fixed on his assailant, as the sound of a dozen patrolmen could be heard running through the apartment. Mrs. Fields was shaking with panic, as fresh tears began running through her mascara. Glaring at Winterbottom, the tendons in her neck were taut, pinned to a mind undone. She was filled with rage. Her shoulders heaved as she turned to see Lucien lying on the floor, bleeding profusely. As the first patrolman entered the room, she turned to Winterbottom with an angry smile. Her eyes frantically bounced around the room as she wrenched a small pistol from her handbag. McCuen shifted his aim toward her. To his surprise, she pushed the gun under her chin and pulled the trigger. The sound of the shot rang out and the tension, once held, was loosened like a severed cord. Her lifeless body folded to the ground, adorned in the dress of a masterpiece, lying amongst the crimson and the Makrana tile.

XI

THE AFTERMATH

What happened following the untimely demise of Mrs. Esmé Fields is best summarized in the way that it was told to me, by McCuen himself. In the immediate aftermath of the shooting, McCuen found himself in a near-impossible situation. Not only was Winterbottom present for, and a witness to, a police-involved shooting, but he was also a precipitating factor in the suicide of Mrs. Esmé Fields. To further complicate the matter, there was unequivocal DNA evidence suggesting that Thomas Fields had committed the murders. As these thoughts churned in his mind, McCuen shutdown the crime scene, and immediately expelled all uniformed personnel from the room, leaving him alone with his team, Winterbottom, and the flaccid corpse of Mrs. Fields. In the silence of the room, Winterbottom began to explain.

Unsurprisingly, Winterbottom had ignored McCuen's instructions to stay in the car, and instead proceeded to meet with the Fields' maid; the same woman he had met with during their first visit to Fields' apartment. While Mr. Fields was being carried away in handcuffs, the maid, Catalina, spoke with Winterbottom about the inner workings of the house. He learned that Mrs. Fields traveled often, and when she did, Mr. Fields would freely enjoy the company of other women. Catalina identified the four victims as being sexually involved with Mr. Fields, and she frequently saw them coming and going from the house in the weeks before they were killed.

Thomas Fields hadn't murdered the wives of his business rivals, he had seduced them. But that was hardly an alibi for murder. His obsession with Sargent's portraits was well established, and the idea of the maniacal billionaire murdering women to satisfy his deranged obsession was hard to overturn. After careful questioning, Winterbottom determined that Mrs. Fields learned of the affairs and began a most peculiar practice. She gave Catalina specific instructions not to change the bed linens. Instead, Mrs. Fields would return from her travels and strip the satin sheets from the bed. She would then proceed to redecorate the entire bedroom, from floor to ceiling. And that was at the heart of why traces of Thomas Fields' DNA were found on the dresses. With knowledge of her husband's obsession for Sargent's portraits, and her experience as a fashion designer, Esmé Fields had carefully tailored her own husband's undoing, exacting revenge in the process. With each act of infidelity, she would sew a dress from the satin bed sheets her husband had slept in, ensuring that his touch-DNA, and skin particles would be found on each victim's Victorian dress. Throughout the series of murders, it had been perplexing to Winterbottom why the red velvet dress from the *Hammersley portrait* was never used by the killer. Now he knew why. The red and gold velvet material of the *Hammersley* dress could never have been used as bed linens, not without raising suspicion.

Leading up to the murders, Mrs. Fields impersonated her husband and sent letters to Willard Somerset, requesting that he deliver the dresses to the unwitting victims. The Gala at the Metropolitan Museum of Art celebrating Sargent's portraits provided her with the perfect opportunity to set out a trail of dead women that would lead directly back to her husband.

Behaviorally, there was even greater evidence that cemented Mrs. Fields as the killer. Not only was she the scorned wife, but she had the added motive of financial gain. It would serve a jealous spouse more effectively to just kill her cheating husband, but in doing so, she would risk losing her livelihood and more importantly his wealth and status. Remember that Esmé Fields was the daughter of a French aristocrat, accustomed to the finer things in life. Wrapped tightly within her family heritage was a notion of dignity and honor, and in circumstances such as these it required retribution, like the Revanchism her ancestors demanded during the Franco-Prussian War. For a woman so refined, yet so infiltrated by anger and greed, it was far more prudent to frame her husband, prolonging his suffering and ensuring her financial stability in one fell swoop. And so she shaped her murderous plot in homage to Bluebeard, the terrifying French folktale she read as a child; the ruthless and bloodthirsty husband; a killer of women.

Of course, the reason the killer acted so unpredictably was because it was not just a killer; it was two. Mrs. Fields had murderous intentions, but there is a difference between wanting to kill and being able to. For that she relied on Lucien de Rais, the Frenchman, who as it turned out had served as her father's private security officer ever since she was a teenager. He served as her teacher. As a member of the French Foreign Legion, he was no stranger to death and killing, having served in Rwanda and Sarajevo. Led on by the promise of her affection, he helped her carry out the murders, one by one. The first victim, he strangled, as she watched. The second, he also strangled, allowing her to place her hands on top of his, so she could better feel the pressure that was required. It was his large hands that formed the bruising on their necks, but it was her anger and unfamiliarity that forcibly created its morbid embossing. That was why the killer's pathology appeared to be so strange. The chimera-like killer was both a novice, and a seasoned technician, all at once. As it turned out, it was Lucien who nearly killed McCuen in the apartment on Marcus Garvey Boulevard.

Above all the other evidence, it was the late onset of physical violence that firmly pointed to Mrs. Fields as the killer. The soft strangulation was a leniency given only to Emma Strauss and Olivia Alford. They were both women of wealth and of her own social class. The subsequent victims were spared nothing. Greta Mallory, *La Carmencita*, was a ballet dancer, a working-class woman from a poor family. In the eyes of Mrs. Fields, this made her husband's affair that much more offensive. It was out of disdain that she beat the woman and severed her tendons, but this was hardly her husband's most egregious betrayal. The last victim incurred the full weight of her wrath. She was stabbed, maimed, and beaten, unrecognizably. Mrs. Fields' hatred for her had little to do with her husband's affair, and everything to do with the woman's age. Infidelity was enough of a reason, but the idea that her husband would have an affair with a woman ten years older than herself, was a torture she couldn't bear. So, with vengeance, greed, and poisonous vanity, she murdered them all and set herself up as *Madame X*, the ultimate desire of her husband's obsession.

Of course, much of Winterbottom's analysis was speculative and relied largely on the testimony of the Fields' housemaid. Fortunately for McCuen, the Frenchman who survived being shot in his stomach, lived just long enough to corroborate Winterbottom's assessment, right down to the finer details.

XII

THE MADNESS

In the weeks that followed, the pieces fell into place. Lucien died a few days after the bullets were removed from his stomach. With both suspects dead there would be no trial, which meant McCuen was off the hook for any sort of explanation. In fact, there was no mention of Winterbottom in any of the investigatory reports. And so, Winterbottom returned to the solitude of Lexington Avenue and became lost to the world again.

Then, nearly four months later, Winterbottom was surprised to find McCuen standing at his doorway again. McCuen could hardly recognize him. Winterbottom's hair had grown out and his face was obscured by a thick, untrimmed beard.

"How are you, Ed?" said Winterbottom, politely.

"I'm well, Anselm—may I come in?"

"Of course," he replied, leading McCuen into the library. "How's Catherine?"

"She's fine—thanks for asking." Without further formality, McCuen continued. "Anselm, there's something I need to talk to you about."

"Sure—but before we get into it, I want to apologize. I should've handled it differently with Mrs. Fields—"

"It's not about that," said McCuen, cutting him off gently. Winterbottom looked surprised and waited for him to continue. He could see that McCuen was troubled.

"I couldn't quite figure it out at first," said McCuen. "But I knew something was wrong. It just didn't add up."

"What didn't add up?"

"How does someone who never drives a car—and seldom leaves his house, know so much about street closures in Midtown?" Before Winterbottom could reply, McCuen held up a manila folder. His expression had become deadly serious. "Help me understand why anyone in their right mind would donate thirty-eight million dollars to the City of New York for street repairs?" Winterbottom made no attempt to counter what was said. He just shook his head and turned away. After a brief pause he turned back to McCuen and smiled.

"I've always had a great love for this city—"

"Fuck you, Anselm!" yelled McCuen, harshly. The words sent a grim look across Winterbottom's face. With his anger rising, McCuen continued. "You knew every detail—hell, you were there that day. You never needed the case file—you just needed a copy of my records request form." McCuen's voice had become gravelly and harsh. "You knew I'd follow the god-damned rules—didn't you?" Winterbottom said nothing but nodded in acknowledgement. "And you knew that an official records request would include my—"

"—signature and authorization number," said Winterbottom, finishing the thought. McCuen's authorization number would have been utterly useless to anyone else, but for Winterbottom, it was the key to his plan.

"You son of a bitch!" snapped McCuen as he began pacing back and forth.

"Do you have any idea what you've done? Did you ever think about what this would mean for me?" After a harrowing silence, McCuen continued. "I need to know why my authorization number was used to obtain six months of video surveillance from the Domain Awareness System?" Winterbottom's expression remained fixed, but it was clear that McCuen had pieced it all together.

For those who don't know, the Domain Awareness System (DAS) was the creation of the U.S. State Department and was implemented in New York City in 2012, as a counterterrorism measure. Consisting of over 18,000 video surveillance cameras and interfaced with over two million license plate readings, and millions of arrest records, it was a technological leviathan. It was the most advanced surveillance system in the world and contained one of the largest caches of personal information ever compiled. Despite its overwhelming presence, even today most New Yorkers don't realize it exists. Given the circumstances, and unsure of how to respond to McCuen's accusations, Winterbottom chose denial.

"Naturally—I don't know what you're talking about," he said unconvincingly.

"Christ, Anselm!", said McCuen. "Six months of video surveillance—from Midtown! There's a god-damned camera on every street corner!"

"Again—I don't know what you're talking about?"

"You've committed the single greatest act of domestic spying in the history of the United States—and you've tied it around my neck!"

"Just calm down," pleaded Winterbottom. "If you're looking for who did this—my first guess would be the Russians. They're usually good for this sort of thing."

"We're past that." McCuen began pacing again, trying to calm his temper.

"Ed, I'm sure whoever did this—and again, my money's on the Russians—but they probably didn't have any other choice."

"If I could figure this out—how long do you think it'll take the FBI?"

Winterbottom knew the risks, and the odds of them coming to fruition. There had always been a possibility that McCuen would discover the breach, but there was no physical way to trace it to Winterbottom. He knew that much for sure. McCuen's knowledge of the accident was the only thing pointing him toward Winterbottom. It was a risk that he tried to manage as best he could. McCuen's proclivity for rule-following had allowed Winterbottom to obtain his authorization code, but it was also the greatest threat to his plan. Would McCuen, the moralist, turn him in? It was a callous gambit, but Winterbottom confidently predicted that he wouldn't. He was McCuen's friend, and what harm had he actually done? Time had rendered the stolen video surveillance effectively useless. What could it possibly be used for aside from everyday voyeurism? But, for all his careful planning, with McCuen standing in front of him, Winterbottom realized that there was one variable he hadn't considered. He never expected to feel ashamed for what he'd done. He had betrayed his friend; his only friend. Worse still, he had underestimated him.

"I need to know why—you owe me that much," said McCuen, beginning to calm down. Winterbottom nodded again, then walked with McCuen into the adjoining room. Without saying a word he stopped in front of the curtain that shrouded the wall, and he pulled it aside. Beneath it was a wall-sized street map of Midtown Manhattan with an extensive arrangement of road closures and street construction sites. Each construction project on the map had been listed in the documents McCuen had retrieved from City Hall. McCuen followed the bright red lines and traffic detours, all leading to a single point, the intersection where the accident happened. McCuen quietly took it all in, and despite its complexities, he began to understand its basic premise.

Through his charitable donation to the Streets Department, which had very specific timelines and locations attached to it, Winterbottom had managed to funnel all southbound streets, for a five-block radius, to pass directly through the intersection of Lexington and East 88th Street. With access to the DAS and its video surveillance, he could monitor and establish the movements of nearly every vehicle in Midtown, over the course of a six-month period. He was gathering information. Suddenly, McCuen broke away from the map and looked at Winterbottom. His eyes appeared somber. He didn't know what to say.

"Did you know that the DAS was implemented two months after the accident?" said Winterbottom, despairingly. Then he shook his head and smiled uncomfortably; an inadequate mask to hide his sadness. "Two months."

"It wouldn't have changed anything," replied McCuen. "It wouldn't have saved them."

"I know," replied Winterbottom. "But they would've found the man who did it." He exhaled heavily. "Ed, can't you see—I'm just doing what should have been done five years ago?"

"So, you're tracking every black Mercedes in Midtown," replied McCuen. "—hoping to find the man who killed them? Do you hear how insane that sounds? This is way beyond grasping at straws, Anselm."

"It's a little more comprehensive than that."

"Well, unless you've managed to build a fucking time-machine—it won't matter."

"Essentially, I have," replied Winterbottom, plainly. McCuen could see that he wasn't speaking of a time machine in the Wellsian sense, but marked his words as the exaggerations of a very desperate man. If he had looked more closely, McCuen would have seen that there were notes of truth to Winterbottom's words. Time isn't much more than a series of choices and events, occurrences that follow and compound upon each other. Past behavioral patterns have always held influence over future choices, and the possibilities touch upon the infinite, but the predictive nature of Winterbottom's work allowed him to trace the lines of history and peer into a blurred and half-shaped future. McCuen was right to question whether a mind could comprehend such an expanse, but Winterbottom was not a singular mind. He was exceptional. With his understanding of quantum mathematics, statistics, and human behavioral analysis, he had manufactured a way forward. He had built an algorithm which harnessed the most sophisticated artificial intelligence in existence, magnifying his own abilities exponentially. It was based on the predictability of humans and the unique street configurations of the Upper East Side.

Winterbottom's system had already begun sorting through the video footage, recording license plate numbers, and the makes and models of the cars that drove by his house on Lexington Avenue. Having detoured all the major traffic routes to pass by his house, Winterbottom was able to capture and record the facial likeness of each driver, through the use of a discrete, high-definition video camera attached to a nearby light pole. The face of every driver was analyzed by facial recognition software which compared it to the overall description of the suspect. If the man he was looking for had driven in Manhattan within the last six months, Winterbottom's machine would find him. McCuen was wrong. He hadn't spent the last five years in quiet seclusion. Winterbottom had been working harder than ever before to solve an impossible equation.

"Anselm, you need to stop this," pleaded McCuen.

"I can find him, Ed."

"This is too big—even for you."

"I know it seems impossible, but it's not—"

"It was five years ago," said McCuen, in disbelief.

"Did you know that 52% of Manhattan's daytime-population consists of people—"

"Anselm—enough!" yelled McCuen, abruptly cutting him off. "I don't care about how it works—none of it matters!" Then McCuen caught sight of something still hidden behind the edge of the curtain. He rushed over and pulled back the curtain even further. Pinned to the wall were twelve forensic sketches of the same portrait. It was the man Winterbottom was looking for.

"I saw him, Ed," said Winterbottom. "I can still see him—every time I close my eyes." He took one of the sketches off the wall and handed it to McCuen. "That's why this can all work. I can follow the numbers—I can rule out the variables. From there—I can sort through the remainders. I can find him!"

"Thirty-eight million dollars," said McCuen. "You spent thirty-eight million dollars." Winterbottom turned away in frustration.

"They wouldn't shut down Park Avenue for anything less," barked Winterbottom. "Just please let me explain—you haven't even heard the best part—"

"I don't want you to explain it me, Anselm!" snapped McCuen.

"Ed, please—"

"No!" shouted McCuen. He couldn't hide it any longer. "You don't get it—it's been five years!"

"I know how long it's been!" yelled Winterbottom, losing his temper.

“The statute of limitations is up!” shouted McCuen. Winterbottom contemplated the words, seemingly confused by what he had said. “Even if you could find him—he can never be charged or tried for what he did. It’s over.” McCuen’s heart sank as he delivered the news. Winterbottom paused for a moment and quietly turned away. “I’m sorry,” continued McCuen. “I should have told you sooner.”

“The statute of limitations?” replied Winterbottom, sharply. The look on his face had changed. There was no confusion; there was no trace of doubt in his voice. “Is that what you think this is about?” Winterbottom stepped closer to him and looked into his eyes. “Ed, I’m not looking for justice. I’m not trying to catch him—I’m going to kill him.” At that moment McCuen knew his friend was lost, and he could no longer be a part of it. Without another word, he turned and left the house, leaving Winterbottom alone with his grand design.

PART II

THE MONSTER OF THE ANDES

XIII

MOONLIGHTING

Knowing who Winterbottom was, did little to curb my habit of watching the house on Lexington Avenue. Resting against a half-reclined seat, I regularly surveyed the comings and goings. It had become a hobby more than anything else. Hobby sounds better than habit. It was like bird watching, only with a person, a particular person who didn't know I was watching him. Sometimes during the day, sometimes at night; it didn't matter. The house was perpetually quiet. Pedestrians and neighbors moved all around him, yet no one seemed to pay him any mind. An absence is often felt, even when it goes unnoticed. And even subtle omissions draw occasional attention.

And that's what he was, an omission. A forgotten man stuck between spaces; between the past, and what was coming. Even if they knew who he was, I can't say much would have changed. I could've told them about the accident, and the losses he suffered, and still most people would find it hard to empathize with him. There were times that I struggled to understand him, and I knew what he had been through. It's something we all do; not necessarily to ourselves, but to others. We venture to understand the people around us, but only on our terms. We make presumptions—simplifications, really. He was a billionaire, so envy would seem far more pertinent than empathy. He had things that we would never have, and it was all too easy to speak of unfairness. That was the glossy finish, the polished enamel. There was no need to chip away at it or look beneath it. There was no interest to go any deeper. What satisfies the eye is of no concern to the mind. That was the box we put him in, but on those nights when I watched him from across the street, it was like I had lifted the lid to look inside—to see things more closely. The view was dioramic, a vivid dimensional display. Putting aside my own selfishness, I could see him for what he was; a remarkable mind, and a deeply-flawed person, incapable of reacquiring something he lost; forever exiled from that which we all take for granted.

On those same nights, it was common for me to question my own perseverance. What was I doing there? And what did I hope to gain, sitting amidst the polarizing rants of the AM radio stations. There was no denying that watching the house was monotonous. I felt akin to a faithful entomologist staring at a chrysalis, waiting for the moth to emerge. I knew that metamorphosis was too much to hope for, but I would settle for a discernible change.

It was the small things that kept me enticed, like following him to Chinatown at 1 AM, or catching the rare courier arriving at his door. To me these were the cupped handfuls of cactus water in the desert. Alone they were of no real consequence, but to watch, in secret, was captivating. It was more than enough to quench my thirst. If I were to put it into words, I'd say I was curious, or even concerned about his arrangement with McCuen, and what that might mean. Then again, that's what a stalker might say to normalize his behavior. Not that I was a stalker; I wasn't. Stalkers have a maligned intent. You know, the kind of obsession that makes people crawl through windows and compels full-grown men to hide in closets, trying on women's underwear. That wasn't me. My compulsion, if you want to call it that, was about finding answers. I was looking for the truth. The road of knowledge leads to the palace of wisdom.

Tom Wolfe said that. Of course, William Blake said that the road of excess leads to the same place. Most of us choose the latter. I suppose if I was ever caught amongst the clothes hangers, wearing a pair of pointed-toe slingbacks, finding justification would be the least of my worries. I could always lean on the fact that I'm an investigative journalist, but these days even that might not hold water.

Perhaps the greatest leap forward came when I was able to follow Winterbottom to LaGuardia. I got as far as the gated section for chartered flights and private jets. As best I could tell he left for four days, then returned to his sanctuary on Lexington Avenue. This occurred on three occasions, and he never used the same taxicab company twice in a row. As far as his trips were concerned, he always left on a Sunday and came back on a Thursday morning. He was traveling somewhere, perhaps even visiting someone, but I had no way of knowing where, or who it was. I could only assume it had something to do with the accident, but there was no way to be certain.

Then suddenly, my moonlighting was suspended indefinitely, thanks to the *Butcher of Bogota*, Alejandro Salas, the boss of the Medellin cartel. Salas had been arrested in Columbia the year before and was extradited to face prosecution by New York's Southern District. I spent weeks preparing for the trial, trying to stay ahead of the media storm. During that time, I was too busy to think about Winterbottom, and in looking back, I felt as though a weight had been lifted. After sleeping consecutive nights on a mattress, the pull of Lexington Avenue slowly faded away. I even stopped scanning the police radio frequencies. If I couldn't immerse myself in it, I wanted nothing to do with it. I tried to pretend like it wasn't there—like it didn't exist. I was burying my head in the sand, an action attributed to ostriches yet only actually practiced and perfected by humans. Regardless of my perspective, the trial had forced a change, and my focus shifted toward the most notorious drug cartel boss in modern history.

Salas was raised in poverty, on the streets of Bogota, and rose quickly through the ranks of the Medellin cartel. Far worse than many of his enemies, Salas was able to hold on to power through a fierce application of violence and brutality which he inflicted on his rivals, and innocent people, alike. His ability to avoid capture and death, which he did on a number of occasions, earned him his moniker, El Gato, as he seemed to have nine lives, or more. After a bloody gun battle on the streets of Villavicencio, he was extradited to United States for trial. It was the trial of the decade, and with it came a host of logistical problems, the most immediate being the safety and security of the judge and jury. The NYPD, FBI, and the United States Marshals Service were all on hand for the show, and I had a front-row seat.

Two weeks into the trial, I had already written my final piece on Salas. Forgone conclusions make for uninteresting stories. Everyone knew he was guilty. The trial was just a formality, and after a few weeks of daytime hours, I was anxious for it to be over. Then, all of a sudden, as if my subconscious had willed it to happen, the trial judge blocked all press coverage from the courthouse. I'd been set free in one sense, and recaptured in another. The nights were mine again, and although I was eager to see where they would take me, I knew where I would eventually end up. I never thought I'd miss driving around Manhattan at night, but I had. The sights and smells of the city, and the euphoric sounds of life in close quarters lent me a heightened awareness. I felt the exuberance of youth again, and the time-acquired wisdom to recognize it as such. I was going to use it all up. Sleep be damned.

On my first night out, despite all the signs and senses, it was dead quiet. And I admit that I was disappointed. It wasn't as though I was hoping for something bad to happen. It was just more interesting when it did. When you find yourself rooting against peace on earth, it's important to recognize that you're doing something wrong. Besides, peace on earth never lasts very long, anyway. As I sat in the cafeteria of the Metropolitan Hospital, I found myself becoming increasingly superstitious. It was like I had done something to change the order of things, as if I had tilted the earth's axis, throwing the whole thing off balance.

I wasn't the only one who felt that way. Police officers and ER doctors are all superstitious; cops more so than docs. It makes perfect sense. It's natural to want to find some reason behind it all, a belief that affords you some control over otherwise uncontrollable circumstances. It doesn't matter if it's rational or not. It's true. If you ever want to see a roll-call room full of cops get upset, just say the word "quiet" out loud. They'll blame you for whatever happens afterward, as if a single spoken word could rule over the universe, like a witch's curse. As a journalist, I can speak firsthand to the power of language, but cynical agnosticism is about as close as I've come to anything supernatural.

By 3 A.M., I was desperate for a change. Just as I was beginning to think that I had worn the wrong color socks, a call came over the radio. If saying the word "quiet" can cause a rollover on the FDR, then I can't imagine what words were spoken that night. I was in luck to have been scanning the emergency channels because the call initially came in through the Fire department. What began as a simple structure fire turned out to be something much more.

I arrived at the scene just after they had extinguished the fire. Smoke was still escaping from the roofline of the warehouse, but as fires go it was relatively small. It was hardly a threat to the greater Ditmars Steinway area. I was about to chalk it up as a gigantic waste of time, when I watched a firefighter come running out of the warehouse, pulling at the sides of his oxygen mask. Once he was free of it, he took in a deep breath and exhaled slowly. With his next breath, he was doubled over vomiting. Another firefighter came to check on him, and was coughing uncomfortably, trying to keep his composure. There was more than fire and smoke in that warehouse. Being the only crime reporter on scene, I spoke to a few firefighters, but they said even less than I expected. I didn't know what it was, but it had to be something terrible. One thing was clear, the fire was out and they weren't going anywhere. They were waiting for someone. I decided to do the same and hoped it would be a reunion of sorts, with an old friend.

Within the hour, the NYPD's Crime Scene Unit had arrived, and I was relieved to see McCuen again. Whelan and Adams were with him and they went to work behind the corrugated metal walls of the warehouse, away from prying eyes. After a few minutes, McCuen emerged. He had seen me when he first arrived, and he knew I was looking for answers. I watched him as he pulled off his latex gloves, carefully folding them over on themselves. I knew to follow him. Stopping just outside the reach of a nearby streetlight, he lit a cigarette. He had started up again.

"It can't be that bad," I asked as McCuen looked down at his cigarette.

"That depends on what we're talking about," he replied. "The fire—or everything else? How's the trial going?"

Of course, he already knew the answer. He was gauging my misery and avoiding his own. I spared him my comparison to the torture of Prometheus, though it was a fitting reference.

"You know I hate the courthouse," I replied. "—but it's almost over."

"You may not be right about that," he said, giving me cause for concern.

"The fire?"

"I don't know—maybe."

"Are you going to tell me what's in there?" He just shook his head slowly and pushed out a conical stream of smoke, like a whistling tea kettle. "You've gotta give me something."

"I'd like to—but this one's not mine," he replied. "The FBI will be here any minute."

"Don't stonewall me, Ed—I know you too well for that." I could see that he was conflicted, but not as much as he was letting on. "Give me more than puke on the sidewalk."

"I'd like to, but you know how the Feds are—"

"The Feds are assholes," I replied. "That firefighter who threw up—he has rank. That tells me that he's already seen some pretty terrible stuff. The fact that he threw up tells me that he hasn't seen anything like this before." McCuen was unmoved, so I continued to push. "You know I'll find out eventually—and if there's even a small chance that it's connected to Salas, I could use the heads up." He was silent. "You don't even have to say what's in the warehouse. Just tell me what would make a veteran firefighter boot all over the sidewalk—and get you pulling on Lucky Strikes again."

He smiled and looked back over his shoulder, along Berrain Boulevard. We could both see two black SUV's moving toward us.

"Three burned bodies," he said quietly.

"And?"

"They were hung by their feet—and set on fire." Then he threw his cigarette on the ground and twisted it into the concrete.

"And you think it's connected to Salas?"

"Not necessarily—but they do. I've got to go."

"Thanks Ed."

He nodded in response and calmly walked back to the warehouse. I knew enough to get out of sight before the FBI arrived, and I was content to watch it play out from the front seat of my car.

Given Salas' history of violence, it made sense that the burnings would draw interest from Federal authorities. It was one of the main reasons he was being prosecuted so far away from his sphere of power. If these burnings were the work of the cartel, it would send a strong signal that even New York City wasn't beyond his reach. As I pondered the killings, I was reminded of a hideous calculation.

In Columbia, when the authorities seized a shipment of cocaine belonging to Salas' cartel, they expected a reprisal. These retributions were as precise as they were grisly. For every 100 kilos of cocaine that was seized, Salas would kill an innocent person. The violence was ruthless and was applied at random, but there was a clear message behind it all. In order to understand it you would have to know that 100 kilos of cocaine, when packaged, weighs roughly 200 pounds, the average weight of a full-grown man. Given this fact, it wasn't hard to understand Salas' terms. If they took his cocaine, he would take revenge, in an equal weight from the people. It was his own "pound of flesh" calculation. It got to a point where officials could reasonably predict murder rates based on how much cocaine had been seized that month. Of course, the number of victims would fluctuate a little, depending on whether they were women or children, on account of them weighing less than 200 pounds. Salas' predilection for killing was ruthless, but the expression of his contempt for human life was far more horrifying. The cartel would often hang their victims from highway overpasses, power lines, and trees. Sometimes they would leave a van filled with dead bodies parked on a public street, or across from a school. That was why they called him a butcher.

In preparation for his trial, the FBI anticipated such reprisals, but the timing of these killings seemed wrong to me. So did the setting. McCuen didn't like it either, but that didn't matter now. The FBI had arrived.

The agent in front was in his forties and had a larger build, the last vestige of his time as a high school Quarterback. He walked with a stern and open gait, the kind that could define a man's character or just as easily hide it. He was either John Wayne reincarnate, or a man deeply imperiled by his own self-image. McCuen didn't have to see through the glaring headlights to know that he was looking at a poor impersonation.

"Captain McCuen," said the man as he approached. "I'm Special Agent Matthew Dempsey." The man extended his arm and delivered a forceful handshake. What was initially mistaken for an athletic build was actually more lumbering and swollen, draped beneath an unfitted polyester suit.

"Good to meet you, Dempsey," he replied. Turning to the other agent, Dempsey continued. "This is Special Agent Dan Gilligan." As the other agent stepped forward, McCuen recognized him immediately.

"Dan—I didn't expect to see you here," he said smiling. "I thought you were at the D.C. field office."

"I was—I transferred in last week."

"I wasn't aware that you two knew each other," said Dempsey.

"We served in Afghanistan together," said McCuen.

"And we were in the same class at Quantico," added Gilligan. "But McCuen was already a living legend at that point."

"I don't remember it that way," said McCuen, dismissively. Sensing that Dempsey was feeling left out, Gilligan turned back to the matter at hand.

"How bad is it in there?"

"I'm not in a rush to go back in, if that tells you anything," replied McCuen.

"Well, let's see what we've got," said Dempsey. McCuen opted to let the wounded Prom King lead the way. It had only been two minutes, and McCuen could already see right through him. Dempsey was everything that was wrong with law enforcement, and the look on Gilligan's face suggested that it was worse than McCuen realized. Dempsey wasn't a new agent. He was Gilligan's supervisor.

As they entered the warehouse they could see that the outer walls were hardly affected by the fire. Everything had been drenched in water, and amongst the falling droplets they could smell traces of fire in the air. As they walked deeper into its steel frame, they could see the bright lights of the portable generators. As they moved closer, they were met by the unmistakable stench of burned flesh. It was a smell that Dempsey had never experienced, and he instinctively pushed it out through his nostrils, only to have it return again in a swarm.

Whelan and Adams were dressed from head to toe in protective forensic suits and face shields, busily examining the suspended bodies. Seeing McCuen and the others approaching, they stopped their work and peeled back their masks. Dempsey and Gilligan stared at the three disfigured bodies.

The smell was horrid but looking at the bodies was much worse. The blackened skin was blistered and cracked; a dreadful testament to the agony they endured. As it often happens, things don't have to be visually gruesome to be horrific. It's something even movies get wrong, because it's never as simple as looking at a dead body. It's the act of seeing it that rattles you. Seeing it, and knowing that you're breathing the same air that they were breathing, not so long before. That's what gets you—the fear of your own mortality. That's the gut punch that folds you over and pulls your head out of the clouds. McCuen recognized it in Dempsey's averted eyes.

"Whelan, why don't you give them a rundown," said McCuen.

"As you can see—we've got three bodies, all suspended by their feet. The killer used quarter inch metal cord—obviously resistant to the fire itself. The victim's hands and feet were bound, and we suspect that they had cloth gags in their mouths. Due to the duration and the overall intensity of combustion, it's not surprising that we've only found partial fibers."

"Identification's going to be a challenge," said Adams. "We've got two males and one female. Their ages range from early thirties to mid-forties. No personal belongings survived the fire, so we'll have to wait for the missing persons' reports to come in. We've obtained swabs for DNA comparison and we'll have the Medical Examiner look into dental records once we get the bodies out of here."

"Are there any other injuries?" asked Gilligan.

"I dug around a little," replied Adams. "There are no obvious bullet wounds, but given the state of the bodies, lacerations would be harder to see."

"So they weren't shot—and you're not sure if they were stabbed?" summarized Dempsey.

"That's right."

"Well, Captain," said Dempsey. "I think I've seen enough—we'll take over from here. We've been preparing for this since Salas was extradited."

"You think this was the cartel?" asked Whelan in confusion.

"It fits the profile," replied Dempsey. "Salas might as well have lit the match himself."

"I understand that it's brutal—but that's a pretty broad profile, don't you think?"

"I'm sorry—who are you?"

"Lieutenant Whelan, NYPD," he replied. "With all due respect, I don't see this being the work of the cartel."

"Okay," said Dempsey, with indignation. "But I do—and in case you're not familiar with Salas' work, I've seen the pictures, and I've read the files. He's stacked up hundreds of bodies over the years—these are no different. He kills without remorse, and he always does it for the same reason—retaliation. He did it when we took his cocaine, and we've expected him to do it ever since we took away his freedom."

"I understand that, but—"

"I don't think you do, Lieutenant," said Dempsey, cutting him off.

"Tom," interrupted McCuen. "We're done here—let's pack it up." Then McCuen turned to Dempsey. "It's all yours."

Whelan watched in frustration as McCuen turned to leave. Adams began shaking her head. She didn't buy it either, and Whelan wasn't finished. Turning to Dempsey again, he continued.

"Have you considered why the cartel would do something like this—away from the public eye? And why would he wait until now—the trial's almost over?

"I don't need to explain it to you, Lieutenant," snapped Dempsey. "We'll handle it from here." Whelan threw down his gloves in protest.

"Let me know how long it takes you to figure out why they're hanging upside down." With that, he turned away and began packing up.

They could all see that Dempsey was unmoved, as he looked over at the hanging corpses again. His lack of field experience was never more apparent, and he was unable to break away from linear advances.

"You should try to get out of the office more often," jabbed Whelan, as he hurried to catch up to McCuen. Dempsey turned to Gilligan, who only raised his eyebrows and shrugged his shoulders, leaving him alone to wrestle with the question. Adams, who was still collecting her gear, couldn't hold back any longer. Watching Dempsey was too much to bear.

"He wanted them to suffer," she said, plainly.

"Thank you—I gathered as much," said Dempsey, sarcastically. "He did set them on fire." Adams just shook her head.

"No," she said sharply. "He didn't just set them on fire. He hung them upside-down—and then he set them on fire." She continued to stare at Dempsey, but the mountain showed no sign of moving. "He lit their feet first, so they'd stay alive longer—while they were burning." The revelation made Dempsey's stomach turn, and he began clearing his nose of the smell again. He was fighting the urge to vomit.

Outside, Whelan had caught up to McCuen just as he reached his unmarked cruiser. The shuffling of his shoes on the pavement had given him away, and McCuen turned to face him.

"The cartel?" shouted Whelan. "You can't believe that bullshit!"

"It doesn't matter what I believe, Tom," replied McCuen, attempting to curb his disappointment.

"It doesn't matter?" repeated Whelan, more upset than before. "Even that asshole thinks it matters! Salas was a butcher, but when he killed people, he killed them quickly. If they had bullets in the back of their heads, then maybe I'd buy it—but this is something very different, and you know it."

"There are idiots everywhere, Tom—this one just happens to be in the FBI."

"Why would the cartel hide the bodies in a warehouse?" continued Whelan, refusing to be led off the subject.

"The FBI has jurisdiction."

"That doesn't mean we can't work it."

"Actually—that's exactly what it means."

"You know they're wrong, and that means no one will be looking for the person who did this—at least not until the trial's over."

"We can't do it all, Tom," replied McCuen. "You have to pick your battles."

"Well, this one's worth fighting!" He showed the kind of defiance that McCuen admired, and once had, but he was more tempered now. At least that's what he told himself. Still, McCuen couldn't bring himself to stifle it in someone else, least of all Whelan.

"I'm going to headquarters in the morning," said McCuen, conceding to the idea. "I'll ask for a joint-investigation. They love that inter-agency, Kumbaya-bullshit." Whelan smiled, and McCuen could see that his proposal was appreciated. "Of course—that would mean you'd have to work alongside that fucking Jack-wagon."

"I can do that," replied Whelan, but his faith in Dempsey to allow such a proposition was far from apostolic.

McCuen had reservations about the idea as well, but for different reasons. Working with the FBI would only complicate matters. He was slowly becoming more and more preoccupied with it every day, but this was the first time it had interfered with his work. He was the only one who knew what Winterbottom had done, and they would both face consequences if the DAS data breach was discovered. He had rid himself of Winterbottom, but he couldn't undo what had been done. It was beyond his reach. It would stay buried between them or it would unfold all on its own.

* * *

The next morning, McCuen arrived at NYPD Headquarters for his monthly meeting with the Chief of Detectives, James Kelly. Kelly and McCuen were old friends, and there was no one in the agency he trusted more, especially within the walls of Police Plaza. As McCuen walked through the lobby, he was followed by a uniformed corporal who had been working the front desk.

“Captain McCuen!” McCuen turned to the officer. “There’s a message for you from Chief Kelly.”

“I’m on my way up to see him now.”

“He insisted that I find you, sir. He said to tell you to bring two extra chairs.” McCuen paused momentarily, at the peculiar request, and nodded to the officer. He had come to headquarters for a monthly meeting, but thanks to Kelly’s cryptic message, he knew it would be anything but routine. After taking the elevator up nine floors, McCuen arrived at Kelly’s office and was escorted inside. He was greeted by Chief Kelly, Special Agent Dempsey, and a third man, who was new to him.

“Gentlemen, this is Captain Edward McCuen,” said Chief Kelly. “Dempsey just informed me that you two met last night on Berrain Boulevard.”

“Yes, we did,” replied McCuen. “Good morning, Dempsey.” McCuen appeared convincingly casual about the situation, which he owed to Chief Kelly’s warning. Dempsey nodded slowly, carefully gauging McCuen’s response and overall demeanor.

“And this is Special Agent Sutherland with the FBI’s Cyber-Crimes Task force.”

“It’s nice to meet you, Sutherland,” said McCuen, shaking his hand.

Sutherland was tall and wiry, and despite being twenty-three years old, he looked more like a high school student. He was stern, especially for his age, and when he spoke his mouth hardly moved at all, causing McCuen to wonder if he had the ability to do so. His shoes were meticulously polished and his suit accentuated his narrow frame. His hair was well-kempt, and he wore retro-style eyeglasses, conjuring up a modern paradox. An Ivy-league computer specialist, working for the FBI, with a fashion sense that harkened back to the good old days of McCarthyism. In McCuen’s mind, one thing was unavoidable. Sutherland was with the Cyber-Crimes Task force, which left little doubt about which direction this was going in.

“I’ll cut right to it,” said Chief Kelly. “The FBI is investigating a breach of the Domain Awareness System [DAS]. An unidentified hacker infiltrated the system and captured video surveillance from various parts of the city. As a user, you know its functions better than I do, so I’m sure you’d agree that a data breach of this magnitude warrants some attention.”

“Absolutely,” replied McCuen, feigning surprise. “When did it happen?”

“Five months ago,” said Dempsey. “We’re still assessing the significance of the breach, and of course, much of what we know is classified. What I can tell you is that it was a highly sophisticated attack.” McCuen knew nothing about cyber-security, but even he could see that Dempsey was treading water in the deep end of the swimming pool.

“Was it the Russians?” asked McCuen, smiling inside.

“Most likely—but we can’t rule out Iran, or the North Koreans.” Dempsey shifted his stance and continued. “They were targeting random traffic points in Manhattan, which indicates it was a pre-emptive hack. We’re monitoring the system in case they make a second attempt.” McCuen listened intently and nodded along until Dempsey was finished.

"Well, I guess the million-dollar question is—what does this have to do with me?" Dempsey took a half-step forward.

"Captain—the hackers used your authorization code to access the system."

"Okay," said McCuen, calmly. "What would you like me to do?" Dempsey paused briefly before softening his stance.

"Nothing, for now," continued Dempsey. "And I hope you're not upset about my little deception last night. When I learned that your authorization code had been used—quite frankly, I was suspicious. I wanted to meet you so I could see what kind of man I was dealing with. Thanks to Salas and the cartel—I was given that opportunity." McCuen listened intently, more conscious than ever of his own body language, as Dempsey continued. "Fortunately, early this morning, Agent Sutherland made an interesting discovery. He found that although the hackers went to great lengths to cover their own tracks—they made no attempt to hide the use of your name and authorization code. It was like they wanted us to think it was you."

"That was nice of them," replied McCuen, sarcastically.

"Of course, such blatant exposure helps to alleviate any direct suspicion around your involvement. With that said, procedure dictates that we notify you that your user account is being monitored." Then Dempsey paused again. "Captain, I feel compelled to warn you that if by some far-off chance you were involved in this breach—you could face prosecution under the Espionage Act."

"Okay, Dempsey," said McCuen, sharply. "Let me just stop you right there." His blood pressure was rising. "Am I to believe that the FBI suspects me of facilitating a cyber attack against the City of New York!" His tone put Dempsey back on his heels.

"No one's accusing you of anything—"

"No—but you're suggesting it, and I have a big fucking problem with that." McCuen was angry, more so with Winterbottom, than with Dempsey and the FBI, but in that moment it didn't matter. "Chief—are we done here?"

"I think so," replied Chief Kelly. "Agent Dempsey, you should also know that because Captain McCuen in under my supervision, our procedures dictate that you notify me of any future contact you have with Captain McCuen regarding this matter. Understood?"

"That won't be a problem, Chief," replied Dempsey, turning to McCuen. "Thank you for your time, Captain—and you should know that I've assigned Agent Gilligan to the Salas killings." The barb had been purposefully thrown. McCuen responded in kind.

"I'm glad you mentioned that," said McCuen, seeing his opportunity. "I was hoping to ask if my team could work alongside Agent Gilligan on the case—maybe they could learn a few things."

"That's fine with me," said Chief Kelly, forcing Dempsey's hand.

"Why not," replied Dempsey, reluctantly. "Happy hunting."

* * *

That same morning, I found myself parked on Lexington Avenue again. By 9 AM, I was about to head home. That's when I saw him. The door to the house swung open just as a taxicab pulled up to the sidewalk. Mrs. Bruce stepped into the daylight, carrying a handbag and a small piece of luggage. She hurried down the steps to the waiting cab where the driver helped her with her bags. I could see Winterbottom standing in the narrow opening, reluctant to come out into the world. His face was ashen, and a thick salt and pepper beard obscured my memory of him. He looked to me like a prisoner, or more like a castaway, exiled to some distant island. He had changed in the weeks since I last saw him, but it was him. As he peered out from the doorway, his eyes seemed to come alive. They darted from the parked cars on the street, to the pedestrians at the corner. Even the upper windows of the opposing buildings drew his suspicion. It was as if he knew I was watching him.

"Agnes, please—," he said, calling out to her.

"I have to go," she replied, turning toward the taxi.

His world was shrinking. The air was growing thin. From the look of him, even the walls of his house seemed to be narrowing. Stepping into the cab, she stopped, unexpectedly.

"She wouldn't have wanted this," said Mrs. Bruce, pleadingly. Winterbottom didn't respond; she didn't expect him to. After a brief pause he retreated back into the house, closing the door behind him. I watched as she ducked into the cab and drove away.

I couldn't have guessed what had happened between them, or if she'd be coming back. It didn't really matter. What mattered was that he was there, and that I had seen him. Given the obvious changes in his appearance, I knew he was working on something profound. Whatever it was, it appeared to be pulling at the most essential parts of him, thirsting on his intellect, as if it were Ambrosia.

On the night of the fire, I was hoping that Winterbottom would show up at the warehouse, but he never did. Speculation had been growing in my mind for weeks, but now it seemed more and more apparent that there had been a rift. McCuen no longer came to Lexington Avenue, and Winterbottom seemingly never left, except for his mysterious excursions by private jet. Now Agnes had left him too. I couldn't help but feel that I was getting closer to his secret. He seemed to be losing hold of things. Maybe he was already adrift. Either way, I'd have to be cautious. Even if distracted, his mind was a formidable opponent. He was becoming increasingly reclusive, perhaps even paranoid, and this made things substantially more difficult for me. I spent the next three days watching the house, and during that time he never left, not until Sunday afternoon, just like he had done the week before. I followed him to the airport, but before I could park, he disappeared into one of the neighboring airfield hangers. I had to find out where he was going.

Earlier I mentioned some of the more peculiar habits that people can develop, and that such curiosity can sometimes bear the fruit of perversion. While at the airport, I discovered such a practice, this one as innocent as it was aimless. It's called "plane spotting." It's a hobby in which people sit outside the perimeter fences of airports in order to record the registration numbers of aircraft that take off and land. These "enthusiasts," as they're called (although one might apply any number of other terms) also monitor and track flight paths of various airplanes. They also listen to the radio transmissions between the planes and air traffic control. Once I got over my initial prejudice regarding anyone who would actually engage in such a mundane activity, I found that it was one of the most popular hobbies in the country. I'm not kidding. Shut down the fucking space program—we've got all the aliens we need right here. It's true. People spend hours every day doing this. Of course, I had no right to judge them. I had just spent the night parked on Lexington Avenue. In a way, we were kindred spirits.

Knowing that Winterbottom was taking off every Thursday, I enlisted the help of a few local "plane spotters" at LaGuardia and offered them a $100 reward if they could tell me which plane he was on, and where he was going. The challenge was happily accepted, though the promise of money was less appreciated than the renewed sense of purpose I had given them.

XIV

HEART OF DARKNESS

Three days later, at around 7 PM, sirens were blaring through the streets of Ditmars Steinway again. It was another warehouse fire in which the building wasn't burned. Inside there were two burned bodies, hanging by their feet, in the same fashion as the previous three. Whoever was behind the killings, they had dispelled any preference for odd numbers, and showed a clear affinity toward the industrial district of the city. This particular warehouse was once owned by the Steinway & Sons piano company and had been used for storage. When Adams and Whelan arrived, they moved through the unlit warehouse, past the wooden skeletons of half-finished grand pianos, and gigantic spools of piano wire. The dampness in the air did little to mask the smell of the burned bodies. Adding to the atmosphere was the fact that the warehouse was currently owned by a private equity firm that manufactured everything from sewing machines to windshield wipers, and even pre-fabricated coffins. The company was using the warehouse as a temporary dumping ground for damaged inventory, resulting in a visual house of horrors.

As Adams and Whelan snaked through the warehouse and the piles of manufactured rubble, they were visited by the eerie sensation that they were being watched. The mood darkened as they neared the far end of the warehouse where they could hear what sounded like footsteps. They stopped and felt the pooling of water underfoot, and they could hear the irregular dripping of water from the ceiling. Neither said a word to each other as their lungs retracted against the particles of smoke in the air. It became heavier the closer they came to the source of the fire. It all merged with the sound of their own breathing, and the voices in their heads, whispering to them.

"God-damned nozzle-heads," said Whelan, trying to avoid the pools of water on the floor.

The hem of his pants and shoes were soaked through.

"At least we know the fire's out," said Adams.

"I'm glad you find this so amusing—just remember, they may have put out the fire, but they washed away all of our forensic evidence along with it."

"We'll figure it out," she said. "Besides, right now I just want to get the fuck out of here —this place is freaking me out."

"I won't argue with that."

Soon they could hear the hum of the generator and saw the distant glow of its portable lights. In the spotlights, they saw the two burned bodies hanging from the ceiling, stiffened and black. Staring back at them was McCuen.

"You got here quickly," said Adams, surprised to see him.

"I decided to follow the fire department for the night—just in case our killer came out to play." As they prepared to process the grisly scene, McCuen continued to look past them into the darkness. Then Whelan noticed that McCuen was holding his gun down at his side, half hidden behind his thigh. Something was definitely wrong. Whelan was suddenly visited by an unsettling thought.

"Don't make any sudden moves," said McCuen sharply and under his breath. "Just act like nothing's wrong." Adams heard him too, and quickly noticed the gun in his hand. They tried to remain calm as grave thoughts ricocheted through their minds. "Put on your gear—just like you would normally do."

"What is going on?" whispered Adams, desperate for an explanation.

"The killer's still here," said McCuen plainly. "He's watching us right now." They paused for a moment as it set in. Adams remained deathly quiet, thinking about the watchful eyes in the darkness. "The fire department only checked this end of the building," continued McCuen.

"If he wasn't on fire—they probably didn't see him," said Adams, as the sickening feeling moved into her stomach. Whelan and Adams looked at each other in disbelief, realizing that they had just walked past the killer, hiding in the darkness.

McCuen was known for having an unshakable disposition, even in the most dangerous situations. But they couldn't imagine he would be this calm with a serial killer still in the building. They had heard the stories about him, from his days on patrol, and from his time in the Army, but that was a long time ago. They had dismissed them as exaggerations, the kind of thing that got bigger with time. As they continued to pull on their forensic suits, Whelan's nerves got the better of him. He instinctively rested his hand on the grip of his Glock.

"It'll be fine," said McCuen, calmly. "I did an initial sweep of this end of the building. " Out of the corners of his eyes, McCuen continued to scan the iron scaffolding of the warehouse as he spoke. "Four more uniforms are on their way—when they get here, I'll help them do a full search. The perimeter units already know to be on high alert." McCuen paused and looked at both of them. "Of course, if you had turned your radios on—you would've known to enter on this end of the building." Quickly, Adams and Whelan both looked down to their belts to see that their portable radios were turned off.

"Shit!" whispered Whelan in disappointment, saying what Adams was thinking. McCuen walked past them, still looking up into the rafters.

"Don't worry about it now," he continued. "I'll handle the search—you just get to work on processing the scene. With any luck, we can end this tonight."

McCuen was never one to hang on to disappointment, but his expectations were high. It was a quality that made them eager to regain their standing. With uneasy minds they began to examine the burned corpses, periodically looking to see where McCuen was. Each time they found him standing with his back to them, facing into the abyss. Then suddenly, they heard a low, radio transmission. The other patrolman had arrived at the far end of the building. McCuen radioed that he would be approaching from the South. With his gun tucked in close to his chest, and his flashlight in hand, they watched him walk into the darkness, alone.

In his absence, Whelan and Adams photographed the hanging bodies and sifted through the ashes, meticulously cataloging any object that might hold the promise of DNA. They scoured the floor and nearby doorways for latent fingerprints. They swabbed every surface and even pulled fingernail scrapings from the scorched and twisted hands of the victims. It was a grim exercise, but if any of the victims had struggled with the killer, it could produce the evidentiary break they needed. They would leave no rock unturned, and nothing to chance.

Then a nearby door opened. It was Special Agent Gilligan. They were relieved to see he was alone. He greeted them and surveyed the charred bodies. Then he quietly surveyed his surroundings looking for McCuen.

"Where is he?" asked Gilligan. Whelan shook his head and pointed into the darkened end of the warehouse.

"In there?" replied Gilligan in surprise. Whelan just nodded. He was still astonished by what had happened. "Let me know if you hear anything on the radio." Then Gilligan turned back to the hanging bodies. "What did he leave us with?"

"Well, they're less burned than the first three, but just as dead," said Adams.

"From the look of things, the killer was interrupted," said Whelan. "He used an accelerant to expedite the burning." Gilligan began rubbing the back of his neck.

"What is it?" asked Adams.

"The prosecution has a key witness set to testify tomorrow—and now, two more burned bodies turn up." Gilligan exhaled heavily.

"You don't think they're connected, do you?"

"No—but the timing isn't helpful," replied Gilligan.

"Dempsey's going to jump all over this one," said McCuen, stepping back into the light.

They all turned to him as he holstered his gun.

"He was already convinced it was the cartel," answered Gilligan. "Now he's never going to let it go." The brief pause that followed was quickly filled by an eagerness to learn what McCuen had found in the far corners of the warehouse.

"Anything?" asked Adams. McCuen nodded slowly in disappoint-ment.

"He was here—watching us the whole time. There are wet shoe prints all over the building. Eventually, he climbed up into the rafters."

"Great," said Adams.

"It's worse than you think." McCuen reached for his cigarettes. "He wasn't cornered, or even surprised—he chose to stay in the warehouse." His words sent a chill up their spines and a feeling of dread into their chests.

"What makes you say that?" asked Whelan. His heart was racing.

"The fire department entered here—on the Southeast side, closest to the fire," answered McCuen. "The killer would have heard the sirens coming from a mile away. He had plenty of time to accelerate the fire, and to get out, if he wanted to." McCuen pointed to a nearby door and their eyes followed an unobstructed path to the exit, just a twenty feet away. "He stayed in the building—to watch them die."

"And to get a very good look at all of us," added Whelan.

They had all come to know killers, but as a profiler, Adams knew them better than anyone. She had studied them, the worst of the worst. Dahmer, Gasey, and Bundy. They were each diabolical reminders of how far we can fall, but this killer was especially troubling. Serial killers often become emboldened, and some have even taunted the police, but she couldn't recall any that had ever taken such a risk of being caught. She couldn't quite understand it, but one thing was clear. They were dealing with a very depraved and dangerous killer.

"He's seen our faces," said McCuen. "And we have to assume he'll continue to follow us. We leave in pairs, and we stay in pairs," he continued. "If anything feels out of place, call me immediately. Any questions?"

"No, sir," replied Whelan.

"Adams—any objections to pairing up with Whelan for the night?"

"That's fine with me," she replied. "I have a very uncomfortable couch he can sleep on."

"Gillie—can you give us a few minutes?"

"Sure thing, I'll be right outside." Once Gilligan exited the warehouse, McCuen moved in closer to his team.

"I need you both to work on bios for each of the victims. We need to know who they are —and when they went missing. If we can't establish some kind of pattern soon, we don't have a chance at catching this guy."

"Consider it done," replied Whelan, confidently. As McCuen turned to leave, Whelan looked at Adams. He hesitated before continuing. "Do you think we should call him?" McCuen stopped suddenly, knowing that Whelan was asking about Winterbottom.

"No, Tom," he replied. "I'm afraid that's no longer an option."

"I just thought maybe he'd be able to help—"

"I know," replied McCuen. "I'm sorry for not explaining things more clearly, but please know that I have my reasons. Anselm can't be a part of what we do—not anymore. I need you to trust me on this."

"Ok," replied Whelan in agreement. McCuen then turned to leave, but stopped short. "About the radios—," he said. They both cringed in disappointment. "It's over and done, but it's my job to keep you both safe. I don't care what you do in your personal lives, but when you're working—you need to act like you're not sleeping together." They both froze in surprise.

"Captain—"

"I don't need an explanation," said McCuen. "If I thought it was a problem, I wouldn't have paired you up together. However, if I noticed, others in the department might, and it'd be a shame to break up a good team."

"Yes, sir," said Adams, reservedly.

"Let's get a few hours of sleep and meet back here at eight. We can go over the warehouse again in the daylight and see what we can find. I'll have the uniforms lock it down for the night."

Adams and Whelan looked at each other wondering if it had really been that obvious, and between themselves they tried to guess at how long McCuen had known. While they waited for the coroner to arrive, McCuen met with

Gilligan in the parking lot.

"Oh, the benefits of arriving late to the party," said Gilligan, gloating about the fact that he hadn't been seen by the killer.

"It's not the time to celebrate, my friend," replied McCuen.

"And why's that?"

"Because you drew the short straw—you're coming with me to breakfast."

* * *

Once McCuen and Gilligan had settled into a corner booth, the waitress delivered two fresh cups of coffee. The sounds and smells of the diner caused him to reminisce. Lifting his coffee cup from the speckled formica, McCuen was reminded of his conversations with Winterbottom, and the many hours they had spent there.

"How is it that every time we get together, I find myself up to my ears in shit?" smiled McCuen.

"Luck of the Irish, I guess," said Gilligan, laughing. "Besides—you fell into this one all on your own." McCuen's mind quickly shifted to the work at hand.

"What can we do about Dempsey?" he asked.

"He's hellbent on the cartel, and until we find something concrete that shows otherwise, he's not going to budge. Salas and the trial—it's all a case for his promotion, and the only person rooting for that more than him—is me. He needs to go, and if it takes a promotion to do that— I'm all for it."

"What if we force his hand?" said McCuen.

"Sure—but how are we going to do that?"

"We could talk to Salas, directly."

"That's a big ask," said Gilligan, shaking his head. "He's in the middle of a Federal trial, and you want to ask him questions?"

"Not about the things that he's on trial for," McCuen continued. "With his lawyers present, we just talk to him about the burnings. Salas knows that he's going to jail for the rest of his life, burnings, or no burnings—what does he have to lose?"

"Maybe nothing—but what good would it do?" said Gilligan. "Even if Salas was willing to talk, the best we could hope for is a denial which Dempsey won't accept."

"True," said McCuen. "It's likely a dead-end, but it's all we have."

"I'll ask, but he'll want to be there for the interview."

"Let him," replied McCuen. "He can get all puffed up and make a fool of himself—and when the dust settles, we can talk to Salas."

"I'll see what I can do." Then Gilligan took a slow sip from his cup and sat back in his seat. "Do you want to talk about what happened back there, at the warehouse?"

"What do you mean?"

"I mean—you going in alone to look for a serial killer."

"There were four patrolmen on scene—"

"It's not like you," said Gilligan plainly.

"Risks come with the paycheck," replied McCuen.

"Yeah—but you don't have to make it more dangerous than it already is." Gilligan leaned forward again. "There are risks, and there are unnecessary risks—there's a difference." Then he paused to draw another sip from his coffee.

"This isn't Fallujah."

"Maybe it's not that different," said McCuen, looking across the diner.

"Maybe not," said Gilligan calmly. "But you can't keep dodging bullets." McCuen half smiled. "See—now you remember," continued Gilligan. "For a minute I thought you forgot. I was there to see all the stupid shit you did in Kandahar. I've never even heard of someone getting shot at so many times—and you always managed to come out unscathed." Gilligan sat back in his seat again. "Most of our unit thought you could walk on water, but you can't do that shit anymore."

There was no point in denying that things had changed. McCuen wasn't that person anymore. He wasn't even the same person he was six months ago.

"Good talk," replied McCuen, signaling that he was done giving it any more attention. Gilligan could see that he had pushed the issue far enough, so he turned to another matter; one that McCuen would like even less.

"Do you want to talk about that other thing?" McCuen's body became rigid, and he knew exactly what Gilligan was driving at.

"I don't want to talk about it," replied McCuen.

"Ed, I don't know the details—but I know Dempsey's looking at you in connection with the DAS data breach."

"There's nothing to worry about."

"How is that nothing to worry about?"

"Thanks for your concern," said McCuen. "I promise—if it turns into something I'll let you know."

* * *

That evening, which happened to be a Thursday, found me reclined behind the steering wheel of my parked car, awaiting Winterbottom's return. This time I brought binoculars. I don't know why it took me so long, but I was finally ready to shed my skin as an amateur. I was all in. At approximately six o'clock, a taxi pulled up and Winterbottom rushed to the front door carrying a satchel over his shoulder. Within seconds the curtained window filled with light, and I could see the faint apparition of his silhouette walking the floors of his secret room. Then I saw him turn suddenly toward the door. Just outside of my narrowed field of view was Whelan, knocking on the front door. There was no answer, so he waited for a moment before knocking again. I was surprised when Winterbottom opened the door.

"I need to talk to you," said Whelan, looking through the partially open door. It was all he could say, before being ambushed by Winterbottom's appearance. His dark hair was longer, and more disheveled, and the traces of gray in his beard made it seem as though he had aged ten years.

"You shouldn't be here, Tom," barked Winterbottom, turning to close the door. "Anselm, please—we need your help." His words sounded futile given Winterbottom's temperament, but to Whelan's surprise, he left the door open and walked back into the house. Reluctantly, Whelan followed him inside. As he followed Winterbottom into the library, he could see that things had changed. Winterbottom seemed more remote than usual, more mercurial than ever before. Whelan had every reason to be hesitant, given their history.

"I don't like visitors, Tom," snapped Winterbottom. "I can only assume it's an emergency, or else McCuen wouldn't have sent you."

"Actually—he doesn't know I'm here." Winterbottom's interest suddenly turned, and he recognized the opportunity.

"How did you find me?" he asked.

"Our cruisers have GPS locators," replied Whelan. "I pulled the data from McCuen's car —it wasn't that hard. He used to come here almost every night."

"Resourceful," said Winterbottom, smiling. "Then of course you realize—he'll be able to find out that you were here."

"Not exactly," replied Whelan. "Adams dropped me off she's circling the block." He appeared confident enough, but inside Whelan was uncomfortable in his own skin, and Winterbottom knew it. He was uneasy and beginning to regret the decision to come.

"You asked him to call me, didn't you?" said Winterbottom, coyly. "And he refused— that's why you're here."

"Five people have been murdered—"

"I'm not interested, Tom."

"What do mean, you're not interested?"

"Sorry—I meant to say I don't care." He said it so matter-of-factly that Whelan didn't know how to respond. "This may come as a shock to you, Tom,—but I don't care about a lot of things—least of all other people. McCuen was right not to call me."

"So, you won't help us?"

"No, I won't." The spring and hammer had been carefully set, and within a very calculated interval of time, Winterbottom's trap would close. "I have my own problems to worry about." Then Winterbottom turned his attention to some papers that had been spread across the desk, as if they were of extraordinary value to him. The presentation was obvious enough, but Whelan could never have guessed the purpose of such a ruse, or see through the artificial movements that were slowly luring him in like a Clouser minnow.

“You look like shit, by the way,” said Whelan.

“I would’ve tried flattery,” said Winterbottom. “But maybe next time—you know the way out.”

“Anselm, I don’t have time for this,” said Whelan, sharply. “We all kept up appearances for McCuen’s sake, and I don’t know why you were doing it—but you were doing it for a reason. You were getting something out of it.”

Seeing his opportunity, Winterbottom interrupted him.

“I want access to the DMV’s photo database.” The specific nature of his request and the speed at which it was delivered caught Whelan off guard. “You heard me,” he pressed on. “And McCuen can never know about it.” Whelan looked at him silently, as he tried to gauge the reason behind the request. “You’re wasting time, Tom,” continued Winterbottom. “You’re asking yourself why—when you should be asking yourself what you’re willing to do to stop a serial killer.”

The Department of Motor Vehicles database contained millions of records, names, addresses, driver’s license photographs, as well as an equal number of vehicle records. It was a vast collection of personal information, which made Whelan trepidatious.

“What kind of access would you need?” asked Whelan.

“All I need is your login and password. I’d access it from a secure network—completely untraceable, and I’d be in and out in less than fifteen minutes.”

“I would need to know why,” said Whelan, grasping for a finger hold, anything that might offer him the slightest bit of control.

“Well—that depends on what you’re willing to believe,” replied Winterbottom.

“I’m listening.”

"Okay—I'm trying to find my high school ex-girlfriend."

"You've gotta do better than that."

"She stole my Pearl Jam t-shirt?"

"No," said Whelan, tired of the sparring match.

"You're right," sighed Winterbottom. "It was the Electric Light Orchestra—I was trying to put it in a context that you might understand. Anyway—it doesn't really matter. You have something I want, and I have something that you need. It's really that simple."

With Winterbottom, there were no safeguards, no guarantees. Whelan was trying to convince himself of the contrary, but there was no way to circumvent it. There was no easy way to avoid the foreboding feeling that he was trying to smother. He thought about McCuen, and the five burned corpses, of which there would surely be more. The decision, like so many in life, boiled down to a simple question. What harm would it do? It was a means to an end, an anesthetic for the conscience, wrong for the sake of what was right. Winterbottom didn't have to say another word, Whelan had already accepted the offer, like Faust before Mephistopheles. It was predetermined in that way, from the moment he knocked on the door.

"Fine," agreed Whelan. "But I'll need you to come with us tonight."

"You drive a hard bargain," said Winterbottom, smiling. "Let's go."

From the house, they drove to the piano graveyard in the heart of Ditmars Steinway. Whelan and Adams quietly badged their way past the patrolmen, and escorted Winterbottom inside. He wasted no time on the surroundings and proceeded toward the two metal strands hanging from the rafters. It was a morbid effigy to what was once suspended there. The charred cables were dangling right above where the fire had burned hottest. Winterbottom approached and began drawing invisible lines in his mind.

"How tall were they?" he asked. Whelan and Adams looked at one another, surprised by such a peripheral question.

"Between 5'8" and 6 feet tall," replied Whelan. "Why do you ask?"

"He hung them upside down—didn't he?" said Winterbottom. He had captured their attention again.

"How did you know?" asked Adams.

"The length of the wire—it's longer than I expected. If he wanted to hang them by their necks, he would have used a noose, or a shorter wire."

"He could have suspended them from their hands—tied above their heads?" said Whelan, trying to test him.

"If he did, then he's an idiot, and we should just wait until he sets himself on fire." Winterbottom didn't wait for a rebuttal. "If they had been hung by their hands, at that height, their feet would've touched the ground. They'd be able to kick and struggle with the killer. No— he hung them by their feet, leaving their heads just inches off the ground. Am I right?" Whelan nodded in response. Then Winterbottom knelt beside the blackened patches on the concrete floor.

"Honestly, as much as I like these puzzles we should probably get on with it. What exactly did you need me for?"

"We need you to find something—anything," said Whelan. "Between the fire and the water used to put it out, we haven't found anything of evidentiary value. No fingerprints—no DNA."

"All we have are a few wet shoe prints, and five burned bodies," said Adams.

"—And a killer who enjoys watching people burn," added Winterbottom.

"Yes—we're dealing with a very deranged person,"

"Most arsonists are opportunistic," continued Winterbottom. "They're motivated by the promise of an insurance payout. Others do it to be destructive, and even then, they typically don't want to hurt anybody. You could even argue that arson, as a means of murder, demonstrates a lack of commitment altogether. It's an incredibly flawed way to kill somebody. The only advantage it offers is the destruction of evidence, or to give the killer time to get away."

"He wasn't interested in getting away," said Whelan. Winterbottom shot him a look of surprise as soon as he had spoken the words. Then he quickly turned to Adams, as if what Whelan said couldn't be trusted.

"He stayed in the warehouse," she said in confirmation. "Even after we arrived." A look of concern washed over Winterbottom's face and his eyes seemed to sharpen their focus. In quiet contemplation, he looked down at the concrete floor as his thoughts drew furrowed lines across his forehead.

"You're absolutely sure?"

"Yes," said Adams. "He was watching us."

"I hope you can appreciate what that means." Winterbottom looked at Adams intently. She didn't reply, and her silence made Whelan that much more impatient to know what Winterbottom was driving at.

"Help me out here, Adams," said Whelan. Winterbottom could sense her hesitation, so he answered for her.

"Every serial killer engages in unusually risky behavior," he replied. "That's not a real shocking statement, I know—but they're all afraid of being caught. All except for one particular type—."

"Pathologically, there are four classifications of serial killers," explained Adams, cutting off Winterbottom. "Thrill-seekers, *Mission-Oriented killers,*

Power-Control seekers, and *Visionary Killers.* Anselm's referring to the latter—*Visionary Killers.* They believe that a god, or some other deity, is commanding them to commit murder. They're typically delusional, and the most mentally unstable of all the killer types—which usually makes them easier to catch." Then she paused. "But—of all the psychological profiles I've studied, there's never been a serial killer so bold, or so careless to stay at the crime scene, not even *Visionary Killers.*"

"There is another type," said Winterbottom. His tone was disconcerting, and Adams stiffened at the suggestion. She reluctantly continued.

"Some profilers have theorized about a fifth type of serial killer. It's referred to as *Divine Command Theory.*" Winterbottom nodded in approval. "But, it's just that—a theory. There's never been a documented case." She could see that Winterbottom wasn't convinced. "Theoretically, just like *Visionary Killers—Divine Command killers* are murderers who believe that a god, or other deity is commanding them to commit murder."

"—or to fulfill a divine rite," added Winterbottom.

"Okay," said Whelan, still confused. "So how are they different from *Visionary Killers?*"

"They're not," replied Adams, in obvious disagreement with the idea. "But the theory infers that these killers are not delusional, or psychotic like *Visionary Killers,* but that they are motivated by a very real belief, or religious zeal." Unsatisfied by her presentation, Winterbottom interjected.

"*Divine Command killers* are reasoned to be the least concerned with getting away with their crimes," explained Winterbottom. "They feel justified in their actions because they've been granted divine permission, and as a result they feel as though they have divine protection. The theory suggests they wouldn't be concerned with evidence, or masking their identity, or even arrest.

For that reason, they'd be far more dangerous than the other killer types." Then Winterbottom shifted his stance. "And it would explain why your killer would stay at the crime scene to watch."

"Hold on a minute," Whelan replied. "I'm not a profiler—but that's not new. Killers have always claimed that God, or the Devil had instructed them to kill their victims. The *Night Stalker* worshipped Satan, and *The Son of Sam* said his neighbor's dog was possessed by a demon and was instructing him to kill his victims. There are dozens of other examples—"

"Many *Visionary serial killers* have claimed *Divine Command*," answered Winterbottom. "But their behavior contradicts their claims. They're just bat-shit crazy. Most say it to shift the blame for their actions away from themselves. The only evidence that the *Night Stalker* was worshipping Satan was a handful of statements that he made to his victims—and there was no physical evidence to corroborate his claims. He used the idea to terrify and intimidate. He was a depraved psychopath, and a colossal asshole. Even the Son of Sam later admitted that he had lied about his neighbor's dog. They say it to justify their actions—it's an excuse, nothing more." Then he looked at Adams before continuing. "If they were truly *Divine Command Killers*, doing sacred work, they wouldn't feel compelled to hide it. There have been a lot of pretenders, but so far—there's never been a true *Divine Command killer*."

"What about suicide bombers?" asked Whelan. "Wouldn't they be considered *Divine Command killers*?

"They would be," said Winterbottom. "But to be a serial killer an individual has to have an established pattern of killing." Winterbottom smiled. "In other words, it's hard to be a suicide-bomber, twice."

"So, our guy's a *Divine Command killer* and doesn't care about getting caught—"

"No," said Adams, sharply. "They don't exist. They're the serial killer equivalent of a unicorn—it's a myth." She continued in a more defiant tone. "There are only four types of serial killers—"

"And the world is flat," snapped Winterbottom.

"Anselm, there's no empirical evidence that—"

"The reason it's so controversial is because it allows for the possibility that it could be true. It requires Science, and more importantly scientists, to acknowledge the possibility that a divine power might actually exist."

"And you do?" she said, in a cutting tone.

"The only thing I can say with certainty is that I don't know," replied Winterbottom.

Adams refused to accept it.

"If God exists, then *Divine Command* is possible. If he doesn't, then the killers are delusional, and just plain-old, *Visionary Killers.* All you have to do now—is prove the existence of God."

Her rejection of the idea was clear and could easily be upheld on scientific grounds, but there was more behind her position than science and pathology. Winterbottom could hear it in her voice. It was fear, not of a new kind of killer, but of greater personal implications. In that moment, Winterbottom imagined her as a young woman, desperately pushing against her parents and their faith. She wouldn't bend or accept any premise that entertained the existence of God. It was all too unsettling for her. She was so adept at keeping those less-tangible things at bay.

Winterbottom saw it for what it was. It was familiar to him, but he was no atheist, not anymore. He had spent too much time in the company of numbers. He had contemplated the infinite; he knew better. He was hardly religious, but to not acknowledge the great magnitude of the unknown was a far greater insult to science than religion ever could be. He could see the divine mystery, or at least its shadow. He saw its role in all things. He wasn't dismissive of it; he despised it. He was angry at it, for all that had been done, for all that had been taken away from him. And maybe somewhere along the line, something had been taken from her as well.

"Okay, so *Divine Command killers* exist—or they don't exist—" said Whelan. "Why does it matter?"

"It matters because if that's what you're up against, you'll be feeling around in the dark. There's no data to draw from." Winterbottom paused momentarily. "There are no predictive indicators to follow. There's no telling what he'll do, or when he'll do it. Not to mention the fact that he was watching you—which puts you all in very real danger."

"And you're confident that our killer is a *Divine Command killer*?"

"There's no way to know," said Winterbottom. "But if he stayed at the crime scene, it's a possibility that shouldn't be ignored."

"Well, if he's got divine protection—then why did he hide from us?" asked Whelan.

"Because his work isn't finished." Winterbottom began scanning his surroundings again, looking up into the rafters, before returning to look at the floor at his feet. "These burnings aren't as simple as they appear to be." He stepped back and thought quietly to himself for a moment. "What if they were sacrificial?" He began walking in a circle around where the bodies were burned. Then he turned to Adams, "Were the victims stabbed?"

"No," replied Adams.

"No cuts. No blood. No ritual," said Winterbottom.

"Ritual?" said Whelan. "He burned them alive—what more do you need? I wouldn't expect him to light candles and draw a bath." Winterbottom curiously surveyed the traces of black ash on the concrete.

"Most likely not," replied Winterbottom. "But if he did—I wonder what might have been thrown out with the bath water." They watched as Winterbottom moved closer and stood at the center of where the fires had burned. Without warning, he began walking to the opposing wall. He followed the trail of ash that had been pushed aside by the artificial current of the fire hoses. Even after it vanished, Winterbottom continued along its invisible path to the far wall of the warehouse, far beyond where the bodies had been hung. At the base of the wall was a thick pile of ash, smoothed over like a dune. He slowly kicked through the ashes, making his way down the length of the wall. Then suddenly he stopped and knelt down. Whelan and Adams rushed to where he was and illuminated their flashlights. In the bright light, they could see that he was holding an archaic carving, a wooden figure. Even at a distance they could make out its distinct tribal appearance, similar in style to the carvings found at Machu Picchu.

"Have you ever known a *Visionary Killer* to carve one of these?" said Winterbottom, handing over the wooden statue to Adams. He didn't wait for a response. "If it survived the fire there's probably another—one for each victim."

"*Divine Command*, or not—this should be enough to show that it's not the cartel," said Whelan.

"I would hope so," said Adams, masking the relief she felt that it wasn't a crucifix, as if the existence of a South American tribal god would somehow be less foreboding.

Walking back to the cruiser, Winterbottom discreetly pulled Whelan aside.

"I'll need that information we spoke of before we go," said Winterbottom.

Whelan was careful to make sure that Adams couldn't hear the details of their arrangement before responding.

"You're that sure I'm going to give it to you?" replied Whelan, smiling.

"We both know you will—and we both know why," said Winterbottom confidently. "It'd be a shame for McCuen to find out about this."

"Yeah, you're right—it would," he replied, handing Winterbottom a piece of paper scribbled with his login information and password. "I don't like going behind his back."

"I know," said Winterbottom with genuine empathy. It reminded him of his own betrayal. "It's always worse when you lie to an honest person." Whelan looked down at the ground and didn't say a word. "He's also a very smart man," continued Winterbottom. "There's a real chance that he knew you'd come to find me. I hope you've considered that." The silence that accompanied them back to the house on Lexington Avenue was a clear indication that he hadn't.

* * *

By morning, the plan had changed. Against expectations, and the advice of counsel, Salas agreed to meet with the FBI. The likelihood that he would say anything was slim to no-fucking-way, but the idea appealed to Dempsey's ego. He leapt at the chance to unload on Salas in person. Over the phone, Whelan told McCuen about the wooden carving, and agreed to bring it to the meeting with Salas.

When McCuen arrived for the meeting, he was escorted to a spacious conference room in the upper levels of the courthouse. He found Salas and his three attorneys seated in front of a gourmet breakfast which had been negotiated as a part of the agreement. Gilligan and Dempsey had arrived early, on account of Dempsey's eagerness, and things were already going in a bad direction.

"I think you know exactly why we're here," said Dempsey, sternly. "And it's my hope that we can put a stop to these killings." Salas was unfazed and continued to eat his breakfast.

"Agent Dempsey," replied one of Salas' attorneys. "My client has agreed to hear what you have to say, and it's his continued position that he has no further comment. You can continue to be vague and cryptic if that serves you—but I must say, as his counsel, I don't even know what you're referring to."

"He knows," said Dempsey, looking sharply at Salas, who calmly turned his attention to a nearby dish of crepes. Out of frustration, Dempsey divulged more details. "The burned bodies that are turning up all over Queens!" Salas raised an eyebrow, but refused to speak. "You may not care now, but you will when we connect them to you and your cartel. It'll be a factor when it comes time for sentencing." In response, Salas leaned over and whispered something to his attorney. After a brief exchange, the attorney nodded his permission for Salas to speak, and Dempsey nearly leapt forward at the hope of progress.

"Agent Dempsey," said Salas. "I'd like to thank you and the FBI for this delicious meal —and I still have no fucking idea what you're talking about." Dempsey turned to Gilligan and McCuen, his face was fuming.

"We're done here!" barked Dempsey, before storming out of the conference room. Salas laughed to himself through a mouthful of crepes.

"Will that be all, gentlemen?" asked Salas' attorney, looking at Gilligan.

"I'd like some coffee—if that's okay," asked Gilligan, hoping to take the charge out of the air. Salas immediately replied.

"Please, senór," he said, pointing to the coffee press on the table. "It's very good—I should know, I'm in the coffee business." He continued to laugh quietly to himself. Gilligan smiled and poured himself and McCuen each a cup. Outwardly, Salas was jovial, but all the while he was assessing them. He was gauging what kind of men they were, and why they were still there. "Your boss is not very polite," continued Salas. "He has a bit of a temper."

"Yes, he does," replied Gilligan, sipping his coffee. "In his defense—you have killed a lot of people." Salas wiped the corner of his mouth with a napkin and placed his silverware back at the sides of his empty plate. He looked at Gilligan and then at McCuen before responding.

"You say I've killed many people," replied Salas, calmly, "—but so have you, and your friend." He was looking at McCuen.

"What makes you say that?" asked Gilligan. Salas' attorney tried to interrupt, but Salas unleashed a tirade in Spanish, putting an end to the disruption. Then he calmly continued.

"I've spent my life surrounded by killers," he said. "I know what they look like. That hilo de puta—your boss, he's no killer. He pushes a desk. He's never had to get his hands dirty, but you two—you're different."

"We were soldiers," said McCuen, entering the conversation. Salas looked at him again.

"And you think I'm not?" Again, his attorney tried to interrupt, but Salas simply motioned his hand to silence him. "I've been at war my whole life, and everything I have—I've had to fight for."

"By butchering innocent people," said McCuen. Salas shrugged his shoulders and raised his eyebrows in frustration.

"Sometimes in war there is—collateral damage."

"Is that what this is?" said McCuen, as he slid photographs of the burned bodies across the table. Surrounded by white porcelain breakfast platters, and an assortment of danishes and croissants, Salas slowly shuffled through the full-color photographs. At one point he turned a few of them upside down, and then right side up again. Then he handed them back to McCuen and sank deeper into his seat. He inhaled through his nose, as if trying to force his words back down into his belly. Then he began shaking his head repeatedly, in silent protest. Clearly, the photographs had stirred up something inside him. Just then Whelan and Adams entered the room and handed McCuen the wooden carving, sealed in a clear plastic evidence bag. McCuen placed it on the table. Salas picked it up, and ran his fingers over it, feeling its contours through the thick plastic. His eyes seemed to darken and the humor he had shown minutes before evaporated completely. He placed the carving on the table, and walked to the large windows that overlooked the city. They could all see that the wooden carving had made him very uncomfortable. After a moment, he turned back to them and spoke.

"This was not my doing!" he said sharply, leaning hard against the tabletop. "If I help you —I want a reduced sentence!"

"That's not going to happen," said Gilligan.

"Then I have nothing to say!" barked Salas.

"Ok—so don't say anything," replied Gilligan. "And my boss will link these burnings to you, anyway. Shit, he's already made up his mind. It might even be enough to stick a needle in your arm."

"*Soldados de misericordia*," replied Salas, angrily.

"Your time has passed," said McCuen. "We all have to face it, eventually. Whether you get the death penalty or not, they're going to put you in general population. You know what that means."

"*Si*—I know what that means, Captain," snapped Salas, defiantly.

"If you're a soldier, like you say you are, why not die like one—with some dignity. I can see that you didn't do this, but by the way you looked at those photographs and that wooden carving—I think you know who did." Salas paused in contemplation and consulted with his attorney in a low and unintelligible voice. After several minutes, he turned back to McCuen.

"Do you believe in ghosts, Captain?" he said, smiling again. "What about the Boogeyman?" McCuen shook his head in frustration. He began to turn away, sensing that Salas was toying with them. "He's the one you're looking for—not me." McCuen and Gilligan were halfway to the door when Salas continued in a more serious tone. "I saw him once in Columbia, at La Cumbre—when the people started disappearing." He had gotten their attention. "He burned them upside down—just like in those pictures." Salas drew a slow sip from a freshly-poured cup of coffee. "It was in the early nineties, when I was young—and much stronger than I am now. The people in the villages knew to stay away from our fields, and even those living in the deep forests knew to mind their own business. Then, one day—the elders from one of the forest tribes came to me asking for help. They said that women and children had been disappearing in the night—sometimes even men were taken. They would find their bodies, hanging from the trees— badly burned. They called him Pishtaco, an old legend of the forest. They thought he was some kind of demon feeding off the fat of his victims—like some vampire in the rainforest. He would carve wooden statues for each of his victims—like that one." Salas then turned again to his breakfast and resumed eating. "I went with my men into the jungle and after tracking him for a week, we found his camp, but he escaped. I saw him as he ran through the trees that night."

“That’s a nice bedtime story,” said McCuen. “But I don’t believe in monsters.”

“Men are monsters, Captain,” replied Salas. “Some of us—more so than others.”

“I appreciate you telling us,” said Gilligan. “But it doesn’t exactly help us—”

“His name is Carlos Javier Lopez,” said Salas. “A few weeks after we chased him from La Cumbre, the authorities arrested him. He confessed to the murders of nearly 200 people. They sent him to prison, but he escaped. In the years that followed, there were similar killings throughout Columbia, but he was never seen, or heard from again.”

“And you think this Lopez is here in New York City—after all these years.”

“I admit it seems strange—but it has to be him,” replied Salas. “The bodies, and the carvings are the same.”

“I find it hard to believe that a serial killer from the Andes would make his way to New York City,” said McCuen.

“That’s not for me to say—but why not?” replied Salas. “It’s not like it’s difficult to cross your border.” Salas couldn’t help but smile. “You don’t have to believe me, look him up in your system—you’ll see.”

“If this is Lopez—why would he all of a sudden start killing again?” asked Whelan. Salas looked at him, unsure of Whelan’s role, but he continued all the same.

“You’ll have to ask him,” said Salas. “But if I were you—I wouldn’t assume that he ever stopped. Monsters can’t change their nature.” Salas then returned to his breakfast, motioning that he was tired, and that the interview was over.

They thanked him for his cooperation and turned to leave. From the doorway, McCuen asked him one last question.

"Why are you telling us this?" Salas stopped eating and wiped the corners of his mouth again.

"One of the young girls that Lopez murdered was the daughter of a childhood friend— she was like family to me. I'm telling you this because now you're my soldiers and I know that in the end—you'll kill him like I promised to do all those years ago."

* * *

That night, Winterbottom was working diligently, attempting to conquer the impossible. His program, which he aptly named *"Winterbottom's Gambit,"* was steadily sorting through six months of video surveillance and the endless number of cars that had passed through the Upper East Side in that time. Thanks to his recent arrangement with Whelan, he was able to expedite his search. With access to the Department of Motor Vehicles database he could now analyze and compare his findings with millions of driver's license photographs.

It was through this process that he hoped to identify the man who destroyed his family, but it wasn't as simple as matching a face to a name. *Winterbottom's Gambit* was just that, a gambit; an action with a risk. It would only work if a series of probabilities and his theoretical assessment of human behavior proved to be accurate. It all hinged on a vast calculation, and the soundness of his mind. Despite the odds, he was uncovering the answers he sought, narrowing in on the man he hoped to kill. He was inching back to that day, and that place, where all things slipped beyond his reach. In a way, he was undoing time itself, and soon the man that eluded him would be found. Then it would only be a matter of natural human volition and a single choice; the seemingly rudimentary act of killing.

XV

CARLOS JAVIER LOPEZ

Carlos Javier Lopez turned out to be everything that Salas said he was, a man and a monster. It took Whelan and Adams twelve hours to compile three dossiers worth of information on the world's most elusive serial killer. After briefing McCuen about what they had learned, they proceeded to Lexington Avenue to meet with Winterbottom, in secret.

"I didn't realize this was going to be a regular thing," said Winterbottom, through the opening in the front door.

"There's been a development," said Whelan.

"I'm very busy, Tom," said Winterbottom coldly.

"Anselm, please," said Adams. "It'll just take a minute." Her voice sounded crisp and her tone was earnest. It reminded him of someone, and he couldn't bring himself to turn her away.

"You'll have to make it quick."

He was careful to close the door to his private room and invited them to sit in the library. He sat at the desk while they took their pick of two distinctly different chairs; an antique wooden armchair with a curved back, and a modern padded seat. As a pair, the chairs seemed horribly out of place. Adams opted for comfort and left Whelan with the rigid wooden chair.

"Salas was right about his name," began Adams. "We confirmed with South American authorities that Carlos Javier Lopez is indeed a real person, and one of the most notorious serial killers in history. Early reports indicate that his mother lived in the villages outside Trujillo but later moved to Columbia to work as a prostitute. Lopez was orphaned at the age of nine, when his mother was murdered by one of her clients."

"The man who killed his mother held him captive for over a year in Bogota," added Whelan.

"Evil begets evil," said Winterbottom, without looking up from the dossier they had given him. As he read quietly, Whelan shifted in his seat, causing the old chair to creak. As he tried to get more comfortable, he began running his fingers over the obvious scratches on the left arm of the chair. More confounding than its condition was why a billionaire would have such a chair to begin with, and not even in a matching set.

"Is there something wrong?" asked Winterbottom.

"No—I'm fine," said Whelan.

"Would you like a different chair, Tom?" he asked.

"No—this one's fine," said Whelan, wanting to avoid any further distraction.

"It should be," said Winterbottom. "It was good enough for Churchill." The realization made Whelan pause, and he leaned less heavily on the priceless antique, as Adams continued.

"After killing his captor, Lopez survived on the streets of Cartegna, stealing cars and selling them to local chop shops. In his twenties, he was arrested for breaking into houses and was sent to Bosque de Barranquilla, one of the most notorious prisons in Columbia. When he was released five years later, he disappeared deep into the Amazonian rainforests. According to reports, he was last seen in the area of Tarapoto. It was around that time that young women in the neighboring villages began disappearing. Within a matter of months, no one was safe. After a massive manhunt, Lopez was finally captured deep in the forests. The authorities found him shirtless, having painted his face and upper body with the blood of his victims." Adams handed Winterbottom a picture of Lopez before continuing. "He confessed to over 200 murders and led authorities to nearly 53 sites, containing the remains of his victims. He was sentenced to life in prison, but escaped two years later."

"You have to admire third-world countries," interrupted Winterbottom. "People are dying in the streets, but as a matter of principle they won't execute a man who has killed over 200 people." He shook his head in disgust. "And the only prisoners who don't escape—are the political ones." Unmoved by Winterbottom's commentary, Whelan continued with a more pressing thought.

"It makes you wonder what happened to him in the forest." He shifted in his chair again. "What makes a man go from stealing cars to setting people on fire?"

"After his escape from prison, he disappeared into the Amazon, again," said Adams. He hasn't been seen since."

"But his trail didn't end there," said Whelan. "Three years after his final disappearance, burned bodies began turning up in the forests in Darien National Park and La Armistad International Park in Costa Rica. Around that time, Interpol investigated a number of burnings throughout South America and Mexico—those photographs are from the Yucatan peninsula." Whelan pointed to one of the dossiers in front of Winterbottom. The photographs depicted dozens of burned bodies, all bound and hanging from their feet. Their charred casings appeared sleek, like graphite, and they reminded Winterbottom of the Tollund Man of Denmark. In each photo there was a wooden totem; a hand-carved figure, set carefully beneath each hanging victim. "If you follow the burnings—it's clear that the killer is moving north through Mexico."

"It's compelling evidence," said Winterbottom. "But you can't ignore the improbability of a South American serial killer leaving the forests of the Amazon for New York City."

"I know it seems unlikely," said Adams.

"No, it seems extraordinarily unlikely," replied Winterbottom, sharply. "The only thing going for you is that it's not physically impossible." Then Whelan handed him a photograph of another burned corpse.

"This was taken three months ago, in Tijuana, just fifteen miles from US border. The body was found in a small patch of trees just outside a migrant camp. According to ICE, the victim's mother crossed the border just a few days before. She came over with a group of migrants who were detained by Border Patrol. When interviewed, she said that several members of the caravan went missing along the journey."

"He was targeting the migrant caravan," said Adams.

"And if the migrants crossed the border—he could've too." Then Whelan paused. His demeanor had changed. It was a discomfort that had nothing to do with his chair. Winterbottom could see that he was holding something back.

"What is it, Tom?" asked Winterbottom.

"It's about the wooden carving from the warehouse," replied Whelan, looking at Adams for reassurance. She picked up where he left off.

"The carving resembles known artifacts from the Chimu civilization dating back to 900 A.D." Winterbottom sat back in his chair, and listened intently as she continued. "The Chimu was an agriculture-based civilization living in the coastal forests of Peru. However, by 500 A.D. that region was devastated by geo-climatic shifts that altered the environment. They endured extreme droughts, and catastrophic flash floods, and were forced to abandon farming. They became increasingly warlike. The land that once provided for them, was turning against them, or so they believed. Archeologists estimate that around that time, like their rivals, the Inca—the Chimu turned to ritual sacrifice."

"Two years ago," said Whelan, "—archeologists discovered mass graves that have been attributed to the Chimu. They contained thousands of skeletal remains. Most were children. The bodies had all been burned alive—a presumed offering to the gods." Adams handed Winterbottom photographs of the excavation. Each corpse had been burned and buried, holding a carved wooden figure.

"The carvings are the same as those linked to Lopez," said Whelan. "And they're identical to the one we found in the warehouse." Winterbottom remained apathetic.

"That archeological site was found deep in the Amazon rain forests," continued Adams, "—in the area where Lopez disappeared. The indigenous people in that region are the descendants of the Chimu, and it's rumored that they practice the rituals of their ancestors— though no outsiders have ever witnessed these rites."

Winterbottom could feel the poignancy of such a revelation. He envisioned a man, lost to the world, retreating into the Amazon. He could see the man digging beneath the forest canopy, sifting through undergrowth and the ochre soil, handling the ancient bones. He thought of all the dark things that were buried there, and imagined what words those spirits might have whispered. He looked up at Whelan and Adams. He could see the concern on their faces, and there was no need to speak of *Divine Command* Theory. Instead, his mind traveled to the place that seemingly held the answers to their questions.

There was nowhere on the Earth more inhospitable to human life than the Amazonian rainforests. Two million square miles of dense forest and treacherous rivers serve as ramparts and parapets against the ambitions of the modern world. It holds the world's highest biodiversity of plant species and is home to many rare creatures, including jaguars, anacondas, and vampire bats. Most deadly of all are the hordes of lethal insects that fill the forest. The rivers are murky, filled with piranhas, eels, and the dreaded Candiru. Most abundant are the parasites which have placed the region under the constant strain of Malaria and Dengue fever. In the Amazon, what doesn't kill you—eventually will. It was long believed that the deadly forests were incapable of sustaining human life, and it wasn't until the mid-twentieth century that scientists and archeologists discovered the remnants of vast ancient civilizations deep in the forests. Such ancient kingdoms had lured the first Europeans into the region in 1542, under the command of Francisco de Orellana. They were seeking El Dorado, and the fabled Fountain of Youth, only to be met by cannibalistic tribes, disease, starvation and death. Even today, few have pierced the deep forests. These were the known characteristics of the land and its people, and the harsh conditions that shaped their way of life. It is an environment where life is closely connected with death. In that moment, Winterbottom had visions of spirits, and flashes of tribalistic dances which passed through his mind. He could see their painted bodies and pierced skin, bathed in darkness and fire. It was easy for such things to infiltrate the mind, to delaminate one's self from reason and understanding. Fear was a skillful manipulator of men, and Winterbottom was quick to return to what was right in front of him.

"Ancient civilizations and cultural ghost stories might shade the killer's complexion, but they won't stop him from killing again—only his victims can do that. They're the only ones who can stop him. What do you know about them?" Adams handed him another dossier.

"Two of the victims were New Yorkers, and the other was from Chicago—here on business. The Medical Examiner's still trying to identify the other two bodies."

"The original three victims weren't reported missing, until after the burnings," said Whelan.

"So, we know the killer works quickly," said Winterbottom. "What about their cell phones?"

"The GPS data is all over the map," said Adams.

Winterbottom began scanning the pages of coded coordinates for each of the known victims. He followed them through the last moments of their lives, along a digital trail, from their houses and apartments, to coffee shops and business meetings. From the numerical data alone, one couldn't know them in any meaningful way. He would never know their thoughts or secrets, but he could see their invisible footprints. He could follow their paths. Suddenly, he pulled a notepad from the desk drawer, and began scribbling, wildly. Whelan and Adams watched as he slowly flipped through the pages, one by one, following in his mind the movements of each person. After nearly fifteen minutes of complete silence, he spoke.

"It's just a sketch—but it's a start."

"Anything will help," said Adams.

Winterbottom pointed to the data which Adams had plotted over a map of Manhattan and began to explain his findings.

"You were smart to pull locations for the entire week leading up to the burnings," he said. "It clearly shows that the two New Yorkers both live in Manhattan—one in Murray Hill, and the other in East Harlem. They don't ever cross paths, or overlap in any meaningful way, but if you look closely, there's a discernible break from their daily patterns." Winterbottom pointed to the map again. "Here's where they were abducted," he said. "And just before their phones were turned off, each victim crossed the Triborough Bridge." Winterbottom stopped to make sure they were following him, then continued. "But the man from Chicago—he's different," said Winterbottom. "He landed at LaGuardia in the early morning hours and turned on his cell phone. The GPS data shows that he traveled west on Grand Central Parkway before eventually heading to Midtown."

"How does that help us," asked Adams, impatiently.

"It doesn't," replied Winterbottom. "Unless you look more closely. On his way to Midtown, his phone turns off. That's when our killer abducted him."

"But you said he eventually traveled to Midtown?"

"According to the GPS data—he did," replied Winterbottom. "Or more accurately—his cell phone did. It was inactivated for twenty minutes in the Ditmars Steinway area, then suddenly his phone turns on and it crosses the Triborough Bridge." Winterbottom paused and set down the dossier. "The killer is covering his tracks." Sitting back in his chair, he continued. "I can't be certain, but based on what I'm seeing—I'm quite confident that your killer is driving a taxicab."

"Shit," replied Whelan, well aware of the fact that there were over 13,000 taxis in New York City.

"You said earlier that Lopez used to steal cars?"

"Yes," replied Adams.

"So that shoe fits." Winterbottom quickly sketched out a very simple map of Manhattan with landmarks representing the Triborough Bridge, the Ditmars

Steinway area, and LaGuardia airport. "He's selecting his victims at random—but he's efficient about it. He's using Manhattan and LaGuardia as his hunting grounds, and the warehouses in Ditmars Steinway as a killing field. But—for all his efforts to cover his tracks, he's still human—he hates driving in New York City. He doesn't want to drive anymore, or for any longer than he absolutely has to. He's getting the most out of his trips." Winterbottom then held up the sketch so they could see it. "Look—he abducted Victim #1 from East Harlem and brought her to the warehouse in Ditmars Steinway. What's next to Ditmars Steinway?"

"LaGuardia," replied Adams.

"Exactly," said Winterbottom. "At Laguardia he abducted Victim #2, our friend from Chicago, and brought him to the warehouse before heading back to Manhattan for Victim #3. The timeline matches up perfectly." Winterbottom smiled. "It shouldn't be too hard. All you have to do is find a single taxicab in New York City."

Returning to headquarters, Whelan and Adams pulled video surveillance from LaGuardia and confirmed that the out-of-towner, the man from Chicago, took a registered taxicab from the airport terminal. That cab had been reported stolen two weeks before. Reviewing video from the intersections that were highlighted on Winterbottom's map, they observed the other two victims getting into the same stolen taxicab. Whelan and Adams briefed McCuen, ever careful not to disclose the source of their information. With the discovery, McCuen applied the full weight of the NYPD to focus on locating the killer's taxicab. Patrols in the Ditmars Steinway area were tripled, and a team of thirty crime analysts and technicians poured through weeks' worth of surveillance from the DAS. They were attempting to follow a broken trail through three hundred hours of backlogged video. After two days, it became glaringly apparent that the scope of their search was insurmountable. They were at least four days behind the killer, and the active license plate readers had failed to produce any sign of the killer's taxicab. He had disappeared into the jungle again—a jungle of streets, poured concrete, and towering buildings.

XVI

THE JUMPING JACK PUMP HOUSE

Due to the killer's connection to the Triborough Bridge, McCuen moved their base of operation to the 25th Precinct and waited for something to happen. They hadn't slept in days, and by 9 PM, McCuen was ready to call it a night. He had been awake for twenty-four of the last thirty-two hours and had nothing to show for it. It was the kind of sleep deprivation that made you feel sluggish—as if your skin was worn thin, like rice paper. Whelan and Adams were only slightly more rested, but just as frustrated with their lack of progress. As they began to surrender to the idea of sleep, Adams' cell phone let out an audible ringtone notification. From beyond the threshold of the door, McCuen stopped and waited for what it could be. Adams rushed to her laptop, searching for an explanation.

"It's his cell phone," said Adams in surprise.

"Whose?"

"Our guy from Chicago," she replied. "It's been powered off for days. Someone just turned it back on."

"Where is it?" asked McCuen.

"It's locating to an abandoned industrial building in Brooklyn, near the waterfront."

"Dead men don't make phone calls," said Whelan. "Some transient probably fished it out of a dumpster."

"It could be our killer," said Adams.

"He knew enough to power off the phone when he abducted his victim," replied Whelan. "He'd know better than to turn it back on now."

"Maybe he wants us to find him?" said Adams.

"Or—it's a potential witness who can tell us something," said McCuen. "Either way, the phone's evidence in a homicide case. Call for three uniforms to meet us there. Let's go see who it is."

McCuen slept in the backseat as they made their way south along the shoreline. His eyes instinctively opened as they emerged from the tunnel, arriving in Brooklyn. They were met at the scene by two patrol officers and a sergeant who had been assigned to help them recover the phone.

"Thanks for coming out fellas," said McCuen, as he pulled on his kevlar vest.

"Happy to help, Captain," said the sergeant. "Which of these lovely deathtraps are we going into?"

"1st and 41st Street," said Adams. "It's the building just east of the pier." The sergeant shook his head. He was familiar with it.

"That's the Jumping Jack Pump House," he replied. "The only people that ever go in there are homeless, or trust-fund kids looking to party. Quite frankly, even the homeless know better than to go in there anymore. It's slowly sinking into the river."

"Well, someone's in there," said Adams. "And we need their cell phone."

"You've all been briefed on who we might be dealing with—so be careful," said McCuen. "Whether he's in there or not—we need to be ready for anything.

"Will do, Captain."

The Jumping Jack Pump House was an abandoned industrial building located on the waterfront, just south of Red Hook. Of the many abandoned places in the city, it was one of the most obscure. And for that reason, it became a destination for adventurous tourists and fanatics of the city's underground places. The building was given its name because it was supported by a configuration of iron beams and thick metal rods that looked like a human figure doing a jumping jack. Some might attempt a reference to Vitruvius, but in doing so you'd have to ignore that the building was a dilapidated shell, held up by a rusted frame. It was riddled with graffiti, adorned with decades of trash, and most of the lower level of the building had been flooded by the East River. It was largely forgotten and industrial, like some post-apocalyptic shrine.

Immediately upon entering the building, they all sensed the difficulty that it presented. The ground level was covered in rubble which had fallen from the upper levels. That, combined with its rusted interior, gave one the idea that the floor might give out at any moment. It was secreting iron oxide, which covered the walls in a coarse orange crust, interrupted only by the balloon-like forms of spray-painted letters. Pressing on, the group of six spread out in pairs, their flashlights cutting into the darkness in discordant cones of light. Whelan and Adams searched the lower level, and its labyrinth of collapsing chambers, while the two patrolmen proceeded up the staircase leading to the upper levels. The sergeant and McCuen remained in the open core of the building, watching and listening for any unexpected signs of life. The initial silence eventually gave way to a heightened acuity for sound. They could hear droplets of water, and the hollow tapping of footsteps on the metal staircases above. It was followed by the thrashing sound of pigeons' wings, and the moaning of steel. Beneath those spikes of sound was a fearful apprehension, as if the darkness was humming against the metal walls of the building, like bees in a hive.

Whelan and Adams moved through the corridor on the ground level and carefully searched each of the adjoining mechanical rooms. The dampness in the air was thick, and the paint on the walls was peeling away from the brick and mortar. Moving into the next room, Adams drew her flashlight across each of its four corners, the most dangerous parts of any room. Suddenly, Whelan grabbed her by the shoulder, forcefully pulling her backward. Before she could turn around, she saw something moving at her feet. Its subtle movements quickly drew the attention of Whelan's flashlight. Adams was standing on the edge of a large opening. Nearly indiscernible from the iron floor was the dark and gentle current of the East River. She nodded her appreciation and stepped around the deep well before walking further into the belly of the beast.

Soon they came to the last room, at the far end of the corridor. The large metal door was partially ajar. Whelan pushed it open, unleashing high-pitched screams from its rusted metal hinges. Entering the room, they saw a narrow passage running through its center. A once elevated walkway now served as a bridge over the waters that had swallowed up the lower half of the room. In the darkness ahead of them, at the end of the bridge, was a pile of crushed metal and bricks. On top of the heap, they could see the eerie glow of a cell phone display. The phone was ringing. With guns drawn, Whelan began scanning the room, while Adams cautiously walked toward it. She moved forward, keeping her flashlight and firearm fixed on the cell phone. They could both sense that something was wrong, and still they moved toward it. What choice did they have? Within arm's reach of the phone, the ringing stopped and its screen went black. In the quiet moments that followed, they heard the startling rise of distant screaming, coming from above them. They looked up at the open ceiling, and saw the devouring glow of fire. The two patrolmen were falling, engulfed in flames and writhing as they plunged into the dark waters, just a few feet away from where Whelan and Adams were standing. Whelan rushed to the edge of the walkway and grabbed one of them by the arm. In the chaos, Adams ran for the cell phone. As Whelan struggled to pull the burned patrolman from the water, a dark figure rose up behind Adams, and wrapped his arm around her neck, knocking her gun from her hand. She watched as her flashlight fell into the water, as she desperately struggling against the killer's grip. Suddenly, the room became filled with light as Whelan fixed his flashlight and gun on the assailant. The man quickly shielded himself behind Adams, allowing her to draw in half a breath.

"Let her go!" barked Whelan, taking aim at the killer's head. His heart was pounding and his vision blurred with a rush of adrenaline, as the killer peered at him from behind her. In the intense glow of his flashlight Whelan could see the killer's face. It was smeared with mud and dirt. They all knew that Whelan couldn't fire without hitting her. As the killer slowly stepped backward, Whelan could see the shining reflection of a knife blade pressed against her side. He eased his stance and slowly moved his gun away from his target. "Just walk away—just walk away," he said.

The killer said nothing and bared his teeth as he moved to the edge of the metal bridge. His eyes widened as his brain swelled with epinephrine and an appetite for murder.

"There's nowhere to go," continued Whelan, desperate to reason with him. The killer just smiled and jabbed the knife into her side, pulling her with him into the cold waters of the East River. Whelan ran the length of the metal bridge and dove in after her, just as McCuen entered the open chamber. The sergeant rushed to help the burned patrolmen, still struggling to stay afloat. McCuen had seen Whelan jumping into the water and rushed to the edge of the floating bridge. He searched for any signs of movement, but his flashlight couldn't penetrate the churning water. Moments passed, and he helplessly watched as the surface began to settle. Finally, Whelan's arm broke through, pushing against the surface. Then Adams' head emerged. She was writhing in pain, struggling to force the water from her lungs. McCuen pulled her out as Whelan kept pressure on the wound.

In the hours after the ambulance came for her, police tactical units searched every square inch of the building. They found snares, tripwires, and incendiary devices hidden throughout the pump house. Other than the traps he had left for them, there was no sign of the killer. One officer was dead, and Adams was in critical condition. And all they had to show for it was a dead man's cell phone.

The next morning, a report came in of a missing woman, she was last seen in St. Nicholas Park. The clock had been reset, and the killer was undeterred. McCuen had to end it. It had been three days since the NYPD had escalated their search for the killer, but the scale of the search had exceeded the capabilities of the DAS. The killer was stalking his victims in the present, video surveillance from the past would never be enough to catch him. He would abduct another, and then another. It was only a matter of time. McCuen's mind was spinning, thinking about Adams, the killer, and the looming FBI investigation. He felt disoriented from the convergence of so many things beyond his control. It made him feel strange in his own skin. Knowing that it was his last and only option, he drove to LaGuardia.

* * *

Earlier that morning, I had received an email from the chairman of the LaGuardia Plane Spotters. He had tracked down the plane I was looking for. According to his findings, Winterbottom had made repeated trips from LaGuardia to the Caledonia County Airport in northern Vermont. In cross-referencing aviation charts with his "colleagues" he found that Winterbottom's plane always flew out on Sunday and arrived back at LaGuardia on Thursday mornings. But what was in northern Vermont that could warrant such regular attention?

Being that it was Thursday, I arrived an hour before Winterbottom's plane was due to land and parked just outside the gate for chartered flights. Peering through my binoculars, hoping to pass the time, I found myself cataloguing the flight numbers of planes as they were taking off.

Plane Spotting—maybe there was something to it after all. Then, out of the corner of my eye, an unmarked police cruiser pulled up to the gate. I immediately wondered if I had done something wrong. To my relief, I watched McCuen exit the car and walk to the gate. After raking his hands through his hair, he lit a cigarette and leaned up against the chain-link fence. He looked like hell, and he wasn't even trying to hide it.

Shortly after he arrived, a Cessna CJ3 touched down and lumbered to a stop near the exit gate. It was the plane I'd been waiting for. Winterbottom had returned. I watched him exit the plane, and I sank lower into my seat, knowing that McCuen was just thirty feet away. Watchers are ever aware of being watched themselves.

"I thought I might find you here," said McCuen as Winterbottom passed through the gate.

"It's Thursday," replied Winterbottom, surprised to see him. "I thought we weren't doing this anymore." McCuen answered with a question of his own.

"Where do you go each week?"

"You didn't answer my question," said Winterbottom.

"I need your help," replied McCuen.

"Now that sounds familiar," said Winterbottom. "Unfortunately—I don't need yours."

"It's about the DAS."

"That's not my problem," said Winterbottom. Then he walked past McCuen toward an awaiting car.

"Did it work?" McCuen's question made him stop. "Did you find him?" His tone was more telling than the words he had spoken. Without turning around, Winterbottom replied.

"Yes," he said. "I found him."

He had done it. Winterbottom had achieved the impossible, and McCuen's next thought was one of both hopeful reservation and dread. Winterbottom was one step closer to that dark threshold, that doorway that can only close behind you. Against all odds, and time itself, he had found the man that had killed his family. McCuen reluctantly pressed forward.

"Could you do it again—if you had too?" asked McCuen. The question gave rise to Winterbottom's curiosity like a bellows to the embers.

"Hypothetically—yes," he replied, turning to McCuen. "I could do it again." His response was both daring and circumspect, all at the same time. "It depends on what you're looking for."

"A taxicab," replied McCuen. "—with no license plate."

"Does it have a cab number?" asked Winterbottom coyly, not wanting to give away his advantage.

"Yes," replied McCuen. "It's the same one Whelan gave you the other night." Winterbottom didn't react, at least not right away, but it was clear that McCuen knew. "They're good," he said. "But they're not that good."

Winterbottom knew what McCuen was after but wondered how far he would go to get it. McCuen wasn't himself. He hadn't been for a while. Winterbottom could feel McCuen's anguish, and he tried to muster feelings of empathy, knowing that it was the correct thing to do, but he couldn't. He could only ever offer the appearance of it, and that was hardly a fitting replacement, especially for his only friend.

"I could find your taxi," continued Winterbottom. "But I would need access to the DAS in order to do it."

"That may be a problem," replied McCuen. "The FBI's assigned someone to look into the breach—your breach. They're monitoring it for any secondary attacks." Winterbottom shook his head and lifted his sunglasses, while McCuen reached for another cigarette. "We're using the system now, but it's just not enough. We can't find him."

"Ed—it would take an act of Congress to approve the changes I would need to make," said Winterbottom. Then his thoughts turned toward self-preservation and to the more subtle details of what McCuen had said.

"Who'd they assign to investigate the breach?"

"What difference does it make?" mumbled McCuen, pinching his cigarette between his lips.

"It makes a big difference."

"Oh—so now you're suddenly worried about getting caught?" snapped McCuen.

"Said the prime suspect—"

"Fuck you!" said McCuen, before answering his question. "It's some young kid named Sutherland, he's with the Cyber Crimes Task force." Winterbottom's expression didn't change, but he shifted his stance in a subtle way. "You know him, don't you?"

"Yes—he's good," said Winterbottom. "He's very good." McCuen had reservations about continuing but, given that a woman's life was on the line, he had no other choice.

"Could you do it again—without getting caught?"

"If the FBI wasn't already waiting for me—yes," replied Winter-bottom. "But with Sutherland watching, encryption would be an issue and I'd never be able to mask the IP for long enough—"

"English, please."

"Basically, in less than twelve hours they'd access whatever terminal I was using and kick down the door. It'd be difficult even if they didn't know I was coming."

"But, it can be done?"

"Hypothetically, yes," replied Winterbottom. "—but not legally. The DAS was designed to limit real-time domestic surveillance, and that's exactly what we'd be doing. It's advanced in a lot of ways, but it's still a reactionary system—"

"But with the program you built—you could make it work for us."

"I could," he replied. "If I was willing to go to prison for the rest of my life."

"It's for a good cause."

"That may be—but it's not my cause," said Winterbottom. "I'm sorry, Ed. I can't risk it— not now."

"A woman was abducted last night and you're—"

"I'm sorry—I can't."

"You can," snapped McCuen. "You just don't want to."

"I've spent five years working on this—and now that I've finally found him, you want me to just give it up? If I helped you it would jeopardize everything I've done—and for what? A random stranger?" Winterbottom was embittered again, more like his usual disposition. "Wake up and remember who you're talking to." Then he abruptly turned and started walking away.

"He got to Adams," said McCuen. "She's alive—but it's not looking good." McCuen could see that the arrow had hit its mark. Winterbottom was moved, but not persuaded.

"I'm sorry, Ed—I just can't."

"I guess I shouldn't be surprised." McCuen shook his head in disappointment. "You're so intent on killing him—but it won't change anything."

"Yes, it will—he'll be dead," said Winterbottom, as he turned to face McCuen again.

"And will that make you feel better?" replied McCuen.

"No, Ed—it won't," conceded Winterbottom, "—but what you consistently overlook is that I rarely feel anything at all. I'm not like you—you'd do well to remember that."

It was true. Winterbottom wasn't like him. He was different, and for that reason, McCuen's appeal for understanding was unavailing. For Winterbottom, it was an intricate calculation. He was intent on murder, and in doing so, he would solve an equation by eliminating the remainder. He was seeking to make it whole again. His mind wasn't so lost as to think that he could bring his family back from the dead; his work was never intended to be a restoration. To Winterbottom, it was every bit a mathematical endeavor, an inferential answer to an equation of crooked numbers.

"You know his name," continued McCuen. "But what about Margaret? Would she have wanted this? Would she want you to kill him?"

Winterbottom had asked himself such questions, but his pursuit was not lacking contemplation as McCuen seemed to imply. It was the result of unceasing self-examination. No assumptions had been allowed. That's what made his machine so veracious. There was no speculation about what Margaret would have wanted. His algorithm wasn't human; it wasn't trying to be. Its conclusions were drawn mathematically, through a system of numbers set towards a solution.

But McCuen wasn't alone in his uneasiness. Winterbottom felt it too, for an entirely different reason. Unlike McCuen, Winterbottom's reservations didn't stem from some moral anchorage. His fear was more complicated.

Since Margaret's death Winterbottom had changed, there was no denying it. Change was inevitable, but the nature of his mind was wild, like the tempest. He'd been running in the dark with no light to guide him, leaving him to wonder. Was it reason that was moving him, or was it madness in disguise? The timbre of their voices was the same. Whichever it was, he could feel it pulling at him and he envisioned the subtle slope. He could feel the deep subterranean convulsions beneath his feet, the predecessor of collapse. He was walking in their footsteps, and was never more close to Godel, Cantor, and Boltzmann, those great minds that fell into madness and eventual suicide.

It was out of this fear that Winterbottom had pressed forward at such a pace, as if it were just a matter of time before his mind would turn. And so, he steeped himself in numbers and sharpened his mind against the pursuit. McCuen had thought that he was helping Winterbottom by distracting him from the accident, by giving him a new purpose. But Winterbottom only saw

McCuen as a hindrance—necessary, but a hindrance nonetheless.

There was no denying that McCuen had become his friend; he was his only friend. But in the vacuum of Winterbottom's mind, McCuen was also a means to an end. Each time he was called upon by McCuen, and with each question answered, Winterbottom felt less like himself. He felt further away from the answers he was hoping to find. And amidst this distraction, his mind was revisited by the events of that terrible day, over and over again. He would see their faces. He would rush towards them, helpless to stop it from happening. It was like he was spinning slowly out of control like the yawing of the tires, and he could feel the weightlessness before the fall. Now, McCuen was pulling at him again, but something was different this time. McCuen had changed.

"I'm sorry, Ed," said Winterbottom. "I can't help you." The moment he said it, he knew it was over. He paused and waited for what had long been in the making.

"You're going to do this for me—one way, or another," said McCuen. Everyone has their limits; Winterbottom had pushed McCuen too far. "I'll turn you over to the FBI myself, if I have to. I'll take the fall right along with you—but either way, you're going to do this for me." McCuen's tone was all the assurance that Winterbottom needed.

"Alright, Ed—if that's the way you want it." Winterbottom paused again, briefly. "I'll have to make a phone call, but I think we can be up and running within the next eight hours. Does that work for you?"

"Yes, that works for me," replied McCuen, returning to a more even state. Winterbottom shook his head, more sorry for the circumstances than for anything McCuen had forced him to do.

"If we get caught—I won't be able to protect you the way I did before.

They'll know you were in on it."

"I understand," said McCuen. "Let's just try not to get caught."

Winterbottom watched McCuen raise the cigarette to his mouth again. It was clear that he was carrying many burdens.

"How long has she been gone for?" asked Winterbottom.

"She went missing from St. Nicholas Park yesterday at—"

"I was talking about Catherine," said Winterbottom. It caught him off guard; McCuen hadn't told anyone.

"Two months ago," he replied, sadly. "She's staying with her sister in Danbury."

"For what it's worth—I'm sorry."

"Thanks," replied McCuen, handing Winterbottom his cell phone. Then Winterbottom walked out of earshot and placed a very brief phone call, before turning back to McCuen.

"It's done," he said. "We'll be ready to go in five hours." McCuen could see that Winterbottom was fatigued, either from the trip, or from what had just transpired.

"We've got time," said McCuen. "A walk in the tall grass might do you some good."

"Thanks, Ed," replied Winterbottom. "I haven't been for a walk in quite a while."

With the passenger's side window open, I had been able to hear their entire conversation. Winterbottom had found the man he was looking for, and he was going to kill him. From that moment on I became inundated by thoughts of a new obsession, and I needed to find out who it was.

XVII

THE HUNT

Anyone can appreciate that vacant lots in Brooklyn are somewhat of a commodity, but they were hardly destinations, at least not for McCuen. He found it difficult to see how the fenced-in lot, and its knee-high grasses could resemble an oasis, but it seemed just that to Winterbottom. He leaned against the car door as Winterbottom began his counter-clockwise walk around the perimeter. It was the same thing every time, and McCuen wondered again why it had to be so. And why of all places on Franklin Avenue. After ten minutes of solitude, Winterbottom returned to find McCuen sitting on the hood.

"Why counter-clockwise?" asked McCuen. Winterbottom smiled.

"It just feels right, I guess." McCuen sensed that there was more to it than that.

"We've been coming here for years," he said. "What is it with you, and this place?" Winterbottom paused and looked at his surroundings as McCuen continued. "At first I thought it was the tall grass, but it's gotta be more than that."

To his surprise, Winterbottom answered.

"Do you see that building over there?" said Winterbottom, pointing across the street. "That's where Ebbets Field used to be—the home of the Brooklyn Dodgers." He smiled again in reflection. "My father lived just up the street from here. He saw Jackie Robinson in 1956—just before they moved the team to Los Angeles." Winterbottom began pushing the loose gravel aside with his feet as he spoke. "With Ebbets Field demolished, and the Dodgers on the West Coast, he was a man without a team. When I was a boy he'd bring me here late at night, when my mother was working, and we'd listen to the games on his portable radio. He'd listen carefully to the announcer while I'd act out each play."

"Counter-clockwise," said McCuen. Winterbottom was walking the base paths. McCuen was no artist, certainly not a philosopher, and he was hardly the kind of person to indulge in anything overly poetic. But he could appreciate the simple beauty of baseball. It had always been a game of numbers, carefully counted out over a span of nine innings. He could see why it would hold Winterbottom's interest. The spirit of the game is found in the percentages, and the players are defined by those calculations. In fact, the game rarely breaks from those averages, and the players that stand out, the great ones, they're great because they're able to be average, or slightly better, for longer than most. Baseball is steady. That's why some describe it as being slow. But it's not confined to being so. With averages there are odds, and the chance to turn them. As a game it holds the promise that a player might just do the improbable. What makes it most beautiful is that those pivotal moments are not reserved for the best players. Those moments are for everyone, even those who would otherwise never be known. It's under the premonition of failure that there is the hope for redemption, and a chance for greatness.

"I hit many home runs right here in this lot," continued Winterbottom. "And when I was just five years old—Sandy Koufax and I threw a perfect game against the Chicago Cubs." Winterbottom laughed quietly to himself, as if he were a child again. "He pitched well that night, but I really carried him through the ninth." Winterbottom took some time to ponder the memory of it and then looked at McCuen again. "We never really understood each other that well, but we had baseball. He passed away when I was fifteen. After that I just kept on coming here. When I made my first million, scaling the fence seemed disrespectful, so I bought it. I was living in a small apartment in Queens at the time, but it seemed like the most necessary thing to do."

"I'm an unapologetic Mets fan," said McCuen, grateful for Winterbottom's sincerity.

"Of course you are," said Winterbottom. He felt nourished by the visit, and McCuen could see the shift happening. He was setting his mind toward the task ahead of them. "I'll need to pick up something from the house on our way to the Triborough."

They hardly spoke on the car ride to Lexington Avenue. Both men knew what they were facing, and the inherent risks involved. McCuen parked while Winterbottom rushed into the house and quickly re-emerged. From there they drove to the Triborough Bridge, just east of Harlem. It was where they would begin the hunt. Not wanting him to be implicated if it all went wrong, McCuen kept Whelan in the dark about Winterbottom and the DAS and assigned him to oversee the search efforts in Ditmars Steinway and at LaGuardia. The fewer people that knew the better.

As they approached the bridge, Winterbottom began typing furiously on his laptop. McCuen watched as he removed a small device from his bag. It was a black cube-shaped box, which he connected to the laptop and placed on the dashboard.

"What the hell is that?" asked McCuen.

"It's better if you don't know."

"Is it safe?"

"Not according to the State Department," replied Winterbottom, turning his attention to his laptop. "Here we go." He quickly entered a sequence of keystrokes and the screen became flooded with alpha-numeric code. "Just keep heading east over the bridge." Within two minutes, the computer flagged a location in Astoria. The DAS, enhanced by Winterbottom's algorithm, had been transformed into a real-time portal of digital information. A bank of remote supercomputers housed on Lexington Avenue fueled their search through the live video feeds from around the city. *Winterbottom's Gambit* had a new target, and a new purpose. It was trolling through an ocean of data, fixed on a particular configuration of bits and pixels, the block shaped characters of the killer's taxicab registration number. Within minutes, the system had picked up the taxicab at the intersection of 34th and 114th Street. "He's near Citi-Field." With the sun plummeting toward the horizon, McCuen activated his lights and sirens and began racing east on Grand Central Parkway. At eighty miles an hour, there was another alert. "Ditmars and 27th— five minutes ago," said Winterbottom.

"He's heading to the airport!" barked McCuen, reaching for his radio. "All units be advised—suspect in the vicinity of LaGuardia—BOL for yellow taxi, registration 4B52, use extreme caution." Suddenly his phone rang. It was Whelan; he was out of breath.

"He just left LaGuardia—we missed him." McCuen could hear the dread in his voice. "He picked up a fare—a woman and her two kids. I'm heading west from the Airport to see if I can catch up with him."

"If you see him get me on the radio," replied McCuen. The stakes had just been raised. McCuen buried his phone in his jacket as the unmarked cruiser barreled toward the exit onto Astoria Boulevard. "Anything?"

"Not since LaGuardia," replied Winterbottom. "But that doesn't surprise me. The DAS cameras are spread thin throughout the Ditmars Steinway area. If he's going there, we may not get another hit." As they turned onto 31st Street, the screen of Winterbottom's laptop lit up again.

"Ditmars Boulevard," said Winterbottom. "He just passed the train station—he's just ahead of us." McCuen floored the accelerator and the engine growled as they began weaving in and out of traffic. As they moved closer, McCuen turned off the strobe lights and sirens, not wanting to give away their position. Not more than a hundred feet ahead of them, in the half-light of the evening, he could see a yellow taxicab. He continued to follow the taxi out toward the industrial buildings and warehouses near the shores of the East River. Beneath the last sliver of daylight, he hurried to get closer, not wanting to lose him in the dark. Then, the taxi unexpectedly pulled up alongside an abandoned warehouse on Steinway Street. McCuen parked just to the south of the building as the garage door opened and the yellow taxicab pulled inside.

"Stay in the car," he said sternly. "I mean it. Under no circumstances are you to get out of this car." Winterbottom nodded in absolute compliance.

"I'll stay in the car," replied Winterbottom, remembering his past promises.

Knowing that lives were at stake, McCuen radioed in his location and requested backup. Then he approached the graffiti riddled facade of the building. Against the distant sounds of the harbor, he continued down the length of the warehouse, where he found a dented metal door. He quietly slipped inside. The building's forgotten purpose quickly became clear. The overhead fluorescent lights glowed at the far end of the building, casting defused light on the nearby conveyor belts, and steel framing. Hanging down from the ceiling in precarious rows were dozens of metal chains and hooks, the last artifacts of a once productive meat packing plant. In the shadows, McCuen made his way toward the light, navigating around the dismantled ventilation system lying broken on the floor.

As he drew nearer to the open end of the warehouse, he could see the taxicab. He could hear the shuffling of footsteps and the muffled cries of a woman struggling to be heard. Still hidden among the heaps of metal and broken appliances, McCuen cautiously paused. He could wait for backup to arrive, but by then it might be too late. Standing at the edge of where the light reached, he surveyed his surrounding and leaned carefully to one side. He could see a woman tied to a metal chair, her cries muted by the cloth gag in her mouth. McCuen watched her as she sobbed. Tears were sliding down her cheeks. At her feet was a wooden Chimu carving. He looked for the other woman and her two children, but he couldn't see them. He heard subtle movements in the space just beyond the parked taxi, but he couldn't see who, or what it was. To find out, he would have to step into the light. He would be exposed.

Pushing a heavy breath from his lungs, he heard the words coming back to him, *this isn't Fallujah*. As he stepped forward, the woman tied to the chair became deathly still and her eyes grew wide. As she stopped crying, all movement ceased. Not a sound could be heard. With his gun in hand, McCuen moved forward to the far side of the taxi. There was nothing there. He pivoted around in a slow circle, with his gun at the ready. Scanning the darkness, he looked for any signs of movement, but all was still and quiet. Slowly he moved to the rear of the taxicab and pulled open the trunk. As the light of the warehouse flooded inside, he could see the woman and her two children. They were alive, bound and packed tightly into the trunk. Their hands and mouths were taped and their struggles only increased at the sight of him. McCuen quickly reached for one of the children. As he did, he was pummeled to the floor, struck by the forceful blow of a tire iron. He fell hard on the concrete and his eyes went black.

As he regained consciousness, his vision faded in and out. He felt a weightlessness that he had never felt before, but soon realized that he was being dragged, half-conscious, across the floor. He was powerless to control his own body, and he watched as the concrete slowly pulled his gun loose from his grip. Sliding past them, he could see the woman and her two children. They had been tied and seated beside the other woman. Unable to move, he instinctively keyed his portable radio which was still in his hand. He tried to speak, but the words never came. It was a silent plea for help, an empty and haunting signal sent out across the police frequency. Then his radio slipped from his hand. In the moments that followed, his vision returned in flashes, as the killer placed a wooden carving on his chest. What followed was the saturating smell of gasoline as his attacker began pouring it over his shoes and pant legs. Instinctively, McCuen raised his arms to cover his face, but to his surprise the pouring had stopped. He felt the killer reaching into his jacket pockets, removing his cigarettes and lighter. McCuen's eyes pulled focus just as the figure standing over him drew in a long breath through the embers at the end of a lit cigarette. He could hear the faint wailing of police sirens in the distance, but the killer remained eerily calm. The smoke spilled from his opened lips and then curled back in through his nostrils. He didn't say a word. Expelling the last traces of smoke from his lungs, the killer held out the cigarette over McCuen's gasoline soaked body. The killer smiled and McCuen closed his eyes.

Suddenly, the entire warehouse shook with the thundering crash of metal on metal, as McCuen's unmarked cruiser exploded through the garage bay door. In an instant, the killer became illuminated, flooded by the headlights that were careening towards them. At the sound, McCuen's legs came to life again, and he leapt away as the car swung sideways, narrowly missing him. It screeched to a halt, grinding against one of the girders and toppling into a nearby heap of scrap metal. As he stood up he was overwhelmed with a sense of artificial vertigo, induced by the swinging fluorescent lights that had been rocked by the crash. Instinctively, he grabbed his gun from the concrete floor, and scanned his surroundings for a shot at the killer. Turning to his cruiser, he saw Winterbottom behind the wheel, raising his hands in utter shock at what he had just done. Suddenly, the wheels of the killer's taxicab spun wildly in reverse as it sped out of the warehouse through the mangled opening. McCuen quickly fired three shots into the front windshield, but the car continued to speed away. His head was throbbing as he raced to free the killer's captives.

Not long after, the warehouse was filled with patrol officers from the 119th Precinct. Winterbottom watched as emergency personnel arrived and tended to the victims. After a brief meeting with Whelan, McCuen returned to his cruiser.

"I'm sorry about the car," said Winterbottom, wrenching open the passenger side door. "I haven't driven in a while." He didn't wait for McCuen to respond. "You told me to stay in the car, which I did—"

"I'm not mad at you, Anselm," said McCuen, rubbing his neck and shoulder. "I'm glad you did what you did." His body sank into the driver's seat. "I'm also glad I was able to get out of the way." He drove his mangled cruiser onto the street as they both looked back at the warehouse. McCuen rested his head against the window. "Has there been anything from the DAS?"

Winterbottom pulled his computer from the floor and placed the mysterious black box on the dashboard.

"He was on Woodhaven Boulevard, but that was almost twenty minutes ago. There hasn't been anything since then."

"We've lost him," said McCuen disappointedly.

"Yes, we've lost him, but there's still a chance—albeit a small one."

Winterbottom scoured the screen of his laptop. After a few minutes, he lifted his eyes from the screen.

"If I go back far enough—the Woodhaven Boulevard camera has picked him up almost every night for the past three weeks."

"Okay, what does that tell us?"

"Even the devil has to sleep somewhere," said Winterbottom. He paused before continuing. "I hit him with the car, Ed. He's hurt, and if it's Lopez, he'll go to a place that's familiar to him. He'll head for the forest." Winterbottom turned the laptop so McCuen could see it. It showed the killer's last location. It was at the entrance to Forest Park.

"How much time do we have left?" asked McCuen.

"I had to make some adjustments that left us pretty exposed—I'd say less than six hours, give or take a few."

Winterbottom could see that McCuen was weighing his options, none of which were any good. Forest Park was too large to set up an effective perimeter, and if he sent patrol officers, they'd surely get the attention of the killer. He decided to call an old friend.

"Gillie, where are you?" said McCuen into his cell phone.

"I'm heading to Steinway Street now."

"Are you alone?"

"Yeah," replied Gilligan, sensing the tone in McCuen's voice. "What do you need?"

"Have you ever gone deer hunting in Forest Park?"

"No—but it sounds fun." Then Gilligan's voice became deathly serious. "Like Fallujah?"

"Like Fallujah," repeated McCuen.

"I'm on my way."

Forest Park was one of the largest parks in New York City, consisting of over a hundred acres of oak trees and shagbark hickories. It was a far cry from the vast jungles of the Amazon, but when compared to the city itself, it seemed as verdant as the Guiana Highlands.

On their way to the park, Winterbottom worked rigorously to narrow the search area. It stood to reason that Lopez would live in the forest, like he had done in the years leading up to the killings, but gauging the precise location would be a challenge. His reliance on the taxicab would require him to stay relatively close to the parking lots and in roads, but those factors were of little use. The park was enormous. Its northeast side offered the most seclusion, with large swathes of trees separating the various walking trails, but the necessity and abundance of water made the area around Strack Pond an ideal site. In an unlit parking area, not far from the pond, they found the killer's parked taxicab. Gilligan arrived shortly after.

"Gilligan, this is Anselm Winterbottom," said McCuen. It felt strange saying his name to another person. "Anselm—this is Special Agent Gilligan with the FBI." Winterbottom paused in reservation, knowing that it was in fact the FBI that was tracking them at that very moment. McCuen sensed his mistrust and did his best to reassure him. "He's a good friend—we served together in the Army." Gilligan only nodded in response, getting the sense that Winterbottom's name was something McCuen wanted him to forget.

"What's the plan?" asked Gilligan as he opened the back doors of his SUV.

"Bounding Overwatch," replied McCuen. Winterbottom could sense that the reference had everything to do with their time in Afghanistan. McCuen looked to Winterbottom and explained. "Deer hunting."

Gilligan then pulled on a green tactical vest and kevlar body armor, the kind typically worn by soldiers. Then he opened a rifle case and removed an

AR-15 assault rifle, fitted with an infrared scope. After slinging the rifle over his shoulder, he pulled a green balaclava over his face and fitted a pair of night vision goggles over his head.

"Deer hunting?" asked Winterbottom. Gilligan smiled, while McCuen helped Winterbottom put on a kevlar vest.

"So, I guess you don't want me to wait in the car?"

"Nope—not this time," said McCuen. "I need you to come with us into the woods."

"I don't think that's a good idea," Winterbottom replied.

"You're coming with us."

"Do I get a gun?" asked Winterbottom.

McCuen didn't respond and handed Winterbottom a flashlight. "I appreciate you getting us here—but that hardly makes us even."

"Okay—I get it, and I deserved that," said Winterbottom. "—but I still don't see why I can't have a gun."

"You can't have a gun," said McCuen.

"Why not?" asked Winterbottom, pointing to Gilligan. "He gets to have a gun." McCuen was silent, while Gilligan quietly chuckled to himself. Winterbottom looked at both men and waited for an answer.

"You can't have a gun," answered McCuen, "—because you're the bait." Before Winterbottom could protest, McCuen continued. "I'll be right there with you—just a few yards back, and Gilligan will have the long gun covering us from a distance."

"You want me to walk in there?" snapped Winterbottom, pointing into the trees. "Without a gun? So you can use me as bait for a serial killer?" He shook his head and started peeling off the kevlar vest that McCuen had given him.

"It won't work any other way," said McCuen. "He knows these woods too well." Knowing that time was running out, McCuen looked him in the eyes. "I need you to do this."

Reluctantly, Winterbottom re-fastened the velcro straps on his vest and took the flashlight from McCuen.

"Keep it turned on—and pay attention to the trail," said McCuen. "I'll be right behind you."

After checking their earpiece radios, Gilligan and McCuen signaled that they were ready. As they approached the parked taxicab, McCuen struggled to see in through the shattered front windshield. Cautiously, he and Gilligan moved down the sides of the vehicle, ensuring that no one was hiding inside. Then Gilligan crouched down beside the rear tire. There were footprints pressed into the silt at the edge of the parking lot. They were leading into the woods. Both men turned to Winterbottom, signaling for him to lead the way. He exhaled forcefully and proceeded into the trees.

At first Winterbottom could hear their footsteps behind him as he walked through a colonnade of tall oaks. But soon even the sound of their footsteps faded away. Looking through the trees, he wished for the daytime, and watched their long shadows running away from his flashlight. It lent to their trunks and branches a more menacing sway. The brittle layers of the shagbark hickory trees were especially haunting. As he walked deeper in the woods, he was only able to see twenty feet in front of him. The night was nearly pitch black.

As he pressed forward, it occurred to him to look back for McCuen, but he couldn't see his friend anywhere. McCuen would never abandon him, but the thought did little to ease his mind. Soon after, he came to a narrow trail, obscured but still visible as it cut through the understory. He proceeded cautiously and stopped at the pulsating sound of a swamp sparrow. Winterbottom's breathing became heavy and his heart began to race, as he walked along the gentle slope toward a dark mass in the distance. It was Strack Pond. Looking ahead to the pond, less than fifty yards away, he saw the diffused glow of a shielded campfire. With each step that he took, his pace naturally slowed. Then out of the darkness came a voice.

"Stop," said McCuen, sharply. "Don't move." Winterbottom froze. Within a few seconds, he could hear the rustling of leaves and the sweeping sound of slow footsteps. Soon, McCuen was standing right beside him. "Look down—but don't move." Nearly invisible in the darkness, was a slim reflection of the moonlight. It was a tripwire. "There will be more as we get closer," said McCuen. "Keep the flashlight and your eyes on the trail—don't step anywhere you can't see the ground." Winterbottom nodded repetitively before cautiously stepping over the wire.

Continuing down the path, his mind pondered the dangers that awaited him and he tried to focus on his footsteps, ever aware that his senses were rising. His attention began to divide and the subtle sounds of the forest began to grow. Soon they were amplified in his ears. His vision blurred and then sharpened, and he began tapping his fingers quietly at his side.

McCuen, who was just a few yards back, was concentrated on their surroundings and the killer. In the darkness he couldn't see the signs that Winterbottom was losing control. Up ahead they could see that the undergrowth had been cut back. At the far end of the clearing, not more than fifty feet away, was a domed hut, fashioned from harvested branches and the leaves of the forest. It was the killer's den. The doorway to the hut appeared to leap out toward them, glowing in the darkness. Winterbottom knew why they were there, and of the danger he was facing. But in that moment he couldn't focus on either thought. The rustling leaves, the sporadic calls of the Nightjars, and the ever-present whispering in his ear, all plagued him equally. He was losing himself to the world around him.

"Wait—stop," whispered McCuen. Something was wrong, McCuen could feel it. He quietly called to Gilligan on the radio, but there was no response. "Gillie?" he repeated. Still, there was nothing. The radio was silent. McCuen's eyes began darting from side to side, attempting to see through the impenetrable darkness. They had come into the woods as hunters. Now, they were the hunted.

He looked to Winterbottom who was standing completely still, staring at the ground. "Anselm—I need you to stay close, okay?" whispered McCuen. "We're going into the clearing." Winterbottom nodded silently, but McCuen could see that he was struggling. He stood close to him and put his hand on his shoulder. "Look at me," said McCuen. "Just make sure you stay close to me—and no matter what happens, you have to stay in the open where I can see you. Stay in the light, okay?"

"Stay in the open—stay in the light," repeated Winterbottom, sensing the gravity of the moment. The killer was close, and he was surely watching them, waiting for the right moment to strike. As they stepped into the clearing, long shadows stretched out behind them, accentuating their movements. Winterbottom's eyes were anxiously darting back and forth, from the dark bushes to the nearby trees on all sides. His pulse was deafening as his mind turned in wild revolutions. As he walked, he heard the words and repeated them to himself; *"Tiger, Tiger, burning bright—In the forest of the night—"* He whispered the words over and over again, focusing his attention on the entrance to the makeshift hut and the glow of the fire. He heard rustling nearby, then the snapping of branches. His chest felt tight as he tried to force his lungs to open. Unable to gain a more even tempo, McCuen's words circled in his mind; *stay in the open, stay in the light.*

Suddenly, a shadowy figure rose up and lunged from the tree line. McCuen snapped his aim on the figure as it lumbered toward him. Winterbottom froze in place as the figure moved closer. McCuen drew in the slack on his trigger and was about to fire, when the figure collapsed on the ground, falling into the light. It was Gilligan. He had been stabbed multiple times. Instinctively, McCuen rushed toward him, while Winterbottom recoiled at the sight, stepping backward into the darkness. As McCuen approached, Gilligan lifted his hand in opposition. In that instant, McCuen remembered Fallujah. With lethal speed he reeled around and drew his gun on Winterbottom, whose eyes widened at the sight of McCuen's aim. Winterbottom clinched his eyes shut and raised his hands as McCuen fired seven shots in quick succession. The bullets whistled past him, punching into the darkness all around him. As the sound reverberated through the trees, Winterbottom felt for his ribs and chest, sure that he had been hit. The pain that he expected never came, and he slowly turned around. Behind him, lying dead on the ground, was the killer. At his feet was a sharp steel blade, a bone-handled knife, lying in the dirt.

Winterbottom turned back to McCuen for an explanation, but no words were offered. In the silence came the realization that McCuen had been willing to risk shooting him in order to end it. It was a chance that Winterbottom would have surely taken if their roles had been reversed. He was alive, and the killer was dead. Nothing else mattered.

Taking comfort in his ability to breathe again, he rushed to help Gilligan.

McCuen called for an ambulance and with Winterbottom's help, he carried Gilligan to the entrance of Forest Park where he was rushed to the hospital. In the hours that followed, they confirmed by fingerprint comparison that the killer who had terrorized the urban jungle was in fact the elusive Carlos Javier Lopez, *the Monster of the Andes.*

* * *

Much later in life, I asked McCuen about that night and about what it was that made him shoot blindly into the darkness. It wasn't something he could put into words. Perhaps he just didn't want to answer. Instead, he told me about his time in Afghanistan. It seemed irrelevant to my inquiry but to him the events seemed intrinsically connected, beneath the surface, like two glacial lakes miles apart from one another.

XVIII

A SECRET REVEALED

That morning, McCuen returned home to an empty house and slept for three hours. He was awakened by an unexpected phone call. There would be no rest for the weary. Over the phone, Chief Kelly told him what he already knew: the hackers had once again accessed the DAS, with undetermined intentions. At Chief Kelly's request, McCuen hurried to Federal Plaza to join him at FBI Headquarters. Along the way, his mind was filled with uncertainty as he tried to brace for what might happen. He tried to call Winterbottom at the house but there was no answer. He was going in blind.

When he arrived, he met with Chief Kelly in the command center of the FBI's Cyber-Crimes Division. The room was filled with a dozen computer technicians, at the heart of which was Sutherland, perched at the helm of three central computer monitors. Standing over his shoulder was Dempsey, watching as if overseeing the moon landing.

"Thanks for coming," said Kelly. "What a fucking mess."

"What have they found?" asked McCuen.

"They haven't told me anything," said Kelly, "—not that I'd understand any of it if they did—fucking computers. All I know is that they're getting close."

"Do they know who's doing it?"

"No—not yet," Chief Kelly, exhaled. "I just figured it would be better to have you here while they track whoever it is." By that time Dempsey had noticed McCuen's arrival and approached.

"Good morning, Captain," he said, confidently. "It looks like they've come back for more, but we've got them this time. It won't be long now." Just then a flurry of alpha-numeric code slid across the central monitors, as a handful of analysts looked back to Sutherland for an answer.

"We've got a second *black hat*," said one of the technicians to Sutherland. Dempsey hurried back to where Sutherland was working.

"What's a *black hat*?" he asked.

"A second hacker just penetrated the system. They're both using the same authorization code, but they're in different locations." Being in the room offered McCuen considerable shelter from suspicion, but he knew that if Winterbottom was caught, they'd both face the consequences.

What confused him the most was why Winterbottom was still using the system.

"It's been almost twelve hours," said Dempsey angrily. "How much longer is this going to take?"

"They're using a very complex algorithm—I've never seen anything like it before," replied Sutherland, "—but it shouldn't be long now." Then he paused before speaking again. "We've isolated the two hackers, but I'll only be able to locate one of them."

"Just get me someone!" shouted Dempsey.

Then the door to the command center swung open and in walked Winterbottom, escorted by an FBI agent. McCuen's heart stopped as

Winterbottom adjusted the lanyard that was hanging around his neck, holding State Department credentials. Sutherland and Dempsey quickly turned to see him. McCuen cringed, but to his surprise, Winterbottom walked right past him and approached Sutherland and Dempsey.

"Anselm," said Sutherland in relief.

"Sorry, I'm late," he replied.

"And you are?" asked Dempsey. Sutherland quickly intervened.

"This is the man who designed and built the DAS," said Sutherland. "Special Agent Dempsey—this is Anselm Winterbottom. I called him last night to see if he could help us with the breach." Anselm nodded to Dempsey, which yielded a slightly more welcomed response.

"Well, I'm glad you're here," replied Dempsey. "But it seems your creation has a few vulnerabilities."

"Don't we all?" said Winterbottom, smiling. "I'll see what I can do."

Within five minutes of Winterbottom's arrival, Sutherland excitedly stood up from his seat and reported their progress to Dempsey.

"We've locked on to the source computer," he said. "The contents of the hackers' computer will begin to come up on the main screen as we narrow in on his location."

McCuen shifted his stance as his palms began to sweat. The initial breach was Winterbottom's responsibility, McCuen hadn't done anything illegal, but this time was different. Not only was this his idea, but he had forced Winterbottom to do it. For most of his life, McCuen had stood between what was right and wrong, upholding one while condemning the other. He could always make out the black and white presumptions of the law against the blurred edges of existence.

But this time, had he done the right thing? In the end, he had saved lives and that was all the justification he needed. He would do it all over again if he had to. And so, there was no need for him to hide it. There was no reason for both of them to go to prison. He was going to end it. He turned to Chief Kelly and was about to speak when one of the technicians called out to Sutherland.

"We just lost one of the *black hats.*"

"They're retreating?" said Sutherland. "Stay with the other one."

"They're operating on the east coast," shouted one of the analysts. "New York—they're in the city." McCuen began watching the geo-location map as it slowly narrowed in on the hacker's location. "Manhattan—Midtown."

McCuen anxiously anticipating the computer's next location.

"Federal Plaza?" replied the analyst in confusion. Sutherland shot up from his chair. A wash of confusion came over McCuen.

"Where is he?" shouted Dempsey.

"He's in the building!" Shouted Sutherland in astonishment. "The hacker is in the building!" Sutherland looked to Winterbottom, who convincingly feigned confusion. "How can that be?"

"Are you sure there were only two *black hats*?" asked Winterbottom.

"Yes, I'm positive."

"Well, we're locked onto someone," said Winterbottom. "You have the IP address?"

"Yes," said Sutherland, entering the address into the system. McCuen looked at Winterbottom, who sat back in his chair, seemingly unaffected by the circumstances. Just then the large monitor on the center wall of the room lit up, mirroring the hacker's desktop screen. It was an FBI computer containing the login name: *Special Agent Dempsey.* Everyone in the room stopped and looked at Dempsey. The whites of his eyes swelled and his face turned red with anger. As he looked around the room, the large monitor suddenly began shuffling through a slideshow of images from Dempsey's computer.

"Shut it down!" he shouted, as Sutherland tried to sever the link. The collection of routine cell phone pictures featured a series of Dempsey's pet cat, an Abyssinian tabby. From there, things took a quick and equally devastating turn, culminating in a series of shirtless selfies.

"God damn it!" shouted Dempsey, spilling his coffee down the lower half of his sleeve. "Shut it down now!" In a rage, he ran over to the monitor and yanked the cables from the display. "What the fuck is going on here!" he yelled as he spun around to leave, throwing his empty coffee cup on his way out. Sutherland was perplexed and slowly lowered himself back into his chair. The hunt was over, though it was hardly a fair fight.

"How did they—"

"You've got more important things to worry about now," said Winterbottom to Sutherland. "Hackers just accessed the most advanced surveillance system in the world. You can push forward and try to catch them—or you can contain the damage." With that he handed Sutherland an ominous looking black thumb drive. "You know what needs to be done." Sutherland nodded in acknowledgement and inserted the thumb drive into the mainframe. With a swift keystroke, he severed the digital connections, and the monitors went black. The code that had been crawling incrementally from the servers suddenly stopped, and the room fell silent. Winterbottom stood up and put on his jacket.

"I'm glad to see you were paying attention," he said to Sutherland, shaking his hand. "You did very well. In fact, you've given me hope. I was beginning to think teaching you Harvard commies was a waste of my time." Sutherland smiled in consolation.

"What happened?" barked Chief Kelly, as if he had watched an entire foreign film with no subtitles.

"They got away, sir," said Sutherland. "They remotely breached the system through Dempsey's own computer." Realizing that clarification was needed, he reframed his response. "We were chasing our own tail."

"And what did they get away with?" asked McCuen.

"Absolutely nothing," replied Sutherland. "They were accessing real-time surveillance, but for whatever reason, they didn't take it with them. It was as if they just wanted to take a quick look around." Then Winterbottom turned to Sutherland before leaving.

"Let me know if you need help with the reboot and diagnostics," he said. Then he swiftly left the room, purposefully ignoring McCuen on his way out.

Leaving Chief Kelly with Sutherland, McCuen followed Winterbottom down the hallway to the elevators.

"What the hell was that?"

"Thank you," said Winterbottom. "I think the words you're looking for are—*'Thank you, Anselm,'* or *'Wow, Anselm, you're a really great friend—thank you so much.'*"

"Oh, you want me to thank you for setting me up—and conspiring to destroy evidence?"

"It's okay, Ed—I won't make you say it."

"And you have State Department credentials now?"

"Well, technically, I always did," said Winterbottom. "I'm not supposed to tell anyone— those are the rules. You know how it is."

"And the DAS?" continued McCuen. "You really built it?"

"In so many words," replied Winterbottom. "Originally, it was much more extensive, but a certain Senator from Kentucky was concerned about it being used to spy on Americans—can you imagine? No one else really cared, but he made enough of a fuss that the State Department ultimately had me rein it in."

"And you didn't feel the need to tell me any of this because—?"

"Would it have mattered?" replied Winterbottom. McCuen kept the answer to himself.

"And the breach?" asked McCuen.

"By severing the connection, Sutherland destroyed any evidence of the breach," answered Winterbottom. "It's over, Ed."

For the first time in six months McCuen could take in a full breath, but he still hadn't lost sight of the horizon. He knew what Winterbottom was planning.

"So it's over—but you're not finished," said McCuen. "Are you?" Winterbottom didn't reply. As they stepped into the elevator, McCuen continued. "The man who you think killed your family, what's his name?" Winterbottom turned to him in silence, surprised that he would even ask.

"I did what you asked," replied Winterbottom.

"And now you're going to kill him," said McCuen, plainly. Winterbottom looked down at the carpeted floor of the elevator and didn't say a word. "Anselm, if there's anything I've learned from you, it's that you can't change who you are—not without paying a terrible price. This isn't who you are, and once you do this—there's no going back." McCuen was desperate for him to understand. "What he did was tragic and cowardly, and maybe he deserves to die for it—but killing is something that you know nothing about." He watched the numbers of the elevator ticking down. "It's one of the few things in life that everyone can do, but no one can fully comprehend—until it's too late."

"I know you're trying to help," said Winterbottom, "—but I need to see this through." McCuen shook his head in disappointment. "I can't just sit back and let that happen."

"I don't expect you to," replied Winterbottom, turning back to the elevator doors. "You're a good man, Ed. You'll do the right thing—you always do. You'll follow the rules—and that's precisely why you won't be able to stop me."

The crux of McCuen's predicament was apparent. It all pointed to a very simple truth. He didn't know the name of the man Winterbottom was chasing. And so, he was helpless to stop him. Coldly, Winterbottom continued. "Ironically, by saving my life last night, you may have inadvertently cost another man his." The words were both cutting and deliberate.

"That doesn't sit well with me," said McCuen.

"Then you have a choice to make," said Winterbottom, as the elevator door opened.

"I suppose so," said McCuen, regrettably. "In the meantime, maybe this will make you reconsider." Then he pulled a copy of *The Post* from his jacket pocket and handed it to Winterbottom. As McCuen walked away, Winterbottom carefully unfolded it. The front page showed a picture of Winterbottom and McCuen walking out of Forest Park; it had been taken the night before. The headline read: *Billionaire Mathematician helps NYPD: Still Searching for the Killer of his Wife and Daughter.* Winterbottom had been forced out into the open. He had been exposed. Of course, his mind naturally turned to McCuen, and the poetic symmetry of it all; a betrayal for a betrayal. For all his careful planning, he could never have foreseen it coming to this. And even in that moment, he wasted no effort on anger or frustration. That would have been inefficient. What was done, was done. He would have to find a way forward.

Like so many things in life, the truth was far from the perception. *The Post* had published the story, but it was my doing, not McCuen's. I had followed them to Forest Park that night. I had taken the photograph, and I had written the story.

But in order to maintain my relationship with McCuen and preserve my anonymity, I leaked the story to a grateful friend at the *Post*. I couldn't risk giving myself away, not now. I would need every advantage if I was going to find out who Winterbottom was after. By publishing the story, I hoped to throw him off balance, maybe even force his hand. If nothing else, I had bought myself a little more time.

PART III

A DEATH MOST QUIET

XIX
PHOTOGRAPHS AND MEMORIES

I woke up to the cold air that often accompanies mid-October; it was the first real sign that winter was coming. It was only after finishing my espresso that I was able to form a clear picture of what had happened the night before. My apartment appeared to have been ransacked. The small breakfast table and most of the living room was buried beneath an assortment of garbage and recycling, crumpled papers, discarded packaging, and empty plastic bottles. It wasn't the work of some unwelcome burglar. This was a mess of my own making. I sat down at the couch and picked up where I had left off, carefully examining each piece of trash as if they held the understanding of some lost civilization. Looking back on it, I can see that I'd crossed a line, and it was far more egregious than a quick dip into the world of dumpster diving.

For the past three months, I'd watched the house on Lexington Avenue, though it seemed unlikely to reveal anything about where he was disappearing to each week. In light of what I had learned, my concern was growing. If his intent was to kill, what could be pulling him away on such a regular basis, to Northern Vermont of all places? Unless the man he was chasing was there. It seemed doubtful, but if that was the case, it was imperative that I learn exactly where he was going, before it was too late. The better part of me knew that I should try to stop him, the other part empathized with him, and even admired what he had accomplished. But what is one's moral obligation? Is it to sit and observe, allowing things to fall as they may? Or is it to intervene and influence the natural progression of things? I wasn't bound by anything, but I could feel the weight of what was happening. I chose to be an observer, a silent witness to whatever would happen.

Learning the man's identity was of paramount concern. Winterbottom had said he was going to kill him, I had heard it with my own ears. But without the man's name, even observation would be difficult. The simple truth was that Winterbottom could've already killed him and I'd have no way of knowing. Months had passed since the newspaper article came out, and I was no closer than before. Despite the uncertainty, I felt there was still time, but watching the house wasn't enough. Eventually, impatience and curiosity conspired against me, and I began stealing his trash, which he placed out on the street every Thursday morning before leaving for Vermont. In a matter of weeks, my already cramped apartment began to feel increasingly so. My Saturday mornings were spent gently ironing crumpled receipts. Then I would catalogue each item and where it was purchased, finally pinning them to the walls of my living room. I taped together torn and shredded documents, most often finding them to be utterly useless.

Then, one Thursday morning, he emerged from the house later than usual. After placing his trash on the street, Winterbottom lingered on the sidewalk. He was waiting for his taxi. The more fearful side of me wondered if he was guarding it, as if wanting to make sure that it would be inseparably crushed together with a thousand other secrets. It sounded like paranoia, but it was a rare occurrence for him to linger for so long out in the open. As he stood there, I could see in my rearview mirror the garbage truck in the distance. It was slowly lurching toward us. I imagined what unknown secrets might be lost, if I couldn't get to it first. Then, as expected, a taxicab arrived and carried Winterbottom away.

My choice not to follow him was easy this time. I knew roughly where he was going, and I knew when he'd be back. The promise of stealing his secrets was too great. There was no telling what was held inside the opaque plastic bag. Once the taxi was out of sight, I rushed toward the unattended trash bag, and quickly tumbled it into the trunk of my car. I landed back in the driver's seat, carefully watching to see if I'd been noticed by the approaching garbage truck. Then it became clear that I was missing the bigger picture. The house was unoccupied.

Whether out of carelessness or neglect, he had left the front door unlocked, making my choice to enter seem less criminal. Having visited the house before, I hurried through the foyer and ran straight for Winterbottom's cloistered room. Knowing that he'd be gone for several days did little to curb the sense of urgency that often accompanies such misadventures. I went straight for his desk, fumbling as I pulled at the drawers. I quickly scanned the papers and documents looking for a name, or an address, anything that might point me in the right direction. Many of his handwritten notes were either illegible or coded in numerical formulas that I had no chance of deciphering. Anything remotely relevant, I shoved into my pockets, constantly looking over my shoulder. It's a heavy feeling to know that eyes are on you. Heavier still to be unsure.

In assessing my surroundings, I saw the dormant computer servers standing in the dark corner of the room. Then my attention shifted to the long folds of the great curtain on the adjacent wall. It had been thrown to the side, exposing the bare wall. What had once been affixed to the wall was now scattered across the floor at my feet and I hastily turned the papers over, one by one. It was then that I found it, a single unnamed DMV photograph. It was him. It was the man Winterbottom was after. But without a name the photo was useless to me. I quickly discarded it and continued to sift through the remaining papers. That's when I discovered his name. It was everything I'd been looking for. On a single printed page was the DMV record belonging to a man named James Dearborn. I quickly folded the paper into my jacket pocket. Then I heard the front door opening. Someone was coming. In a panic, I rushed for the darkest corner of the room, narrowly fitting between two of the monolithic computer servers. I squeezed myself tightly between them, hoping they would give me enough cover. As I drew in a deep breath a lone figure entered the room. I could hear his footsteps and the quiet brushing of his coat sleeves. Not wanting him to sense that he was being watched, I closed my eyes tightly. Then, he stopped, as I had done. He was surveying the room. Then I heard him pulling at the drawers of the desk and rummaging through the stacks of papers. Slowly, I opened my eyes, and turned away from the wall, hoping to get a better look at him. He was just out of view.

Informed by its shape and the furnishings of the room, his movements followed my own, increasing the chance that I'd be discovered. As I had done, he walked across the center of the room toward the curtain. It was McCuen. He gently pushed aside the discarded papers on the floor and knelt down to find the unnamed photograph that I had discarded on the floor. Taking the picture with him, McCuen rushed back to the desk, neatly covering his tracks, sliding the drawers back into place. He left as quickly as he had entered, and I listened for the sound of the latch. At the closing of the front door, I exhaled in relief before quickly drawing in another breath. McCuen and I were looking for the same thing, the only difference was that I had his name and address, and McCuen didn't. He only had a photograph. This revelation compounded the moral dilemma I spoke of earlier. McCuen would be helpless to stop him—unless I told him. Unsure of what to do, I continued on my current path.

Shaken, but still confident that the house was empty again, I crawled out from my hiding place. Rushing out of the room, the staircase caught my attention. Burglary had never occurred to me before that day, but since I was already inside the house, I might as well be thorough about it.

Being a stranger to the upper levels of the house, it pulled at my curiosity. Before I could think too much about it, I had climbed the steep carpeted stairs. As expected, I found myself staring down a narrow corridor, lined with doorways. Its length was accentuated by the daylight pouring in from the room at the end of the hall. The first doorway led to the bathroom, a simple and small space, lined with aging porcelain tile. Inside was a small sink, and a clawfoot bathtub. The next doorway led to a study, which was filled with stacks of books and empty moving boxes. Stepping into the room, I saw that the curtains and once hanging picture frames had also been taken down. Having pierced its outer shell, the mystery that the house once held began to fade. In some ways, it was as common as any other, and at the same time, I felt a sense that each room might hold new secrets. In that way the house and all its mysteries were continually rising and falling, like the fluctuations of a chambered nautilus.

Aware that I had nearly been caught in the lower levels of the house, I forged ahead into the master bedroom. There was no time to waste. It was essentially empty, aside from a few sealed boxes and subtle hints of habitation. As I approached the bed, I could see that one side had seen more use than the other. And although the sheets and comforter favored one side, it was clear that the mattress was intended for two.

The only other sign of occupancy was a single picture frame, angled on the bedside table. It was an older photograph, most assuredly not digital. It depicted his wife, Margaret, and their daughter, Grace, standing near a rustic cabin on a lake. The blurred edges of a distant pine tree, and the soft light around the child's hands suggested that the moment was fleeting. It was Margaret's smile that gave Winterbottom away as the photographer and the only living witness to a memory long passed. I carefully turned over the frame and on its reverse there was a handwritten caption: *Lake Willoughby, 2003.*

It was the intimacy of the photograph that compelled me to leave the house as quickly as possible. There are few things more precious than the sanctity of someone's home, surpassed only by those intimate things they keep inside it. For that offense, I felt deeply ashamed, and it dulled the excitement of what I had learned.

Back at my apartment, I began sifting through the most recent bag of trash, looking for anything that might help me. Most of the items were irrelevant, but amongst them I found an electricity bill from a power company located in Vermont. Winterbottom's name was listed as the customer and it contained a service address on Lake Willoughby, in the rural town of Westmore, Vermont. It was the cabin from the photograph. That's where he was going each week. With one mystery solved, I turned my attention to another. I focused on finding out as much as I could about James Dearborn.

From my cubicle at the *Times*, I began to dive into his life. On the surface, Dearborn wasn't that much different from any other thirty-six-year-old, white man living in upper Manhattan. He had an above-average apartment in Sugar Hill and was a successful Marketing Manager for one of the larger firms in the Lower East Side. He drove a black Mercedes and played golf at Van Cortlandt every weekend. On all accounts, he had done pretty well for himself, aside from the secret he was keeping.

James Dearborn came to New York City from Elkhart, Indiana seven years ago, leaving behind his parents, and two older brothers. Empire State horizons could never be physically broader than those of Northern Indiana, but he had grown to resent the limitation of the small town. He was looking for something new and different. He loved his family, but their view of the world, and what little they had seen of it, spurred him to look for something more. He knew the odds that were stacked against high-school sweethearts and feared a lifetime of Friday nights spent drinking beneath the water tower. Both of his brothers had followed in their father's footsteps, working for the Indiana-Michigan Power company. It was something he could never understand. It was like they hadn't even considered a different way, or so it seemed to him. They would never know the luxuries that existed just outside the reach of the working middle-class. And those were the things he had come to hold dear. That was the promise of New York City.

Earlier that week, he had secured the largest advertising account at the firm, proposed to his girlfriend of three years, and shot three over par. Things were going very well for James Dearborn.

XX

MOMENTO MORI

Winterbottom returned home to find a shadowy figure standing at his doorstep. The shallow archway aided in shielding the man's face, but the streetlights ultimately gave him away. From the solemnity of the man's posture, he could tell it was McCuen. Tired from his trip, Winterbottom walked slowly up the steps to the front door.

"Let me guess—someone died?" he said, coldly.

"No—someone's been murdered," replied McCuen. "There's a difference." Winterbottom turned to the door and reached for his house keys.

"It's unlocked," said McCuen. Winterbottom paused momentarily before opening the door. McCuen reluctantly followed him inside.

"It must be dire if you're coming to me for help," said Winterbottom, standing next to the secretary's desk.

"It is," answered McCuen. "If I had a choice—I wouldn't be here." His words implied a fixed number of possibilities, and Winterbottom's thoughts jumped to the newspaper article which had outed him as an investigatory consultant for the NYPD.

"Did they order you to consult with me—wouldn't that be ironic?" He smiled, thinking how frustrating that would be for McCuen.

"I hate to disappoint you, but that's not it."

"Then why are you here?"

McCuen handed him an already opened manila envelope. "It arrived this morning." Curious to know what was inside, Winterbottom pried at its contents. The envelope itself was common enough, but what was inside was anything but mundane. It contained medical records, photographs, and a death certificate associated with a man named Moshe Potok. Winterbottom paid special attention to a newspaper clipping of the man's obituary, from two years before. According to the announcement, Potok was an Orthodox Jew who had lived in Borough Park for most of his life. He had a wife, two children, and seven grandchildren. According to the attached death certificate, he died of a heart attack at the age of seventy-two.

On the verge of losing interest, Winterbottom turned to the next document. It was a single piece of paper, sealed in evidence plastic to prevent fingerprint contamination. Adhered to the page were a series of letters and words, cut from the pages of magazines and newspapers. In varying colors, proportions and fonts, the text read:

"I am Death, and this man is one of many who did not die from natural causes."

The letter was attached to an etching by the famous French Symbolist, Marcel Roux, from his series known as *Danse Macabre,* or *Dance of Death*. This particular etching was entitled *The Miser.* It portrayed an older man clutching at a pile of coins on the table in front of him, while Death looms over his shoulder. The association with Moshe Potok, an Orthodox Jew, highlighted the ugliness of the sender's anti-Semitic intentions. Winterbottom noted its hateful representation, but he didn't linger on the etching, or the cryptic message. Instead, he ran his fingers over the corner of the page where he noticed a single staple. It seemed out of place. Quickly, he turned it over and saw the front-page newspaper article featuring him and McCuen. The sender had circled their faces with a red, broad-tipped marker.

"It seems as though we've gotten someone's attention," said McCuen.

"No good deed goes unpunished," grumbled Winterbottom. "Do you know anything about who sent it?"

"No," replied McCuen. "We've tested it for touch DNA, and latent prints—but no luck."

"And you think it's something to take seriously?"

"I do."

Winterbottom's attention was elsewhere, but his instincts agreed with McCuen. As much as he wanted to dismiss the whole thing, this wasn't some innocuous letter.

"I assume there was no autopsy performed on Mr. Potok," said Winterbottom, shuffling back through the papers.

"No, there wasn't," replied McCuen. "There's nothing suspicious about a seventy-two-year-old man who dies of a heart attack."

"Well, then you'll have to dig him up to find out what really killed him."

"It was two years ago," replied McCuen. "And in the Orthodox Jewish community there are strict rules prohibiting disinterment." McCuen could see that Winterbottom was already moving on as he carefully closed the clip at the top of the envelope. "This isn't something that's going to just go away."

"So, you came to warn me then?" continued Winterbottom.

"Yes—"

"I appreciate your concern, and I hope you find the person who sent it."

As he was handing the envelope back to McCuen, he stopped suddenly. A noticeable look of concern washed over his face. The envelope had been sent to McCuen's home address. McCuen didn't have to say another word. In that moment, Winterbottom realized the true reason why McCuen had come. He hurried to the front door and opened the hatch to his mail slot. He pulled out the mail that had been collecting since he had left for his trip. Standing out amongst a few smaller envelopes, was a manila envelope. It was identical to the one McCuen had received. Resentful at the inconvenience, he gave it to McCuen.

"Don't look so disappointed," said McCuen. "It's not every day you get a letter from a serial killer." It was hardly enough to soften Winterbottom's mood. McCuen pulled on a pair of nitrile gloves before carefully cutting open the envelope. Inside was an obituary for a man named Samuel Whitaker. He had died just two weeks before. Then McCuen removed another grim etching by Marcel Roux, this one known as *The Cabaret*. In crosshatched lines, was the depiction of a man, hunched over against a bar top, seated beside an illuminated skeleton holding a bottle. Behind the etching was a note forged from cut-out letters, repeating the same haunting proclamation as the previous envelope:

"I am Death, and this man is one of many who did not die from natural causes."

The arrival of the second envelope had instilled a change in both of them. It was especially felt by Winterbottom. Whoever was sending the envelopes, regardless of their intentions, knew where he lived. He had to assume that he was being watched.

Winterbottom had grown increasingly distrusting of the outside world, but he questioned whether it was out of imbalanced paranoia or, in fact, the result of a valid suspicion. By watching him in secret, as I had a done for months, I had introduced turmoil into an already tumultuous mind. I had unintentionally caused him to distrust his instincts, and despite the arrival of the unpleasant packages, I imagined that Winterbottom felt relieved to know that his feelings were warranted. It brought to mind an old, forgotten poem. He, in his madness, prays for storms and dreams that storms will bring him peace.

Inner suspicions aside, the envelopes themselves were hardly definitive proof that these deaths were in fact murders, but circumstances dictated that something had to be done. Winterbottom wouldn't be able to pursue Dearborn, if he was being watched, perhaps even targeted. It needed to be dealt with, and it was clear from the red circles drawn around their faces that the sender wanted him to work with McCuen.

"Will you come with me?" asked McCuen.

"I don't have much of a choice—do I?" replied Winterbottom, grabbing his jacket.

McCuen was tired of the conflict between them, but he couldn't help feeling unsettled. Winterbottom had always been driven by self-interest, and the nature of these killings, if they were in fact murders, was disconcerting. He became haunted by a dark probability. Was Winterbottom trying to rid himself of watchful eyes, or was there added incentive to finding a killer who could make murder look like a natural death? It stayed with him as they drove to the 19th Precinct to see what more they could learn about the alleged victims of Death.

Once inside the police station, Winterbottom's worries subsided. He was happy to see Adams again. And he could see that her encounter with a serial killer had no lasting influence on her work ethic. He was glad to see Whelan again too, which surprised him. They'd been working diligently to compile as much information as possible about the two decedents, Moshe Potok and Samuel

Whitaker. The walls and whiteboards of the conference room were cluttered with full-color photos, names, and medical records, and Winterbottom was quickly pulled in.

"Let's not waste any time," said McCuen. "Adams, what do we have on Mr. Potok?"

"He grew up in Borough Park and lived there his whole life. He was a respected member of the Orthodox Jewish community and a family man. As far as his medical history goes, he was presumed to have died of coronary artery disease. He'd been treated for the condition for nearly fifteen years, and his post-mortem exam showed no signs of physical trauma, or irregularities. According to the coroner's report, they checked for marks, bruises, and injection sites—but nothing was found."

"That's it?" asked Winterbottom. "I mean—is that typical?"

"They don't perform full autopsies on seventy-two-year-old men," said Whelan. "Especially when they have a history of heart failure. All signs point to natural causes."

"Except for the envelopes," added Winterbottom. "What about the other guy?"

"Samuel Whitaker," said Whelan. "He was a sixty-eight-year-old, black male from Brooklyn. In 1968, while serving in Vietnam, he was awarded the Bronze Star, and the Distinguished Service Cross for heroic action during the Tet Offensive. According to reports, he saved the lives of four men and was subsequently injured by an enemy land mine, resulting in the amputation of both of his legs."

"Cause of death?" asked McCuen.

"Coronary Artery Disease—a heart attack," said Whelan. "There were no signs of recent physical trauma, and no history of drug abuse—though he struggled with alcoholism. He had heart and lung disease, and in the months before he died he was moved to a VA nursing home. He had no living relatives, and there was no autopsy. He was later cremated."

"Which eliminates the option to exhume the body," said Adams.

"Okay, so we've got a Jewish grandfather, and a black war hero—and the only thing they have in common is their cause of death." McCuen then looked to Winterbottom, who was still scanning the documents affixed to the wall. By the way he was standing, it was clear that the lack of dependable information was frustrating to him. In spite of that, McCuen could see that he was following the strands. Then, like an impulsive child, Winterbottom began pulling at loose threads.

"They both lived in Brooklyn," he said. "Just five blocks away from each other." He pointed out the addresses, but it did little to muster any significant feelings.

"In Brooklyn—five blocks may as well be a hundred miles," said Whelan, dispelling the idea that such a broad similarity could be relevant. "Are you suggesting our victims knew each other?"

"No," replied Winterbottom. "Not necessarily—but it increases the likelihood for crossover. Living in the same geographical area reduces the degrees in which they're separated." Winterbottom cleared his throat and continued. "Despite different backgrounds and life experiences, their lives revolved around the same places, and therefore, many of the same people." Then he turned back toward the center of the room. "If they were in fact murdered, they weren't chosen at random. They knew the killer, at least in some small way, and he most certainly knew them." Winterbottom pulled the two etchings from the wall. "These etchings prove as much. Both victims shared characteristics with

Roux's subjects. Aside from his obvious anti-Semitic views, the killer knew that Potok was Jewish, and that Whitaker struggled with alcoholism. That can't be a coincidence."

"Yes—but I wouldn't go as far as to say they knew the killer," said Adams.

"You may be right," said Winterbottom, diplomatically. He had missed the way she spoke to him. "But if the killer was a stranger—then why kill them so quietly?"

"We don't even know if they were murdered," said Whelan. "Until we know for sure—I don't see the point in guessing at motive."

"I think we have to assume that they were murdered," said Winterbottom. "He told us about them for a reason."

"Yes, but he waited until two years after Potok died," replied Whelan, "And weeks after Whitaker was cremated—why would he do that?"

"I'm not sure," said Winterbottom in a grim tone. "Maybe he's hoping that we doubt him —so he can prove us wrong." He paused before continuing. "I think it's a question the killer will answer soon enough."

In the silence that followed, Winterbottom focused on the most intriguing aspect of the whole ordeal, the manner of death and the method of murder.

"I think we can all agree that if they were murdered, poison is the most likely means."

"It would have to be," said Adams. McCuen and Whelan agreed.

"Good," said Winterbottom. "Because there are at least a dozen more efficient ways to kill someone—other than poison. Our killer chose it for a reason."

"It can be easily concealed from the victims," said Adams. "And it's relatively easy to obtain."

"It can be administered, or ingested," added Whelan.

"And in different doses," said McCuen, "—which would allow our killer to be hours away when the victim dies."

"Exactly," acknowledged Winterbottom. "The fact that the killer needs such distance implies that he's close to the victims. It's the reason why poison is preferred by political rivals and spouses." Winterbottom turned again to the papers and photographs surrounding him. "If it's poison—I'm inclined to think our killer's name is in these documents. And for that reason, the killer knows we can find him. He won't waste any time in killing again."

"We'll have to work quickly," said McCuen. Winterbottom had given them much to consider, but it was all theoretical. McCuen needed more than vague assumptions about the killer. "If he's so worried about being caught—why would he send the envelopes?"

"Because he wants us to try to stop him," replied Winterbottom, plainly. "He's also quite confident that we can't." Just then the door to the conference opened.

"Sorry to interrupt, Captain," said a uniformed patrolman. "This just arrived by courier." He handed McCuen an ominous manila envelope. Its arrival brought a somber air into the room. The timing of the delivery was especially noteworthy. They were being watched. McCuen opened the envelope and emptied its contents onto the conference room table. On top of the pile was a reproduction print of Marcel Roux's etching known as *A Piece for Four Hands.* It portrayed a woman sitting at a piano. Seated beside her is Death, in the form of a skeleton. Accompanying the work was a copy of a New York Driver's License belonging to an elderly, Vietnamese woman named Hau Phan, with a listed address on Greenpoint Avenue. Beneath the photograph was a haunting message which read:

"I am Death, and I am coming for Hau Phan."

The killer was no longer hiding; he was no longer sheltered by the past. The arrival of the letter and its inscription had shifted to the future tense. The prospect that she was still alive sent them racing to her apartment. As they sped through the Midtown Tunnel, Winterbottom, who was in the front passenger seat, was visibly shaken by the ongoing accelerations of the car. With each turn, he braced against the door and closed his eyes.

"There's no need to rush," he shouted, "—she's already dead."

McCuen didn't respond and continued to weave in and around the remnants of the morning commute as if every second mattered. As they emerged from the tunnel, he radioed for an ambulance to standby, in case it was needed.

Nearing their destination, Winterbottom breathed deeply, trying to regulate his aversion to the forces at work, and the confines of the car itself. For the remainder of the drive, he closed his eyes and placed his hand on his forehead. He could hear the rear seatbelts unbuckling as the brakes engaged. The car lurched to the side, and suddenly stopped.

McCuen, Whelan and Adams rushed up the steps of the four-story apartment building, while Winterbottom loitered on the sidewalk, observing the paint that was peeling away from the building. It was a pale yellow, with brown trim. The windows on the first floor were barred, and from the sound of their footsteps, he guessed that her apartment was on the third floor. Slowly, he followed after them, at his own pace. When he arrived, they were all standing around an upholstered chair, holding the lifeless body of Hau Phan.

Her eyes were open in a frozen stare, unresponsive to the colors and sounds of the television. Against the back wall of the room was an upright piano. The fall board had been left open, exposing the yellowed ivory and intermittent black keys. One of the white keys at its center was broken; stuck in place from when it was last played.

Much about Hau Phan could be learned from the state of her apartment. It was clean, and the few possessions she had were neatly arranged. The solitude and overall emptiness of the apartment were familiar to Winterbottom. Much like him, she was utterly alone in the world. To the sound of the television playing in the background, Adams and Whelan went to work examining the body. McCuen searched the kitchen cabinets and the rest of the house while Winterbottom peered out at the neighboring buildings.

Adams was unable to find any signs of trauma. The body itself was room temperature, and her slackened jaw showed no sign of rigor mortis. She had died within the last hour. Beside her chair was a tepid cup of tea, hauntingly half-filled. Finally, McCuen emerged from the bedroom, empty handed.

"Whelan, call the Medical Examiner," he said. "Make sure he knows about the likelihood of poison and brief him on the details of the case. I want a full-spectrum screening." Then he turned to Adams. She was already dusting for fingerprints. Then he looked across the room at Winterbottom; he was still looking out the window onto Greenpoint Avenue. "Are you doing alright?"

"I'm fine," replied Winterbottom, stoically. The physiological effects of the high speed car ride had subsided, but McCuen could tell that something was bothering him. Winterbottom was a thousand miles away. Unperturbed, Winterbottom turned to face Phan's reclining corpse. It reminded him of unfinished things. "It looks like you'll be tied up with this for a while," he said. "Would you mind calling me a cab?"

"I can," replied McCuen, "—but I think we should all stay together. He's out there—and he's watching us."

"Yes, he is," said Winterbottom. Then he smiled. "But if I go—he can't watch us both at the same time."

* * *

That afternoon, I welcomed a change in scenery, and traded in my observations of Lexington Avenue for the ambling scenery of Sugar Hill. It was a quiet neighborhood, and Dearborn's small apartment building consisted of a street level apartment with three upper tiers.

His was on the second floor, which was convenient for me. From my parking space, I had a clear view of the steps and the painted front door. Most importantly, the street-facing windows allowed me to peer into the living room of the apartment. The most ideal vantage point was two spaces ahead of me, currently occupied by a gray Lexus, but availability was scarce. I was lucky to get as close as I was. As I was settling in, a taxicab dropped off a man at the corner. I didn't recognize him at first, but as he came closer I could see it was Winterbottom. His eyes seemed menacing and he was walking straight toward me. I fumbled with the car keys and struggled to get them into the ignition. Suddenly, he stopped and unlocked the rear door of the parked gray Lexus, quietly slipping inside. For the next two hours, I divided my attention between Dearborn's apartment and Winterbottom's parked car, but nothing changed. I was about to drive away when Dearborn emerged, carrying his golf clubs. He walked a short distance, to a black Mercedes, and placed his clubs in the trunk.

The sight of his car must have been jarring to Winterbottom. I could only imagine how its sleek black finish must have stirred him. Whether it was the same car, or a new replacement, it didn't matter. Such a thing was so easily fixed, as if the accident had never happened. In that way, Dearborn's greatest crime wasn't the accident itself. It was the audacity he had to keep living, to go about his life as if nothing had happened. After the Mercedes pulled away, Winterbottom exited the Lexus, and was quickly picked up by a passing taxicab. For the first time, I felt like I had something in common with him. As soon as they were both out of sight, I stole Dearborn's trash.

XXI

THE AUTOPSY OF HAU PHAN

The following morning, Winterbottom was running late. When he arrived at the Chief Medical Examiner's Office, he was greeted by Whelan and Adams and saw McCuen pacing the width of the corridor.

"I can see I haven't missed anything," said Winterbottom.

McCuen looked up from his wristwatch.

"Just because he's late—doesn't mean that you're on time."

Just then a man in a dark gray suit and tie pushed through the double doors.

"Captain McCuen," he said, smiling. "It's been awhile."

"How are you, Ethan?" said McCuen, shaking his hand. McCuen turned to them and continued.

"Everyone, this is Dr. Ethan Howard, the Assistant to the Chief Medical Examiner. He'll be taking us through the findings from Phan's autopsy."

Dr. Howard nodded to them before turning back to McCuen.

"You know, I was trying to remember the last time we worked together—"

"It's all a blur to me," said McCuen, "—what did you come up with?"

"Six years ago—the Hunts Point Murders," he replied, directing them to a nearby conference room.

"That sounds about right," replied McCuen.

"You know, I rarely have to deal with this shit anymore—not unless the brass at Police Plaza ask me to."

"Well, I really appreciate you taking the time—this one's got me worried."

"I'm happy to help," he said. "Just promise me another six years of peace—and we'll call it even."

Inside the conference room, Dr. Howard pulled a file from the nearby cabinet and sat down at the opposing end of the table.

"Okay, so Hau Phan," said Dr. Howard. "She was a sixty-eight-year-old Vietnamese woman with no living relatives. I won't get into how she was found—because you found her. From the onset of rigor mortis, I put her time of death roughly around when you found her— certainly no more than an hour before you arrived. As for her medical history, she had a congenital heart defect, but the condition was mild, overall. It looks like she had bi-annual doctor's visits, which were routine. At autopsy, we couldn't find any signs of physical trauma, other than a lateral bruise on her thigh, right above the knee."

McCuen turned to Winterbottom; they were thinking the same thing. She must have bumped her leg on the underside of her piano. Uninterrupted, Dr. Howard continued.

"We tested all of her major organs and there were no observable issues, but the toxicology report will be more definitive."

"How long before that comes in?" asked McCuen.

"I sent my assistant to pick them up from the lab," replied Dr. Howard. "I know how impatient you get when it comes to lab results." Dr. Howard grinned.

"Between hospital rom-coms and cop-shows, the expectations are getting pretty fucking out of control. He should be here any minute."

Howard took a sip from his coffee before continuing.

"We ran toxicology just after autopsy, and I conducted affirmation testing last night."

"Just tell me you're not thinking she died of natural causes," replied McCuen, cutting to the chase.

"Based on what you've told me, and the envelopes the killer sent, toxicology will give us the answer. If she was poisoned, then it—"

Before he could finish, his assistant entered the room and handed Howard the lab results. He was a young med student, not more than twenty-four years old, and he glanced reverently at them before leaving the conference room. As Dr. Howard reviewed the lab report, Winterbottom began pacing. After a few minutes, Dr. Howard removed his eyeglasses and sat back in his chair.

"Toxicology is negative," he said, appearing lost in his own words.

"How can that be," replied McCuen.

"We found traces of known medications that she was taking, and the concentrations were well within—if not below, normal levels."

"You're saying there are no traces of chemical toxins, or poison?" asked McCuen.

"That's correct," he replied, finding it hard to believe what he was reading.

"How is that possible?" said McCuen.

"It's not," he replied, plainly. "If the killer used poison—it would've shown up in the test. Ed—I'm sorry, I'll run the tests a third time just to be sure, but there's nothing here." Amidst the confusion, Winterbottom broke his silence.

"Could it be something new?" he asked. "Something more advanced?"

"There are new toxins engineered all the time," replied Dr. Howard, "—but they all leave traces in the body."

Howard could follow Winterbottom's line of thinking, and it was logical to suspect a new toxin, but certain truths couldn't be ignored.

"It's medically impossible," continued Dr. Howard. "There's a lot happening in the field of molecular biology, but to engineer a compound that is completely untraceable—that would be an incredible leap, although I'm not sure in what direction."

"It has to be poison," said McCuen. "How else could the killer have predicted her death?"

"I agree with you, Ed," said Howard. "Poison is the only plausible explanation—except for the fact that there's no trace of it in her system." Dismayed, McCuen stood up from his seat.

"There are only a few absolutes in medical science," said Dr. Howard, "—but this is one of them. Toxins leave obvious traces in the body, there are no exceptions to that. Even the most advanced neurotoxins leave traces. They can be odorless, tasteless, and undetectable to touch, but they all leave their mark on the body. Not to mention, in general, the more advanced the toxin, the more identifiable it becomes. They leave a more unique signature and induce obvious post-mortem changes."

Howard stood up and walked to the other side of the table.

"I'm sorry, Ed—I wish I had better news."

"It may not be what I wanted to hear, but I appreciate your help," said McCuen. "Of course, it's likely I may call on you again, soon."

"You know where to find me," he replied. "In the meantime, I'll run the tests again and let you know if anything changes."

As they were leaving the room, Dr. Howard noticed a note affixed to the file folder.

"Ed, hold on—there's something else."

McCuen turned to see what it was.

"I don't know if it necessarily matters, but it came up in our database when I was pulling her files. Ten years ago, Hau Phan was a patient of Dr. Emile Taub. Is that name familiar to you?"

"No," replied McCuen.

"I didn't recognize it either," he continued. "It doesn't say the reason, but according to our records, Dr. Taub had his medical license revoked in 1998."

"Thanks, Ethan. We'll look into it."

* * *

Looking for solace, and answers, Winterbottom and McCuen retreated to the Odessa. They settled into a booth in the back of the diner, far away from the windows, and the prying eyes of the other patrons.

"There's no use pretending," said McCuen, "—we've got nothing." Winterbottom slowly sipped his coffee.

"You can't stop something that doesn't exist," said Winterbottom. "If there's no poison— there's no murder." It was that simple, and it had the makings of the perfect crime. "Molecular biology is way outside my wheelhouse," continued Winterbottom, "—but Dr. Howard's right. Chemical compounds leave traces. It's a fundamental scientific principle. I've been trying to come to terms with that for the last few hours."

"What'd you come up with?" asked McCuen.

"Essentially—we can't rule out the possibility that our killer has developed something new—an undetectable poison."

"If that's true," replied McCuen, "—it would explain why he wants us to know about it." Sipping from the black abyss of his coffee cup, through the oily sheen of ground Arabica came a feeling of dread. "What if he stops sending envelopes?"

"Well, that's when it happens," replied Winterbottom in a more serious tone. "That's when murder would begin a strange metamorphosis. And from that point on there would only be Death. He'd be able to kill with absolute discretion. There would be no way of telling a murder from a natural death."

McCuen listened intently and watched him closely as he spoke. Winterbottom's words were solemn, but the subtle shifts in his mannerisms gave away the fact that his mind was preoccupied. It had been from the moment McCuen arrived at Lexington Avenue.

"Absolute discretion," repeated McCuen. "You won't have that advantage." His tone made Winterbottom sit back in his chair. "You won't be able to hide it." Then McCuen removed the photograph from his pocket and placed it on the table. "You won't be able to kill him quietly. His murder will be loud, and it will scream your name."

"Burglary—," said Winterbottom, looking at the photograph. "Ed, you should be ashamed of yourself." Then he smiled, dismissively. "You still don't know his name—do you?"

"Does it matter?"

"It does if you plan on stopping me," snapped Winterbottom.

"It's murder, Anselm!"

"Are we really going to do this now?" said Winterbottom. "Maybe we should eat first?"

"Why wait?"

"Well, it might not be the best thing for our friendship," replied Winterbottom. "You know how easily my feelings get hurt." Winterbottom drank his coffee and cleared his throat. "Here's how it would go," he continued. "You'd try to convince me not to kill him, and like all your previous attempts you'd fail—miserably. For all your efforts, as honorable as they are—I'd kill him, anyway. Now, for the sake of argument, let's just say that you manage to identify the man in that photo, and you also miraculously find enough evidence to charge me with his murder. Then you would arrest me. Have I missed anything?"

"Yes," replied McCuen. "You left out the part where you go to prison for the rest of your life."

"I'm already serving a life sentence!" barked Winterbottom in anger.

"You could make a different choice."

"So could you?" said Winterbottom. "You could let me get away with it?"

"You know I can't do that," conceded McCuen, "—and those are two very different things."

They were at a standstill, like two equal forces pushing against one another. Eventually, Winterbottom eased back into his seat. McCuen said nothing. He just gently turned his coffee cup in slow circles on the table.

"You keep making the same mistake," muttered Winterbottom, quietly.

"And what mistake is that?"

"There are two, actually," he replied. "You think I care about getting away with it." Then he paused in an almost sorrowful way. "And you assume that I don't know how to."

"Anselm—"

"Ed, you're my friend," he interrupted. "That may not mean much in this world, but it means a great deal to me. I don't expect you to change, and whatever happens, you'll have to do what you think is right."

There was a finality to his words that left little room for argument. And so they sat quietly, drinking their coffee and watching the people coming and going through the doors of the restaurant. Not long after, Whelan and Adams arrived and occupied the remaining seats at the table.

"Dr. Emile Taub," said Adams, placing an extensive dossier on the table. The file had a daunting weight to it.

"Can you give us the highlights?" asked McCuen.

"All three of our victims were patients of Taub at one time, or another." Adams had gotten his attention. Winterbottom dragged the folder in front of himself and began flipping through its contents as she continued. "We had to go back twelve years to find the connection."

"Which is?" asked McCuen, eager for answers.

"Dr. Taub specialized in the treatment of congenital birth defects," replied Whelan. "Everything from common heart arrhythmias to spina bifida and various other genetic disorders. Outside of that, he managed a small family practice in White Plains. Our three victims were all patients at his primary care practice."

"That can't be a coincidence," said McCuen.

"No, it's not, and there's more—much more," said Whelan. "Taub graduated from Harvard Medical School in 1968 with a doctorate in Molecular

Biology and Biomedical Sciences."

"Which suggests that he's far more interested in Molecular Biology than family medicine," said Winterbottom.

"You're right about that," replied Adams. "In 1998, he was arrested for medical negligence for conducting unauthorized and undisclosed genetic experiments on a number of his patients."

"The evidence and trial testimony were somewhat cloudy," added Whelan, "—given the fact that he targeted patients with limited cognitive abilities, and those with a history of mental illness."

"There were also allegations that Taub was operating an illegal abortion clinic out of his basement," said Adams, "—but authorities weren't able to prove it. In the end, his license to practice medicine was revoked, and he was sentenced to twelve years at Altona Correctional."

"Where is he now?" asked McCuen.

"He has an apartment in Red Hook, on Columbia Street."

* * *

You can learn a lot about a person by what they throw away. Public records can tell you all the hallmarks of a person's life: birth dates, marriages, divorces, and deaths. But to learn who they truly are, you have to watch them when they're alone. It wasn't something that could be done in a week but required observation over a significant length of time. Of course, I didn't have that luxury. I had to work quickly and from a distance. I already knew why Winterbottom was looking for Dearborn and that he planned to kill him, and the more I watched him, the more difficult it became. My conscience was burdened. I considered telling McCuen, but what good would that do? The reality was that Winterbottom hadn't done anything illegal, at least not that I was aware of. In fact, in pursuing Winterbottom, I was the only one engaging in criminal activity. I had illegally obtained cell phone records, engaged in stalking behavior, broken into his house, and I had even stolen his trash. Of the two of us, I was more culpable. Besides, I knew that McCuen was following the same trail I was on. It was only a matter of time before he would find Dearborn all on his own. I decided to leave it to chance and focus my attention on the items in his trash, as if I were an oracle reading the tea leaves.

As I had explained before, Dearborn was a successful marketing manager. He enjoyed playing golf and recently became engaged. However, his garbage implied a more complicated story. I found several receipts for various purchases at gas stations, the golf course, and the grocery store. The items he purchased were informative, but what he didn't buy was equally telling. There was a notable absence of alcoholic beverages which led me to think that he either never drank at all, or that he used to drink too much. I also found two empty prescription bottles for lansoprazole and lorazepam, medications prescribed for anxiety, stomach ulcers and sleep disorders. After I followed him for a few days, it all became clear. On his way to and from work each day, he was careful to follow a self-imposed detour around the intersection where the accident happened. The next night, I followed him to 58th Street, where he attended a weekly Alcoholics Anonymous meeting.

On the outside, to friends and strangers alike, everything was going well for James Dearborn. But on the inside, he was feeling the burning pains of stomach ulcers and frequent vomiting. He was haunted by voices that kept him up at night. He was hiding it from everyone, even his fiancée. He had a handle on his drinking, at least for the time being, but the stress of keeping such a secret, knowing that he had killed a mother and her child was slowly devouring him. He was living a double life: the successful marketing manager and the fugitive. He was running from himself. Perhaps the most compelling item that I recovered from the trash was a disposable pregnancy test.

XXII

DR. EMILE TAUB

It was mid-morning and McCuen was knocking on Winterbottom's door, again. This time he had been summoned. Another package had arrived. Winterbottom cautiously opened the door and welcomed McCuen inside.

"Have you opened it?"

"No—I was waiting for you."

McCuen sat down at the desk and carefully placed the envelope at its center, while Winterbottom turned on the nearby desk lamp. The heavy curtains had been pulled over the library windows, making the room feel almost cave-like. Rather than open them, Winterbottom continued around the room, turning on the ceiling lights and torchieres in each corner of the room. Time was of the essence, they both felt it. But knowing the killer's affection for poison required caution. McCuen reached into a black, hard shelled case that he had brought with him, pulling out arms-length plastic gloves, a mask, and a respirator. The killer's interest in them had been well established, but there was no telling when his intentions might shift. Risks needed to be taken, but it would be foolish to rely on the whims of a poisoner, a man claiming to be Death itself. Winterbottom stood back as McCuen carefully cut open the seal on the envelope. Like the others, it contained a series of documents accompanied by another work by Marcel Roux. This time it was the etching known as *The Clergyman,* depicting a bearded priest walking inside a cathedral, as a skeleton lurks in the shadow of a vaulted archway. McCuen read the killer's inscription, forged from cut-out letters. It read:

"I am Death, and I am coming for Jean Gerard."

The last page in the envelope was a photocopy of the New York State driver's license belonging to Jean Gerard, a retired Catholic priest.

* * *

Later that afternoon, McCuen found himself back at the Odessa, impatiently waiting for Winterbottom, who was over an hour late. Despite McCuen's objections, they had gone their separate ways, agreeing to meet up once Whelan and Adams had a chance to learn more about Jean Gerard. McCuen was beginning to worry, not for Winterbottom's personal safety, but for what he might do if left unsupervised for too long. After ordering another cup of coffee his attention turned to the photograph he had taken from Winterbottom's house. It had been two days since he secretly submitted it to the DMV database for identification. Soon he would know the man's identity. He hoped that it would be enough to stop a murder, but he was running out of time.

It hardly required any imagination to consider how Winterbottom might do it. Given present circumstances, poison was at the forefront of McCuen's mind, but Winterbottom's own words dismissed it as being less effective than other means. There were so many ways at his disposal, and given his work with McCuen over the years, he had acquired firsthand knowledge of each. Nothing could be guessed at, and nothing could be ruled out, not even the cold-blooded. Each was as likely as the next, be it electrocution, or gunshots. Then, of course, there was his intellect to contend with. Winterbottom could easily turn any anticipated theory on its head at any moment. It was anyone's guess, but McCuen leaned toward a more complicated design. He feared that it would be made to look like a suicide, a murder hidden within a violent death; the proverbial reaper's sleight of hand.

Just as McCuen was about to ask for the check, Winterbottom pushed his way through the door to the diner. McCuen watched him approaching. Winterbottom's eyes darted from face to face as he neared the table. It was happening again. McCuen had only seen it a few times before.

Whatever it was, be it anxiety or paranoia, it showed in subtle gestures and eventually magnified Winterbottom's more apparent eccentricities. He would be more irritable, and even more unpredictable. Crashing down into his seat, Winterbottom pressed his hands deep into the pockets of the field jacket. He was in no mood for a lecture, so McCuen buried his observations and proceeded to the matter at hand.

"Father Gerard was admitted to Tisch hospital, yesterday," said McCuen. "He had a scheduled surgery to remove his gallbladder."

"Interesting," muttered Winterbottom, in a voice that was monotone. He proceeded to look over his shoulder.

"I just came from the hospital," continued McCuen. "They're monitoring him closely and I've assigned two patrolmen to guard the room. I've limited his care team and no one is allowed into the room alone."

Winterbottom nodded to the waiter for coffee, saying no more than was absolutely necessary. Before the server arrived with a hot pot of coffee, Winterbottom switched his mug with one from an adjacent table.

"Naturally, I'm curious how our killer plans to get to him," said Winterbottom.

"I don't see any way that he can," said McCuen. "But clearly he likes a challenge."

"I think it's more a matter of confidence on his part," said Winterbottom. "I hate to be the pessimist, but I'm afraid it's already too late for Gerard." His demeanor was obstinate, even as he sipped his coffee. "He wants you to know just how helpless you are to stop him."

"Don't you mean how helpless 'we' are to stop him?" replied McCuen.

"No—I mean 'you'. Something's come up for me—I can't put it off any longer."

"Anselm—"

"Look, this killer likes to play games," said Winterbottom, sharply, "—but he only plays when he can win. I'm not interested in playing anymore. Hell, the only reason I got involved to begin with was because he knew where I lived—"

"He still knows where you live."

"Yes—but he doesn't seem to care," replied Winterbottom. "I'm quite content getting his envelopes and passing them off to you. Is that really so bad?"

"A serial killer is sending you letters—that's a very bad thing," replied McCuen.

"Come to think of it, I'm only involved because of your stunt with that goddamned newspaper article."

"How many times do I have to tell you—that wasn't me," replied McCuen.

"Okay," said Winterbottom in disbelief, "—there just happened to be a reporter waiting in Forest Park that night." Winterbottom smiled in disgust.

"Not to mention that it seemed to serve your purposes quite well. The house phone's been ringing off the hook day and night—and people are asking questions. I liked it better when they thought I was dead."

"Good," replied McCuen. "I'm glad it's making things difficult for you—but it wasn't me."

"I wish I could believe that."

McCuen looked down at his coffee and a stern expression came across his face, as if disappointed by himself.

"They suspended me for three weeks," said McCuen, quietly. Winterbottom paused on the words. "And that was far less than I expected. Another mistake—and I'm done. They were pretty clear about that."

Winterbottom had never considered what the newspaper article might mean for McCuen's career. The news seemed to make Winterbottom soften a little.

"Of course, now that the killer's roped you into this case—the brass at Police Plaza have given you their blessing—temporarily," said McCuen. "I was hoping you'd come with me to talk to Taub."

"What good would that do?"

"Hardly any," joked McCuen. "It's probably a terrible idea—but why start making good decisions now?"

"That may be your most compelling argument yet," replied Winterbottom.

"I could have you back in a few hours."

Winterbottom was eager to get out from under the killer's watchful eyes, and although he preferred to ignore it all together, that was hardly a solution.

They had to catch him. It was the only way.

"You've waited five years to get your revenge," said McCuen. "—What's one more day?"

"When you say it like that it seems so easy," said Winterbottom, coldly. Looking out the window of the diner, he continued. "I guess one more day won't hurt."

As they drove through Red Hook, Winterbottom looked out over the harbor and the soft gray patina that masked the city skyline. He was overtaken by a sense of longing, one he often felt that time of year. Like the fog stretching over the water, his mind had become clouded.

Constant analysis and the labors of extreme neuroplasticity were compounded by a lack of sleep. It was leading to physiological changes that he had never experienced before. He felt divorced from himself, and if he had taken the time to look in the mirror, he would have seen a hollow likeness of his former self. It was midday, and yet to him, it seemed like twilight. A greater consciousness resurfaced as the tires bumped against the wet cobblestone streets. They were almost there. When they arrived on Columbia Street, Whelan and Adams were waiting for them.

"Did you get the search warrant?" asked McCuen.

"It took some doing, but we got it," replied Whelan.

"If he's willing to talk, Anselm and I will meet with him while you two search the house."

From there, they approached the brick-faced housing complex and made their way to the second floor. The door was answered by a middle-aged woman, Taub's in-home caregiver. She escorted them into the living room where Taub was seated in a high-backed leather armchair.

His slender frame had the appearance of being swallowed up by the cushioned leather, and the deep wrinkles that crept from corners of his eyes and mouth showed his age. Given the yellowish tint of his white hair, it was no surprise that his blue eyes seemed empty and pale. He sat quietly, scowling as the nurse introduced McCuen. He didn't immediately respond, and sat for a moment, staring at them amidst the hissing sound of his oxygen tank and nasal cannula. His brow became furrowed as he pulled the plastic tubes from his nose.

"What do you want?" he said sharply.

"Mr. Taub, we have a search warrant for your apartment," said McCuen.

"Of course you do," he replied, begrudgingly. "As you can see—I'm a great danger to society."

"All the same—we're going to search your house."

McCuen handed him a copy of the search warrant as Whelan and Adams went to work. Taub carefully adjusted his large, square-framed eyeglasses and scanned over the warrant, looking for the alleged offense. "We'd also like to speak with you—if you're willing." Then Taub's eyes rose up from the page.

"Murder?" he said, chuckling to himself. "And who is it I'm supposed to have killed?"

"We're looking for any evidence of the crime of murder," replied McCuen, "—several murders, actually."

Taub's smile slackened before hardening into a sneer.

"I'm intrigued," he replied, "—but I have nothing to say to you."

It wasn't an outright refusal, but it left McCuen with little room to move. Then Winterbottom interjected.

"Moshe Potok, Samuel Whitaker, and Hau Phan."

Taub's eyebrows bent and hardened at the presentation of their names. He shifted in his seat and looked out the nearby window. A smile curled into the angle of his mouth.

"*Dr. Taub*," he said, defiantly. "I'll speak with you—but you must refer to me as *Dr. Taub*." The request seemed insidious, given his past conduct, but McCuen was willing to appease him if it would help their case.

"That's fine with me—Dr. Taub," said McCuen.

Then Taub motioned with his hand that he was ready for questioning. As they continued, he gently lifted a cup of amber tea to his lips.

"We're looking into the deaths of several of your past patients," said McCuen. "From your response to their names, I assume you remember them."

"I remember them," he said. McCuen was about to continue when he was interrupted. "I remember them—because they were different from my other patients."

"How so?" asked McCuen.

Taub began to smile again. He could see where it was leading, and he saw no point in beating around the bush.

"Do I disgust you, Captain?" he asked, rhetorically. "You don't have to answer—because the answer depends greatly on your perspective." A short and gravelly cough made him stop momentarily. Then he pressed the oxygen tubes to his nostrils again, filling his tired lungs. "You know about my experiments—that's why you're here." His voice crackled, as he continued at a softer volume. "I am a man of science—and I believe in absolute biology. It's been my religion, and I've spent a lifetime in its service." In that moment a change came over him, like a cloud obstructing the Sun. "In my opinion," he continued, "—you shouldn't be asking who killed these people, but instead—who is responsible for letting them live." Taub could see the look of disdain on their faces. He was wallowing in it.

"They all had birth defects," said Winterbottom. Taub nodded in affirmation.

"Some were more noticeable than others," he replied, "—but they were biological errors, nonetheless. Potok and Phan had heart arrhythmias, and Whitaker had a mild form of late onset muscular dystrophy—something that would have been far more noticeable if he hadn't lost his legs in Vietnam."

"And Jean Gerard?" asked McCuen, pressing through the underlying intent of Taub's admissions. Taub's face soured at the name.

"His condition went beyond physical irregularity," grumbled Taub. "Genetic weakness doesn't always result in physical defect, but it can be equally offensive to our humanity. Inferior genetic combinations result in maladaptive behaviors such as inferior cognitive abilities, alcoholism, mental illness, and criminal behavior—"

"Potok was a Jew, Whitaker was black, Phan was Vietnamese—," interrupted Winterbottom. "Isn't that what you're saying?" He had summarized Taub's wicked ideology in a concise and appropriately accusatory manner.

"Yes," snapped Taub, angry at the interruption. "And Gerard was a mutt! His father was French Canadian, and his mother was Abenaki." Taub's face turned wretched as he bit into the words. "Being a Catholic priest was a deformity of his own choosing." Then Taub drew in another serving of oxygen. As he exhaled, he focused again on his inquisitors, as Winterbottom continued.

"You said that Gerard *was* a mutt?" noted Winterbottom. "It gives me great pleasure to tell you that he's very much still alive."

"A pity," replied Taub, cautiously. "Something that time will surely rectify."

"The same could be said for you—Dr. Taub," said McCuen, coldly.

"Yes, Captain," he snapped back. "I don't need to be reminded that I'm dying—but I have no regrets."

"You experimented on vulnerable patients," replied McCuen. "And now they're being murdered—killed off, one by one. You may not be the one killing them, but I was hoping you might help us find out who is."

"Oh, is that right—you've come here for my help?" he said, smirking passively. It soon turned to laughter. "I'm afraid you've come to the wrong man, Captain. If I'd had my way—I would have ended their burdensome lives a long time ago."

"Burdensome for whom?" asked Winterbottom.

"Again, that's a matter of perspective," replied Taub.

"And your illegal abortion clinic?" said McCuen, attempting to draw him out further. "Was that just a matter of perspective?"

"Now, Captain—those allegations were never proven in a court of law. But, that issue in particular is a matter of perspective. Despite your personal feelings about me, it's important that you know—I was only trying to help them."

"Of course, you were," said McCuen. "I'm sure it had everything to do with helping young women—"

"No, no, no—you've misunderstood me, again," continued Taub with a fixed expression. "I wasn't helping those women—I was helping their babies."

In that moment, the ugliness of Taub's nature was laid bare for them to see. He was enjoying himself, and McCuen had lost the stomach for peripheral conversation. He reverted to a more direct approach.

"Did you kill Phan and the others?"

"No," said Taub. His casual tone prevented any truth from being affixed to the denial. He was toying with them. "Death comes for us all," he added, giving rise to their suspicions.

"As a man of *Science*," said McCuen, "—if you're so proud of your work, why make it appear as if they died of natural causes?" His words struck an uncomfortable chord, and he watched as Taub's jaw tightened, protruding out to one side.

"Hiding my work?" he said, in surprise. "Is that what you think I'm doing?" Taub's grin widened. "Captain, I expected more from you." Then Taub became deathly serious. "The best way to get away with murder isn't to make it look like natural causes—"

"—it's to make it look like someone else did it," said Winterbottom, cutting him off. For a moment no one said a word. Even McCuen was taken aback by the deliverance of the idea. In that time, Taub's expression hardened with anger toward Winterbottom for usurping his response. In a rage, he stared at Winterbottom before continuing.

"I can see that you're one of them," snapped Taub. "You hide it well—but you can't hide it from me. The lack of inflection in your voice, the way you move. Yes, I saw you tapping your fingers together, struggling to focus on my words and your thoughts—all the while fighting the urge to re-arrange the objects on my bookshelf. I bet the drumming of this old heating system sounds like an orchestra in your ears. And then, of course, there's the pacing—or perhaps I should say the urge you have to pace—back and forth, back and forth. Yes, you hide it better than most, but I can smell it all over you." Then his eyebrows jumped inquisitively. "Is it Autism or Asperger's?"

Winterbottom said nothing as Taub chuckled to himself.

"It's a pity your mother didn't come to me—I could have helped you." Then his wicked smile erupted into laughter again. Unbridled, it soon turned into a violent coughing fit. The wrinkles on his face gripped him more firmly, and he fumbled for the oxygen tube that had fallen to his side. Winterbottom callously watched, expressionless, as Taub struggled to reach for it. Soon he was laboring to breathe, culminating in a desperate gasp for air. It was like watching a balloon slowly deflate.

McCuen watched it happening, but soon he became uncomfortable. Stepping forward, he handed Taub the oxygen tube, which he quickly pressed to his nose for relief.

Once he was relatively present again, Winterbottom responded.

"For all of your smooth sounding words, a simple undeniable fact, remains. You, Dr. Taub, are a coward." His words were cutting, but he wasn't finished. "You've deemed others unfit to live, and yet, here you are—rotting away from the inside out, clinging to that machine for every breath it can give you." He leaned over and looked Taub in the eyes. "You're afraid of the very thing you've prescribed to so many."

Taub's face became red with anger, as his oxygen tube hissed like an *Inland Taipan.* He was too weak to sustain such passion, and his temper soon faded into fatigue. He clamped his pursed lips shut and turned the knob on his oxygen tank, increasing the flow. Then Winterbottom continued.

"Your time has passed, doctor—and soon, the world will be rid of you." Surprisingly, Taub smiled gently.

"Your little fit insinuates that I've failed in some way," he said, "—when in fact, quite the opposite is true. Of course, I know that names like Goebbels and Mengele will never be openly celebrated in our society, but what of Theodore Roosevelt and Margaret Sanger? They advocated for Eugenicist policies, and they have statues in prominent places. Do you know why that is?" Then Taub paused and carefully sipped his tea. "It's because our society is more interested in the way things look—than how they really are. Right or wrong is an afterthought—and a distant one at that. I'm content in knowing that our society feels the same way that I do."

"White supremacy and genocide are hardly societal values—"

"Mr. Winterbottom, you're not hearing me," he said more firmly. "Most people don't celebrate the idea of a superior race—I don't deny that. But even you must admit that in their innermost thoughts most people believe themselves to be better than those around them." He paused again for a moment and looked at McCuen before continuing. "Have you ever asked yourself the question—if racial supremacy is so appalling to everyone—then why is there still such inequality?" He was smiling again. "The eradication of the feeble-minded, the disabled, the poor, *the inferior*—these ideas make people feel very uncomfortable—but not on moral grounds. They deny them because they're afraid of what other people might think. What matters to them is the appearance. And so they've learned to cringe publicly, while quietly embracing each of these things under more palatable names." He stopped to clear his throat and drew in another long breath through his nose. "Different means to the same, ultimate end. What was once called eugenics is now genetic-engineering. What we once referred to as ideology, we now call Science. We can't just advocate for the extermination of certain races and populations, the way that we used to—but the beauty of my work is that we don't have to." Taub drew another sip from his teacup. "Those we can't exterminate—we control, alienate, and even incarcerate, either through the criminal justice system, or just good old-fashioned economics. I've always said, 'keep them poor, but well-fed—life will take care of the rest.' The poor are sent to prison, and the elderly are exiled—left in isolation." He began chuckling again. "The more progressive states allow them to voluntarily end their lives.

It's done under the guise of mercy, but how long before that changes? Frankly, I couldn't have designed a more perfect solution. And true to form, they call it *Death with Dignity*. Isn't that so humane sounding? For the wealthy who are suffering the choice is a comfort. But to the poor and less fortunate—well, what other choice do they really have?" He finished his tea and placed it gently back on the side table. "So many wonderful things can be done—with the best of intentions." Taub didn't wait for a response; his lecture had ended. Grabbing his cane, he walked slowly into the kitchen where his nurse was waiting for him.

Winterbottom and McCuen lingered in the living room while Whelan and Adams continued their search. With Taub in the kitchen, Winterbottom was free to re-arrange the items on his bookshelf, which gave him great satisfaction. The majority of the shelves were occupied by books, ranging from Molecular Biology, and Family Genealogical Surveys from the turn of the century to the present. He carefully ran his fingers along the spines, passing over *The Eugenics Survey, The Pivot of Civilization*, and *The Goebbels Diaries*. As he moved down the shelf, he came to a glass display, housing a collection of pinned butterflies and moths. Beside it were a few succulent plants and peculiar looking flowers. Then he glanced to the wall in front of him. It held a small photograph portraying Dr. Taub with another man standing beside him. It was taken at Harvard University in 1968. Winterbottom remained fixed on the picture until something else caught his eye. A neighboring mahogany frame showcased an etching from the 17th-century. It portrayed a skeleton, Death, wearing a billowing robe, while carrying a small infant under its arm. Speaking with Dr. Taub did little in terms of clarity, but one thing was certain. They were closing in on the killer.

Leaving the apartment complex on Columbia Street, McCuen was confident that Taub was involved, but some things just didn't add up.

"He's too decrepit to kill anyone," said McCuen, "—and yet, he's practically bragging about committing the murders." McCuen shook his head in frustration. "Not to mention—if Taub was the killer, he would have known that Gerard is still alive."

"It's strange," agreed Winterbottom. "But I'm not ready to rule out Dr. Taub—especially, if we think that poison is a possibility. Some toxins can take days to induce death, and I think he's far more capable than he's letting on. It's possible that Gerard's already been poisoned—and it just hasn't killed him yet."

"We have to get to the hospital."

"If the poison is undetectable—we can't help him," replied Winterbottom. McCuen remained undeterred and headed for Tisch hospital. Along the way, Winterbottom became withdrawn. He seemed almost fearful.

"What is it?" asked McCuen.

"At his apartment—Taub called me, *Mr. Winterbottom.*"

"So?"

"You never told him my name—and neither did I."

Taub could have recognized Winterbottom from the newspaper article, but given his connection to the victims, it seemed more and more likely that he was deeply involved.

As they exited the elevator on the third floor of the hospital, Winterbottom seemed troubled. McCuen could see that something was wrong. Winterbottom was shaking, he couldn't hold still. He'd been drumming his fingers nervously against his leg, and his body became more rigid. After a few more steps, his breathing became labored and he began to sweat profusely.

"Are you alright?" asked McCuen, grabbing him by the arm. McCuen feared the worst. They had just come from Taub's apartment. Was it something he touched? McCuen's own collar tightened thinking of the possible exposure to poison. Before McCuen could call out for help, Winterbottom grabbed him by the sleeve.

"It's not that," said Winterbottom, trying to calm his nerves. "I'll be fine—just give me a minute."

"Like hell you will!"

"Ed—it's not poison," insisted Winterbottom. "It's just that I hate hospitals—this one in particular." In that moment, McCuen realized what it all meant. The accident, Tisch hospital; it was where Winterbottom had lost everything.

"We should go," said McCuen.

"I'll be all right," replied Winterbottom. Then suddenly, McCuen saw hospital staff rushing into Gerard's room. In the commotion, he could hear the uninterrupted tone of a flat-lined heart monitor. They were too late.

* * *

It was just after midnight when they arrived at the Odessa for coffee and a late-night meal. The death of Jean Gerard, and the disgust that had followed them from Taub's apartment affected their appetites. Whelan and Adams had joined them, but with their cups only half empty, McCuen thought it best to get some sleep.

"It's late, Anselm," he said. "Let me bring you home." Winterbottom sipped his coffee as he stared out the window. The night was pitch black.

"That's all right, Ed," he replied. "I think I'll stay a bit longer."

He'd hardly spoken a word since the hospital, and it was clear to everyone that he was still troubled by old memories. Whelan slowly pulled on his coat and yawned.

"Well, I'm exhausted," he said. "And unless mathematicians are exempt—I suggest you try to get some sleep."

"Goodnight, Tom," replied Winterbottom, as he waved to the server for another cup.

"Are you sure I can't give you a ride home?" asked McCuen.

"No, I'm fine."

"Suit yourself."

That left Winterbottom and Adams sitting on opposite sides of the table. She had already pulled on her jacket, but something stopped her from leaving. She could see it in his face. It was as if the table between them was a raft, set loose on an endless ocean. From the adjoining room of Taub's apartment she had heard the things that Dr. Taub had said about him. Adams had always known that Winterbottom was different, but Taub's assessment of Asperger's Syndrome had given her a more clear picture.

"I never knew what happened to your family—until I read the newspaper," she said. "I'm so sorry, Anselm."

"We're all visited by tragedy—at some point," he replied plainly.

"Yes," she replied. "And it's rarely delivered in equal portions." To her surprise, Winterbottom continued.

"I have trouble remembering what she looks like," he said. "It's only been five years, and already I can't quite see her." He began shaking his head slowly. "I remember her face, and how she moved, but when I try to picture her in my mind, it never looks quite right."

"I think that's fairly common."

"The man who did it—I can see his face just fine," he replied quickly. "But the memory of my own wife is a blur." He raised his cup to his lips and paused. "What does that say about me?"

"I think it says that you miss her very much," replied Adams.

He nodded in response and looked into her eyes.

"You know something about that too—don't you?" he said.

The question made her uncomfortable, but he was right. And in that moment, it would have been more hurtful to deny it.

"My father died last year," she replied. "And there's not a day that goes by that I'm not reminded of him."

"Were you close?"

"We used to be," said Adams, "—despite our differences." She sat back in her chair. "He was a Baptist minister, and I've always been—skeptical. But he never held it against me or pushed me to change how I felt. I guess he thought I'd come around to it, eventually."

"And have you?"

"No," she said bluntly. "When he died, it just pushed me even further away from believing in anything. He had ALS." Then she paused for a moment. "I heard what Dr. Taub said about euthanasia—but all of his hatefulness aside, I wish my father could've had the option to end his suffering. Toward the end—he was in a lot of pain."

"Pain can be a terrible thing," replied Winterbottom. "It's agony for those afflicted by it —and nearly as bad for those that have to watch it happening. Worse still, there never seems to be a reason for it."

"So, what's the answer then?" she asked.

"The answer?"

"Is it so wrong—to end your own suffering?"

"That's not a question I can answer," said Winterbottom. "What would your father say?"

It was as if she could hear her father speaking the words.

"He'd say—what he always said." Then she smiled. "He'd say—that no matter who you are—or what you believe, life is precious. And the world would be a much better place if we all had a greater respect for human life."

XXIII
THE AUTOPSY OF JEAN GERARD

In the morning, McCuen and Winterbottom returned to the basement of the Chief Medical Examiner's Office, looking for answers. They hoped that Gerard's autopsy would produce different results. As they waited, McCuen remained on edge. He regretted leaving Winterbottom at the Odessa the night before. He should have been more vigilant, and it made him wonder if it was already done. There was no way to know for sure, but Winterbottom's behavior seemed to suggest he was still sliding toward it.

McCuen could have dismissed the changes he saw in Winterbottom's behavior as Asperger's syndrome, but he'd be wrong. That was only a part of it. This was different. Winterbottom often shied away from direct eye contact, but lately, it was getting worse. Even the way he walked and moved was affected. And McCuen could only see what was on the surface. In Winterbottom's mind, the synapses were all firing simultaneously. Fueled by thoughts of revenge and murder, his mind and his emotions were imbalanced. They magnified his greatest attributes alongside his most virulent fears. It was dividing him, making him less grounded and more susceptible to the effects of the outside world. Lights and sounds, even smells, began to rule over him. He was becoming less aware of his own body, which had become rigid and mechanical. What McCuen didn't realize was that the incident at Tisch hospital was just the beginning. Far from view, and in the middle of conversations, Winterbottom was silently calculating *Birch and Swinnerton-Dyer Conjecture*. In his head he was jumping between the elements of murder and the *Riemann hypothesis*. McCuen could never gauge the extent of it, but he could see its effects. It was becoming more obvious that Winterbottom was approaching a choice that could never be reversed. McCuen was about to speak when the office door opened. Dr. Howard motioned them inside.

"I'm afraid it's just like the last one," he said. "Gerard's lab results came back completely clean." McCuen was visibly frustrated. "I also re-tested the samples from Phan's autopsy—and we got the same result. I don't know what we're dealing with."

"It has to be poison," said McCuen.

"I don't know," replied Dr. Howard, still pushing against the idea of an untraceable poison. "I even tested his IV lines and bed linens—there's no signs of any toxins." McCuen glanced over at Winterbottom, who suddenly emerged from contemplative silence.

"If we can't identify the poison," said Winterbottom, "—we can at least try to find how it was administered."

"His nurses were closely monitored," said McCuen, "—and there was a patrolman in the room the entire time."

"What compounds were found in his body?" asked Winterbottom.

"He had normal levels of saline, presumably from his IV fluids, and low-levels of hydrocodone, which he was prescribed post-surgery."

"Could the hydrocodone have been altered?"

Dr. Howard shook his head in doubt.

"Technically, yes—but it's very unlikely," replied Dr. Howard. "Pain medications are sealed in carefully monitored electronic dispensers. Even if the killer knew what kind of medication Gerard was prescribed, he would've had to poison all the drugs in the unit. There would have been incidental patient deaths."

"What about the pre-scheduled surgery?" asked McCuen. "It would've given the killer ample time to plan, and an opportunity to administer the poison."

"It could've been mixed with the anesthesia during the surgery," said Howard.

"Who would've had access to him pre-op?" asked McCuen.

"Not many people," replied Howard. "I'll track down a list of names."

* * *

As they drove back to Lexington Avenue, thoughts of the killer weighed on them. They both understood the significance of time, and that they had no control over it. They were closing in on him, but not nearly fast enough. He would kill again. It was inevitable. And without another envelope, there was no telling who might be next. The mood within the car was sullen, and the distance between them seemed to increase. Each man was carrying a burden which the other couldn't fully understand, and they were haplessly tied to one another. Winterbottom preferred the silence, but as they crept through the morning traffic, he could see that McCuen was troubled by it.

"When does this end for you?" asked Winterbottom.

"Soon, I hope," replied McCuen.

"Do you really mean that?"

"Yes," said McCuen. "I do."

"Then why wait?" continued Winterbottom. "Why not just walk away—right now? You've done your time, and you've helped a lot of people. Why not just go—before it gets the better of you?"

"Is this you being concerned for me?" said McCuen. "Or are you just trying to get rid of the only person who knows what your plans are?"

"I'm being serious," said Winterbottom. Then he paused and looked at the surrounding cars and passing pedestrians. They were unaware of the true ugliness in the world. Most were sheltered from it entirely. And for all they didn't know, they were no happier for it. "Did you know most people live their entire lives without ever seeing a dead body?"

McCuen quietly turned to listen more intently.

"Of course, I don't mean on television," continued Winterbottom, "—or in a video game, or even at funerals. I mean in real life, in person." He turned slightly toward McCuen. "Not even one," Winterbottom reiterated. "How many have you seen? I'm just guessing, but I imagine its well over five hundred. And those are violent deaths. When you're that near to death, you're near to the suffering that accompanies it." McCuen bowed slightly before looking out the driver's side window. "This work that you're doing—it's not normal," continued Winterbottom. "It takes from you in ways you don't realize—a little each time."

McCuen nodded in quiet agreement. Then he spoke.

"When I first started, I didn't even notice it." His voice was low in reverence. "I knew that what I was doing was right—it was as clear as day. Yes, it takes a toll, and there's a heavy price to pay. But the ugliness that you see also brings clarity—about what's right and wrong. And the longer you do it, the more clear it becomes." He paused along with the starts and stops of the traffic ahead of them. "You begin to see the limits of everyone and everything around you—the failures of the system that we're all a part of." Then he looked at Winterbottom, directly. "And then you realize that there are fewer and fewer good people willing to do the work. The longer

you do it—the more necessary you become. And that's why I can't leave just yet. There's more good to be done, and I'll keep doing it—until I can't do it anymore."

Winterbottom said nothing and turned to look out his window. At that moment, McCuen received a text containing a single name: James Dearborn. It was the answer he'd been looking for. His contact at the DMV had identified the photograph. He had hoped that Winterbottom would abandon the pursuit on his own, but clearly there was no reasoning with him. McCuen had tried.

"Are you really going to kill him?" asked McCuen. It pulled Winterbottom away from the window. "Ed—"

"James Dearborn," said McCuen. "Are you going to kill him?"

Winterbottom paused on the name and looked down in disappointment. He knew McCuen had the photograph, it had only been a matter of time.

"I suppose you think this changes things," said Winterbottom.

"Doesn't it?"

"No—not really," Winterbottom said defiantly. "So, you know his name—now what? What are you going to do—tell him?" McCuen had no way of answering. He wasn't sure what he was going to do, he hadn't gotten that far. "Actually—I'd like to see that," continued Winterbottom *"Hello, Mr. Dearborn—I'm here to tell you that the eccentric billionaire, whose family you killed in a hit-and-run, is going to try to kill you, I think."*

"Anselm, you can't go through with it—not now," barked McCuen. "I know his name. If you kill him, I'll have no choice but to come after you—"

"Assuming he doesn't die of natural causes," said Winterbottom, coldly.

The way that he said it gave McCuen pause. It was said as if he had learned the killer's secret, or perhaps he had known it all along. These thoughts remained with him, as he weighed his own culpability. He had brought Winterbottom into this world. He had given him an open invitation to an exhibition of death and murder. McCuen had inadvertently shown him a hundred different ways to kill. Winterbottom had studied what he didn't already know, and he was able to see what ultimately led to the undoing of each perpetrator. What he wasn't able to learn from a lifetime of studying human behavior, he had been shown by McCuen and the others. As this grim realization took shape, McCuen broke the silence.

"Killing isn't as easy as it seems," he said. "You can plan it out a thousand different ways, but it never happens the way you think."

Winterbottom stared blankly at the dashboard, as McCuen continued.

"You think you won't feel anything," said McCuen, "—you've gotten used to that by now. And you might be surprised to know that it was that way for me when I was in Afghanistan." McCuen cleared his throat. "I wondered what it would feel like. Would I feel regret, would I feel shame, or disgust? Then it happened, just like that. In an instant it was over."

Winterbottom seemed gripped by his tone. It wasn't forceful or accusatory. It wasn't even trying to be persuasive.

"Anselm, I didn't feel a thing—nothing," said McCuen. "Then it happened again, and again after that—still nothing. Then five months later, deep in the Hindu Kush, I took the midnight watch. We were in hostile territory, so there were no campfires. My unit was sleeping fifty yards away, and I was alone, awake in the freezing cold. So, there I was in the darkness and out of nowhere an Afghani man in tattered clothing, with a rifle slung over his back, walks right up to me and sits down. He just sat there, ten feet away from me. He didn't say a word, he just kept looking at me—and I was looking at him. It took me a while to realize that he was the first man I had ever killed—a few months before." McCuen took a slow sip from his styrofoam cup, as if the story had made him cold. "In that way, you're right—you don't feel anything," said McCuen, "—not at first, or even in the hours after it happens. That's what allows you to do it in the first place. But they all come back, again and again. They do it to remind you of what you've done—and that is something that you will feel for the rest of your life."

"Ed—"

"I've killed a lot of people, Anselm," interrupted McCuen, "—and most were, particularly, bad men. Even those I regret." He looked over at Winterbottom. "And I'm reminded of them whenever I'm alone."

XXIV

HART ISLAND

Three days went by before McCuen returned to Lexington Avenue. It was an intrusion that even Winterbottom was beginning to get used to. He knocked several times before Winterbottom answered.

"Good afternoon, Ed," he said warmly. McCuen followed him inside to the library, which felt more empty than before, though McCuen couldn't figure out what was missing.

"We received another envelope this morning," he said, holding it out in his hand.

"Is that good news?" replied Winterbottom. "Every time we get an envelope somebody dies."

"This one's a little different."

"How so?" asked Winterbottom.

"Well, as you can imagine, there's another creepy etching. This one's entitled *The Feast*." McCuen removed it and showed it to Winterbottom. It depicted a group of people seated at a table, in various levels of intoxication and debauchery. At the center, illuminated by candlelight, stood the hostess of the dinner, Death.

"There's not much different about that," replied Winterbottom.

"There's a list of sixty-three names attached to it," said McCuen "They're all deceased, all except one—"

"—George Barrett," said Winterbottom, jumping in.

McCuen froze.

"How did you know that name?" he said. Winterbottom didn't answer right away and McCuen's thoughts foamed with suspicion again. Then Winterbottom smiled.

"Relax, Ed—I'm not the one sending the envelopes." Then he walked to the other side of the desk. "Unless James Dearborn's name is on that list, I can assure you that I have no intention of killing anyone." His reply did little to ease McCuen's mind.

"How did you know that name?" scowled McCuen.

"Ed—"

"Anselm!"

"You ask—but you never like the answers."

"The name!" shouted McCuen. "How did you know that name?"

"I received that same envelope—three days ago," he replied. McCuen quietly turned away in frustration.

"You son of a bitch!" shouted McCuen. "Why didn't you call me?"

"I was preoccupied."

"Bullshit!"

"Look at it this way—I may have bought George Barrett a few more days."

McCuen suddenly realized what Winterbottom was doing, and it certainly wasn't out of concern for George Barrett.

"You were testing him," said McCuen. "You wanted to see if he was watching you."

"He won't let you save them, Ed—but he wants you to keep trying. That's why he sends the envelopes—that's why he's telling you their names."

"Anselm—"

"Don't you get it?" pleaded Winterbottom. "You're giving him just want he wants!"

"You risked a man's life!" said McCuen. "Because if you're being watched—you can't kill Dearborn." He had shattered the whole thing wide open, but Winterbottom wouldn't let it go.

"And you're going after Barrett—knowing that it will get him killed." Winterbottom's tone was cutting. "Is that really so different?"

"We can stop him this time," said McCuen.

"You're out of your depth,"

"And you've lost your footing!" snapped McCuen.

"He got to Gerard, and he was in a guarded hospital room!" Winterbottom's face was red with anger. "Stop being so goddamned naive!"

McCuen paused as his temper slowly settled.

"George Barrett is the groundskeeper on Hart Island," said McCuen. It was never mentioned in the envelope, and the detail caused Winterbottom to pull back, slightly.

"Whelan and Adams are outside," continued McCuen. "We're heading there now. The killer can't get to him unless he goes to the island himself."

"Ed, he won't let you stop him—"

"I know it's a game to him," said McCuen, "—but I don't have a choice. And this time we have a chance." With grave reservations, Winterbottom pulled on his jacket.

For those unfamiliar with it, Hart Island rests on the western end of Long Island Sound, just off the shores of the Bronx. But be sure not to affix any idyllic notions to the place. It's a dreadful stretch of ground, as hollow as it is narrow. Hart Island is New York City's potter's field; an isolated graveyard for unclaimed decedents. It's one of the largest mass graves in the United States. Anyone who dies in the city and whose body goes unclaimed for seventy-two hours is buried on Hart Island. Some are disinterred once family members are identified, but most remain at rest on the island. There are an estimated 850,000 unclaimed or unidentified people buried there. Prison inmates from Riker's are paid fifty cents an hour to bury the coffins in groups of one hundred, stacked five deep in rows of twenty. At present, most of the buildings on the island are abandoned, the last remnants of a Union Army prison camp and a forgotten psychiatric hospital. Public access is carefully restricted. There's no electricity, and the only way to access the island is a ferryboat run by the Department of Corrections. For the last twenty-five years, the island's only living resident has been its groundskeeper, George Barrett.

Winterbottom's doubts about the excursion to Hart Island accompanied him aboard the ferryboat, but seeing the brooding waters, made him feel more uneasy. The evening air was cold, and the wind coming off the water cut through his jacket as he paced the deck. McCuen, Whelan and Adams were huddled together against the rail, reviewing a map of the island, as a team of tactical officers waited anxiously at the back of the ferry. Eventually, Winterbottom broke from his isolation and joined McCuen and the others.

"The groundskeeper's cabin is on the southern half of the island," said

McCuen, pointing to the map. "When we arrive, the tactical team will break into three groups. We'll follow the main group to Barrett's house while the other teams sweep the remainder of the island. Where do we stand on Barrett?"

"The only telephone on the island is at the ferry dock," replied Whelan. "We haven't gotten through to him yet—but I'll keep trying. He was alive less than an hour ago, when the work crew took the last ferryboat back to the mainland."

McCuen looked at Winterbottom who was leaning against the rail. His back was turned to them as he looked out over the water.

"Do we know why the killer's after Barrett?" asked Winterbottom, with his back still turned.

"I've been over the records a dozen times," replied Adams. "Barrett was never a patient of Dr. Taub's—and he doesn't seem to have any connection to the other victims."

McCuen said nothing.

"I suppose we'll know soon enough," said Winterbottom, looking out at the dark mass looming on the horizon. Surprisingly, Whelan joined him at the rail.

"Strange, isn't it?" he said, watching Winterbottom staring at the island. "They say that Barrett was once a prisoner at Rikers Island." Winterbottom kept his eyes fixed on the dark waters. "Rumor has it that his wife died ten years into his twelve-year prison sentence. Without any other living relatives, she was buried on Hart Island. He spent the last two years of his sentence tending to the grounds where she was buried. After he was released, he'd row out to the island every Sunday, and put flowers on her grave. Of course, access was restricted then, just like it is now. They even threatened to send him back to prison, but he kept coming—every Sunday. Out of sympathy more than anything else, they offered him one of the abandoned houses on the island in exchange for overseeing the groundskeeping efforts. They say he's been out there ever since."

Winterbottom nodded to Whelan and turned to McCuen.

"If the story's true," he said, "—then the killer can just as easily access the island by boat." He had listened to Whelan's story, but against the sharpened edge of reason, he amputated and quickly discarded all of its lore and sentiment.

"A boat can be put ashore," answered McCuen, "—but not easily. I've had patrol boats circling the island for the last two hours. If the killer wants to get through—he'll have to wait until dark."

The sun had nearly set and seeing the glowing orbs of the ferry dock, they followed McCuen to the lower deck. Once the ferryboat was secured to its moorings, they drove McCuen's unmarked cruiser down the gravel road to the groundskeeper's cabin.

Barrett's house was clad with irregular wooden planks, not unlike the Clutch Plague shanties of the 1920s. Through the single-paned windows they could see that the lanterns inside were lit, and there was smoke creeping from the stovepipe chimney. McCuen knocked on the door, and called out to Barrett, but there was no answer. With a sense of urgency, they cautiously entered. Inside the cabin they found simple comforts, a tattered wool rug, and a folding metal table, repurposed from the old psychiatric hospital. The kitchen consisted of a tea kettle, two pans, and a small sink, and in the corner of the room was a simple cot, its wool blankets carefully folded. McCuen and Winterbottom moved through the space as Whelan and Adams proceeded into the only other adjoining room. They quickly re-emerged.

"He's not here," said Whelan. "But you need to see this." In the room they found a wooden desk and five dark green filing cabinets. On the wall there were maps of the island indicating the locations of the thousands of gravesites.

"He's been cataloging the names and burial locations."

"Look at this," said Adams, pointing to the opposing wall. It was covered with pinned documents and medical records, representing hundreds of deceased people. They had all gone unclaimed; they had all been buried on Hart Island. Upon closer inspection of the pages, they could see short lines of highlighted text. The documents all shared a common trait, the highlighted name of Dr. Robert Bishop.

"Who the hell is Dr. Robert Bishop?" asked Whelan.

"I have no idea," said McCuen, "—but we had better find out." This new evidence compelled McCuen to radio the tactical units. They would have to search the entire island. It was more important than ever to find George Barrett.

McCuen and his team joined the search and hurried north along the gravel road to the nearest cluster of buildings. It was the abandoned psychiatric ward. When he parked, McCuen pointed the headlights straight at the building, casting eerie shadows inside. As they fanned out, Winterbottom lingered, captivated by its menacing facade. He was struck by the lack of reflection in the windows and soon realized that the panes were missing, broken by time and weather. Rising from his observations, Winterbottom rushed to catch up with McCuen just as he was entering the eroded walls. Adams and Whelan broke away to search the outer perimeter of the building while Winterbottom and McCuen pushed through the broken front door. McCuen's flashlight washed across the crumbling interior, which proved to be a massive open space. There were no chairs, no tables, no beds. Everything had been stripped away. They walked the length of the tiled floor and exited through the far end.

In the open air again, they found themselves surrounded by sweeping tall grass. Fifty yards away was a thick grove of honey locusts. McCuen paused a moment, looking down at his feet. In the glow of the flashlight, there was a noticeable parting of the grass leading into the grove of trees. What first appeared to be a windswept trail soon showed signs of recent travel. They could see the tread of a man's boot prints. He had been running.

"Stay close," said McCuen, quietly. Winterbottom nodded in response, but inside his mind he had never left Barrett's cabin. He kept hearing the words in his head. That name—he had heard it before: Dr. Robert Bishop. As they moved along the trail, Winterbottom had visions of the trees in Forest Park. He saw flashes of painted portraits and carved wooden statues. Then McCuen stopped suddenly, as his flashlight fell upon the unmistakable shape of a human form. Lying on his side, bent and still, was the body of George Barrett. He had been stabbed twice in his left side and once in the neck. The body was still warm, as if its last breath had just left it.

McCuen called to the others on the radio, notifying them of his location. Then there was a rustling in the trees ahead of them. Before Winterbottom knew it, he was chasing after McCuen, running through the grasses and between the trunks of trees. What little the waning crescent could offer was soon obscured by dark clouds and hovering branches. A stillness accompanied them into the grove as McCuen pressed himself against the wide trunk of a nearby tree. Winterbottom did the same, finding shelter behind an adjacent oak. Whoever had been running from them had stopped. Sensing the killer nearby, McCuen listened for any sign that might give him away. Picking up a handful of small rocks, McCuen threw them into the thicket. As they collided against the boughs and branches, a shadowy figure shot out of the darkness, pushing through the trees. He was heading for the shoreline. McCuen watched as the tall, thin frame of the killer vanished into another thicket of trees.

Between strides, McCuen raised his Glock and followed after him.

His heart was pounding wildly and he felt the air grating against his lungs. Surrounded by trees, he stepped amongst their shadows, listening for any sign of the killer. Then, bullets struck all around him, two at his feet, and one that strayed off to his left, splintering the tree bark beside him. He dropped to the ground and rolled to the side as another three shots narrowly missed. McCuen sent three rounds in the direction of the killer's last muzzle flash, hoping they would find their target.

He turned away just in time to see Winterbottom entering the thicket. Winterbottom was consumed by panic and the chaos of the gunfire. Covering his ears with his hands, he clinched his eyes shut and began rocking back and forth. The precipitating moments had taken hold and the physiological tides of his mind swelled, carrying him to some far-off place. In the turbulence, he saw them again. He could see his wife and daughter walking across Lexington Avenue. They were looking back at him.

McCuen shouted out to him from the ground and watched as the dirt shifted and danced at his feet, but his voice couldn't be heard. Winterbottom was screaming. He was calling out to them, as the killer's gun thundered toward him. In his mind, he watched it all over again; an audience unto himself, as their bodies were thrown into the air. Amidst the chaos and the cracking, he felt his body being lifted up, as if the world had stopped spinning. It closed around him, it pushed him forward, before throwing him to the ground.

Then there was silence, and the shuffling of the killer's footsteps disappearing into the distance. With the clouded vision that often follows sound sleep, Winterbottom emerged, and lifted himself up onto his knees. Miraculously, he was unharmed. As he turned to see what had knocked him to the ground, he was overcome again. Lying beside him was Whelan, bleeding from a gunshot wound to the neck. Winterbottom instinctively pressed his hands against the wound as Whelan struggled to open his eyes. Within seconds McCuen was there, helping to compress the wound, as Whelan began to swallow hard. He was struggling to breathe. Not a word passed between them. Neither man could speak. When Adams arrived, she paused quietly. She didn't need to ask. Whelan was gone.

* * *

There is nothing more somber than the sound of bagpipes. Not the volley of rifles, or kind words of remembrance, maybe not even the flag, carefully folded and presented to his parents. The droning notes lingered and instilled a feeling that made McCuen and Winterbottom stay at the cemetery long after the crowds had left. It had been three days, but neither man had talked about what had happened that night. The silence remained unbroken as they walked the green hills of the Calvary Cemetery. It was during that walk that Winterbottom finally spoke.

"I'm so sorry, Ed," said Winterbottom.

"It wasn't your fault, Anselm."

"I just kept running," he continued. "Without even knowing it—"

"Anselm, you can't do this to yourself," said McCuen sternly. Winterbottom turned to him after staring blankly out over the headstones.

It would never quite look like sorrow or remorse, but he could see that Winterbottom was feeling both in his own way. He could hear it in his voice. It was wrong to think that Winterbottom didn't feel pain or sadness; he did. His share in those sorrows was far greater than most would ever realize. In some ways, he felt emotions more strongly than we ever could. But his mind and body would never respond quite like ours. He felt sadness in isolation, filtered through childhood memories and the pain he witnessed others feeling.

There would be no tears, but it would emerge in some other way, like in the abrasiveness of a wool sweater on his skin or the unabating ringing in his ears. Grief is complicated, but for Winterbottom, it lived in a thousand tortures.

"It just doesn't make sense," said Winterbottom. "Why would he do that for me? He died saving my life—even after I treated him so terribly."

"I don't know that it's meant to be understood," replied McCuen. "That's what makes it so remarkable." McCuen paused a moment before continuing. "But I'm not surprised that he did what he did. Given his father's rank in the department, most people thought Whelan became a police officer out of some kind of family obligation—to make his father proud. But that wasn't it. In the first five years of his career, he worked patrol in Port Morris in the Bronx—one of the most violent neighborhoods in the city." McCuen gently cleared his throat. "His father was a Deputy Inspector, he could have had any assignment that he wanted. Instead, he turned down three promotions. When I recruited him to the Crime Scene Unit, I asked him why. His answer was simple. He said that he wanted to protect people from harm. That was ultimately why I chose him."

"Ed—"

"It was his choice to make, Anselm," interrupted McCuen. "And he made it a long time ago. It didn't matter that it was you—he would have done it for anyone." McCuen could see that the words had reached him, and firmly continued. "Whatever you choose to do—from this point on—he'll share in that with you. I hope you honor that."

Winterbottom nodded quietly, unsure if he could. Shifting his attention back to the living, McCuen spoke.

"The killer is the only one responsible for Tom's death," he said. "And I need your help to find him."

"Whatever you need," said Winterbottom.

"I need your undivided attention," said McCuen, sternly. "I can't afford to be distracted. I can't be worrying that you'll kill Dearborn as soon as my back is turned."

"Ed, I want to help—"

"I need your promise that you won't do anything until we've caught the killer," said McCuen.

"You have my word—I promise."

XXV

DR. ROBERT BISHOP

Closing herself off from any feelings surrounding Whelan's death, Adams diligently searched the documents from Barrett's cabin. She had sorted through thousands of pages by the time Winterbottom and McCuen arrived. Every inch of the conference room was covered with photographs and death certificates.

"There are over twelve-hundred death certificates," she said. "All from people who died and were subsequently buried on Hart Island. And those are just from the previous two years. All of them have some connection to Dr. Robert Bishop."

"Who is he?"

"He's a surgeon," she replied. "He spends his time between the Brooklyn Surgical Center, New York Methodist, and Tisch Hospital."

"Where Gerard had his surgery," added McCuen. "What do we know about him?"

"He's in his late-sixties—tall, thin build." She could see that McCuen was concerned by what she had said.

"I wouldn't have guessed him to be that old," said McCuen, "—but the physical description matches the man I was chasing."

Then Winterbottom interrupted.

"What exactly is the connection to Dr. Bishop?" he asked. "I'd like to think that bells and whistles would go off somewhere if a doctor lost twelve-hundred patients in less than two years."

"That would've raised a big red flag," replied Adams. "But they didn't all die in his care. Most of these people weren't ever his patients."

"And yet his signature is on each of these death certificates," replied Winterbottom. "In addition to being a surgeon," said Adams, "—he also assists the Coroner with the examinations of any medical-related deaths."

"So, if you die in the hospital—he determines the cause of death?" asked McCuen

"Yes."

"That's a lot of unclaimed people," said Winterbottom. "Barrett noticed that too."

Winterbottom stepped back and folded his arms across his chest, before cradling his head in his right hand.

"Barrett worked on the island for twenty-five years," said Winterbottom. "He oversaw the burials and the disinterments. He would have known the seasons of the island, better than anyone. As the groundskeeper he would have known the rhythms of life and death in a deeply personal way, with an appreciation for the passing of time that only a prisoner can have." He turned around to face them as he continued. "Barrett recognized that something was wrong. He saw that too many of the deaths were going unclaimed."

"How could he know that?" asked McCuen.

"Because death doesn't discriminate between those who have loved ones, and those who don't," replied Winterbottom. "If Barrett noticed an unnatural uptick in unclaimed deaths, maybe he became suspicious that someone was putting their finger on the scales." The idea prompted Adams to pick up her phone and walk out of the room.

"Then what about Taub?" said McCuen.

"In his condition he couldn't have been Whelan's killer," said Winterbottom. "But that doesn't mean he's not involved somehow."

Just then Adams came rushing back into the room.

"I just spoke with the Medical Examiner's Office," said Adams. "It turns out that George Barrett filed a formal complaint against Dr. Robert Bishop, two weeks ago. He was preparing to turn over his findings to the Medical Examiner this week."

"There's our motive," said McCuen.

"And an explanation," added Winterbottom, "—for why the killer chose to stab Barrett instead of poisoning him. If the killer had found out that Barrett was turning over the documents, he would needed to be sure that Barrett's death was swift and unwitnessed. Poison wasn't certain enough for the killer. And on the island, he couldn't risk us hearing the gunshots. Under those circumstances, nothing is more certain than three stab wounds to the neck and chest."

Just then Adams pulled Bishop's photograph from the nearby printer and tacked it to the wall. It immediately drew Winterbottom's attention.

"It's him," said Winterbottom. "He's the man in the picture—from Dr. Taub's apartment. They went to Harvard together."

"Let's go have a talk with him," said Adams, holding up a search warrant for Bishop's apartment. Moving toward the door, McCuen turned to see Winterbottom still looking at Bishop's photograph.

"Are you coming?" asked McCuen.

"Yes, I'm coming."

When they arrived at Dr. Bishop's apartment, there was no answer at the front door. McCuen continued to pound on the oak door, but no one answered. His initial instinct was to not touch anything, even the doorknob, knowing that poison could be in play. Adams was wearing forensic gloves, and with her Glock drawn, she slowly twisted the doorknob. It was unlocked. The killer had a penchant for poison, but their recent encounter proved that he would resort to other means, if necessary. McCuen was especially aware that they could be walking into a trap. Winterbottom felt it too and waited in the hallway. McCuen and Adams nodded to each other and silently entered.

From outside, Winterbottom waited in quiet contemplation until he heard McCuen calling to him. It was safe to go in. The mid-morning light was pouring in through the windows and after walking the length of the entryway he was standing in the living room. It was a large space, adorned with various pieces of antique Austrian furniture. The adjoining wall immediately drew his attention. It held a vast collection of 17th-century German Fraktur manuscripts, in a variety of colors and styles. As he made his way toward the master bedroom, he found himself facing a reproduction of the same Medieval etching that was in Dr. Taub's apartment. Such a unique and morbid choice in Art could hardly be a coincidence. Winterbottom's mind continued its orbit around the atmosphere of evidence, the timing and behaviors, even the names of everyone involved. It all seemed to be spinning. As he crossed the threshold of the bedroom door, he saw Dr. Bishop's lifeless body lying on the bed. McCuen and Adams were quietly examining the room, as Winterbottom approached. Bishop's eyes were peacefully closed, and his hands had been reverently folded across his chest, as if he were lying in State. On his bedside table was an empty cup of tea and a small etching. It was a copy of Marcel Roux's *The Genius*, depicting the artist in front of his easel. Next to the etching on the bedside table there was a note in cutout letters. It read:

"I am Death, and great is the work I have done."

After hours of searching, a number of Bishop's possessions were seized. Most significant was a .40 caliber handgun. It had been fired recently. Other items of interest included a pair of muddy boots, a boat key, patient lists, and medical records, as well as several handwritten journals containing indecipherable chemical formulas. In his closet they found photographs and address information for all the known victims and thousands of other patients. All the pieces had fallen into place. All except one. Not a single drop of poison was found in the apartment, though Winterbottom suspected that some would likely to be found in the residue at the bottom of Bishop's teacup.

"You were right, Anselm," said McCuen. "He was never going to let us catch him."

"I guess not," replied Winterbottom.

"Taub may have been skilled enough in Molecular Biology to develop an undetectable poison," said McCuen, "—but he was too infirm to track down and administer it to the victims.

"He provided the method," said Adams, "—and Dr. Bishop put their plan into action."

"It seems they were ideologically tied to each other," said Winter-bottom, scanning the books on a nearby shelf. Then Winterbottom turned to the notebooks and boxes of patient records they had found in the closet. McCuen watched as he began scanning.

"What are you looking for?" asked McCuen.

"I don't know—I'm just disappointed, I guess," said Winterbottom as he continued to flip through the records. "I wanted to get him—for Whelan."

Then Winterbottom looked back to the bed. "But he's gotten away with it." Then three patrolmen entered the apartment to assist. Winterbottom nodded to them as he continued. "Do you think there's enough to connect Dr. Taub to the murders?"

"Given all the evidence and his connection to Bishop, I think we can get him," said McCuen, "—if he hasn't already committed suicide. We'll go after him next."

"Well, you don't need me for that," replied Winterbottom. "I'm going to head home and get some sleep."

"Okay," said McCuen. "Thank you for the help." Winterbottom nodded stoically.

On his way out the door, Winterbottom gave a cordial goodbye to the patrolman in the hallway, shaking his hand as he passed by. McCuen watched from the second-floor window as Winterbottom moved out to the street corner to wait for a taxi. His hands were buried deep in his jacket pockets. It wasn't long before McCuen turned to the nightstand again. His eyes ran along Bishop's bedside table to the etching. *The Genius*. Suddenly, a feeling of dread poured over him. In that instant, McCuen knew where Winterbottom was going.

Rushing out of the apartment, he ran down the stairs to the street. Winterbottom's taxi was just pulling away. McCuen hurried to his unmarked cruiser and followed the cab as it moved through Midtown. The sun had just dropped below the horizon and the darkness allowed McCuen to follow the cab more closely. As they continued, his mind began to churn with an eerie feeling of helplessness. Winterbottom had kept his promise, the case was over. The terms of their agreement had been met. He was going after Dearborn. Of course, nothing Winterbottom did was ever that simple, and McCuen was visited by more complex insinuations.

Why would Winterbottom be interested in the names on Bishop's patient list? Was there something there, or was he just buying time? What was he waiting for? Winterbottom had left the apartment just after the patrolmen arrived, but why? Then McCuen came upon a more perplexing thought. When had Winterbottom ever given such a warm greeting to anyone? Least of all a patrolman? Then it came to him. Winterbottom was building a near perfect alibi. The patrolman would remember his face. He'd remember that Winterbottom was there at Bishop's apartment. And who would ever suspect that a police consultant would leave a crime scene, in order to commit a murder of his own? If Winterbottom succeeded in killing him, there would be no way to prove that Dearborn was responsible for the car accident. Proof of Winterbottom's motive would die with Dearborn. There would be no way to connect him to Winterbottom at all, except for what little information McCuen had found. McCuen had to stop him.

Suddenly, the taxicab turned off Madison and came to an abrupt stop, forcing McCuen to drive past the parked taxi. He parked his cruiser and hurried to find Winterbottom in his rear-view mirror. Even in the darkness, he could see Winterbottom's silhouette walking across the street. McCuen followed him on foot for six blocks, winding through side-streets, beneath the intermittent glow of the streetlights. Suddenly Winterbottom stopped and turned toward an adjacent row house. He was waiting in the darkness, only his breath was visible in the cold night air. He looked down the street, and then over each shoulder, before moving across the street. That was when McCuen saw it. There was a black Mercedes parked on the street.

The lights of the house were out, and it appeared to be unoccupied, but the apartment above it was well lit. Winterbottom looked at his watch. Another two minutes passed, as Winterbottom continued to pace back and forth on the sidewalk. McCuen waited at the corner, watching as he began to feel the cold.

Then suddenly, the lights in the upper apartment went out. Soon after, an older woman exited the front door, walked to her car, and drove away. Before the car was even out of sight, Winterbottom rushed for the front door. McCuen quietly followed after him.

From inside the foyer, McCuen could see Winterbottom entering the second-floor apartment, carefully closing the door behind him. McCuen hurried down the corridor to the apartment door. He paused and exhaled slowly before unholstering his gun. As he quietly opened the door, Winterbottom was nowhere to be seen. As he entered the apartment and turned the corner into the living room, he found Winterbottom standing in the open space. With his back turned to McCuen, he reached into his right jacket pocket. McCuen slowly raised his gun, he couldn't let it go any further.

"Don't move," said McCuen, forcefully.

Winterbottom froze at the sound of his voice.

"Put it down, Anselm." said McCuen.

Winterbottom's head sank in frustration. He held up the object in his hand and slowly turned to face McCuen. He was holding a flashlight.

"What the hell are you thinking?" grumbled McCuen.

"Well, I couldn't exactly ask for your help—"

"This is your plan?" continued McCuen, careful not to raise his voice. "You were just going to kill him right here—in his own living room?"

"Kill him?" replied Winterbottom, appearing genuinely confused. Then he tilted his head in thought before continuing. "You don't know whose house this is—do you?" said Winterbottom.

"James Dearborn's," replied McCuen.

"No," said Winterbottom, sternly. "This is Dr. Howard's house." McCuen was astonished at the revelation.

"Dr. Howard," said McCuen. "The Assistant to the Chief Medical Examiner?" Before Winterbottom could respond, McCuen holstered his gun. "We need to leave—now!"

"I know he's your friend—,"

"Anselm!," shouted McCuen in anger.

"It was him all along," yelled Winterbottom. "—Dr. Howard is the killer."

"Do you have any idea how crazy you sound?" replied McCuen. "We're leaving!" McCuen grabbed Winterbottom by the arm.

"No—look!" shouted Winterbottom pulling away from McCuen's grip. McCuen stopped just long enough to see what Winterbottom was pointing at. In the circular glow of Winterbottom's flashlight, on the far wall, he could see a simple wooden frame holding a copy of Roux's etching, *The Feast*. The discovery solidified his suspicion of Dr. Howard, forcing McCuen to approach the etching for a closer look. As they wandered further into the house they came upon other etchings from Roux's *Danse Macabre* series, but most telling was a small photograph hanging in the corner of the living room. It was a copy of the photograph from Dr. Taub's apartment, the one from Harvard, depicting Taub and Dr. Bishop.

"Don't you see?" said Winterbottom. "There were three of them—Taub, Bishop, and the man who took this photograph—their apprentice, Dr. Ethan Howard. Dr. Taub fostered the ideology, Dr. Bishop had access to the patients, and Dr. Howard had the means to cover it all up."

"I still can't believe that he—"

"I know it's hard to accept," said Winterbottom. "It's a testament to how masterfully he's planned it. He practically told us that he was killer when we first met with him."

"What do you mean?" said McCuen.

"He said it himself," continued Winterbottom. "It's impossible for a poison to be undetectable in the body—and he was right. And if that's true, there can only be one explanation —"

"He was falsifying the toxicology reports," said McCuen.

"Yes—to make it appear as if the killer had created an undetectable poison. He played to our worst fears in order to undermine our logic."

"But why send us the letters?"

"Because George Barrett forced his hand," replied Winterbottom. "Once Barrett discovered that Dr. Bishop was involved, he filed a complaint with the Chief Medical Examiner. The moment that happened, Dr. Howard was forced to act. He had to shield himself. He sent the envelopes claiming to be the personification of Death, knowing that a high-profile case would land in his hands, and that he'd be able to steer our suspicions."

"And what about the evidence from Dr. Bishop's apartment?" asked McCuen, still feeling uneasy about the idea.

"Dr. Taub answered that question for us," said Winterbottom. "Do you remember? The best way to get away with murder isn't to make it look like natural causes—"

"—it's to make it look like someone else did it," said McCuen.

The hard edges and deep curves became clearer, and the pieces began to align. "Between the three of them they may have already killed thousands," said Winterbottom,"—but Dr. Howard has no intention of stopping."

As he spoke, Winterbottom pushed through a closed door at the end of the hallway. Upon entering they were blinded by bright lights. The entire ceiling was flooded by UV lights which were hovering above racks of strange plants and flowers. It was a garden nursery; a botanical paradise. Taking a closer look, Winterbottom could see that the plants were all of the same species, in various stages of growth. The most mature plants had long green stems and vibrant purple flowers of a most peculiar shape.

"Aconite," said Winterbottom. "It's more commonly known as *Monkshood*, or *Wolfsbane*."

Then he moved to a nearby countertop filled with racks of test tubes, boiling flasks, and laboratory beakers. They were filled with a clear substance.

"He didn't use a chemically-engineered toxin," continued Winter-bottom. "He used one of the oldest poisons known to man. Greek shepherds used aconite to poison wolves that were threatening their flocks. Hence its name—*Wolfsbane*." Then he turned to McCuen again. "Physiologically, it mimics cardiac arrest."

The plant and its poisonous properties made McCuen think back to Bishop's apartment. Then he was reminded of Winterbottom's peculiar behavior, and the fact that at present, they were both trespassing.

"Anselm—we need to leave!" he said sharply.

"I can't," replied Winterbottom, "—not yet."

McCuen could see that he was intensely focused, and it prompted him to think further back, to that moment when Winterbottom first saw Dr. Bishop's picture.

"That's what it is," said McCuen. "At the station when you saw Bishop's photo—you recognized him—didn't you?"

Unimpeded, Winterbottom clawed through the notebooks on the nearby desk, flipping hurriedly through each page. McCuen continued, knowing that he was listening.

"You were looking through his patient files—why?"

Still, Winterbottom didn't answer. Then without warning, McCuen slapped the notebook from his hands. "Answer me!" shouted McCuen. Winterbottom was shaken by the forcefulness of his voice.

"Yes," replied Winterbottom. "I recognized him from the photo-graph!"

"And in his apartment—what were you looking for in his patient files?" repeated McCuen. "I can only assume it's the same thing you're looking for now!"

Winterbottom bowed his head slightly.

"I'm looking for a name," replied Winterbottom, "—my daughter's name."

McCuen stopped and attempted to make sense of the knotted puzzle he had been presented with. Before he could speak, Winterbottom continued.

"Dr. Bishop was her surgeon."

"I don't understand," said McCuen. "Grace died in the accident."

A look of deep concern came over Winterbottom's face, and he reluctantly continued. "Margaret died in the accident," he said. "Grace survived—barely. She's paralyzed from the waist down."

"She's alive?"

"Yes," said Winterbottom. "Every day she wakes up in unbearable pain—but she's making progress."

"And that's where you go each week," said McCuen, "—to visit Grace." Winterbottom nodded in confirmation as his face took on a more sorrowful expression.

In that moment, McCuen could understand him. James Dearborn hadn't just killed his wife. He hadn't just caused irreversible injury to Grace. He was continuing to cause her pain, over and over again, each day, and for the rest of her life. Hidden amongst her physical injuries were the added outgrowths, the desultory nightmares and fears that haunted her, least of all the unyielding sorrow for the loss of her mother. Winterbottom was a witness to it all, and he was helpless to stop it. He was unable to protect her from it. That was why he wanted to kill James Dearborn.

"I took steps to make sure the newspapers reported that she died," said Winterbottom as he continued to rummage through the notebooks. "She had her first two surgeries with Dr. Bishop, but her condition needed more specialized care. So, I moved her to a cabin on Lake Willoughby, not too far from the Dartmouth Hitchcock Medical Center, where she receives regular treatment." As he spoke, he moved over to a nearby shelf and continued to shuffle through a collection of small notebooks. His voice was becoming more serious, and his eyes looked desperate. "I need to make sure she's not on his list of patients." As Winterbottom spoke, McCuen envisioned the newspaper article and their faces circled in red marker. "I need to make sure he's not targeting her."

McCuen moved to the filing cabinets in the corner of the room. He pulled at the top drawer and then suddenly, he stopped. Inside was a sealed envelope addressed to Winterbottom. He called to Winterbottom as he pulled its contents onto the desk. On top of the pile was a picture of Grace. Winterbottom grabbed at the pages which included a map of Lake Willoughby. A red circle had been drawn over the thin lines of topography. It was the location of Winterbottom's cabin. With trembling hands, he lifted another grim etching from the pile of papers. It showed a young girl, walking beside a skeleton, holding its hand.

Accompanying the picture was a note that read:

"I am Death, and I am coming for Grace Winterbottom."

As they turned to leave McCuen saw something that made him stop. Above the door was a video surveillance camera. Its red light was flashing.

"He knows we're here," said McCuen, "—we have to get to her first."

XXVI

LAKE WILLOUGHBY

As luck would have it, I arrived in Westmore, Vermont, early that morning. Given Winterbottom's persistent absence outside Dearborn's apartment, I decided to make the long drive to Vermont. It took me six hours to drive along the Connecticut River, crawling through the low lying hills of the Green Mountains. Most of the leaves had already fallen due to the rain and wind that arrived early that year. It left the mountains cold and colorless, all but for the evergreens. It was certainly not the ideal time for a retreat to the glacial lake, but my motivations were hardly recreational. I drove to Winterbottom's property, but the driveway was gated and surrounded by acres of forest. Back in town, I inquired about cottage rentals, and, it being the off-season, I had my pick of available cabins. I settled on a small, two-bedroom cottage about two hundred yards from Winterbottom's property, by rowboat of course. The cottage was strangely comforting, adorned with wood paneling and furnishings that were at least thirty years past their prime.

While I was settling in, Winterbottom and McCuen raced to LaGuardia and took Winterbottom's private jet to the Caledonia County Airport. From the plane, Winterbottom attempted to reach Mrs. Bruce at the cabin, but there was no answer. McCuen had sent a patrolman to the Chief Medical Examiner's Office, but Dr. Howard was nowhere to be found. He had taken an impromptu vacation. Throughout the flight, McCuen prepared for what might lie ahead of them. Howard knew they were onto him, and his disappearance made it all the more likely that he would be coming for Grace. He had been exposed and that would make him more unpredictable, and much more dangerous. There was no telling how many people he had killed over the years, or how many more would die if he wasn't stopped. Most upsetting to McCuen, was that the murders were committed right under his nose, by a man he considered to be a friend. He held his thoughts in silence, knowing that Winterbottom was unreachable. McCuen could see it in his eyes. He was untethered.

They arrived late that night, and Winterbottom rushed to the cabin. Exiting the car, McCuen drew his gun and began scanning the woods all around them. Having heard the car doors slamming, Mrs. Bruce came out onto the porch to greet them.

"Anselm?" she said. "We weren't expecting you—is everything alright?"

"I tried calling," he said in a panic. "There was no answer—"

"I've been here all day—the phone never rang." She could see he wasn't himself.

"Where's Grace?" he demanded sharply.

"She's down by the lake—with Dr. Howard."

His eyes widened as he turned to the broad waters. In the darkness, he could just make out a figure standing on the shoreline. Beside him, seated in her wheelchair, was Grace. They hurried to the water's edge, unsure of what they would find when they got there. At the sound of their footsteps, Dr. Howard glanced over his shoulder at them. He was smiling. Still running alongside Winterbottom, McCuen slowed his pace, discreetly drawing his gun. He was preparing for what might be needed; calm nerves and a steady hand.

"Mr. Winterbottom," said Dr. Howard in greeting. Then he looked to McCuen. "Ed—I'm glad you could make it." Dr. Howard slowly turned Grace's wheelchair around so she could see her father. "Grace and I were just getting some fresh air—it's so good for the lungs."

Winterbottom could see that she was uneasy. She could sense that something was wrong.

"It's ok, Grace," said Winterbottom. "We're going to get you back to the house."

Dr. Howard could see that McCuen had drawn his gun, concealing it behind his back. McCuen stared into his eyes with lethal resolve, nodding slowly. It was a clear message that the slightest unpredictable movement would result in a violent end. In response, Dr. Howard just smiled at him and slowly raised his open hands out to his sides in compliance.

"Your father's right, Grace," said Dr. Howard, "—we should get you back to the cabin." A crooked grin stretched across his mouth. "But don't worry, Grace. Just like we talked about—I think I might be able to help you."

By then, Mrs. Bruce had joined them, and to Winterbottom's surprise, Dr. Howard turned over Grace without incident. As Mrs. Bruce escorted her back toward the cabin, Dr. Howard continued.

"You can put the gun away, Ed," he said. "I'm not foolish enough to come here armed." Winterbottom rushed at him and grabbed him by his jacket collar, nearly lifting him off his feet.

"What did you do to her?" shouted Winterbottom.

Dr. Howard smiled again and made no attempt to stop him. Instead, he kept his hands out to his sides where McCuen could see them.

"Did you poison my daughter?" continued Winterbottom. His eyes shook with anger.

"Mr. Winterbottom," replied Dr. Howard, casually. "You're upset that I'm here—,"

"Answer me!"

Dr. Howard didn't respond and a spiteful sneer crept across his face. Realizing that it was futile to force the answer, Winterbottom let him go. Stepping backward, Dr. Howard straightened his shirt and jacket.

"Now, that's better," he said. "To answer your question—no, I didn't poison your daughter." He smiled facetiously. "But I do want to help her." His tone was wicked and deceitful.

With his gun in hand, McCuen interrupted.

"Ethan, turn around and put your hands behind your back."

"If I must," scoffed Dr. Howard in compliance. McCuen carefully patted him down, searching his clothes and pockets. Against expectation, Howard was unarmed. His pockets were completely empty. After walking him back to the cabin, McCuen sat him down, handcuffed to one of the kitchen chairs. While Winterbottom helped get Grace into bed, McCuen called for an ambulance and the Vermont State Police. Not long after, Winterbottom joined him and Dr. Howard in the kitchen.

"I suppose we have a lot to talk about," said Dr. Howard, looking out the window over the lake. McCuen said nothing. "Did you really think I would come here to harm her?" said Howard, plainly.

"Then why are you here?" asked McCuen angrily.

"Because I wanted you both to know how committed I am to helping her," he replied. There was a maniacal tilt to the way he was speaking. "I've helped so many like her to find an end to their suffering. It's been my life's work."

Winterbottom couldn't bring himself to look at him. Instead, he turned to face the window, wishing that the cabin floor would open up and swallow Dr. Howard whole. Then Dr. Howard adjusted his position in the chair, before continuing to speak.

"Now, it's important to understand that it can take some time," he said. "It may be a week —a month—maybe even years. You can never really know when it's going to happen. It might come in the morning, or in the middle of the night—but rest assured the pain will end." He smiled and laughed quietly to himself. After a brief pause, he looked to McCuen again, and raised his handcuffed wrists in front of him. "You haven't exactly thought this through—have you, Ed?"

McCuen didn't respond and shifted his weight from one leg to the other, while Winterbottom contemplated the audacity of Howard's comments. Bewildered as to why he wasn't more concerned about the situation, he looked to McCuen for reassurance.

"What's he talking about, Ed?" asked Winterbottom.

McCuen didn't say a word. He didn't know how to explain it in a way that Winterbottom would understand. The answer was unbelievable, and remarkably simple, all at the same time. There was no evidence that Dr. Howard had killed anyone. Given what they had been through and what they had learned, it seemed impossible, but the fact remained. There was no evidence that Dr. Howard had committed the murders. In fact, there was no evidence he had committed any crime at all. Since finding Howard at the shoreline, McCuen had been going over it in his head. As much as he tried, there was no willing it to be any different. The lack of evidence against Dr. Howard was compounded by the substantial evidence which implicated Dr. Taub, and Dr. Bishop in the murders. Their crimes were not his crimes, at least not in the eyes of the law. The inference, as strong as it was, couldn't be supported. They knew that Dr. Howard was behind it all, but what could they prove? There were no fingerprints, no DNA evidence, no cell phone records, and not even any medical records that connected Dr. Howard to any of the victims. There was no provable connection to Hart Island or the murder of George Barrett. He couldn't be connected to Whelan's murder either, though they both knew he pulled the trigger. They both knew he had done it; nothing was more certain in their minds. Howard's expression and demeanor had confessed as much, but what proof was that? He had planned it all to perfection. He had committed the perfect crime. He knew the disparity between his involvement, and their ability to prove it. It was why he had traveled to the lake to begin with. He wanted to see it in their eyes and on their faces. He wanted them to know just how helpless they were to stop him. They could both feel it coming off him. He was the dark hand of *Death*, and his work was not finished.

"You falsified the toxicology reports," said McCuen.

"Those people died of natural causes," smiled Dr. Howard, ever careful with his choice of words. "I'm sure you can exhume the bodies and run the analysis again. That should put to rest any doubts you have."

McCuen was well aware that any traces of the poison would have long since dissipated.

"And the *Wolfsbane* in your apartment?" asked Winterbottom curiously. "What about the etchings, the envelope—the letter targeting Grace?"

"I assure you, Mr. Winterbottom, I have no idea what you're talking about." Then he paused and cleared his throat. "Besides, such things are quite irrelevant."

"Irrelevant?" scoffed Winterbottom in disbelief. Howard's face soured in disappointment.

He was frustrated that Winterbottom still couldn't see it.

"Do you want to tell him, Ed—or should I?"

McCuen looked angrily at him, refusing to admit that he was right. Arrogantly, Howard explained.

"First, *Wolfsbane* is a common variety flower," he said, "—unregulated in every way. You can buy it at garden nurseries. Secondly, you and Captain McCuen entered and searched my apartment—quite illegally, and more specifically, without a search warrant." Dr. Howard calmly cleared his throat again. "And there is video evidence documenting that illegal search. The plants, the poison, the etchings—and the letter you spoke of—they're all fruits of the poisonous tree, as they say. Any evidence—"

"—any evidence obtained in an illegal search is inadmissible in court," interrupted McCuen, not wanting to give Howard the satisfaction of saying it out loud. Then McCuen turned to Winterbottom. "We can't use it against him," he explained.

Winterbottom's unorthodox approach and methods had outpaced the evidence. He had pushed too far, too fast. Once again he had defied the odds. He found the killer, the executor of *Death*, all without the assistance of tangible facts. It was only after several minutes of contemplation that Winterbottom could see the whole picture.

Dr. Howard found joy and ebullience, not just in the killings themselves, but in the entire process of death. He had lived in the morgue, examining the cold remnants of life, and the post- mortem decay of death. What began as an exercise, a means to a genocidal end, soon became something more. After years of quietly murdering those deemed unfit to live, Dr. Howard became transfixed on death itself. He found himself basking in the hours before their deaths. He came to savor it and found joy in the masterful control he held over their lives.

Ultimately, his satisfaction came through the knowledge of the exact time of their death, the precision of its timing, and the scientific certainty of when his victims would succumb to his poison. His excitement only increased when he began sending the envelopes, watching McCuen and Winterbottom working tirelessly toward an unreachable end. In the course of his career, alongside Taub and Bishop, he had orchestrated thousands of flawless murders, untraceable and beyond the reach of prosecution.

It left Winterbottom staring blankly out the window, unable to come to terms with the reality. Dr. Howard couldn't be stopped. He would walk away and disappear. There would be no protection from him, and no telling when Death would come for her. That had been his aim from the beginning. In that moment, Winterbottom was revisited by the same helplessness that he had felt on the day it all changed. He was unable to protect her, unable to stop it. He would lose her all over again.

"Ed, please," said Winterbottom, his hands were trembling. "There has to be something you can do."

McCuen paused and stared at Dr. Howard.

"I'm sorry, Anselm," he replied. "He's right."

They could hear the sirens of the ambulance approaching in the distance, as Mrs. Bruce wheeled Grace out of her room toward the front door.

"Don't you worry, Grace," said Dr. Howard. "I'll see you again—very soon." Winterbottom picked her up in his arms and carried her to the front door. Following Mrs. Bruce out of the cabin, he turned to McCuen. There were tears in his eyes. Nothing was said as Winterbottom turned to leave. Dr. Howard smiled as McCuen approached and removed the handcuffs from his wrists.

Holding Grace close to his chest, Winterbottom walked out of the cabin. As the porch door closed behind him, there was a clamoring of furniture. It was the sound of two men struggling, followed by two quick flashes of light, as gunshots rang out across the lake.

XXVII
CONCLUSION

The gunshots woke me that night and I spent the proceeding hours drifting in a rowboat, watching the comings and goings of the Vermont State Police and emergency medical personnel. McCuen's official report and affidavit of the shooting carefully detailed the events that led up to Dr. Howard's death. He laid out all the circumstantial evidence connecting Dr. Howard to the murders, including the evidence obtained during the illegal search of Howard's apartment. Most interesting was his account of what happened after he had removed Howard's handcuffs.

According to McCuen's report, Howard became agitated and initiated a physical altercation. During that struggle, he attempted to take McCuen's gun, and in fearing for his life, McCuen fired two shots, striking Dr. Howard in the chest. The fatal shooting was investigated by the Vermont State Police, who ruled it a justifiable police shooting. Two weeks later, McCuen resigned his position and retired early from the NYPD.

In all our subsequent conversations, and throughout the remaining years of our friendship, he never told me what happened that night, though the realities seemed obvious to me. Something in him had changed. I've often wondered what it was exactly, and when it began to shift. Maybe it was there all along, even when he was a child, waiting for a righteous purpose. Or maybe it was just the precipitation of the moment? Then again, maybe the answer lay elsewhere, amongst the ghosts of Afghanistan. There was no way of knowing for sure. It could have been a spoken word, or a silent gesture. Or maybe it was the fear that he saw in Winterbottom's face that night? Maybe it was the darkness that loomed across the deep end of the lake. I had felt it too that night. I'm inclined to think it was the sum of all these things, not that it matters much anymore. Whatever the reason, McCuen chose to surrender the best part of himself that night. He did it to protect them. In the end, he did what had to be done.

After the shooting, I returned to the city and found that the house on Lexington Avenue had been sold. More importantly, I never saw or heard of Anselm Winterbottom ever again. I continued on as a crime reporter and met with McCuen twice a week to play chess. We were both amateurs, but it was an excuse for good company. Over the course of the next year, I watched him salvage his marriage to Catherine. Six years after that, we lost him to cancer.

It was in the latter part of those years, during one of our weekly chess meetings, that I came upon an interesting discovery. He was a far more patient player than I was, and in between turns I had the habit of reading the newspaper. On that particular afternoon, just as we had entered the middle game, I came upon a familiar name in the obituaries: James Dearborn. With all that had happened, I had long forgotten about the man that Winterbottom had so ambitiously hunted. I couldn't imagine that he would seek out a closer relationship with death, but in reading Dearborn's name, feelings of concern came flooding back. I showed McCuen his picture and proceeded to read the obituary out loud. McCuen only briefly looked up from the chessboard, before leaning back in his chair. Then he quietly turned his attention back to the game. As I continued to read, he spoke.

"How did he die?" he asked stoically. I quietly scanned the remainder of the announcement.

"He died—in a car accident," I replied.

McCuen nodded slowly in acknowledgement, but the gesture was far from telling. Perhaps he thought it was an incidental end for a man who caused so much pain and suffering. Or was his silence an indication of disappointment? If it had been an accident, it would be a comfort to him. I think McCuen chose to believe that, but a small part of him was still suspicious. I had to believe that his thoughts followed my own, pondering how one might orchestrate a fatal car accident, and what planning that would take.

CPSIA information can be obtained
at www.ICGtesting.com
Printed in the USA
LVHW090710161121
703452LV00015B/664/J

9 780578 935669